EIGHT

The *Novelle* is the German equivalent of what in English is named, after the Italian, the novella. It really established itself as a key literary genre in the German tradition only around the end of the eighteenth century. Its influences derive, in particular, from the outstanding Medieval and Renaissance exponents of the genre, especially Boccaccio and Cervantes. Most of the examples which flooded the German literary market in the course of the nineteenth century were at best of ephemeral interest, crude anecdotal narratives dressed in the clothes of a more dis-

EIGHT GERMAN NOVELLAS

The *Novelle* is the German equivalent of what in English is named, after a very long time, the novella. It really established itself as a key literary form in the German tradition only around the end of the eighteenth century. Its influences derive, for instance, from the outstanding historical and Renaissance examples of this genre, equally Decameron and Cervantes. Most of the examples which flooded the various different markets, in the course of the nineteenth century, were in want of ephemeral interest, crude anecdotal narratives dressed in the clothes of a more distinguished form. But many of the leading German writers of the nineteenth century found in the *Novelle* a particularly appealing form for the narration of tightly organized, dramatically shaped stories. The sort of tales of the unexpected assembled in this volume can be read as a digest of narrative styles and themes throughout the period from Romanticism to Naturalism. They enact a most acute form of the struggle for mastery of experience in an age driven by an ideology of progression in the various fields of knowledge. As such, they represent a particularly telling gauge for the broader developments of German culture in the nineteenth century and must count as some of the most significant works of nineteenth-century European literature.

MICHAEL FLEMING was born in Lancashire and studied at London University, where he read Oriental History and Japanese language and literature. He has been living and working in southern Germany since 1966.

ANDREW J. WEBBER is University Lecturer in German at the University of Cambridge. He is the author of *The Doppelgänger: Double Visions in German Literature* (Oxford, 1996) as well as articles on nineteenth-century German literature.

THE WORLD'S CLASSICS

Eight German Novellas

Translated by
MICHAEL FLEMING

With an Introduction and Notes by
ANDREW J. WEBBER

Oxford   New York
OXFORD UNIVERSITY PRESS
1997

Oxford University Press, Great Clarendon Street, Oxford OX2 6DP

Oxford New York

*Athens Auckland Bangkok Bogota Bombay Buenos Aires
Calcutta Cape Town Dar es Salaam Delhi Florence Hong Kong
Istanbul Karachi Kuala Lumpur Madras Madrid Melbourne
Mexico City Nairobi Paris Singapore Taipei Tokyo Toronto*

*and associated companies in
Berlin Ibadan*

Oxford is a trade mark of Oxford University Press

*Translation, Translator's Note © Michael Fleming 1997
Introduction, Select Bibliography, Explanatory Notes © Andrew J. Webber 1997*

First published as a World's Classics paperback 1997

British Library Cataloguing in Publication Data

Data available

Library of Congress Cataloging in Publication Data

Eight German novellas/ translated by Michael Fleming; with an
introduction and notes by Andrew J. Webber.
(The world's classics)
Includes bibliographical references.
Contents: Blond Eckbert/ Ludwig Tieck — The marchioness of O/
Heinrich von Kleist — Lenz/ Georg Büchner — The Jew's beech/
Annette von Droste-Hülshoff — Tourmaline/ Adalbert Stifter —
Mozart on the way to Prague/ Eduard Mörike — Clothes make the man
/ Gottfried Keller — The white horse rider/ Theodor Storm.
1. Short stories, German—Translations into English. 2. German
fiction—19th century—Translations into English. I. Fleming,
Michael. II. Webber, Andrew. III. Series.
PT1327.E35 1997   833'.0108—dc20   96–41401
ISBN 0–19–283218–2

1 3 5 7 9 10 8 6 4 2

*Typeset by Graphicraft Typesetters Ltd., Hong Kong
Printed in Great Britain by
BPC Paperbacks Ltd.
Aylesbury, Bucks.*

CONTENTS

CONTENTS

INTRODUCTION

This volume aims to present a more-or-less representative sample of what is generally viewed as *the* representative genre of nineteenth-century German literature—the *Novelle*. Of course, the eight texts collected here cannot fully represent the variety of practices in the genre through the century, but they should give a sense of the range of forms, styles, and contents which *Novellen* of the period covered. To misappropriate the title of Cervantes's famous collection—the *Novelas ejemplares*—the texts gathered here are, paradoxically, exemplary novellas precisely in as far as they exceed the conventional shapes of the genre. It is worth recalling that Cervantes not only characterized his cycle of novellas as exemplary or didactic, but also as imbued with an element of exceptional mystery. The strategy of selection in the present volume—looking for paradigms, for exceptional rather than more general examples—might, therefore, be peculiarly appropriate in the case of a genre which is distinguished precisely by its depiction of mysterious, excessive, or out-of-the-ordinary examples.

This principle of the exceptional case is perhaps the only secure element in any attempt at a generic definition of the *Novelle*. It is set out, most famously, in Goethe's axiomatic pronouncement in conversation with Eckermann, that the *Novelle* is nothing other than 'an unheard-of event which has occurred'. On the basis of this, Goethe apparently determines to lend his own text exemplary status by entitling it *Novelle*. It might thus appear that the genre has no other specificity than its denominative novelty. And as Ludwig Tieck pointed out, this is not a properly specific characteristic, as evidenced by the denomination of the novel in English. It might indeed seem that the relation of exceptional occurrences is the condition of narrative writing as a whole, the motor of readerly interest. Accordingly, the *Novelle* might work as an exception, once again, only in as far as it exceeds this norm by singling out an occurrence which is more exceptional than those novelties purveyed by other narrative genres.

In its origins, then, the status of the *Novelle* appears to be a function of its material, which would put it on a level with anecdote. Tieck suggests that the generic label often only signals the transient character of the narrative novelty, hence the proliferation of vulgarities in the early Italian examples. At the same time, the application of the Italian term *novella* to any 'narrative or event' which is new and unfamiliar, suggests that the literary genre might not have any determining characteristics on the level of form. The only formal requirement appears to be the general one that the *novella* should be of short or medium length (in practice it proves to be as short or medium-sized as a short or medium-sized piece of string). The logic of Tieck's account of the *novella* heritage transfers to Goethe's definition, which collapses the 'occurence' with the fictional construction of its narration. Goethe's title—*Novelle*—shifts between a formal designation and the more conventional function of labelling what will happen in the text. This effacement of matters of form exposes the status of the *Novelle* at the beginning of the nineteenth century as a sub-genre (though the novel hardly enjoyed any more aesthetic privilege at that time). Even if Cervantes, with his *Novelas ejemplares*, provided a sort of *exemplum* for a more elevated kind of novella writing, where the narrative novelty would produce an exemplary moral, the nineteenth-century *Novelle* inherited at best a mixed generic tradition.

The literary history of the *Novelle* in nineteenth-century Germany charts the development of a form and of its status, and this in the domain of theory as much as of practice. From its initial, inferior position the *Novelle* climbs the aesthetic scale to find a place amongst the master genres of lyric poetry and drama. It assumes a particular relation to the latter, as a series of theoreticians of the *Novelle* recognize its distinctive, forceful profile as akin to dramatic structure. Both August Wilhelm Schlegel and Ludwig Tieck identify, in particular, the characteristic use of dramatic *peripeteia* (the *Wendepunkt* or turning-point) as a shared feature. And, in an unpublished preface to an 1881 collection, Theodor Storm confirmed that the erstwhile poor relation was now none other than the 'sister of drama'—with its tight structure, a vehicle for the most substantial subjects. Thus, in such cases as Kleist and Büchner, dramatists find in the

Novelle a vehicle for the dramatic organization of narrative form. At the same time, the proliferation of verse inserts in the texts collected here serves as a reminder of the lyrical potential of a more elliptical prose form (many *Novelle* writers were primarily, or equally, poets).

The *Novelle* is subject, in the course of the nineteenth century, to a catalogue of prescriptive and descriptive theories, but if Storm's preface, which might be read as the culmination of these, failed to go to press, then this perhaps indicates that a viable regulating formula for the genre remains elusive. However conventionalized it may seem to become in relation to other prose genres, in practice the *Novelle* remains a highly slippery commodity. The history of the genre in the nineteenth century shows an entangled dialectical relationship between theory and practice, presenting as many exceptions as it does rules. As we will see, this dialectic extends in its turn to the shifting relations between principles of ordering and of disorder on every level of the genre's form and content.

The novella has its origins, then, in such serial texts as the *Novelas ejemplares*, the *Arabian Nights*, Chaucer's *Canterbury Tales*, and especially Boccaccio's *Decameron*. Many of the foremost German contributions to the genre also form part of textual series or cycles, either as exchanged between multiple narrators or assembled by one (including those by Tieck, Stifter, and Keller in this volume). The *Decameron* sets up a sort of symposium in the form of a society of story-tellers who seek to assert a sense of community and order even as they are on the run from life-threatening disorder. Here, as elsewhere, the narrative diversions are deployed in the face of a catastrophic event. In this case it is the plague, in Goethe's *Conversations of German Émigrés* (1795) the French Revolution, in Storm's *White Horse Rider* the cataclysmic storm, and so on.

As to the subject-matter, *Novellen* always operate at, challenge, and extend the margins of what is accepted as real. If Boccaccio's story-tellers escape from social disaster, their tales represent a catalogue of smaller-scale disasters and disorders. While there is no escaping the plague except through flight, an order can be established for these narrated disorders in the form of pleasurable and regulated exchange between the various parties: the fugitives set up a mock court at the queen's pleasure, and the novellas are arranged according to a sort of decimal exchange system, with ten narrators, telling ten tales each, in ten days.

So not only do key texts in the novella tradition arise out of radical upheaval in the order of things, but the genre is devoted largely to the depiction of natural, social, familial, and interpersonal crisis. In terms of the nineteenth-century German tradition, it deals in plague, in cases like Kleist's *The Foundling* or Stifter's *Granite*; in earthquakes (Kleist's *The Earthquake in Chile*); tempests and flood (*The White Horse Rider*); war and insurrection (Kleist's *Michael Kohlhaas*); murder (*The Jew's Beech*); rape (*The Marchioness of O...*); adultery (*Tourmaline*); imposture (*Clothes Make the Man*); insanity (*Lenz*); and the supernatural (*Blond Eckbert et al.*). The *Novelle*, in other words, specializes in the various manifestations of what might be called the 'other' of enlightened social order.

It is conventional to stylize nineteenth-century European culture as governed by the spirit of positivism, the progressive faith in the empirical gaugeability and regulation of the world and its affairs. The *Novelle* might be seen at once to counter this historical narrative and to bear witness to its power. It might be argued that nineteenth-century culture depended upon the depiction of these forms of otherness precisely in order to test the security which it derived from the progress of science, democratic advances, and the institutions of domestic well-being. It may have needed to engage dialectically—that is, in a contradictory dialogue—with its mysteries and disorders, even as these threatened its very foundations. By so doing it both challenges its official narrative of its own development and finds an opportunity to reassert its powers of control over those challenges. This establishes something akin to the carnival as analysed by the Russian literary theorist Mikhael Bakhtin: an arena for deviation from, and transformation of, the prevailing order, but one which may at the same time be used by that order to sustain its authority at all other times. *Novellen*, from the tales of Hoffmann to Keller's *Clothes Make the Man*, indeed assume the costumes and unconventional conventions of the carnival. It remains open to question, however, whether the carnivalesque spirit of the *Novelle* tradition is always safely returned to social order.

By telling tales of scandal and transgression, of the weird and the wonderful, the *Novelle* sustains a dialogue with a series of other types of narrative devoted to the anti-social and the mysterious: the detective story, the fairy-tale, the case-history. A particularly suggestive model in terms of the nineteenth-century tradition in English would be Stevenson's *Strange Case of Dr Jekyll and Mr Hyde*, which has elements of all three types of narrative. Novellas are always more or less strange cases of this kind. And while these three types of narrative can of course find resolutions—the whodunnit solved, the fairy-tale couple living happy ever after, and the psychiatric case-history ending in therapeutic success—they can also all three resist any such narrative resolution, and reflect darkly on the disordered order out of which they arise. Thus the strangeness of the case of Jekyll and Hyde, for instance, remains unamenable to resolution or familiarization.

The fairy-tale, as the primary narrative genre of Romanticism, provides a particularly ambiguous influence on the development of the *Novelle* in the post-Romantic age. Paul Heyse, the practitioner, theorist, and anthologist of the genre, celebrates Tieck for having 'led the *Novelle* out of the magical night and dusk of Romanticism into the bright light of day', but it will be clear from the magical mystery of *Blond Eckbert* that some of Tieck's most compelling contributions to the genre, much like Hoffmann's, have an abiding allegiance to the obscurities of the fairy-tale forest. Indeed, Heyse's contemporary and collaborator Theodor Storm, in his *Immensee* and elsewhere, is still subject to the ambiguous lure of that prime site for the unfolding of fantastic tales.

These anachronistic Romantic attractions account in large part for the hybrid status of Realism in Germany, which has accordingly been differentiated from the more epic social Realism of its European counterparts as 'Poetic Realism'. The 'Poetic' in this formulation extends beyond the inclusion of conventionally poetic topics to principles of aesthetic economy: the Poetic Realist text tends to distil experience into more-essential forms by isolating and highlighting its symbolic potential and giving relatively short shrift to more mundane social effects. The *Novelle* enjoys a particular affinity with this mitigated form of Realism, hence its characteristic embroidering of symbolic fairy-tale fantasy into the fabric of socio-historical realities. Again, we might cite Bakhtin to describe the disposition of the *Novelle* of Poetic Realism as fundamentally dialogical, a form of narrative negotiating between two types of voice, two master discourses. For Bakhtin, the dialogical principle means a resistance to structures of finalization, and this is certainly the case with many nineteenth-century *Novellen*, interminably strung as they are between the different modes of understanding which can be subsumed under Romanticism and Realism. Neither fantasy nor reason ever really has the last word here.

Typically, the subversive potential of Romantic fantasy is regulated by the key device of formal control in the *Novelle*, and the signature of its anchorage in the real, that of frameworking. Of course, fairy-tales have at least rudimentary frames which set their extraordinary narratives up for the expectations of readerly consumption; but 'Es war einmal' or 'Once upon a time' are frames so indeterminate and conventional as to be self-effacing. When the fairy-tale is adapted as a model for a *Novelle*, as in the case of *Blond Eckbert*, its framing becomes complex and multi-layered, and, in particular, there is an unsettling sense of confusion between frame and narrative. This should alert us immediately to the fact that the framing mechanisms of the *Novelle* must be handled with great care.

A key exponent of the *Rahmennovelle*, or framed novella, in the Romantic period was E. T. A. Hoffmann. In what he called his *Nachtstücke*, or night-pieces (most famously *The Sandman*), Hoffmann wrote demonic real-life fairy-tales of desire and terror. It is not for nothing that Hoffmann's tales provided the material for the first experiments in psychoanalytic criticism. They read as psychopathological case-books. Freud's reading of Hoffmann's *Sandman* tale forms the basis of his essay on *Das Unheimliche* ('The Uncanny' (1919)). He pointed out that the apparent opposites of *heimlich* and *unheimlich*, 'homely/secret' and 'uncanny', in fact share common meanings in their etymological origins. This serves his argument that the *unheimlich*, the uncanny stuff of psychological trauma, is in fact rooted in the *Heim*, in home-life and its darker secrets. It is conventional to view much nineteenth-century *Novelle* writing as parochial in its scope, limited to the trials and tribulations of domestic life. But the 'homeliness' of many a post-Romantic *Novelle* writer is far from ensuring cosy familiarity, as home-life is revisited by traumas of the uncanny. The domestic scenes of nineteenth-century German fiction are recurrently a host to dark, repressed secrets.

The ambiguity of frame-hold is not limited to tales with uncanny thematics; rather, it seems that the frame all too often reinforces an uncanny sense of uncertainty on the level of structure. The guidance it gives is typically only partial, luring readers into some sense of security in the fictional world only in order to expose them to radical challenges to understanding. In other words, it may only serve to complicate what Martin Swales has called the 'hermeneutic gamble' involved in the reading of *Novellen*. The reader must always take the risk that she or he may be being 'framed' by a narratorial confidence trick.

It is worthwhile to scrutinize the narrative implications of the frame metaphor. A picture frame encloses a two-dimensional image of a three-dimensional space—an evident, highly conventional illusion. Its Greek form is *parergon*—that is, that which stands around or against the work. It is contiguous with the picture, but utterly blank or extraneously ornamental, and so invariably discontinuous with its representation. The frame is both of the work and other to it, marking out the arbitrary limits of its illusory space, and representing its function as an artefact of domestic or institutional decoration. Through the mediation of the frame the picture is both radically separated from, and set within, the domestic space it cohabits with the viewer.

How does all this relate to the principle of frameworking as part of the rhetorical design of narration? Narrative frameworking is about a manipulation of positions and a marking out of limitations. It both secures and excludes readerly involvement. It is a device of closure, serving strategies of containment and of isolation. It squares things up. It establishes the points of view and perspective within the narrative picture: that which the reader—indeed, that which the narrator—may see from a given vantage-point, and that which is closed off by curtains, walls, obstacles, darkness, and above all the arbitrary geometry of its margins.

Novellen are time and again framed by theorists and practitioners in the imagery of painting and drawing, aligned with genre pictures, water-colours, woodcuts, silhouettes, and, latterly, photographs. At their most colourful they represent a model for the more vivid domestic show of the magic lantern (this is how Storm describes his reading of the tales of Hoffmann). These images will always imply, though, as much what cannot be shown (contextual breadth, causal development, etc.) as what is pictured in the graphic poetry of the captured moment.

The architectural blueprint for the narrative frame in nineteenth-century culture is perhaps that conventional framework for the telling of tales which will be encountered more than once in the narratives collected here, the domestic hearth. The fireside provides the comfort of warmth and light; it contains, even as it displays, a potential for destruction of the home. This communicative framing is at the same time metaphorically transposed to the book in the hands of the solitary domestic reader. The book, and not least that which contains *Novellen*, is an artefact like the picture, one which both introduces other potentialities into the home and apparently contains them. Books, of course, may be opened and closed, but there is always the possibility that the frame may remain open when the book is shut. The domestic rectangles of book or picture are not always as benign and orderly as they may seem; in tales ranging from Hoffmann to Storm, pictures and texts are prone to come uncannily to life.[1]

The *Decameron* set up an apparently intact model of framing for its series of novellas, which are co-ordinated by a framework of discourse between the tellers and the listeners. The conversational frame seems to ensure some sense of interpretative community. But while it remains a distinctive, if not universal, feature

---

[1] A particularly telling instance of this is the painting *Der Nachtmahr* (*The Nightmare*) by Johann Heinrich Füßli (Fuseli) which hung in Storm's home and comes to life in his work. I have discussed this uncanny escape from the control of the frame in my chapter on the Novelle of Poetic Realism in *The 'Doppelgänger': Double Visions in German Literature* (Oxford, 1996).

of the genre, framing rarely manages to secure closure in any simple sense. It tends, indeed, to complicate the direct act of narration by reflecting upon the relative positions of the narrator and the audience or readership. It raises questions about narrative authority, about the conventions of this form of narration and the expectations it elicits. This is the effect of the *Rahmengespräch*, or framing conversation, in what is perhaps the formative text in the German tradition: Goethe's *Conversations of German Émigrés* (*Unterhaltungen deutscher Ausgewanderten*). Here, the priest who plays the narrator within the narrative reflects upon the novellas he purveys, and various members of the aristocratic circle of listeners are made to express different types of reader demand and response. The model of an unmediated and apparently omniscient narrative voice is subverted by the dubious credentials of the tale to be told, which, it transpires, may be true or tall, and perhaps in the service of some mysterious conspiracy. The narrator's preamble questions the whole business of suspension of disbelief through the conceits of fiction-making. In particular, the extraordinary tale to be told skirts the realm of the *Märchen*, or fairy-tale; the 'unheard-of', in Goethe's famous formulation, typically confuses the parameters of the real and the fantastic. Where the credulity of the reader is to be radically stretched, an acute strain is put upon the powers of narrative guile and persuasion. It is typical of the genre that the story, which will depend for its effect on a massive suspension of disbelief, is so often not so much told as retold. The priest tells a story of which he has heard tell and is thus apparently set apart from the role of fictionalizer; the prime issue is whether the narrator recounts his second-hand tale in good faith—for he is unable ultimately to vouch for the truth of what he documents.

The sort of narrative community set up here may spawn others, the stories pass into ever-expanding circulation, and assert their authentic value only by continuing to be as compelling as they are 'unheard-of'. This is also, of course, how they are tested by readers as the narrative product of a given nineteenth-century author. As the stories are reproduced, as listeners become tellers, and as books are printed, the novella, however strange it may be to tell, becomes woven into the edges of the social fabric. As new novellas are negotiated into circulation, so the framework of expectation and credibility is extended. Recurrently in such texts, the *faits divers* of newspapers serve as a model for the passage of the hitherto unheard-of into public discourse (thus *The Marchioness of O…* and *Tourmaline*). Indeed, many *Novellen* were published in serial form in journals of the day (*Mozart on the Way to Prague*, for instance, first appeared in the pages of the Stuttgart *Morgenblatt*). The case of the lovers' suicide in Keller's *Village Romeo and Juliet*, misreported in the news-sheets as a negative example to public morality, exposes the double-standards of this form of mediation, attracted by sensation and yet quick to exploit any exemplary potential for its own ideological ends. Again and again, nineteenth-century *Novellen* show the various social authorities and institutions, from the press to the Church, government, and judiciary, recuperating their own sense of order from the scandals in question, so establishing an exemplary reading for popular opinion to follow.

These authoritative reading models pose further questions about the relationship of the *Novelle* to history, both literary and socio-political. If it is indeed the representative form of nineteenth-century German literature, then to what extent may it be said really to *represent* the society in question? The first thing to say is that the novella is never properly social in the way that a novel may be. The 'occurence' tends to be punctual, focusing with narrative economy on an event which is at odds with historical developments rather than upon history itself. And the *Novelle* tends to focus on the individual rather than the social. Friedrich Schlegel, in his essay on Boccaccio (1801), saw the genre as the vehicle of individuality, but not in what might be called the properly subjective lyric form. In fact, it effects an acute balance between the subjective and the objective, casting personal experience in an impersonal, or stylized form. The *Novelle* also has an exemplary function, that is, in the sense of portraying forms of experience which are not constrained by the particularities of their context, but which have a more universal character. It is, therefore, in Friedrich Schlegel's terms, a vehicle for an 'indirect and concealed subjectivity'.

This accords with Heyse's view that the *Novelle* accommodates the latter-day equivalent of Classical myth, where the exemplary struggle between the individual and Fate is transferred to conflict with the collective in the form of social order. It may serve, in other words, as an *exemplum* for existence in the age of bourgeois individualism, privileging the eponymous likes of Kleist's Michael Kohlhaas or Storm's Rider, Hauke Haien. If not all of the heroes and heroines qualify as bourgeois (for instance, the Marchioness of O...), then this highlights the aristocratic origins of a genre co-opted now by a new order. Bourgeois heroics in the *Novelle* are defined, at least in part, by the aristocratic conventions to which they are heir. They thereby adopt but also adapt the prerogative of tragedy, and the formalities of its representation from their aristocratic antecedents. The Baroness in the framework of the *Conversations of German Émigrés* calls for decorous standards of 'good form' in the narration of the priest's novellas, but such aesthetic courtesies appear increasingly anachronistic. The extraordinary powers and the tragic potential of paradigmatic personalities as displayed in the cases of the bourgeois rebels Michael Kohlhaas or Hauke Haien puts a strain on inherited forms. The fate of another exemplary, eponymous hero—Büchner's Lenz, the poet-preacher—indicates the susceptibility of bourgeois individuality at its limits to the sort of crisis which must find alternative forms of representation, creating new examples, new manners.

In both these and less-critical cases, the *Novelle* would seem to have an in-built bias away from social control and towards the individual angle. It will always sacrifice the epic sweep of social history to an economic narration of personal exploit or crisis. It is, according to the terms elaborated by György Lukács in his *Theory of the Novel* (1920), an intensive rather than an extensive form. It can thus be said to chronicle various kinds of alternative histories. In the Boccaccio essay, Friedrich Schlegel writes that the *Novelle* stands in an ironic relation to history, never properly belonging to it. His brother, August Wilhelm, in his *History of Romantic Literature* (1803), saw the genre as representing a hidden history, recounting the 'curious events which have, as it were, occurred behind the back of bourgeois constitutions and regulations'. As what he calls a 'poetic counter-image' to the official accounts of political historiography, the *Novelle* may both poetically embellish and subvert the grand narrative of history.

This ironic and hidden relation to history is accentuated by a dual tendency in much *Novelle* writing: on the one hand, to frame the action of the narrative in a more-or-less distant past, and on the other, to adopt a rather parochial perspective as compared with the epic sweep of post-Industrial Revolution metropolitan life in the manner of a Dickens or Balzac. But by specializing in what might be called forms of micro-history, and telling stories from behind the back of the bourgeois order, the *Novelle* can have a significant corrective function. A good example might be Droste-Hülshoff's *The Jew's Beech*, a tale which is cast in the domestic manner of the Biedermeier age as a 'Moral Portrait from the Hills of Westphalia'. The narrative focuses on a time-locked 'patch of land', which is 'of historical note' primarily because it is inured to the Age of Enlightenment and Revolution in which it is set. The story is brought to a close in 1789, the year of revolution on the world-historical stage, which points up its function as an ironic 'counter-image' to the historical process. In fact, as we shall see, this story from the back of beyond questions the whole notion of accountability which underlies the project of history in the nineteenth century. Such hidden histories paradoxically challenge the very project of precise empirical research through isolation and analysis which Heyse saw as a model for the *Novelle* in the Age of Realism. By leaving the case it appears so assiduously to document tantalizingly open at its end, this tale of a community which resists historical developments can be seen to reflect ironically upon the image these project.

Theodor Storm based his description of the contemporary *Novelle* as the 'sister of drama' not least on its characteristic economy as 'the most closed of forms'. The closed form may be given a key, a signature, in the form of an emblematic object or action at its core. This feature has come to be known by the term *Falke* or 'falcon', the symbolic bird at the centre of one of Boccaccio's tales, adopted as a programmatic model by Heyse. Heyse and subsequent afficionados of the *Novelle* have specialized in hunting such falcons, according to the presumption that to bag the bird is to find the key which will open up the tale. The example of *The Jew's Beech*, with its emblematic tree, shows, however, that the novella can be a closed form in more senses than one. The key evidence that the tree bears for the tale is, as we shall see, profoundly dubious. Of course there are tales such as Stifter's *Granite* which, as it were, set their narration of personal and local history in the emblematic substance of stone. *Granite* effects a sort of narrative closed circuit, starting and finishing with the incontrovertible weight of a granite keystone. The old patriarch recounting history to his grandson stands as a model for the unquestioned authority of a paternalistic narrator, a legislator of the 'gentle law' which Stifter laid down as the guiding principle behind the world as depicted in his *Coloured Stones* (*Bunte Steine*) collection. But Stifter himself also creates mysterious, darker stones, such as *Tourmaline*, the one featured here, where the 'gentle law' encounters limits to its control.

The darker pieces in Stifter's collection point up a tension within so many nineteenth-century *Novellen*, between an economic tightness of form and a partial or fragmentary narrative perspective. Even Heyse is forced to admit that the frame and falcon model cannot accommodate the vicissitudes of contemporary existence; the keystone is at odds with a cultural life which Heyse recognizes as 'multiply fractured'. The fragmentation of experience opens up new narrative perspectives, but can also break with the guiding principles of understanding. The most closed form, to recall Storm's definition, may also be closed off in various ways from the reader. The graphic narrative silhouette is often liable to appear as a mysterious shadow, with the features which might have guided recognition blanked out. The principle of narrative isolation may isolate the stuff of the story—its characters and 'occurrence'—from readerly access. Economy of means frequently equates with lack of narrative explanation or detective work.

The 'exclusion of the inessential' which Storm prescribes for the genre extends from the level of social contextualization to the domain of psychological investigation. August Wilhelm Schlegel notes that what distinguishes drama from the *Novelle* is the requirement of thorough and detailed motivation for the action; the *Novelle* may present the most improbable scenarios, but should refrain from 'dissecting' their motivation. Storm concurs with Schlegel, attributing his distaste for the parading of 'motivation before the eyes of the reader' to his abiding investment in the 'golden gleam of Romanticism'. For Storm, the Romantic narrative furnishes a model free of excessive psychological rationalization; he dubs this sort of treatment 'symptomatic'—in that it represents human motivation through symptoms without engaging in their analysis. The symptomatic principle converges with the symbolic tendency which informs the genre. An action, event, or object will frequently assume a symbolic value for the psychology of character, a value which the reader will have to assess without the help of the narrator as psychologist.

Storm's use of the language of nineteenth-century psychiatric medicine in his principle of 'symptomatic treatment' looks towards the involvement of the *Novelle* genre with the therapeutic and discursive models of the new science of psychoanalysis which was emerging at about the same time. The early case-histories of hysteria, in particular, were famously compared by Freud to *Novellen* (often mistranslated, following the *Standard Edition*, as 'short stories'). And conversely, the Austrian Modernist Robert Musil aligns his experiments in *Novelle* writing with psychoanalytic case-work, when he transfers the familiar model of the silhouette to that of 'symptomatic actions', actions which, like hysterical symptoms, will represent the 'story' of the 'patient' with exemplary economy.

What will clearly distinguish the symptomatic *Novelle* from the case-history is narratorial intervention. While the analyst's case-book is devoted to establishing an unbroken narrative of cause and effect, trauma and symptom, the narrators of nineteenth-century *Novellen*, from Hoffmann and Kleist to Storm, recurrently fail to fulfil the analytic function. The case narrative of the *Novelle* is more often than not never properly developed into a case-study. The omniscient guidance of the reader by the narrator is only ever given by degrees. Thus, to pursue the case-history model, the reader is placed in the position of analyst, aiming to reconstruct some sort of sustained narrative meaning out of the symptomatic evidence. Again and again, the discursive possibilities of narrative communication are diverted into forms of body-language which rarely yield a straightforward reading. The epidemic blushes and swoons of Kleist's characters and the looks and gestures which substitute for verbal communication in Storm's texts are but two examples of a general feature. Access to the thinking of individuals faced with the crisis situations of *Novelle* narratives is typically absent, partial, or switched to encoded forms. Readerly security in the world of the nineteenth-century *Novelle* is, not least in this respect, a profoundly relative business.

What emerges, then, from the theories and practices of the *Novelle* in nineteenth-century German literature is a thing of many contradictions. It is a genre with a peculiar mixture of courtly and vulgar credentials, appropriated as the representative form of the age of bourgeois realism; it is all too often a curious hybrid of fantasy and workaday rationality—as Roger Paulin has depicted it,[2] part fabulous beast and part domestic animal (we need only think of Storm's White Horse); it is subject to stringent structural controls and yet only, it seems, in order to challenge their hold. Fritz Martini expresses this in terms of what he calls the dialectical relationship between form and fragmentation, order and disorder, knowledge and unknowability in the *Novelle* genre. As a compendium of irregular elements—'individual, coincidental, contradictory, confused, and even "demonic"'— the *Novelle* can only sustain a particular kind of narrative organization. Even though the genre tends to present a 'closed fable', the conventions of step-by-step causality are superseded by a deregulated, often fragmentary form of narrative.

It is these and other contradictions which ultimately make the *Novelle* so fit a representative for nineteenth-century German culture with all its contents and discontents. And that representative or exemplary status may apply beyond the borders of German culture—the parishes, provinces, and cantons of Storm's Schleswig-Holstein, Droste-Hülshoff's Westphalia, and Keller's hypothetical Seldwyla—to the wider domains of nineteenth-century Europe. The *Novelle* remains an exceptional case, perhaps, but an exemplary one none the less.

[2] Roger Paulin, *The Brief Compass: The Nineteenth-Century German Novelle* (Oxford, 1985), 1–2.

LUDWIG TIECK, *Blond Eckbert* (*Der blonde Eckbert*, 1796)

This tale is often viewed as the prototype for the Romantic *Novelle*, with its appeal to fairy-tale conventions and to the feudal world of an indeterminate medieval setting. Arranged before a roaring fire, the narrative circle of the knight, his lady, and a noble guest fulfil the archetypal requirements of the *Novelle* genre as a particular object of Romantic nostalgia. In fact, *Blond Eckbert* proves an acutely unsettling revival of this narrative model as it proceeds to confuse its apparently secure domestic framework with the uncanny events of the tale told within it. This confusion provides an ambiguous model for the *Novelle* genre in both its Romantic and post-Romantic modes. Indeed, the collapsing of the 'real' world of the frame with the 'fairy-tale' world of Bertha's childhood story establishes a confused relationship between those two modes which will prevail throughout the nineteenth century. As Bertha insists that her story, as strange as it may seem, should not be taken for a fairy-tale, thus staking a realist claim for this archetypal Romantic story, so the narratives of Realism will be drawn to revisit this strange world. Like Eckbert, a whole series of post-Romantic protagonists will find their ostensibly real lives seeming 'more like a strange fairy-tale'.

The power of this *Novelle* lies not least in the sense it gives of compulsive recurrence. While, like the *Novelle* genre itself, Bertha's quest is driven by the desire to see 'something new', all experience in this text seems bound to turn back on itself. Her search for novelty is programmed by story-book romances and is converted in its turn into a narrative which turns out to be circular. The repeated song serves as a sort of *leitmotiv* for a more general sense of the past revisiting the present, an effect emphasized by its self-reflexive structure. The story has a stock of reflexive features, from the partial mirroring of the names of the couple, to dreams within dreams, to the proliferation of Walther's identity in the figures encountered by Eckbert in the final sequence. Identity is prone here to the sorts of compulsive divisions, projections, and reflections which characterize the world of German Romanticism. The story of the brother and sister divided and then united in incest represents the sort of nightmare which haunts the family romance of perfect union in the home. The variety of experience is reduced to serial repetitions, leaving only a sense of radical isolation for the protagonist.

In common with the tales of Hoffmann, *Blond Eckbert*, with its elements of dream and madness, can be read as a psycho-analytic case *avant la lettre*. As such, it provides a potentially catastrophic model for the case-stories of the nineteenth-century *Novelle*. In the Age of Realism this model will rarely recur with such terrible consequences, but the threat of the unknowable, and more especially of repressed knowledge, remains a potent element in the construction of the genre.

HEINRICH VON KLEIST, *The Marchioness of O...*
(*Die Marquise von O...*, 1808)

This tale is typical of Kleist's *Novellen* in dispensing with a mediating framework. It retains only the vestige of a frame in the prefatory note that it is recounted after a real event which has been transferred southwards from home-ground to Upper Italy. This device at once gestures towards the *Novelle* standard of an actual occurrence whilst indicating that it is transposed on to fictional ground. This principle is carried over to the naming of places and people (in this aristocratic tale the two converge) by their initials and/or titles. The initial at once vouches for real identities to be protected and signals a potential inclination towards narratorial secrecy and disguise, an unsettling feature in a story which turns on a mystery of identity. If these initials are reminiscent of those used in judicial reports and psychiatric case-histories (not least Freud's case-studies in hysteria), then this is only too apt in a *Novelle* which incorporates both the model of the detective story and that of the case-history (the pregnancy as a hysterical fantasy).

Stylistically, *The Marchioness of O...* represents a particularly fine example of Kleistian idiosyncrasies. If the narrator is appar-ently non-interventionist, the reader is none the less made aware of the process of mediation. The most striking feature is the extraordinary proliferation of reported speech, a device which converts the drama of the spoken word into an estranged narra-tive form. Given that the dramatic 'event' of the narrative is advertised at the outset, it may not be far-fetched to compare the narration to Brechtian strategies of alienation. The story, with its strong sense of scene and dramatic turning-points, certainly exemplifies the *Novelle* form as 'sister of drama', but also suggests that this relationship is partially estranged. This stylistic tension is characteristic of the involvement between passionate, often violent physicality and forms of decorum throughout the story.

The Marchioness of O... thus embodies (as does its heroine) the paradoxical combination of order and disorder which is the proper stuff of the *Novelle* genre. Kleist pits feeling against reason, personal honour against the prevailing moral code, exposing the fragility of the social structures, not least that of the family, when confronted with the 'unheard-of event'. The polarizations which are created through this event (the count transformed from angel to devil; the murderous father converted into doting lover) test the structures of order and understanding to the limit. In the version of the classic recognition scene when the Marchioness and her mother recognize how obvious the identity of the mystery man should have been, Kleist plays with the potential for destruction familiar from the *Decameron* and elsewhere by having the Marchioness flee the count as if he were carrying the plague. When the family ultimately assents to the incorporation of the rapist as father, they do it for the sake of preserving a fragile arrangement. This must remain a paradoxical accommodation, arguably as much an endorsement of fragility —the susceptibility to being plagued by further disorders—as the affirmation of a sense of order.

GEORG BÜCHNER, *Lenz* (1839)

While Tieck's and Kleist's stories display certain elements of the case-history model, *Lenz* has a more sustained rapport with psychiatric narratives. If the account of this episode of insanity in the life of the late-eighteenth-century writer has often been seen as previewing psychoanalytic insights, then it does so in distinctly ambiguous ways. Above all, *Lenz* lacks the sort of controlling, analytic framework which would feature in a case-history, and, accordingly, the potential for a therapeutic treatment of the case.

The much-vaunted modernity of this text lies in the way in which it subjects the reader to the disordered experience of its protagonist. Not only is the Novelle itself a fragment, but it recurrently fragments conventional structures of language and continuities of perspective. The opening sequence of the text is characteristic of the whole as it gravitates between incomplete syntactic units (through various effects of parataxis—the assembly of linguistic elements without normal cohesion) and almost unbearable accumulations of experience within a single sentence structure (through the excessive continuity effects of hypotaxis). This radically inconsistent style is only apparently under the control of the third-person narrator, whose sober voice ascertains the essentials of time, place, person, and action in the opening model sentence. Before the reader is directly challenged by the extraordinary point of view of the disturbed individual who wishes he could walk on his head, the narrative has set about inserting the reader's perspective into the text via that of the protagonist. The bizarre animation of the landscape is accentuated in the German text by a proliferation of prefixes indicating motions to and from a perceiving subject, subtle markers of the subjective perspective which defy adequate translation.

The modulation between first- and third-person perspectives which operates throughout the story, not least through forms of *erlebte Rede*, or free indirect speech, is characteristic of a more general rhythm of alternations in the text. It is tempting to see a sort of proto-Expressionism at work in the text, as the swinging moods and perceptions of Lenz are transferred to the extraordinary landscape descriptions. Indeed, the term 'abstract expressionism' might be most appropriate, as the shapes of the outer world are recurrently stylized into a topography of lines and planes. Line and plane represent one element in the alternation between extremes in this landscape, between contraction and expansion, intimacy and alienation, rigidity and animation, peaks and abysses. It is the pulse of these alternations which gives such a powerful picture of Lenz's disturbance as he is driven into forms of repetition compulsion in his actions and speech. The notion of the 'unheard-of occurence' as the basis of the *Novelle* is converted here into a form of unheard-of recurrence. It finds its ultimate expression in the oxymoron of the screaming silence which takes up the circumference of Lenz's perception at the end of the text. The final line of the *Novelle*—'And so his life went on'—marks the fact that it must remain incomplete in a case where the strange event is the ongoing life of the insane subject.

ANNETTE VON DROSTE-HÜLSHOFF, *The Jew's Beech*
(*Die Judenbuche*, 1842)

As we have already seen, *The Jew's Beech* is an exemplary novella which can only offer an ambiguous example for moral judgements. The poem which frames it can only make the judgement that judgements are fallible, likely to rebound upon the arbiter. As a detective story, it might easily comply with classic models like the Sherlock Holmes stories, where the carefully constructed mystery is always ultimately solved by a competent sleuth. This is the detective as a model agent for the work of disclosure in both narrative fiction and historical research. But in the case of this *Novelle* we have a detective story without a detective. Instead, we have a scrupulous narrative voice which certainly on occasion fulfils the conventional role of an omniscient and freely informative guide to the fictional world and its obscurities, but remains for the most part limited to an external perspective on the psychological motivation of the key players. The text leaves certain mysteries in the dark even as it appears to offer revelation at its end.

The refusal on the part of the narrator to fictionalize the solution of the Brandis murder mystery only serves to point up the limitations of the narrative or historical or criminological quest for reliable sources and attributions. It is arguably less a guarantee of narrative honesty than a frank admission of obscurity. This unsolved crime also reflects upon the final disclosure, which might appear successfully to consign the case of *The Jew's Beech* to the case-book of criminal history. Here we have the old feudal squire as a stand-in for the detective, more Dr Watson than Holmes; and it is on his questionable authority that the historical riddle of Aaron's murder is solved. But the evidence for this disclosure is itself an unresolved mystery. The squire recognizes the identity of the hanged man by means of a distinguishing mark almost as old as the history of Western literature: the scar which reveals the identity of Homer's Odysseus. And yet this scar is not recognizable to the reader, as it has no documented source in the narrative. We are left with a personal history which is written off on the strength of a mysterious clue. This unaccountable trace of violence must reflect problematically on the narration of history as a whole, the project of historiographical source-work which Heyse identifies as the model for *Novelle* writing in the Age of Realism. This exemplary *Novelle* would appear to reveal above all that the moral regulation of society is made to rely upon dubious and circumstantial evidence.

ADALBERT STIFTER, *Tourmaline* (*Turmalin*, 1853)

This text, perhaps the most opaque amongst Stifter's *Novelle* collection of *Coloured Stones*, incorporates both the detective-story and the case-history models. It is a stone which seems to enjoy a steady setting in its narrative framework, starting out in the assured voice of the collection's master narrator and then contracted to that of a respected benefactress with good judgement. This is a framed narrative, however, which encloses highly questionable examples of narration and communication. The case of adultery, missing persons, and a strange underground existence is never properly accountable.

The institutions of public order and information can gain no real purchase on the strange case of *Tourmaline*; twice newspapers are used, much as in *The Marchioness of O...*, in an attempt to trace the missing party, but without success; and when the local officials intervene they can only repeat the inventory of his possessions already provided by the narrator. Stifter indulges here in the sort of excessive listing of materials which is so characteristic of Gottfried Keller's narratives, and which only accentuates the lack of information in the real substance of the case.

If the judicial post-mortem also fails to cast light on the case, then this reveals the ambiguous function of the body in this mystery. The grotesque distension of the daughter's head serves as a most graphic embodiment of experience which defies normal judgement. The body is incorporated into the breakdown of communication in the tale: the girl's age cannot be 'read' from her distorted features, and even when she has been treated her face is only partly regularized, with the features 'more expressive' (literally, 'speaking more clearly'). It is a form of 'body language' which is echoed in parody by the jackdaw whose speech is 'mutilated' and 'scarcely human'. The girl's communication represents the collapsing of excessive order with disorder, as she speaks a 'written language' which is largely incomprehensible and can only be approximately translated into the terms of the narrative.

By the end of the narrative the child has been socialized and domesticated to a degree. The facts of her case are, however, never properly disclosed. The description of death, removal, demolition, and rebuilding in the final frame arguably only serves to reinforce the sense of lost experience in this strange case. Not only does this *Novelle* go 'behind the back' of the bourgeois order, but it sheds an unclear light on the sort of underground existences which threaten to undermine by their example its exemplary controls.

EDUARD MÖRIKE, *Mozart on the Way to Prague*
(*Mozart auf der Reise nach Prag*, 1856)

Mörike's text, like *Lenz*, is a version of the *Künstlernovelle*, the genre which depicts the exemplary fate of the artist. Unlike *Lenz*, this *Novelle* adopts a secure Realist mode, with an assured narrator taking his cue from a contemporary source to elaborate freely on the story of a station on Mozart's journey to Prague. The narrator paints in the picture of the Mozarts' coach with a sense of detail which appeals to his reader as connoisseur, and thereby establishes a contract of shared knowledge. The tone of the narration is controlled, humorous, and engaging, but even here there are darker undertones. Mörike effects, that is, a sort of toned-down imitation of his protagonist's disposition and compositions: exuberant, melancholic, lyrical, and morbid by turns. Here too, the *Novelle* provides the vehicle for a combination of oppositions, 'as proof', to cite the text, 'of how extremes sometimes converge'.

While the tale as a whole is overlaid by a sense of affirmation, it would be wrong to be too easily seduced by this. On the social-political level, the appeal is to a sort of retrospective community in narrative and other forms of cultural communication. This is a *Novelle* cast in the classic mould of gentility and benevolent patronage. As in the case of *The Jew's Beech*, however, it is a fragile reconstruction, overshadowed by the imminent crisis of the *ancien régime* in the shape of the French Revolution. In both cases there would seem to be a dubious prognosis here for the feudal structures of mid-nineteenth-century German culture.

This sense of political death-throes is matched by the shades of mortality around the vivid characterization of Mozart. The two combine in the object which fits the example of Heyse's falcon, the orange. This fruit serves as an emblem for the interpolated narrative of the Italian spectacle which is, in its turn, a 'perfect reflection of the Mozart spirit'. It is, however, an emblem which is split and disjunctive. The fantasy of the orange tree's perfect revival as a 'living symbol' of the pre-revolutionary heyday must thus carry signs of mortification. The tree is figured by the count as a sort of aristocratic Odysseus, recognizable and legitimated by its old scars. But the new scar of the plucked and spliced orange cuts across the mythical model; as in *The Jew's Beech*, there is more to the recognition scene than meets the eye.

This narrative so given to fruition then, bearing a profusion of tales and interludes which flout the economic prescriptions of the genre, also recognizes that the fruit must fall or be broken off. When the company divides 'into two groups', so must the narrative split and follow one half. The story gives and it takes away. Its ending, where the narrative is diverted into the form of a lyrical poem, represents the culmination of this double movement. The narrative celebration of musical composition is cut off in order to bear a final fruit—the music in words of one of Mörike's lyrics. It is a sort of premonitory elegy, figuring death in the growth of less fruitful plants—the fir-tree and the rose which are meant for the grave. It consummates the combination of gain and loss which is the stuff of this *Novelle*.

GOTTFRIED KELLER, *Clothes Make the Man*
(*Kleider machen Leute*, 1874)

This tale, part of the *People of Seldwyla* (*Die Leute von Seldwyla*) cycle, represents another, more satirical form of challenge to the order of bourgeois realism. The framework to the cycle establishes Seldwyla as the exemplary case of an exemplary community. The assembled stories describe exceptional bits of what the framework calls 'discarded' experience, but none the less the sort of thing which 'could only happen in Seldwyla'. The logic of this is that the throw-away fiction of Seldwyla might equally serve as an exceptional example of nineteenth-century bourgeois order as a whole.

Clothes Make the Man is a satirical exposé of the double economy regulating the moral and cultural affairs of the bourgeoisie. The impostor can only be so successful because of the regime of false appearances which operates in the host community; the 'novel' of the mysterious aristocratic visitor is co-authored by the bourgeois hosts in order to fulfil the lack of romance in their existence. They misread the signs of the tailor's status in much the same way as they attach misleading signs to their houses and sleighs. The false investment in the aristocratic other is a sign of bankruptcy in their material culture.

Keller crowns and breaks this illusion by enacting one of the exemplary scenarios of Romanticism: the *Doppelgänger* encounter. He sets this amidst the mockery of a carnival parade. The Romantic nightmare of a double identity is visited both upon the impostor and on the no-less inauthentic communal identity of Goldach. The 'novella' of the Polish count is debunked as a twopenny fiction and with it the would-be poetic realism of those who helped to construct it. And while narrator and reader have apparently enjoyed the privilege of critical knowledge from the very start, Keller's satires invariably also expose the investments made by author-producer and reader-consumer in the fictional text. We too have been made a party to the alluring fantasy of Romantic imposture.

While Nettchen comes to recognize Wenzel for what he really is and returns him to the order of realism with her call for 'No more story-book romancing!', what is left is a story of rags to riches which carries no real narrative interest. Wenzel is now more like the bourgeois than they are themselves, and, left with such realities, the reader is likely to feel a certain, albeit guarded, nostalgia for the false count and for what Keller, in a letter to Storm, called the 'plastic and drastic' scenario of his *Novelle*.

THEODOR STORM, *The White Horse Rider*
(*Der Schimmelreiter*, 1888)

This text is perhaps the closest that the *Novelle* genre comes to the broader sweep of Realism in its characteristic European format. It depicts the major stations of a life-span and sets this within a fairly extensive social and natural picture. If the narrative none the less qualifies as a *Novelle* rather than a short novel, then this is due to its personal form of narration, its intense symbolic fabric, and its dramatic construction. In the crisis scenes on the dike, Storm achieves a perfect embodiment of the 'falcon' principle, as the turning-points in the action literally turn upon the ghostly white horse.

   The White Horse Rider gives the lie to the criticism that Storm's is a parochial world with only domestic interests. It joins the other examples here in presenting a radical challenge to conventions of knowability. The frame is here raised to a new level of sophistication, as the core story is mediated through time by a string of narrators, and interrupted more than once by the central narrator, the schoolmaster. The tension inherent in the framing device between control and containment on the one hand and distance and relativization on the other is nowhere more acute than here. The framework cannot properly keep hold of the enigma of the supernatural which returns here to haunt the culture of Realism at its peak. Nor does it serve to display the psychology of character; Storm's 'symptomatic treatment' of his characters' motivation subjects the reader to the same problems of communication and of understanding as afflict his isolated protagonists. Hauke Haien is never psychologized for the reader; rather, we are either left to read the symptoms of gesture and word or, as in the case of *Lenz*, immediately subjected to the thought processes of a subjectivity in chaos through the use of free indirect speech.

The ambivalence of the framing controls, the contesting claims of the real and the fantastic, order and disorder, and the crisis of isolated subjectivity all mark this text out as an exemplary case of this, the exemplary genre of German literature in the age of bourgeois individualism.

TRANSLATOR'S NOTE

Traduttore, traditore—translator, traitor. The old proverb is as true as ever, for the work of the translator can only be, at best, a compromise, an attempt to produce upon the reader, as far as possible, the effect of the original version upon the original reader. And yet, I hope that the present collection of nineteenth-century German novellas will give the reader an idea, at least, of the original flavour.

I have sought to remain faithful to any idiosyncrasies of style in the original texts. Thus, in *The Marchioness of O...*, I have reproduced the proliferation of subordinate clauses and the 'excessive' use of reported speech. Similarly, the English version of *Lenz* does not seek to 'correct' the text where the German may seem eccentric, even nonsensical (reflecting as this does the heightened and disturbed mental processes of the protagonist). In the case of *The White Horse Rider* I opted to render the elements of the text originally in Plattdeutsch into Yorkshire dialect. Whether or not I have succeeded (being in fact a Lancashireman), I respectfully leave to any readers from Yorkshire to decide.

The present translations are based on the editions published by Philipp Reclam Jun., Stuttgart, with the exception of *The Jew's Beech*, for which the Insel Taschenbuch edition (Frank-furt/Main 1979) was used.

I would like to thank Judith Luna of Oxford University Press for her patience and support in the considerable liaison work involved in the preparation of this book; Jeff New, for his copy-editing; and above all Andrew Webber, for his valuable help and suggestions on difficult points of translation—especially with the verses: the renderings, of the poem and Christmas carol in *The Jew's Beech*, and the verses from *Blond Eckbert* and *Lenz* are, in fact, his entirely.

Aalen, Germany
June 1996

SELECT BIBLIOGRAPHY

On the Novelle genre

E. K. Bennett and H. M. Waidson, *A History of the German Novelle* (Cambridge, 1965).

J. M. Ellis, *Narration in the German 'Novelle': Theory and Interpretation* (Cambridge, 1974).

R. Paulin, *The Brief Compass: The Nineteenth-Century German 'Novelle'* (Oxford, 1985).

M. Swales, *The German 'Novelle'* (Princeton, 1977).

A. J. Webber, *The 'Doppelgänger': Double Visions in German Literature* (Oxford, 1996).

On the authors featured here

J. Adams (ed.), *Mörike's Muses: Critical Essays of Eduard Mörike* (Columbia, 1990).

J. Guthrie, *Annette von Droste-Hülshoff: A German Poet Between Romanticism and Realism* (Oxford, 1989).

J. McGlathery, *Desire's Sway: The Plays and Stories of Heinrich von Kleist* (Detroit, 1983).

R. Paulin, *Ludwig Tieck: A Literary Biography* (Oxford, 1985).

J. Reddick, *Georg Büchner: The Shattered Whole* (Oxford, 1994).

T. J. Rogers, *Techniques of Solipsism: A Study of Theodor Storm's Narrative Fiction* (Cambridge, 1970).

E. Swales, *The Poetics of Scepticism: Gottfried Keller and 'Die Leute von Seldwyla'* (Oxford, 1994).

E. and M. Swales, *Adalbert Stifter: A Critical Study* (Cambridge, 1984).

LUDWIG TIECK

Blond Eckbert

In a region of the Harz Mountains there once lived a knight who
was generally known simply as 'Blond Eckbert'. He was around
forty years of age, barely of middle height, and his short light–
blond hair hung thick and unadorned about his pale, haggard
face. He lived a very quiet and withdrawn existence, was never
involved in his neighbours' feuds, and was only seldom to be
seen outside the curtain wall of his small castle. His wife was
just as fond of this solitary life as he, and they seemed to love
each other dearly; but they frequently lamented that heaven did
not bless their union with children.

Only rarely did Eckbert receive guests and, when he did so,
hardly anything in the normal course of life was changed for
their sakes; moderation reigned in the castle and thrift itself
appeared to rule over everything. On such occasions Eckbert was
good–humoured and merry; when he was alone, however, a sort
of reticence, a quiet reserved melancholy, could be seen in him.

No one came to the castle as often as Philipp Walther, a man
with whom Eckbert had formed a friendship because he was
more or less of the same way of thinking as Eckbert. Walther's
home was in Franconia, but he often stayed for more than half
a year in the vicinity of Eckbert's castle; here he would gather
herbs and stones and spend his time in sorting them; he was not
dependent upon anyone but lived on his modest fortune. Eckbert
often accompanied him on his lonely walks and the friendship
between the two deepened with every year.

Sometimes a man is anxious when he must keep a secret from
his friend, a secret which, until then, he has most carefully
concealed; then his soul feels an irresistible urge to reveal itself
completely, to open its innermost depths to his friend in order
to secure his friendship even more. In moments such as this, the
two gentle souls reveal themselves to each other and it sometimes
happens, too, that one shies away from the other's acquaintance.

It was already autumn when, one misty evening, Eckbert was sitting with his friend and his wife Bertha before the hearth. The flames were casting a bright light throughout the room and playing upon the ceiling; the blackness of the night peered through the windows and the trees outside trembled in the wet cold. Walther was grumbling about the long way home which faced him. Eckbert suggested that he should stay to spend half the night in pleasant chat and then sleep in one of the rooms in the castle until morning. Walther agreed; now supper and wine were brought, more logs were piled upon the fire, and the conversation became merrier and more intimate.

After supper had been cleared away and the servants had gone, Eckbert took Walther by the hand and said: 'My friend, you must hear from my wife the story of her youth—a strange enough tale it is.'—'With pleasure,' replied Walther, and they took their places before the hearth once more.

The clock had just struck midnight and the moon was shining intermittently through the clouds scudding past. 'You must not think me intrusive,' Bertha began, 'but my husband says you are such a noble-minded man that it would be unjust to conceal anything from you. But please do not consider my story a mere fairy-tale, however strange it may sound.

I was born in a small village; my father was a poor herdsman. My parents had such difficulties managing their household that they often did not know where the next crust of bread was to come from. But what saddened me far more was that my father and mother often quarrelled because of their poverty, and that one would reproach the other bitterly for it. What was more, I was always having to hear that I was a stupid, silly creature not capable of doing even the simplest task, and I was indeed very clumsy and awkward; I used to drop everything, I could not learn either sewing or spinning, I was of no help in the fields— but I understood my parents' plight only too well. I would often sit in the corner and dream of how I would help them if I were suddenly to become rich, how I would shower them with gold and silver and rejoice at their amazement; I imagined spirits appearing who showed me buried treasures or gave me little pebbles which turned into jewels—in a word, I busied myself with the strangest fantasies, and then, whenever I had to stand up to help with something or carry something, I was even more clumsy, because my head was spinning from all those odd imaginings.

My father was always very angry with me because, he said, I was such a useless burden on the family; he often treated me quite cruelly and it was seldom that I heard a friendly word from him. I was now about eight years old, so that they began to make serious efforts to have me work or learn something useful. My father believed it was only stubbornness or laziness on my part, making me wish to spend my days in idleness; and he was unbelievably hard on me and used to threaten me; but as this was all to no avail, he punished me in the cruellest possible manner, saying that this punishment would be repeated every day, because I was such a good-for-nothing creature.

I wept bitterly the whole night through; I felt so dreadfully forsaken and so sorry for myself that I wished I was dead. I feared the coming of the dawn; I did not know what to do; I wished for every possible talent and could not understand why I should be more stupid than the other children I knew. I was on the brink of despair.

As dawn approached I rose and, hardly knowing what I was doing, opened the door of our little hut. Soon I was in the open fields and, a short time later, I found myself in a forest where the light of day was hardly to be seen. On and on I ran without looking back; I did not feel tired at all, always imagining that my father would overtake me and, angry at me for running away, treat me even more cruelly.

The sun was already quite high in the sky when I came out of the forest; now I could see something dark ahead of me covered in a thick mist. Sometimes I had to climb hills, sometimes I had to walk a winding path through cliffs; now I guessed that I must be in the neighbouring mountains and I began to be afraid in the midst of the solitude; I had never seen mountains on the plain where we lived, and the very word 'mountains' was a dreadful sound to my ears whenever I heard it mentioned. I had not the courage to go back and my fear drove me on; often I looked around in terror whenever the wind rushed through the trees above me or the sound of a distant axe echoed far through the still morning air. When at last I encountered some miners and charcoal burners and heard their outlandish accents, I almost fainted with fright.

Then I came through a number of villages where I had to beg, for now I was hungry and thirsty; I was able to get along fairly well with my replies whenever people questioned me. I had been wandering for about four days when I came to a narrow, steep path which led me farther and farther from the highway. The crags around me now took on another, far uncannier aspect: cliffs, piled one upon another in such a way that it seemed the first puff of wind would topple them. I did not know whether I should go on. Until now, I had always slept in the forest at night—for it was just then the loveliest time of year—or in shepherd's huts off the beaten track; but here I could see no human dwelling, nor could I expect to find one in this wilderness; the cliffs became more and more frightening; often I had to walk past dizzying chasms and at last even the path came to an end beneath my feet. I was in despair, I wept and shrieked and my voice echoed dreadfully in the rocky valleys. Now night was falling and I looked for a mossy spot where I might rest. But I could not sleep; during the night I heard the most eerie sounds; sometimes I took them for wild animals, sometimes for the wind moaning through the cliffs, and sometimes for strange birds. I said my prayers and did not fall asleep until it was almost morning.

I awoke with daylight shining in my face. A steep cliff rose in front of me, and I climbed up in the hope of discovering a way out of the wilderness, and perhaps of seeing houses and people. When I reached the top, however, everything, as far as my eye could see, was just like the scene around me; everywhere was veiled in a misty haze; the day was grey and gloomy, nowhere could I espy a tree, a meadow, or even a bush, save for some single shrubs which had sprouted, lonely and dreary, out of narrow cracks in the cliffs. I cannot describe how I yearned to see just one human being, even if it should be someone I would fear. At the same time I was tormented by a ravaging hunger. I sat down and made up my mind to die. But after a while the desire to live gained the upper hand, and I dragged myself to my feet and walked on, weeping and sighing broken sighs the whole day; at last I scarcely knew who I was, so tired and exhausted was I; I hardly wished to live, yet I was afraid to die.

As evening approached, the surrounding district seemed somewhat more friendly; my thoughts and wishes revived and the desire to live awoke in all my veins. Now I thought I could hear the clatter of a mill in the distance, I doubled my pace—and oh! how happy, how relieved I felt when at last I came to the end of those barren cliffs; I saw woods and meadows with smiling, far-off hills ahead of me once more. It was as if I had walked out of Hell into Paradise, and my loneliness and helplessness no longer seemed so frightening.

Instead of the mill I had hoped for, I came upon a waterfall, which naturally lessened my joy a great deal; I was just scooping a handful of water from the brook when I thought I heard a gentle sound of coughing some distance away. Never have I been so pleasantly surprised as at that moment; I went closer, and there at the edge of the wood I glimpsed an old woman who seemed to be resting. She was dressed almost entirely in black, a black hood covered her head and a large part of her face, and she was holding a crutch in her hand.

I went up to her and begged her to help me; she bade me sit down beside her and gave me bread and some wine. Whilst I was eating, she sang a hymn in a grating voice, then, when she had finished singing, she bade me follow her.

I was very pleased at this request, even though the old woman's voice and manner seemed so strange to me. With the help of her crutch she walked quite nimbly, though pulling a face at every step, so that I could not help laughing at first. The wild crags lay farther and farther behind us; we went across a pleasant meadow and then through a fairly wide forest. The sun was just setting as we came out of the forest, and I shall never forget the sight and my feelings on that evening. Everything was melting in the softest shade of red and gold, the trees were standing with their tops against the setting sun; the fields were bathed in its beautiful light, the woods and the leaves of the trees were still, the clear sky seemed like an open paradise; the whispering of the streams and, from time to time, the rustling of the trees resounded through the pleasant stillness as if in melancholy joy. For the first time, my soul began to gain an inkling of the world and what went on in it. I completely forgot myself and my guide, and my eyes and mind were lost in wonder amid the golden clouds.

Now we went up a hill on which birch trees were growing; from the top you could look down into a green valley filled with birches and in the midst of the trees was a small hut. We heard the sound of excited barking, and soon a lively little dog appeared, leaping up at the old woman and wagging his tail; then he came to me, looked at me from all sides, and went back to the old woman again, jumping happily about her.

As we walked down the hill I heard a wonderful sound of singing, like that of a bird, which seemed to come from the hut. The song went like this:

> The woods lonely
> A joy to me
> Each day will be
> In eternity.
> What joy to me
> The woods lonely.

These few words were constantly repeated; I would say it sounded almost as if a horn and a shawm were playing together far, far away.

In a fit of extreme curiosity I walked into the hut without waiting for a word from the old woman. It was already twilight; everything in the hut was neat and tidy, there were some cups standing on a cupboard and some curious vessels upon a table; there was a bird in a gleaming cage near the window, and it was indeed the bird that was singing those words. The old woman began coughing and wheezing, and I thought she would never recover; sometimes she would stroke the little dog, sometimes she would speak to the bird, which only answered with its usual song; all in all she behaved as if I were simply not there. I could not help shuddering whenever I looked at her, for her face kept twitching, and she kept nodding her head as well, as if from old age, so that I could not see at all what she really looked like.

After she had recovered she lighted a lamp and laid a tiny little table, on which she placed our supper. Then she looked around for me and bade me bring up one of the basket chairs; now I sat facing her with the lamp between us. Folding her bony hands together she began to pray aloud, her face twitching all the while, so that again I almost laughed; but I took care not to do so, not wishing to make her angry.

After supper was over she prayed again; then she showed me to a bed in a low, narrow room; she herself slept in the outer room. I did not remain awake for long, I was half dazed with weariness, but I awoke several times in the night to hear the old woman talking to the dog and, now and then, to the bird, which seemed to be dreaming and only sang a few words of its song. All this, together with the birch trees rustling in front of the window and the song of a distant nightingale, made such a strange medley that I had a feeling of not being awake, but only of falling into another, even stranger dream.

Next morning the old woman woke me and, shortly after, showed me the work I was to do. I had to spin for her, and this I learned quickly; I also had to look after the dog and the bird. I was soon able to cope with the household, and I became familiar with all the things around me; I now felt that everything had to be just as it was; nor did it occur to me any more that there was something strange about the old woman, that her house was bizarre and far away from other human dwellings, and that there was something extraordinary about the bird. Naturally I was always aware of its beauty; its feathers gleamed in every possible colour, the loveliest pale blue and the most fiery red alternated on its throat and body, and when it sang it swelled its breast proudly, so that its feathers seemed more splendid than ever.

The old woman often went away and did not return until evening; then I would go with the dog to meet her and she would call me her child and daughter. At last I became fond of her with all my heart, just as we grow accustomed to everything, especially in our childhood. In the evenings she would teach me to read; I learned to do so easily and later it became a source of endless pleasure to me in my loneliness, for she had some old, handwritten books with wonderful stories.

The memory of how I lived in those days seems strange to me even now; never visited by any human creature, living in such a narrow family circle—for the dog and the bird were like old friends to me. I have never been able to recall the dog's strange name since, in spite of all the times I called him.

I had been living with the old woman for four years in this way, and I must have been about twelve when she at last began to trust me more and revealed a secret to me: every day the bird used to lay an egg with a pearl or a jewel inside it. Already I had often noticed her furtively busying herself with the cage, although I had never taken any particular notice. Now she gave me the task of taking out the eggs when she was away and keeping them safe in those curious vessels. She used to leave me my food and remain away for longer periods—for weeks, for months; my spinning-wheel would hum, the dog would bark, the wondrous bird would sing, and yet everything around was so quiet that, all the time I was there, I cannot recall ever hearing a gale or a thunderstorm. No human soul ever strayed to our house, no wild animal ever approached our door; I was contented and worked from one day to the next.—People might perhaps be very happy if they could live like that, undisturbed until the end of their days.

From the little that I read, I formed strange fantasies about the world and its people; all these I deduced from myself and the beings around me: whenever merry people were mentioned, I could only imagine them to be like the little dog; splendid ladies always looked like the bird, and all old women looked like that strange old one of mine. I had also read something about love, and enacted wondrous tales in my own imagination. I thought up the most handsome knight in the world, I endowed him with every possible virtue, without really knowing what he looked like after all my efforts; but I was also able to feel genuine pity for myself when he did not return my love; then I would deliver long, moving speeches to myself, at times aloud, only to win his love.—I see you smiling! Well, of course, we are all of us past that time of our youth.

By now I preferred to be alone, for then I was the mistress of the house. The dog was very fond of me and did everything I wished; the bird replied to all my questions with its only song, and my spinning-wheel turned merrily so that, truly, I never wished for things to be different. Whenever the old woman returned from her long travels she would praise me for my work; she said that her house was kept much more orderly since I lived there. She was pleased to see how I was growing and how healthy I looked; in a word, she treated me just like a daughter.

'You're a good girl, child,' she once said to me in her grating voice; 'if you continue this way, life will always be kind to you; but no one who strays from the path of righteousness will ever prosper, and punishment will follow, no matter how late'.—I did not pay much heed as she said this, for I was always a very lively child in all my deeds and all my being; during the night, however, her words came back to me, yet I did not understand what she had meant. I thought them all over very carefully, for I had indeed read about riches, and at last it occurred to me that her pearls and jewels might well be something valuable. Soon this thought became clearer and clearer to me. But whatever could she mean by the 'path of righteousness'? I still did not fully understand the meaning of her words.

I was now fourteen years of age, and it is always man's misfortune that he only gains his wits in order to lose the innocence of his soul. For I fully realized that I alone could decide whether I should take the bird and the jewels while the old woman was away and go out into the world which I had read about. At the same time, I thought, perhaps I might be able to meet that very handsome knight who still lived in my memory.

This thought was at first no more vivid than any other but, whenever I sat at my spinning-wheel, it would always come back to me against my will and I would immerse myself so deeply in it that I could imagine myself splendidly adorned with jewels and surrounded by knights and princes. And whenever I had forgotten myself in this way, I would feel very gloomy when I looked up once more and found myself in the little dwelling. While I was at my work, by the way, the old woman did not trouble herself about me.

One day my hostess again set out, saying that this time she would remain away longer than usual, that I should take good care of everything, and not waste my time. It was not without a certain anxiety that I said farewell to her, for I had a feeling that I would not see her again. I stood watching her for a long time as she went off, though I did not know myself why I was so afraid; it was almost as if my plan lay directly before me without my really knowing it.

Never did I make such efforts to care for the dog and the bird; they meant more to me then than ever before. The old woman had already been gone for several days when I rose one morning with the firm intention of taking the bird with me and going off to seek the world, as it is called. My thoughts oppressed me and weighed heavily upon me. I wanted to remain there and yet the idea was repulsive to me; a strange struggle raged in my soul, like a quarrel between two conflicting spirits within me. One moment the calm solitude seemed so pleasant, the next, I was captivated by the thought of a new world with all its wonderful variety.

I did not know what to make of myself; the dog kept jumping up at me, the sunshine spread joyfully across the meadows, and the green birch-trees glistened; I felt as if I had something very urgent to do; I seized the little dog, tied him up in the room, and took the cage, with the bird in it, under my arm. The dog twisted and turned, whining at such unaccustomed treatment; he looked at me with pleading eyes but I was afraid to take him with me. Then I picked up one of the vessels filled with jewels and put it in my pocket, leaving the others where they were.

The bird turned its head in a curious manner as I walked out of the door carrying it, and the dog did everything he could to follow me, but he had to remain behind.

Avoiding the path which led to the menacing cliffs, I went in the opposite direction. The dog was barking and whining, which deeply affected me; the bird made as if to sing several times but, since I was carrying it, did not much care to do so.

The farther I went, the weaker became the sound of the dog's barking, until at last it died away completely. I wept and almost went back again, but the urge to see something new drove me on.

I had already crossed the mountains and passed through several forests when evening approached and I had to spend the night in a village inn. I was very shy as I walked in; I was given a room and a bed where I slept quite peacefully, except that I dreamed of the old woman threatening me.

It was a rather tiresome journey, yet the farther I went, the more frightened I was by my thoughts of the old woman and the little dog; I thought that he was bound to starve without me to care for him, and often, when I was in the forest, I imagined the old woman would suddenly appear before me. And so I went on my way, sighing and weeping; and whenever I halted and set down the cage, the bird would sing its wondrous song and I would vividly recall my happy sojourn, now left behind me. So forgetful is human nature: I now believed that my first journey during my childhood had not been as sorrowful as the present one and I wished myself back in my childhood again.

I had sold some of the jewels, and now, after wandering about for many days, I came to a village. Even as I entered it I had an odd feeling; I was afraid, though I did not know why, but soon I realized where I was: it was the very same village where I had been born. How astonished I was! A thousand strange memories flooded over me, and tears of joy ran down my cheeks. Many things had changed; new houses had been built, whilst others, which had only just been built when I lived there, had now fallen down; I could also see where houses had burned down; everything was far smaller, far more cramped than I had expected. I looked forward with boundless joy to seeing my parents again after so many years; I found the little house again, the familiar threshold and the door-handle were exactly as before, it seemed as if I had pulled the door to only yesterday; I quickly opened it, my heart pounding furiously—but the faces in the room were completely strange to me and stared at me in surprise. I asked them about Martin the shepherd and they told me that he and his wife had been dead for three years.—I left the house hastily and went away from the village, weeping loudly.

I had imagined how wonderful it would be to surprise them with my riches; by the strangest chance, the things that I had dreamed of as a child had now come true—and now everything was in vain; they could not share my happiness, and what I had always hoped for most in life was now lost to me forever.

In a pleasant town I rented a little house with a garden and engaged a servant girl. I did not find the world so wonderful as I had supposed but, little by little, I forgot the old woman and my former home and lived, on the whole, quite contentedly.

The bird had not sung for a long time, and so I was more than a little frightened when, one night, it suddenly began to sing again, though it was now a different song:

> The woods lonely
> How far from me!
> Regrets there'll be
> In time, you'll see.
> Alas, the only joy for me,
> The woods lonely.

I could not sleep the whole night through; it all came back to me once again and I felt more than once that I had done wrong. When I arose, the sight of the bird was perfectly hateful to me; it looked at me all the time and its very presence made me anxious. Now it did not cease its song at all, but sang louder and more strongly than it had used to sing before. The more I watched it, the more frightened I became; at last I opened the cage, put in my hand, and seized it by the throat; then I closed my fingers firmly; the bird looked at me with pleading eyes, and I released my grip, but it was already dead.—I buried it in the garden.

Now I was often afraid of my maidservant, I thought back to my own days as a servant and believed that she, too, might rob me some day or even murder me.—For a long time I had known a young knight whom I liked very much; I gave him my hand in marriage—and that, Herr Walther, is the end of my tale.'

'You should have seen her in those days,' broke in Eckbert hurriedly; 'her youth, her beauty—what a strange charm her lonely upbringing had given her. To me she seemed a miracle and I loved her more than words can tell. I had no fortune of my own, but came into this wealth through her love for me; we came here and, until this day, we have not regretted our marriage for a single instant.'

'But with all our chatting,' went on Bertha once more, 'it is now the middle of the night—we should go to bed.'

She rose to her feet and made to go to her chamber. Walther kissed her hand, wishing her good night, and said: 'Thank you, noble lady; I can well imagine you with that wondrous bird and giving little *Strohmian* his food.'

Walther, too, then went to bed, only Eckbert remained walking back and forth in the hall.—'Is not man a foolish creature?'

he said at last to himself; 'I of all people was the cause of my wife telling Walther her story, and now I regret the trust I placed in him.—Will he not abuse my trust? Will he not tell it to others? Will he not perhaps—for that is man's nature—feel a base desire to possess our jewels and secretly make plans to steal them?'

It occurred to Eckbert that Walther had not taken leave of him with such heartfelt fondness as would have been natural after such a display of trust. Once suspicion is aroused within a man's soul it finds confirmation of this suspicion in every little detail. Then Eckbert reproached himself for his ignoble mistrust of his good friend, yet he could not banish it from his mind. He busied himself with these fantasies all night and slept very little indeed.

Bertha was ill and unable to appear at breakfast; Walther did not seem to be greatly concerned about this and took leave of Eckbert in a rather indifferent manner. Eckbert could not understand his friend's behaviour; he went to see his lady, in bed with a high fever; she said that the tale she had told that night must have excited her.

Since that evening, Walther very seldom visited his friend's castle; and when he did so, he would leave again after a few trivial words. This behaviour troubled Eckbert very deeply; he did not betray his feelings either to Bertha or to Walther, yet no one could have failed to notice his inner restlessness.

Bertha's illness became more and more disturbing; the physician grew anxious, the rosy colour had vanished from her cheeks and her eyes were more and more feverish.—One morning she summoned her husband to her bedside and the maids were ordered to leave.

'Dearest husband,' she said, 'I must confess something which, small and insignificant though it may be, has almost driven me out of my mind and is destroying my health.—You know that, whenever I came to speak of my childhood, I could never recall the name of the little dog that I took care of for so long, no matter how much I tried; when Walther was taking leave of me that evening, he suddenly said to me: "I can well imagine you giving little *Strohmian* his food." Was that mere chance? Did he guess the name? Does he know the name and did he pronounce it intentionally? And how is this man bound up with my fate? At times I struggle with myself, as if I were only imagining this curious incident—but it is true, only too true. I was struck by an awful terror when this unknown person helped my memory in this way. What do *you* think, Eckbert?'

Eckbert, deeply moved, looked at his suffering wife; he said nothing, but pondered for a while, then, with a few words of consolation, he left her. In a remote room of the castle he walked back and forth in a conflict of unspeakable anxiety. For many years Walther had been his only friend, but was now the only person in the world whose existence oppressed and tormented him. Eckbert felt he would be happy and free of care if only this one person could be got out of his way. In search of some distraction he took his crossbow and went off to hunt.

It was a rough, stormy winter's day; the hills lay covered in deep snow which bent the branches of the trees. He wandered about aimlessly, his brow beaded with sweat; he did not find any game, which only served to increase his ill humour. Suddenly he saw something moving in the distance; it was Walther, gathering moss from the trees. Without knowing what he was doing, Eckbert raised his crossbow. Walther turned round and made a silent, threatening gesture, but then the bolt flew on its way and Walther fell to the ground.

Eckbert felt relieved and free of care, yet a cold fear drove him back to his castle; he had a long way to go, for he had strayed deep into the woods.—When he reached the castle Bertha was already dead; before she died she had spoken a great deal about Walther and the old woman.

Eckbert now lived a long while in deepest solitude. He had always been of a melancholy turn, for his wife's uncanny tale disturbed him, and he was afraid that something dreadful might happen—now, however, he was entirely at odds with himself. In his mind's eye, he kept seeing the murder of his friend, and could not stop reproaching himself for what he had done.

In order to take his mind off these matters he sometimes went off to the nearest large town to attend banquets and take part in festivities. He was moved by a wish to fill the emptiness in his soul with the help of some friend or other, yet whenever he thought of Walther he would shudder at the idea of finding a new friend, for he was convinced that friendship with anyone at all would only bring him unhappiness. He had lived so long in peace and harmony with Bertha, and his friendship with Walther had brought him happiness for many a year, and now both had been torn away from him so suddenly that, at certain moments, his life seemed to him more like a strange fairy-tale than real life.

A young knight, Hugo, sought the acquaintance of the quiet, melancholy Eckbert and seemed to have a genuine liking for him. Eckbert was surprised in a strange way; the unexpectedness of the young knight's friendship led him to respond all the more quickly. Soon the two men were often in each other's company; the stranger showed Eckbert every possible form of kindness, and one would scarcely ever ride out without the other; they would meet at every festivity; in short, they seemed inseparable.

Yet all the time Eckbert was happy only for a few brief moments, for he clearly felt that Hugo was fond of him only because he was mistaken in him; Hugo did not know him and was not familiar with his story, so that Eckbert once more felt the same compulsion to confess everything to him in order to be certain that Hugo really was his friend. But again he was restrained by his doubts and his fear that Hugo would feel revulsion for him. Many a time he was so convinced of his own unworthiness that he believed no one to whom he was not a complete stranger could possibly have respect for him. Yet he could not resist the urge; while they were out on a lonely ride together he revealed the whole story to his friend, and then asked him whether he could feel affection for a murderer. Hugo, deeply moved, tried to console him; Eckbert, now relieved, went with Hugo into the town.

But it seemed to be his fate always to harbour suspicion in the very moment of taking someone into his confidence; hardly had they entered the banquet hall when he felt displeased by his friend's expression, seen in the light of the many lamps. He thought he could detect a mocking smile on Hugo's features; he noticed that Hugo spoke very little to him, that he spoke a great deal to the other guests whilst seeming to pay no attention to Eckbert at all. There was an old knight present at the feast who had always shown himself to be Eckbert's enemy and had often displayed an odd interest in Eckbert's wealth and in Bertha. Hugo took his place beside the knight and the two conversed secretively for a while together, pointing to Eckbert as they did so. Eckbert saw his suspicions confirmed; thinking himself betrayed, he fell into a dreadful rage. As he continued to stare at the two men, he suddenly saw Walther's face with all its features, Walther's entire form that was so familiar to him; he went on staring, convinced that none other than *Walther* was speaking to the old knight.

The terror which he felt was indescribable; storming wildly out of the hall, he left the town that very night and returned to his castle by many devious paths.

There he ran like a restless spirit from one chamber to the next, unable to think clearly, and his mind raced from one dreadful fantasy to another, yet more dreadful; he could not close his eyes in sleep even for a moment. Often he believed himself to be mad, and that everything was a product of his own imagination; then he would recall Walther's features once again and everything would become more and more a mystery. He decided to go on a journey in order to collect his thoughts; his hopes of finding friendship, his desire for company, he had now given up for ever.

He set off without determining which way to take; he scarcely noticed the scenery which lay in front of him. After having pressed on for several days as fast as his horse could go, he suddenly realized that he was lost in a labyrinth of rocks, from which no way out was to be seen. At last he met a peasant who showed him a path which led past a waterfall; he tried to give him a few coins by way of thanks, but the man refused.—'What am I thinking of?' said Eckbert to himself; 'I could easily believe it was none other than Walther!' He looked back once more and indeed it was none other than Walther.—Eckbert spurred his horse on through forest and meadow as fast as it could gallop until at last, worn out, it collapsed beneath him.—Unconcerned, he now continued his way on foot.

In a dream, he climbed a hill; he thought he heard the sound of lively barking nearby, mingled with the rustling of birch-trees, and a strange song came to his ears:

The woods lonely
Once more a joy to me.
No pain there'll be,
Here's no envy
But joy once more for me,
The woods lonely.

Now his consciousness and senses failed him completely; he could find no answer to the mystery, whether he was now dreaming or whether he had once dreamed of a woman named Bertha; the most fantastic things were mingled with the most commonplace; the world around him seemed enchanted, and he himself incapable of any thought, of any memory.

A bent-backed old woman leaning on a crutch crept up the hill, coughing. 'Have you brought me my bird? my pearls? my dog?' she screeched at him. 'There, you see—evil punishes itself—I and no other was your friend Walther, your friend Hugo.'

'Almighty God!' murmured Eckbert to himself—'in what awful loneliness have I spent my life!'

'And Bertha was your sister.'

Eckbert fell to the ground.

'Why did she leave me so treacherously? All would have been well and ended well—her trial years were over. She was the daughter of a knight who had her brought up by a herdsman; she was your father's daughter.'

'Why have I always had these dreadful forebodings?' cried Eckbert.

'Because when you were very young, you once heard your father tell the story; because of his wife, he could not bring up his daughter in his home, for she was the child of another woman.'

Eckbert lay crazed and dying upon the ground; in dim confusion he heard the old woman speaking, the dog barking, and the bird repeating its song.

HEINRICH VON KLEIST

The Marchioness of O...

(Based on a true occurrence, the scene of which has been
transposed from the north to the south.)

In M..., an eminent city in Upper Italy, the widowed Marchioness of O..., a lady of unimpeachable reputation and mother of two well-bred children, made the following announcement through the newspapers: that she was with child, an event which had occurred without her knowledge; that the father of the child that she was to bear should communicate with her; and that, out of consideration for her family, she had decided to marry him. The lady, who, under the pressure of immutable circumstances, had taken such an unusual step with such a degree of self-confidence, thus drawing the mockery of the world upon herself, was the daughter of Colonel G..., Commandant of the citadel near M.... Some three years before, she had lost her husband, the Marquis of O..., to whom she had been most deeply and tenderly devoted, on a journey which he had made to Paris on family business. Following his death, and at the wish of the Colonel's wife, her worthy mother, she had left her country estate near V..., where she had previously lived, and returned with her two children to her father in his official residence. Here she had spent the following years reading, painting, educating her children, and looking after her parents, in the deepest seclusion imaginable, until the ... War suddenly filled the region with troops of almost every nation, including those of Russia. Colonel G..., who had received orders to defend the position, bade his wife and daughter withdraw, either to the daughter's country estate or to that of his son, which was situated near V.... But before the troubles with which they were faced in the fortress, on the one hand, and the horrors to which they might be exposed out in the country, on the other, had been weighed and compared in the balance of female consideration, the citadel had been beset by the Russian troops and its occupants called upon to surrender. The Colonel explained to his family that he would now act as if they were not present, and replied to the Russians with bullets and grenades. The enemy responded by bombarding the citadel: they set fire to the magazine, overran an outer defence position, and, when the Commandant, after a second call to surrender, still hesitated, carried out a night attack and took the citadel by storm.

Just as the Russian troops, under heavy cannon fire, were forcing their way inside, the left wing of the Commandant's house caught fire, so that the women were obliged to leave. The Colonel's lady, hurrying after her daughter who was fleeing downstairs with her children, shouted that they should all keep together and take refuge in the vaults below; but a grenade, bursting in the house that same moment, completed the entire confusion within. The Marchioness, with her two children, reached the front terrace of the house where, amidst fierce fighting, shots were already flashing in the darkness and drove her—not knowing where to turn—back into the burning building. Here, unfortunately, just as she was about to slip through the back door, she encountered a group of enemy sharpshooters who, on seeing her, immediately fell silent, shouldered their rifles, and, to the accompaniment of disgusting gestures, dragged her away. In vain did the Marchioness, pulled now in one direction, now in another by this dreadful rabble, who were fighting among themselves, call for help to her trembling handmaids as they fled back through the gate. The men dragged her into the rear courtyard where, having been manhandled in the most infamous manner, she was on the point of falling to the ground when, attracted by the lady's screams, a Russian officer appeared and, with fierce blows, drove apart the mad dogs ravening for their prey. To the Marchioness he seemed like an angel of heaven. With the hilt of his sword he struck the last bestial assassin, who was still tightly embracing her slender body, in the face, so that the fellow stumbled backwards with blood pouring from his mouth; then, speaking kindly to her in French, he offered the lady his arm and led her, speechless as she was after all that had happened, into the other wing of the residence, which had not yet been reached by the flames, where she fell down in a profound swoon. Here—her terrified handmaids having soon afterwards appeared—he ordered a doctor to be called; then, donning his hat, he assured them that she would soon recover, and went off to rejoin the fighting.

In a short time the entire area was taken, and the Commandant, who continued to offer resistance only because the enemy would not offer him quarter, was retreating with failing strength to the main gate of the house when the Russian officer, his face highly flushed, appeared from the gate and called upon him to surrender. The Commandant replied that this was the very order he had been waiting to hear, offered him his sword, and requested permission to enter the fortress and attend to his family. The Russian officer, who, judging from the role he was playing, appeared to be one of the leaders of the attack, gave him permission to do so under the supervision of a sentry; then, with some haste, took command of a detachment of troops, determined the course of the fighting wherever this was still in doubt, and swiftly occupied the strategic points of the fortress. Soon afterwards he returned to the scene of the fighting, gave orders to put out the fire, which was beginning to spread, and displayed wondrous efforts himself in doing so when his orders were not obeyed with the appropriate zeal. One moment he was clambering about with the fire-hose in his hand, beneath burning gables, directing the jet of water; the next, he was busy in the arsenals, to the horror of the Asian soldiers, rolling powder barrels and live bombs out into the open. The Commandant, who had meanwhile entered the house, was absolutely horrified on hearing of the misadventure which the Marchioness had suffered. The Marchioness, who, without benefit of medical attention, had already completely recovered from her faint as the Russian officer had foretold, and in her joy at seeing all her loved ones safe and sound, kept to her bed only in order to assuage their excessive anxiety, assured her father that she had no other wish save that of being allowed to leave her bed in order to offer thanks to her rescuer. She already knew that he was Count F..., Lieutenant-Colonel of the . . . Rifle Corps, Knight of a Legion of Honour and of several other orders. She asked her father to request him earnestly not to leave the citadel without first having called at the residence for a moment. The Commandant, who had great respect for his daughter's feelings, returned to the fortress without delay and, for want of a better opportunity, reported his daughter's wish to the Count (who was moving ceaselessly back and forth issuing battle orders) there on the ramparts, where he was reviewing his battered troops. The Count assured him that he was only waiting for a moment in which he could be spared from his duties, in order to come and pay his respects to the lady. He was on the point of enquiring about the state of health of the Marchioness when he was summoned back into the storm of battle by the reports of several of his officers. At daybreak the Commanding General of the Russian forces appeared and proceeded to inspect the fortress. He assured the Commandant of his great esteem, expressed his regret that the Commandant's courage had not been matched by his luck, and gave him, upon his word of honour, permission to depart to wherever he wished. The Commandant assured him of his gratitude and declared how greatly indebted he was, on that day, to the Russians generally, and to the young Count F..., Lieutenant-Colonel of the . . . Rifle Corps, in particular. The General then asked what had happened; and, after he had been informed of the outrageous attack upon the Commandant's daughter, declared himself to be absolutely scandalized. He summoned Count F... by name. After first briefly praising the Count for his gallant conduct, whereupon the Count blushed deeply, he finally stated that he intended to have the shameful ruffians shot who had disgraced the name of the Emperor, and ordered him to reveal their names. The Count replied, in some confusion, that he was not in a position to reveal the men's names, since it had been impossible for him, in the dim light of the lamps in the courtyard, to recognize their faces. The General, having heard that the fortress had been in flames at the time, was astonished; he remarked that it was certainly possible to recognize at night people whom one knew, by their voices; and ordered the Count, who had shrugged his shoulders with an expression of embarrassment on his face, to investigate the matter with the greatest haste and severity. Thereupon, one of the officers present, pushing his way to the front of the group, reported that one of the scoundrels, who had been wounded by the Count and collapsed in the corridor, had been dragged off to a cell by the Commandant's men, where he was still confined. The General immediately ordered a sentry to bring the man, subjected him to a short interrogation, and, after the man had confessed the names, he ordered the entire pack—five altogether—to be shot. After this had been carried out the General, leaving behind a small contingent to occupy the fortress, gave the order for the remaining troops to march off; the officers hastened to their separate units. The Count, making his way through the bustling throng of soldiers as they hurried away, approached the Commandant and expressed his regret that, under the circumstances, he was obliged to send his respects to the Marchioness; and, less than an hour later, the fortress was completely empty of Russians.

The family now fell to considering how they might in the future find an opportunity of offering the Count some expression of their gratitude; how great, then, was their consternation when they heard the news that, on the very day of his departure from the fortress, he had met his death in a skirmish with enemy troops. The courier who brought the news to M... had with his own eyes seen the Count, mortally wounded by a shot through the chest, being carried away to P... where, according to a reliable report, he had died just as the bearers were about to lower him from their shoulders. The Commandant himself went to the post house where he made enquiries regarding the exact details of this incident, and further learned that the Count, in the same moment that the shot struck him on the battlefield, had cried out: 'Julietta! This bullet has avenged you!' and then closed his lips for ever. The Marchioness was inconsolable that she had not availed herself of the opportunity of throwing herself before his feet. She reproached herself most bitterly that she herself had not gone in search of him following his refusal —which, she thought, was perhaps prompted by modesty—to appear at the residence; she grieved for the unhappy person, her namesake, to whom his thoughts had turned at the moment of his death; she made every effort, though in vain, to discover the lady's whereabouts, in order to inform her of this unfortunate and touching incident; and several months went by before she herself was able to forget him.

The family was now obliged to leave the Commandant's residence in order to make room for the Russian Commanding General. At first, they considered whether they should not go to live on the Commandant's estate, to which the Marchioness was very much attached; but, as the Colonel did not much care for life in the country, the family moved into a house in the town and made it their permanent dwelling. Circumstances now reverted completely to their accustomed order. The Marchioness took up once more the education of her children, which had been interrupted for so long, and brought out her easel and books for use in her leisure hours; then, however, she—otherwise the very picture of health—was overcome by repeated attacks of illness, which for weeks on end made it impossible for her to show herself in society. She suffered from fits of nausea, dizziness, and fainting, and did not know what to make of this strange condition. One morning, as the family was sitting drinking tea and her father had just left the room for a moment, the Marchioness, awakening from a long stupor, said to her mother: if a woman were to tell me that she had had the same feeling as I had just now as I took hold of that cup, I would think that she was with child. Madame G... declared she did not understand her. The Marchioness explained once again that she had just experienced a sensation like that which she had felt when she was expecting her second daughter. Madame G... replied, perhaps she was about to give birth to Phantasus, and laughed. 'Morpheus,* at least,' countered the Marchioness, 'or one of his retinue of dreams, would be the father'—continuing the joke. Then the Colonel returned, the conversation was broken off, and, since the Marchioness recovered within a few days, the entire matter was forgotten.

A short while later, just when Forestry Inspector G..., the Commandant's son, had arrived at the house, the family was strangely shocked by the news of a footman, who entered the room to announce the arrival of Count F.... 'Count F...!' cried father and daughter simultaneously; and all were speechless with astonishment. The footman assured them that he had seen and heard correctly, and that the Count was already standing waiting in the ante-room. The Commandant himself immediately leapt to his feet to open the door for him, whereupon, as beautiful as a young god, though a little pale of visage, he entered the room. After the scene of uncomprehending amazement was over, and the Count, in reply to the parents' accusation that he was dead, had assured them that he was alive, he turned to the daughter, his face filled with emotion, and his very first question concerned her health. The Marchioness assured him that she was very well and asked, in her turn, how *he* had been resurrected to life? But the Count, holding fast to his original question, answered that she was not telling him the truth; her face, he declared, betrayed a strange weariness; she was ill and suffering, or he was very much mistaken. The Marchioness, put in good humour by the heartfelt manner in which he spoke, replied: Well, then; this weariness might, if he so insisted, be considered small evidence of a sickliness from which she had suffered some weeks ago; meanwhile, however, she had no fear that this would have any further consequences. To which the Count rejoined, flushing with pleasure: nor did he! and further asked her, whether she would marry him? The Marchioness did not know what to think of this strange performance. Blushing crimson, she looked at her mother, who, in turn, looked in embarrassment at her son and husband; meanwhile, the Count stepped forward to the Marchioness and, taking her hand as if intending to kiss it, asked again, whether she had understood him? The Commandant asked him whether he would not sit down and, in a friendly though somewhat grave manner, placed a chair beside him. Then the Colonel's lady spoke: 'We shall indeed believe that you are a ghost, until you have explained to us how you rose again from the tomb in which you were laid at P....' The Count sat down, releasing the lady's hand from his, and said that, by force of circumstances, he must keep the story very short; that he had been brought to P..., mortally wounded in the chest; that he himself had despaired of his life for several months; that during this time, the Marchioness had been the sole object of his thoughts; that he could not describe the pleasure and the pain which had embraced each other in these thoughts; that at last, following his recovery, he had returned to the army again; that he himself had been tormented by the keenest anxiety; that, more than once, he had taken up his pen to write to the Colonel and the Marchioness in order to pour out his feelings; that now, he had suddenly been sent with dispatches to Naples; that he did not know whether he would receive orders to proceed from there to Constantinople; that it was even possible that he might have to go to St Petersburg; that meanwhile, it was impossible for him to live any longer without coming to terms with such an undeniable yearning of his soul; that, while passing through M..., he had been unable to resist the urge to take steps towards the fulfilment of this purpose; that, in short, he wished to have the happiness of marrying the Marchioness, and he begged, most respectfully, most honourably, and most fervently to be given a favourable reply.—After a long pause, the Commandant declared that such a request, if meant earnestly, which he did not doubt, was most flattering to him; however, following the death of her husband, the Marquis of O..., his daughter had determined not to enter into a second marriage. But, since the Count had placed such a great obligation upon her a short time ago, it was not impossible that her resolution might have undergone a change in accordance with the Count's desire. The Commandant therefore requested, on his daughter's behalf, to be permitted to consider the matter for a time. The Count assured him that such a kind declaration fulfilled all his hopes; that, under other circumstances, it would have made him completely happy; that he realized how perfectly unseemly it was for him not to be satisfied with it; that, owing to urgent circumstances, however, which he was not in a position to explain in more detail, he greatly desired a more precise reply; that the horses which were to bring him to Naples were already harnessed to his carriage; and that he therefore earnestly requested that, if anything at all in this house should speak in his favour—here he looked at the Marchioness—he should not be allowed to depart without a kindly word. The Colonel, a little embarrassed by these remarks, replied that the gratitude which the Marchioness felt for the Count did indeed entitle him to far-reaching assumptions, though not to assumptions as great as these; in consideration of such a step, which would have a bearing upon her lifelong happiness, she would not act without applying appropriate judgement. It was imperative, he said, that his daughter, before declaring her intentions, should first have the pleasure of becoming more closely acquainted with the Count. He invited the Count to return to M... after completing his official journey, to be the guest of the family for some time. If the Marchioness could hope to find happiness with the Count, he himself would rejoice when he heard—though not before—that she had favoured him with a definite answer. The Count, blushing, replied that, throughout the entire journey, he had prophesied such a fate for his impatient desires, because of which he meantime found himself plunged into extreme difficulties; that in view of the inauspicious role which he himself was obliged to play at present, a closer acquaintance could only be of advantage; that he believed he could vouch for his reputation, if this most ambiguous of all characteristics were to be otherwise taken into consideration; that the only unworthy act which he had ever committed in his life was unknown to the world at large, and he was now on the point of atoning for it; in short, that he was an honest man, and requested them to accept his assurance that this assurance was true.—Smiling a little, though without any trace of irony, the Commandant replied that he concurred with all these remarks; he had not, he said, made the acquaintance of any young man who, in such a short time, had revealed so many admirable traits of character. He quite believed that a brief period of reflection would dispel the uncertainty which still prevailed; before he had consulted with his family, however, and with the Count's own family, no declaration other than the one already given could follow. To this the Count rejoined that his parents were both dead and that he was a free man. His uncle was General K..., whose permission he could guarantee. He further added that he possessed a considerable fortune and would be ready to make Italy his home.—The Commandant bowed to him in good grace, explained his wishes once again, and requested the Count to undertake nothing further in this matter until after he had completed his journey. After a brief pause, during which he displayed every sign of extreme uneasiness, the Count turned to the Marchioness's mother and said that he had done everything possible to avoid making this official journey; the measures which he had therefore ventured to adopt with regard to the Commanding General and General K..., his uncle, had been the most decisive possible; it was thought, however, that this journey would cure him of a mood of melancholy which had still prevailed after his illness; now, as a result, he felt himself plunged into the depths of misery.—The family did not know what to reply to this statement. If there were any hope, he went on, rubbing his forehead, of coming closer to attaining his wishes by doing so, he would postpone his journey by one day, or even longer in order to try.—As he spoke, he looked in succession at the Commandant, the Marchioness, and her mother. The Commandant looked down at the floor in displeasure and made no reply. Then the Commandant's lady spoke: 'Go now, Count, go to Naples and, when you return, let us have the pleasure of your company for some time; everything else will resolve itself.'— The Count remained seated for a moment and appeared to be considering what he should do. Then he rose to his feet, put aside his chair, and spoke: since he was now obliged, he said, to recognize that the hopes with which he had entered this house were premature, and since the family insisted upon a closer acquaintance—of which he could not disapprove—he would send back his dispatches to his headquarters in Z..., so that they might be conveyed in another way, and accept for some weeks the family's kind offer to receive him as their guest. With these words, he remained standing by the wall for a moment, his hand on the chair, looking at the Commandant. The Commandant replied that he would be most sorry if the passion which the Count appeared to have conceived for his daughter were to occasion him unpleasantness of the most serious nature; that he, nevertheless, must know what he should do and not do, and that he should send off the dispatches and occupy the rooms intended for him. At these words the Count was seen to turn pale; whereupon he respectfully kissed the hand of the mother, bowed to the rest of the company, and took his leave.

After he had left the room, the family did not know what to make of it all. The Marchioness's mother said it was not possible that he should send back to Z... dispatches with which he had been travelling to Naples, merely because he had not succeeded, while passing through M..., in the course of a conversation lasting five minutes, in obtaining the consent of a lady completely unknown to him. The Forestry Inspector declared that such a reckless deed would be punished with nothing less than incarceration! And by being cashiered as well, added the Commandant. However, he went on, there was no danger of that: it was merely a shot in the air, and the Count would certainly come to his senses again before sending back the dispatches. The Marchioness's mother, however, when informed of this danger, expressed her keenest fear that he would send back the dispatches. His impetuous desire, concentrated on one single point, she said, seemed to her to be eminently capable of provoking such an act. She earnestly begged the Forestry Inspector to follow the Count immediately and dissuade him from taking such a step, which could only result in unhappiness. The Forestry Inspector replied that such an attempt would have exactly the opposite effect and merely fortify his hopes of achieving victory by means of a military strategem. The Marchioness expressed the same opinion, though she assured them that the return of the dispatches would inevitably follow if the attempt were not made, since the Count would surely plunge himself into unhappiness rather than lose face. All present agreed that his behaviour was extremely strange and that he appeared to be accustomed to taking ladies' hearts, like fortresses, by storm. At that moment, the Commandant noticed the Count's carriage, with horses harnessed in readiness, in front of the door. He called the family to the window and, astonished, asked a servant who had just entered whether the Count was still in the house. The servant replied that the Count was in the servants' quarters downstairs, in the company of his adjutant, writing letters and sealing packages. The Commandant, controlling his consternation, rushed downstairs together with the Forestry Inspector and, seeing the Count concluding his business at a table unsuited for the task, asked him whether he would not rather come to his rooms? And whether he had any further requirements? The Count, continuing to write with great haste, replied that he thanked the Commandant most respectfully, and that his business was now concluded; then, sealing the letter, he asked the time of day and, giving the entire portfolio to the adjutant, wished him *bon voyage*. The Commandant, unable to believe his eyes, said, just as the adjutant was leaving the house: 'My dear Count, unless you have very important reasons—' 'Decisive reasons!' interrupted the Count and, accompanying the adjutant to the carriage, opened the door for him. 'In that case,' continued the Commandant, 'I would at least suggest that the dispatches—' 'It is not possible,' replied the Count, helping the adjutant into his seat. 'The dispatches are of no value in Naples without my presence. I, too, thought of that. Drive on!'—'And your uncle's letters?' called the adjutant, leaning out of the carriage window. 'Will reach me in M...,' replied the Count. 'Drive on!' said the adjutant, and the carriage bore him away.

Thereupon the Count turned to the Commandant and asked him if he would be kind enough to have him shown to his rooms. 'I shall have the honour of doing so myself,' replied the bewildered Commandant; bidding his own and the Count's servants to take care of the Count's baggage, he led him to the rooms reserved for visitors to the house, where, with a grave expression, he left him. The Count changed his clothes; then he left the house in order to report to the governor of the town and, having remained unseen in the house for the remainder of the day, made his appearance again only shortly before dinner.

Meanwhile, the family was in a state of extreme uneasiness. The Forestry Inspector pointed out how firm had been the Count's replies to several of the Commandant's remarks, offered the opinion that the Count's conduct suggested a fully premeditated step, and asked, what in the world could be the reason for such a courtship by courier horse? The Commandant declared that he understood nothing of the affair and bade the family not to speak of it any further in his presence. The mother looked out of the window at every moment, to see whether he would come to express regret for his reckless deed and take steps to repair the harm. At last, for dusk was drawing in, she sat down by the Marchioness, who was working most diligently at a table, seemingly desirous of avoiding conversation. She asked her daughter in a low voice, while the father was pacing back and forth, whether she knew what would become of all this? The Marchioness, looking shyly at the Commandant, replied: if her father had succeeded in persuading him to go to Naples, everything would be in order. 'To Naples!' cried her father, who had heard this remark. 'Should I have sent for the priest? Or should I have had him put under close arrest and sent to Naples under guard?'—'No,' replied the Marchioness, 'but vigorous and urgent persuasion would have had their effect;' and, somewhat annoyed, she looked down at her work again.—At last, towards nightfall, the Count appeared. They only hoped that, following the usual expressions of politeness, the matter would be broached, so that they might persuade him, with their combined efforts, to revoke, if at all possible, the step which he had ventured to take. But in vain, during the entire meal, did they wait for this moment. Studiously avoiding everything which might lead to that subject, he conversed with the Commandant about war, and with the Forestry Inspector about hunting. When he came to mention the skirmish near P... during which he had been wounded, the Marchioness's mother involved him in a conversation about his illness, asked him how matters had gone with him in that little town, and whether he had found there the appropriate comforts. Thereupon he related a number of matters which were of interest by reason of his passion for the Marchioness: how she had always sat at his bedside during his illness; how, in the delirium of his fever, he had continually confused his vision of the Marchioness with that of a swan which he had seen, when a boy, on his uncle's estates; that one memory in particular had been touching for him, since he had once thrown mud at this swan, whereupon the bird had dived under and then risen again, perfectly clean, from the water; that she had been coasting about amid flaming waters, and that he had called out 'Thinka', which had been the name of the swan, but that he had not succeeded in luring her to him, for she had taken pleasure only in gliding about and preening herself; suddenly, blushing crimson, he declared that he loved her passionately; then he looked down at his plate once more and fell silent. At last they had to leave the table; and the Count, after a brief exchange with the mother, immediately bowed to the company and withdrew to his room; the remainder of the company remained standing, not knowing what to think. The Commandant expressed the opinion that they must let matters take their course: the Count, he said, was probably relying upon the help of his relatives in taking this step. Without such help, shameful dismissal would surely follow. Madame G... asked her daughter what she thought of the Count? And whether she could bring herself to say something to him which would ward off a calamity? The Marchioness replied: 'Dearest mother! That is not possible. I am sorry that my gratitude must be put to such a severe test. But it was my decision not to marry again; I would not wish to risk my happiness a second time, nor in such a careless fashion.'—The Forestry Inspector remarked that, if this was her determined will, then even such a declaration as this could help the Count, and that it appeared almost a necessity to give him a definite statement of some kind. The Commandant's lady retorted that, since this young man, who was distinguished by so many extraordinary traits of character, had declared himself desirous of taking up residence in Italy, his proposal of marriage, in her opinion, deserved some consideration, and the Marchioness's decision ought to be reconsidered. The Forestry Inspector, sitting down beside his sister, asked her how the Count pleased her as far as his person was concerned? The Marchioness replied, with some embarrassment: 'I like him and yet I do not like him;' and she asked the other members of the company what their feelings were? The Commandant's lady said: 'When he returns from Naples, and provided the enquiries which we shall be able to make concerning him in the meantime are not contrary to the overall impression which you have had of him, how would you reply if he should then repeat his proposal?' 'In that case,' answered the Marchioness, 'I would—since his wishes indeed seem so intense—' here she faltered and her eyes shone as she spoke— 'I would, for the sake of the civility which I owe to him, fulfil these wishes.' Her mother, who had always cherished the wish that her daughter should marry again, had difficulty in concealing her joy at this declaration and began to consider what advantage was to be gained from it. The Forestry Inspector rose uneasily from his chair and said that, if the Marchioness really considered it possible that she might sometime please the Count by agreeing to marry him, a necessary step must follow immediately in order to obviate the consequences of his reckless conduct. Her mother was of the same opinion, and declared that the risk was not really so great, after all, since, in view of the excellent character which he had displayed that night when the Russians attacked the citadel, it was scarcely to be feared that his usual way of life would run contrary to this. The Marchioness cast down her eyes with an expression of the greatest uneasiness. 'We could', said her mother, grasping her daughter's hand, 'give him a promise that you will not undertake a union with anyone else before his return from Naples.' The Marchioness said: 'This promise, dearest mother, I can indeed give him; I only fear, however, that this promise would not set his mind at rest, and would involve us in difficulties.' 'Let that be my concern!' replied her mother with tremendous joy, and looked towards her husband. 'Lorenzo!' she asked, 'What do you think?' and made to rise from her chair. The Commandant, who had heard everything, was standing at the window; he looked out into the street and made no answer. The Forestry Inspector said that he was willing to rid the house of the Count by means of this harmless declaration. 'Then do so, do so!' cried the Commandant, turning around from the window; 'it is now the second time that I am obliged to submit to this Russian!'—At this, his wife leapt to her feet, kissed him and her daughter, and asked—whilst her husband smiled at such zealousness—how they might best communicate this declaration immediately to the Count? At the suggestion of the Forestry Inspector, it was decided to send a footman to request him, if he had not already undressed, to be so kind as to attend for a moment upon the family. The Count replied that it would be an honour for him to attend directly! And scarcely had the footman returned with this message when the Count himself, his feet winged with joy, entered the room and, in a display of the deepest possible emotion, fell at the Marchioness's feet. The Commandant was on the point of saying something when the Count, rising to his feet, declared: 'say no more!' kissed the Commandant's and the mother's hands, embraced the brother, and only requested the favour of being assisted immediately to his carriage. The Marchioness, though deeply moved by this scene, said: 'I have no fear, Count, that your hasty expectations—!' 'Nothing! nothing!' replied the Count; 'nothing will have occurred if the enquiries which you may please to make concerning my person should run contrary to the feelings which summoned me back to you in this room.' Thereupon the Commandant embraced him most warmly; the Forestry Inspector immediately offered him his own travelling carriage, a groom was dispatched directly to the coaching station to hire post-horses at a premium, and such joy was felt at this departure as had never been felt at an arrival. He hoped, declared the Count, to overtake the dispatches in B..., from whence he would take a shorter route to Naples than via M...; in Naples he would do everything possible to decline to make the further official journey to Constantinople; and since he was determined, in the event of the most extreme circumstances, to report himself too ill for duty, he would not fail, he assured the company, unless prevented by unforeseen difficulties, to be back in M... again in four to six weeks. Just then the groom reported that the horses were harnessed and that everything was ready for the Count's departure. The Count picked up his hat, walked over to the Marchioness, and took hold of her hand. 'Well, then, Julietta,' he said, 'I am to some extent consoled'—and he laid his hand in hers—'although it had been my dearest wish to marry you even before my departure.' 'Marry!' echoed the entire family. 'Marry,' repeated the Count, kissed the Marchioness's hand, and assured her, when she asked him whether he had taken leave of his senses: the day would come when they would understand him! The family was on the point of becoming angry; but he immediately took his leave of them all in the most heartfelt fashion, begged them to think no more about this last remark, and set off on his journey.

Several weeks went by, during which the members of the family, with very mixed feelings, awaited the outcome of this curious situation. The Commandant received a polite letter from General K..., the Count's uncle; the Count himself wrote from Naples; the enquiries which they had made about him spoke pretty much in his favour; in short, the engagement was already considered as good as concluded, when the Marchioness's indisposition returned again with greater intensity than ever before. She observed an inexplicable change in her figure. With perfect frankness, she unburdened herself to her mother, saying that she did not know what to think of her condition. Her mother, who, because of these strange circumstances, was extremely anxious about her daughter's health, demanded that she should consult a physician. The Marchioness, hoping that her robust nature would finally conquer, resisted; and she spent several more days of the most painful suffering without following her mother's advice, until the ever-recurring sensations which she felt, of such a strange nature, afflicted her with the keenest anxiety. She therefore summoned a physician, in whom her father placed great confidence, urged him to sit down on the divan—her mother being absent just at that moment—and, after briefly leading up to the matter, jokingly revealed to him what she thought of her condition. The doctor gave her a searching glance; after having examined her thoroughly, he remained silent for a while and then replied, with a most grave expression, that Her Ladyship was absolutely correct in her supposition. The lady asked him what he meant by this. He replied very plainly, and with a smile which he was unable to suppress, that she was perfectly healthy and did not need a physician, whereupon the Marchioness, with a sidelong glance of extreme severity, rang the bell and asked him to leave. In a low voice, as if he were not worth speaking to, she murmured to herself that she had no desire to jest with him about matters of this nature. The doctor replied in an injured tone that he wished she were always so disinclined to jest as now; then he picked up his stick and hat and prepared to leave. The Marchioness declared that she would inform her father of these insulting remarks. The physician replied that he could swear to the truth of his statement before a court of law; he opened the door, bowed to the lady, and made to leave the room. Just as he was picking up a glove which he had dropped upon the floor, the Marchioness said: 'How should what you say be possible, doctor?' The doctor replied that he hardly needed to explain to her the cause of her condition, bowed to her once again, and left.

The Marchioness remained standing as if thunderstruck, then she pulled herself together and was about to hasten to her father; but the strange earnestness of the man whom she considered to have insulted her completely paralysed her. In a fit of overwhelming emotion she threw herself down upon the divan. Mistrustful of herself, she recalled in detail every event of the past year, believing herself to be mad when she thought of what had just happened. At last her mother appeared and, in reply to her dismayed question, why she was so perturbed, the Marchioness told her what the doctor had said. Madame G... proclaimed him an insolent and worthless individual, thus strengthening her daughter in her determination to inform her father of the insult she had suffered. The Marchioness assured her mother that the physician had been perfectly serious, and that he had seemed determined to repeat his scandalous assertion to her father's face. Madame G..., not a little startled, asked her daughter whether she believed in the possibility of such a condition? I could rather believe, retorted the Marchioness, that graves might become fruitful and that infants might be born from the loins of the dead! 'Well, then, you dear, extraordinary creature,' said the Commandant's wife, pressing her daughter firmly to her bosom, 'what is troubling you? If your conscience is clear, how can a diagnosis disturb you at all, even if it were given by an entire college of physicians? Whether his diagnosis was given in error or was due to malice: surely it must be a matter of complete indifference to you? But it would be best if we were to inform your father.'—'O God!' cried the Marchioness with a convulsive movement: 'how can I possibly calm myself? Do not my own innermost feelings, which I know only too well, speak against me? If I knew that another woman experienced this feeling of mine, would I not myself believe that my judgement was correct?' 'This is dreadful!' exclaimed the Commandant's wife. 'Malice! Error!' the Marchioness continued. 'What possible reason can this man, who until today seemed to us an estimable person, have for injuring me in such a wilful and base manner? Me, who had never insulted him? Me, who received him with trust and a presentiment of future gratitude? To whom he appeared, as his first words proved, with the pure and simple desire to help, and not to cause worse pain than that which I felt already? And if'—she went on, while her mother continued to look at her steadfastly—'in the necessity of making a choice, I wished to believe that he was in error: is it possible that a physician, even one of mediocre ability, should be mistaken in such a case?'—Her mother replied, in a somewhat biting tone: 'nevertheless, it must have been either one or the other reason.' 'Yes! my dearest mother,' answered the Marchioness and, with an expression of injured dignity and flushing crimson, she kissed her mother's hand: 'it must! Although the circumstances are so extraordinary as to permit me to doubt it. Yet, because an assurance is required, I swear that my own conscience is as clear as that of my children; your own conscience, most respected mother, could not possibly be clearer. Yet I ask you to have a midwife called, so that I may know what it is and, *whatever* it is, put my mind at rest.' 'A midwife!' exclaimed Madame G... with indignation. 'A clear conscience and a midwife!' And she was lost for words. 'A midwife, dearest mother,' repeated the Marchioness,

kneeling down in front of her; 'immediately, or I shall go mad!'
'Oh, willingly,' replied the Colonel's wife; 'but do not let the confinement take place in my house, if you please.' With this remark
she rose to her feet and made to leave the room. The Marchioness
followed her mother with arms outstretched and fell prostrate
before her, clasping her knees. 'If ever an unimpeachable way
of life'—she cried, with the eloquence of despair—'a life led in
accordance with your example, gave me the right to your respect; if ever a mother's feeling in your bosom should speak in
my favour, only so long as my guilt is not perfectly clear: do not
abandon me at this dreadful moment'—'What is it that disquiets
you?' asked her mother. 'Is it nothing more than the doctor's
remarks? Nothing more than your innermost feelings?' 'Nothing
more, mother,' replied the Marchioness, placing her hand upon
her breast. 'Nothing, Julietta?' continued her mother. 'Think
well. A lapse on your part, though it would cause me unspeakable pain, would be permissible, and I would have to pardon it,
after all; but if, in order to escape your mother's reprobation,
you were capable of inventing a fairy-story, overturning the
order of the world and uttering blasphemous oaths with which
to burden my heart—which would all too willingly believe you—
that would be shameful, and I would never forgive you for it.'—
'May the Kingdom of Heaven some day lie as open to me as my
soul before you now,' cried the Marchioness. 'I have concealed
nothing from you, my mother.'—This declaration, filled with
emotion, shook her mother to the heart. 'Good God!' she cried:
'my darling child! How you move me!' And she lifted her daughter to her feet and kissed her, and pressed her to her bosom.
'What in the world are you afraid of, then? Come, you are very
ill'—and she tried to bring her daughter to bed. But the Marchioness, weeping profusely, assured her mother that she was
perfectly healthy and that there was nothing wrong with her
except this strange and inexplicable condition.—'Condition!'
exclaimed her mother; 'what condition? If your recollection of
the past is so clear, what mad fear has seized you? Is it not possible that an inner feeling, that is so dim and vague, is deceiving
you?' 'No, no!' cried the Marchioness, 'it is not deceiving me!
And if you will summon the midwife, you will hear that this
dreadful tale, which threatens my very being, is true!'—'Come,

my dearest child,' said Madame G..., beginning to fear for her sanity. 'Come with me, and go to bed. What did you think that the doctor was saying to you? How burning hot your face is! And you are trembling in every limb! What was it that the doctor said to you?' Whereupon she led the Marchioness away, completely disbelieving all that her daughter had told her of the encounter.—'Dearest! Most excellent mother!' said the Marchioness, smiling despite her tear-filled eyes. 'I am in full possession of my senses. The doctor told me that I am with child. Have the midwife called; as soon as she says that it is not true, I shall be at ease once more.' 'Very well,' replied the Colonel's wife, suppressing her fears. 'She shall come directly, she shall appear immediately—if it is your wish to be derided by her— and tell you that you are a dreamer and a foolish creature.' Whereupon she rang the bell and immediately sent one of her servants to fetch the midwife.

The Marchioness was still lying in her mother's arms, her breast heaving uneasily, when the midwife arrived; and the Colonel's wife explained to the woman the strange delusion from which her daughter was suffering. 'Her Ladyship the Marchioness,' said her mother, 'swears that she has conducted herself virtuously, and yet, deceived by an inexplicable feeling, considers it necessary that an experienced woman should examine her.' As she examined the Marchioness, the midwife spoke of young blood and the insidious ways of the world and, after concluding her examination, explained that such cases as this were already familiar to her; all young widows who found themselves in such a condition cherished the belief that they had been living upon a desert island; then she spoke words of consolation to Her Ladyship the Marchioness and assured her that the gallant corsair who had landed at night upon the island would surely be found. At these words the Marchioness fell into a swoon. The Colonel's lady, unable to suppress her maternal feelings, succeeded—with the help of the midwife—in restoring her to her senses; but as soon as the Marchioness revived, her mother's indignation won the upper hand. 'Julietta!' exclaimed her mother, afflicted by the most awful pain—'will you not confess to me? Will you not reveal to me the name of the father?' And she still seemed willing to become reconciled with her daughter. When, however, the Marchioness declared that she would go mad, her mother, rising from the divan, cried: 'Go! go! you worthless creature! Cursed be the hour in which I bore you!' With these words she left the room.

Almost fainting a second time, the Marchioness drew the midwife to her side and, trembling violently, laid her head upon her breast. In a broken voice, she asked what was the natural course of events? And whether it was possible for a woman to conceive without her knowledge?—The midwife smiled, loosened the Marchioness's kerchief, and said, that was certainly not the case with Her Ladyship. 'No, no,' replied the Marchioness; she had conceived with her knowledge; she merely wished to know whether, in general, such an event was within the bounds of Nature's possibility. The midwife answered that this had not happened to any woman on earth, with the exception of the Holy Virgin. The Marchioness trembled even more violently. She believed that she was about to give birth that very moment and, clasping the midwife to her in a fit of fear, begged the woman not to leave her. The midwife reassured her. She declared that the Marchioness's confinement was still a considerable time ahead, advised her by what means public rumours might be avoided, and said that everything would turn out well in the end. But these words of consolation pierced the unhappy lady like a dagger through her breast; then, composing herself, she declared that she felt herself better and requested the midwife to leave.

Scarcely had the midwife left the room when a servant brought a letter from the Marchioness's mother, who expressed herself in the following terms: Under the circumstances, Colonel G... desired the Marchioness to leave his house. He enclosed the relevant documents concerning her fortune, he said, and hoped that God would spare him the sorrow of ever seeing her again.— The letter was wet with tears and, in one corner, was a smudged word: 'dictated.'—The Marchioness's eyes were filled with pain. Weeping bitterly at her parents' error and the injustice which these excellent people had been deceived into making, she went to her mother's apartments. There, she was met with the information that her mother was with the Commandant, whereupon she stumbled to her father's apartments. Finding the door locked, she collapsed on the floor in front of it, calling in a sorrowful voice upon all the saints to witness her innocence. She had been lying upon the floor for perhaps several minutes when the Forestry Inspector appeared at the door and, his face aflame, said: she had heard that the Commandant did not wish to see her. 'My dearest brother!' cried the Marchioness, sobbing violently; she forced her way into the room crying: 'My dearest father!' and stretched out her arms towards him. As soon as he saw his daughter, the Commandant turned his back upon her and hastened into his bedchamber. 'Away!' he cried, as she made to follow him into the room, and he tried to slam the door; weeping and wailing, she prevented him from closing it, so that he suddenly gave up his attempt and ran to the far end of the room whilst the Marchioness followed him. Though he had turned his back upon her, she threw herself at his feet and was clasping his knees, trembling, when a pistol which he had seized discharged just as he snatched it from the wall, and the shot struck the ceiling loudly. 'God in Heaven!' cried the Marchioness, and rising, pale as death, to her feet, she ran from her father's apartments again. Returning to her own rooms, she gave orders for the horses to be harnessed immediately; deathly tired, she sank into an armchair, then she hastily dressed her children and ordered their belongings to be packed. She had just taken her younger daughter upon her knee and was wrapping a scarf around the child's neck before they climbed into the carriage, everything now being ready for their departure, when the Forestry Inspector entered and demanded from her, on behalf of the Commandant, that the children should be left behind in his care. 'These children?' she asked, and rose to her feet. 'Tell your inhuman father that he may come and shoot me, but that he cannot take my children away from me!' And, with the absolute pride afforded by innocence, she took her children into her arms, bore them to her carriage—her brother not daring to stop her—and drove away.

Having, as a result of these splendid efforts, become aware of her own capabilities, she suddenly drew herself, as if by her own hand, out of the deep morass into which Fate had plunged her. Once they were in the open, the tumult heaving within her breast subsided; she kissed her children—her precious booty—

again and again; then she fell to thinking, with the greatest satisfaction, about the victory which she had won over her brother
thanks to her consciousness of her innocence. Her power of
reason, which was strong enough not to collapse despite the
unusual position in which she found herself, yielded entirely to
the great, holy, and inexplicable order of the world. She realized
that it was impossible to convince her family of her innocence;
she understood that she must learn to accept this, if she were
not to perish and, only a few days after her arrival in V..., her
grief had entirely given way to a heroic determination to face
with pride the attacks of the world at large. She made up her
mind to withdraw completely into her inmost soul, to dedicate
herself—with an enthusiasm excluding all other duties—to the
education of her children and to devote her care to the gift
which God had made her in the shape of the third child, with
perfect maternal love. She made preparations to restore, in a few
weeks time—as soon as she had recovered from her confinement—her beautiful estate, which had somewhat fallen into
neglect as a result of her long absence; sitting in her garden
arbour, knitting tiny bonnets and stockings for tiny legs, she
considered how she should plan the rooms in the most suitable
manner; which room she would fill with books and in which
room her easel would best be placed. Thus, even before the time
at which Count F... was due to return from Naples, she was
already perfectly accustomed to her fate of living in permanent,
cloistered seclusion. The door-keeper received orders to admit
no one into the house. To her, the thought was unbearable that
the child that she had conceived in perfect innocence and purity,
and whose origin, for the very reason that it was so mysterious,
also seemed more divine than that of other men, should bear the
mark of disgrace in the eyes of bourgeois society. An unusual
means of discovering the identity of the father had occurred to
her: a means which, as she first thought of it, made her drop her
knitting in sheer fright. For entire nights on end, during which
she lay sleepless and uneasy, she considered and reconsidered
the idea in order to familiarize herself with its nature, which was
injurious to her innermost feelings. She still hesitated to enter
into a relationship of any kind with the person who had so
abused her; for she very rightly concluded that this person must

irrevocably belong to the lowest level of his species and, of whatever rank one might consider him to be, could only originate from the most abject and disgusting dregs of society. But, because her mood of independence was growing stronger and stronger within her, and because she considered that a precious stone retains its value no matter what the setting may be—one morning, as the young life within her was stirring once again, she plucked up courage and had that astonishing advertisement, which the reader has already seen at the beginning of this narrative, published in the newspapers of M....

Count F..., who had been detained by unavoidable business in Naples, had meanwhile written to the Marchioness for the second time and appealed to her—whatever unfavourable circumstances might arise—to remain true to her silent declaration already given to him. As soon as he had succeeded in refusing to make an additional official journey to Constantinople, and as soon as his other circumstances permitted, he would immediately leave Naples and would arrive in good time in M... only a few days later than the date which he himself had fixed. The Commandant received him with an extremely embarrassed expression, declared that urgent business obliged him to leave the house, and instructed the Forestry Inspector to entertain him in the meantime. The Forestry Inspector invited him to his room and, after some brief words of greeting, asked him whether he already knew what had taken place in the Commandant's house during his absence. The Count paled for a second and replied that he did not. Thereupon the Forestry Inspector related to the Count the shame which the Marchioness had brought upon the family and repeated the events of which the reader has just been informed. The Count clapped his hand to his forehead. 'Why,' he exclaimed, forgetting himself, 'why have so many obstacles been laid in my path? If the marriage had taken place, we would have been spared all this disgrace and unhappiness!' The Forestry Inspector, staring at the Count, asked him whether he were so mad as to wish to be married to this worthless creature? The Count replied that she was worth more than the entire world which so despised her; that her declaration of her innocence was absolutely credible to him; and that he would travel to V... that very day and make his proposal to her a second time.

Immediately picking up his hat, he took leave of the Forestry Inspector, who believed him to have completely lost his senses, and departed.

Mounting his horse, he galloped away to V.... When he had dismounted at the gate and was just about to enter the court-yard, the door-keeper informed him that the Marchioness would not speak to anyone. The Count asked whether this rule, devised for strangers, also applied to a friend of the family; whereupon the door-keeper replied that he was not aware of any exception, and immediately asked, in an ambiguous manner, whether per-haps he was Count F...? 'No,' replied the Count, giving the man a searching look; then, turning to his servant, he said—though loudly enough for the other to hear—that, under the circum-stances, he would stay at an inn and communicate with the Marchioness by letter. As soon as he was out of sight of the door-keeper, however, he turned a corner and crept alongside the wall of a large garden which extended behind the house. Finding a gate open, he walked through it into the garden, went along the path, and was just about to ascend the slope at the end of the garden when he saw, in an arbour at the side of the garden, the Marchioness, her figure transformed in a lovely, mysterious way, working busily at a small table. He approached her so cautiously that she did not see him until he was standing at the entrance to the arbour, three short paces from her feet. 'Count F...!' exclaimed the Marchioness, opening wide her eyes, and a flush of astonishment spread over her face. The Count smiled and remained standing at the entrance for a moment without moving; then he sat down beside her, yet with such a degree of modest importunity that she had no occasion to be startled; and before she was able, in her unaccustomed situation, to make a decision, he put his arm around her lovely waist. 'Where have you come from, Count?' asked the Marchioness, and gazed shyly at the ground in front of her. 'From M...,' replied the Count, and pressed her gently to him; 'through a back gate which I found open. I thought that I might count upon your forgiveness and entered the garden.' 'Did they not tell you in M...—?'—she asked, remaining perfectly motionless in his arms. 'Everything, beloved lady,' replied the Count; 'never-theless, being completely convinced of your innocence—' 'What!'

exclaimed the Marchioness, wresting herself free and rising to her feet—'and you have come here none the less?' 'In spite of the world at large,' he continued, holding her tightly, 'in spite of your family, and even in spite of this lovely apparition;' and he pressed a fiery kiss upon her breast.—'Begone!' cried the Marchioness.—'So convinced, Julietta,' he said, 'as if I were all-knowing, as if my soul dwelt within your breast.'—'Leave me!' cried the Marchioness.—'I have come,' he concluded—but did not leave her—'to renew my proposal and, if you will hear me, to receive the reward of the blessed from your hand.' 'Leave me this instant!' exclaimed the Marchioness; 'I command you!' and, freeing herself from his arms by force, she fled. 'Beloved! Divine creature!' he whispered, rising to his feet once more and following her. 'Do you hear me!' cried the Marchioness, turning away and avoiding his embrace. 'One single, secret, whispered——!' said the Count, and hastily made to seize her smooth arm as it slipped away from him.—'*I do not wish to hear anything*,' replied the Marchioness and, fiercely pushing him away from her, she ran up the slope and vanished.

He was already half-way up the slope, with the intention of making her listen to him at whatever cost, when the door slammed in his face and the bolt was thrust home violently and with distraught haste before him. Uncertain, for a moment, what to do under such circumstances, he remained standing and considered whether he should climb through an open window beside him and pursue his aim until he achieved it; yet, hard as it was for him, in every sense, to return, nevertheless, on this occasion it seemed absolutely necessary to do so and, bitterly angry with himself for having allowed her to escape from his arms, he crept down the slope and left the garden in order to find his horses. He felt that his attempt to pour out his declaration of love on to her bosom had failed for ever, and rode slowly back to M..., meditating upon a letter which he was now condemned to write. That evening, having entered a hostelry in a most evil temper, he met the Forestry Inspector, who immediately asked him whether he had been successful in making his proposal in V...? The Count replied curtly: 'No!' and was strongly inclined to send him about his business with a bitter remark; but a moment later he added, for politeness's sake, that he had decided to communicate with her by letter and that he would bring matters to a satisfactory conclusion in a short time. The Forestry Inspector replied: he regretted to see that the Count's passion for the Marchioness had robbed him of his senses. He must inform the Count, he said, that she was already on the point of choosing another; then he rang for a servant to bring the latest newspapers and gave him the page containing the Marchioness's appeal to the father of her child. The Count scanned the text, his face flushing crimson as he did so, and a host of emotions ran through him in succession. The Forestry Inspector asked him whether he believed that the person whom the Marchioness sought would be found?—'Undoubtedly,' replied the Count, bent intently over the newspaper and avidly devouring the significance of the message. Then, having folded the newspaper again, he walked to the window for a moment. 'Very well,' he said, 'now I know what I must do;' he turned around immediately and, in a courtly manner, asked the Forestry Inspector whether he might hope to see him again soon, took his leave of him, and, completely resigned to his fate, departed.—

Meanwhile, the Commandant's house had been the scene of great commotion. The Colonel's wife was bitterly angry at the destructive vehemence displayed by her husband and at her own weakness in allowing herself to be overridden by him on the occasion of the tyrannical expulsion of her daughter. When the shot was fired in the Commandant's bedchamber and the Marchioness rushed out of the room, Madame G... had fallen into a swoon from which she had, admittedly, soon recovered; but the moment she awoke, the Commandant had merely said that he regretted that his wife had suffered such a fright without good reason, and had thrown the discharged pistol upon a table. Afterwards, when the question of keeping the Marchioness's children was under discussion, she ventured to declare timidly that no one had the right to take such a step; in a voice which was weak and affecting as a result of her frightening experience, she begged him to avoid such violent scenes in the house; but the Commandant made no further reply except to turn to his son and, foaming with rage, to cry: 'Go! Bring them to me!' When the Count's second letter arrived, the Commandant had ordered that it should be sent to V... to the Marchioness who, as they later learned from the messenger, had laid the letter aside and said, 'Very well!' The Colonel's wife, to whom so much of the entire affair was unclear, in particular the Marchioness's inclination to embark upon a second marriage to which she was completely indifferent, vainly attempted to commence a discussion on the subject. The Commandant, in a tone approaching that of a military command, requested her the whole time to be silent; taking down a portrait of the Marchioness which was still hanging upon the wall, he said that he wished to delete her entirely from his memory and declared that he no longer had a daughter. Then the Marchioness's strange appeal appeared in the newspapers. The Commandant's wife, extremely disturbed by this, went carrying the newspaper, which her husband had given her, to his room, where she found him working at a table, and asked him what on earth he thought of it. The Commandant went on writing and said: 'Oh! she is innocent.' 'What!' exclaimed Madame G... in absolute astonishment: 'innocent?' 'She conceived in her sleep,' said the Commandant without looking up from his work. 'In her sleep!' echoed Madame G.... 'Could such a monstrous event be—?' 'She's quite mad!' cried the Commandant and, pushing his papers together, he left the room.

The next morning, as they were both sitting at the breakfast table, the Colonel's wife read in a newspaper, on which the ink was still wet, the following reply:

'If Her Ladyship the Marchioness of O... will attend at 11 o'clock in the morning on the 3rd of . . . in the house of her father, Colonel G..., the person whom she is seeking will be there to throw himself at her feet'—

The Colonel's wife was speechless even before she had reached the middle of this shocking message; she quickly scanned the remainder of the text and then handed over the newspaper to her husband. The Colonel read the item three times as if he could not believe his own eyes. 'Tell me, Lorenzo,' cried his wife, 'for heaven's sake—what is your opinion of it?' 'Oh! the shameful creature!' replied the Commandant, rising to his feet; 'Oh! the scheming hypocrite! Not the tenfold shamelessness of a bitch coupled with the tenfold cunning of a fox could equal hers! Such a face! Such eyes! A cherub's eyes could not be more true!'—he wailed, and was not to be comforted. 'But,' asked the Colonel's wife, 'if it is indeed a trick, what on earth can she hope to achieve by it?' 'Achieve by it? She intends to accomplish her worthless deception by any means possible,' replied the Colonel. 'And the fairy-tale which they both—she and he—intend to serve up to us here at 11 o'clock in the morning of the 3rd, is one they have learned by heart. "My darling daughter," I am supposed to say, "I did not know; who could possibly imagine? forgive me, my blessing be upon you, and let bygones be bygones." But whoever steps over my threshold on the morning of the 3rd will be met by a bullet! It would be more proper for me to have the servants throw him out of the house.'—Reading the newspaper item once more, Madame G... declared that if she were required to believe one of two incredible things, she would rather believe in a scandalous trick of fate than in this base conduct of her otherwise excellent daughter. But before she had finished speaking, the Commandant exclaimed: 'Would you kindly hold your tongue!' whereupon he left the room, adding: 'It disgusts me even to hear of it.'

A few days later the Commandant received from the Marchioness a letter regarding this newspaper item in which, in a respectful, moving tone, she begged him, since she was denied the mercy of being permitted to appear in his house, to be so kind as to send the person who was to appear before him on the morning of the 3rd to her in V.... The Colonel's wife happened to be present just as the Commandant received this letter; and seeing clearly from his expression that he was confused in his feelings—for what motive could be imputed to the Marchioness, if it were a deception, since she apparently laid no claim to his forgiveness?—she now, made bold by her observation, renewed a plan which she had for a long time been carrying about with her in a heart so plagued with doubt. Whilst the Colonel, with a neutral expression, continued to look at the newspaper, she said that she had an idea: would the Commandant permit her to drive out to V... for one or two days? Should the Marchioness really already know the person who had anonymously replied to her through the newspapers, she would be able to place her daughter in a situation in which she would have to reveal her

innermost thoughts, even if she were the most cunning dissembler
of all time. With a sudden, violent gesture, the Commandant
tore up the letter and replied: she knew that he did not wish to
have anything further to do with his daughter, and he forbade
her to have any contact with her whatsoever. He placed the torn
pieces in an envelope, sealed it and addressed it to the Marchioness, and gave it back to the messenger as reply. The Colonel's wife, secretly angered by her husband's wilful obstinacy
which put paid to any possibility of an explanation, now determined to implement her plan against his will. Taking one of the
Commandant's grooms, she drove off with him next morning to
V... while her husband was still asleep. Arriving at the gate of
the estate, she was informed by the door-keeper that no one was
to be admitted to the Marchioness. Madame G... replied that
she was quite aware of this order but that he should none the
less go and announce the arrival of Madame G... to Her Ladyship. To this the door-keeper replied that that would be of no
avail, since Her Ladyship the Marchioness absolutely refused to
speak to a living soul. Madame G... retorted that the Marchioness
would most certainly speak to her, since she was the Marchioness's mother, and that he should go about his business without
any further delay. Scarcely had the door-keeper entered the house
on this—as he thought—vain errand when the Marchioness
came forth, hurried to the gate, and fell upon her knees in front
of her mother's carriage. Madame G..., assisted by the groom,
stepped down from the carriage and, not without emotion, helped
the Marchioness to her feet again. Overcome by her feelings, the
Marchioness bowed deeply over her mother's hand and, with
tears flowing down her cheeks, led her mother into the house.
'My dearest mother!' she exclaimed, after having invited her to
take a seat upon the divan whilst she herself remained standing
and dried the tears from her eyes.—'To what happy chance do
I owe the inestimable pleasure of your visit?' Taking her daughter
by the hand in a friendly manner, Madame G... replied, she
must say only this: that she had come to beg her daughter's forgiveness for the harsh manner in which she had been expelled
from her father's house. 'Forgiveness!' exclaimed the Marchioness, interrupting her, and attempted to kiss her mother's hands.
Her mother, however, evaded her kisses and continued: 'not

only did the message which appeared in the latest newspapers in answer to your original appeal convince me, as well as your father, of your innocence; I must tell you, too, that he himself, to our great and joyful astonishment, appeared at our house yesterday.' 'Who?'—asked the Marchioness, and sat down beside her mother;—'whom do you mean by "he himself appeared"—?' and her entire body was tense with expectancy. 'He,' replied Madame G...; 'the author of the reply, in person, to whom your appeal was directed.'—'Well, then,' said the Marchioness, her breast heaving with anxiety, 'who is he?' And again she repeated: 'Who is he?'—'That,' replied Madame G..., 'I would like you to guess. Just imagine: yesterday, as we are sitting at tea and reading that curious newspaper, a person whom we know very well bursts into the room with gestures of despair, and falls at your father's feet and then at mine. Not knowing what to make of this, we order him to speak. Thereupon he begins to speak: his conscience leaves him no peace, he says; he is the shameful wretch who has so ill-used Her Ladyship the Marchioness; he knows how his crime will be condemned and, if vengeance must fall upon him, he has come of his own accord to face it.' 'But who? who? who?' exclaimed the Marchioness. 'As I have said,' went on Frau von G..., 'a young, otherwise well brought-up person, whom we would never have considered capable of such base conduct. But you must not be dismayed, my daughter, when you learn that he is of low birth and lacking all the attributes which one could otherwise expect in your husband.' 'No matter, excellent mother,' said the Marchioness, 'he cannot be totally unworthy, since he has already thrown himself at your feet before throwing himself at mine. But who? who? Only tell me, who?' 'Well, then,' said her mother; 'it is Leopardo, the groom, whom your father recruited from Tirol not long ago, and whom, as you may have noticed, I have brought with me to present to you as your bridegroom.' 'Leopardo the groom!' exclaimed the Marchioness, pressing her hand against her forehead with an expression of despair. 'What affrights you so?' asked the Colonel's wife. 'Do you have cause to doubt what I have told you?'—'How? Where? When?' asked the bewildered Marchioness. 'That', replied her mother, 'is something he will tell only you. His shame and love, he said, made it impossible for him to speak of it to anyone but you. But if you wish, let us open the door to the ante-room, where he is awaiting the out-come with a pounding heart, and you shall see whether you cannot coax his secret from him when I am not present.'—'Our Father in Heaven!' exclaimed the Marchioness; 'once, when I had fallen asleep in the midday heat, I saw him walking away from my divan when I awoke!'—And she held her little hands in front of her face flushed with shame. At these words, her mother sank down on her knees before her. 'My daughter!' she cried; 'O noble child!' and she threw her arms around her. 'Worthless creature that I am!' and she hid her face in her daughter's lap. 'What is the matter, mother?' asked the Marchioness, alarmed. 'I must confess to you,' continued her mother, 'you who are purer than the angels, that nothing is true of all that I have told you; that my abandoned soul was unable to believe in such innocence as that which shines around you, and that only through this shameful deception was I able to convince myself of it.' 'Dearest mother!' exclaimed the Marchioness, deeply moved, and, bending over her mother, she tried to raise her to her feet. 'No,' replied her mother; 'I shall not move from your feet until you say that you can forgive my monstrous behaviour—you perfect creature, you angel!'—'*I*, forgive *you*, my mother! Stand up, I beg you,' cried the Marchioness.—'Hear me,' said Madame G..., 'I wish to know whether you can still love me and still honestly respect me, as before?' 'My adored mother,' exclaimed the Marchioness, and she, too, fell upon her knees before her mother; 'my love and respect for you have never left my heart. Who could have been capable of trusting me in such unheard-of circumstances? How happy I am that you are convinced of my blamelessness!' 'Well, then,' replied Madame G..., and, supported by her daughter, she rose to her feet: 'I will help you in every way I can, my dearest daughter. You shall give birth to your child in my house; even if the circumstances were such that I might expect a young prince from you, I could not care for you with greater tenderness and respect. I shall never leave your side for the rest of my days. I defy the entire world; I do not wish any other honour save your shame; as long as you love me again and no longer think of the harshness with which I drove you away.' The Marchioness attempted to console her mother, caressing her and entreating her repeatedly, although evening approached and midnight struck before she succeeded in doing so. Next day, the old lady's indisposition—which had brought about a fever during the night—having improved a little, mother and daughter and grandchildren drove back as if in triumph to M.... They were in extremely good humour during the journey, made jokes about Leopardo the groom, who was sitting on the driver's seat in front; and Madame G... said to the Marchioness she noticed that her daughter blushed whenever she looked at his broad back. Half sighing, half smiling, the Marchioness replied: 'Who knows who will appear before us at 11 o'clock on the morning of the 3rd, after all!'—Thereafter, however, the closer they came to M..., the graver became their mood, in premonition of the decisive scene which still awaited them. When they descended from the carriage in front of the house, Madame G..., her demeanour such as to allow no one to suspect her plans, brought her daughter to her old apartments again; she should make herself comfortable, her mother said; she would be with her again in a short while; whereupon she quickly left. She returned an hour later, her face quite flushed. 'No! such a doubting Thomas!' she said, secretly amused; 'such a doubting Thomas! I was a whole hour convincing him. And now he is sitting weeping.' 'Who?' asked the Marchioness. '*He*,' answered her mother. 'Who else but the one who has most reason to weep?' 'Not my father?' exclaimed the Marchioness. 'Like a child,' replied her mother; 'so much so that, if I myself had not had to wipe the tears from my eyes, I would have laughed, the moment I was outside the door.' 'And because of me?' asked the Marchioness, standing up; 'and you would have me stay here——?' 'You shan't go one step!' said Madame G.... 'Why did he dictate the letter to me? He shall seek *you* here, if he wishes to see *me* again as long as I live.' 'Dearest mother!' implored the Marchioness—'I'm not to be moved!' the Colonel's wife interrupted her. 'Why did he reach for the pistol?'—'But, mother, I beg you——' 'You *must not*,' said Madame G..., pressing her daughter back on to her armchair. 'And if he does not come here by this evening, I shall depart tomorrow with you.'—The Marchioness considered such a procedure harsh and unjust. But her mother replied: 'Calm yourself'—for, at just that instant, she heard from far away someone sobbing his way towards them—'he is coming!' 'Where?' asked the Marchioness, listening. 'Is there someone at the door? This loud knocking—?' 'Of course,' replied Madame G..., 'He wishes us to open the door.' 'Let me go!' cried the Marchioness and rose impetuously from her armchair. 'If you love me, Julietta,' said her mother, 'remain where you are;' and at that moment the Commandant entered the room, holding his handkerchief to his face. The mother placed herself directly in front of her daughter, her back turned to her husband. 'Dearest father!' cried the Marchioness, stretching out her arms towards him. 'Not a step!' commanded Madame G...; 'do you hear!' The Commandant remained standing and went on weeping. 'He must ask your forgiveness,' Madame G... continued; 'Why does he weep so bitterly? And why is he so stubborn? I love him, but I love you, too; I respect him, but I respect you, too. And if I must choose between you both, then you are more admirable than he, and I shall remain with you.'—The Commandant bent double, and wept so that the room echoed with the sound. 'My God!' exclaimed the Marchioness, suddenly giving way to her mother and, taking out her handkerchief, she herself began to weep.— 'Yet he cannot speak!' said Madame G..., moving aside a little. At this, the Marchioness rose to her feet, embraced the Commandant, and begged him to compose himself. She herself was weeping bitterly. She asked him whether he would not be seated; she attempted to pull him on to an armchair; she pushed an armchair towards him so that he might sit down; but he made no reply; he could not be moved from the spot; nor would he sit down, but remained standing, his head bowed deeply, and continued to weep. Holding him upright, and half turning towards her mother, the Marchioness said: 'He will make himself ill;' then, as he began to jerk convulsively, the Marchioness's mother herself seemed on the point of losing her tenacity. At last, in obedience to his daughter's repeated appeals, the Commandant sat down, and the Marchioness, caressing him without cease, sank down at his feet; whereupon his wife, addressing him once more, said that he quite deserved it; that he would certainly now come to his senses; then she went from the room, leaving them alone.

As soon as she was outside the room, she herself wiped away her tears; then she considered whether the severe agitation which she had caused her husband might not be dangerous, and whether it would not be advisable to have a doctor called? She went to the kitchen and herself prepared for him everything she knew in the way of tonic and soothing concoctions; made and warmed his bed for him in order to put him into it the moment he should appear, led by his daughter; and, as he had still not appeared though the table was laid for supper, crept to the Marchioness's room in order to hear what was happening. Quietly laying her ear to the door, she heard the last echo of some soft whisperings which seemed to proceed from the Marchioness; and, as she was able to observe through the keyhole, the Marchioness was sitting on her father's lap—something which he had never before permitted in his life. At last she opened the door, and her heart filled with joy at what she saw—her daughter, with head thrown back and eyes tightly closed, was lying in her father's arms; whilst he, sitting in the armchair, his eyes wide open and filled with shining tears, was covering her lips with long, glowing, thirsty kisses: just like a lover! The daughter did not speak a word, nor did he; his head bent over her, as if she were the girl he had first loved, he tended her lips and kissed her. Her mother was overcome with bliss; standing unseen behind her husband's chair, she refrained from disturbing the pleasure of the heavenly reconciliation which had returned to her house once more. At last she drew close to the father and, bending over the chair, looked at him from the side as, with unutterable pleasure, he was once more engaged in caressing his daughter's mouth with fingers and lips. On seeing her, the Commandant lowered his face, now quite puckered once again, and attempted to say something; but she exclaimed: 'Oh what a face is this!' whereupon she herself now kissed her husband's face so that it too became composed once more, and with jesting remarks put an end to this moving scene. She summoned them to supper and led them —walking like a bridal couple—to the table; though the Commandant was in very good spirits, he nevertheless sobbed from time to time; he ate and spoke little, but gazed down at his plate and played with his daughter's hand.

At dawn the following day the burning question was: who on earth would appear at 11 o'clock tomorrow? For tomorrow was the dreaded 3rd of the month. The Marchioness's father and mother, and her brother too, who had come to be reconciled with her, were unconditionally in favour of marriage, provided the man was to some degree acceptable; everything possible should be done in order to restore the Marchioness's happiness. However, should the man's circumstances be too much inferior to those of the Marchioness, even if the family were to come to his aid, then her parents opposed the marriage; they determined to keep the Marchioness with them as before and to adopt the child. The Marchioness, on the contrary, seemed willing, whatever happened, to keep the promise she had made, provided the man was not of disreputable character, and to provide her child with a father, at whatever cost. That evening, her mother asked what reception should be accorded to the man? The Commandant was of the opinion that it would be best if they were to leave the Marchioness alone at 11 o'clock. The Marchioness, however, insisted that both parents and her brother, too, should be present, since she did not wish to share any secrets whatsoever with this man. The same wish, she said, also seemed to be expressed in the answer to her announcement, namely, by proposing the Commandant's house as the scene of the meeting; a reason why this answer, as she freely admitted, had greatly pleased her. Her mother commented upon the awkwardness of the roles which the father and the brother would have to play in that case, and asked her daughter to agree to their not being present; she herself agreed to her daughter's wish and would be present when the man was received. After the Marchioness had considered this proposal for a while, she at last consented. Following a night spent in the most feverish expectations, the morning of the dreaded 3rd arrived. As the clock struck eleven, both women, sumptuously dressed as if for a marriage engagement, were sitting in the reception room; their hearts were pounding so hard that they would have been heard if the sounds of everyday life had suddenly ceased. The eleventh stroke of the clock was still sounding when Leopardo the groom, whom the Marchioness's father had recruited from Tirol, entered the room. At this, the two women turned pale. 'Count F... has arrived,' he said, 'and requests the honour of being admitted.' 'Count F...!' they exclaimed, plunged from dismay of one kind to dismay of another. 'Lock the doors!' ordered the Marchioness; 'we are not at home to him.' She rose in order to bolt the door herself and was just about to thrust the groom, who was standing in her way, from the room, when the Count, wearing exactly the same uniform, with weapons and decorations, as he had worn during the storming of the citadel, entered and walked towards her. The Marchioness was so bewildered that she thought she would sink into the ground; she seized a shawl which she had left lying upon her chair and attempted to flee into an adjoining room. But Madame G… seized her by the hand, crying 'Julietta—!' then, overcome by her racing thoughts, was struck speechless. 'Julietta! I beg you!' she repeated, her gaze fixed firmly upon the Count, and drew her daughter back. 'Who is it we are expecting —?' The Marchioness turned abruptly and exclaimed: 'Why— not him, surely—?' and hurled a look like a bolt of lightning at the Count whilst a deathly pallor flitted across her face. The Count had fallen upon one knee before her; his right hand laid over his heart and his head slightly bent upon his breast, he stared at the floor in front of him with his eyes burning, and said not a word. 'Whom else?' exclaimed the Colonel's wife, 'whom else should we expect save him—? demented creatures that we are!' The Marchioness stood, unbending, over him. 'Mother,' she said, 'I shall go mad!' 'Fool!' retorted her mother and, pulling her daughter to her, whispered something into her ear. The Marchioness turned away and, her hands held in front of her face, fell upon the sofa. 'Unhappy child!' exclaimed her mother; 'what is the matter? What has happened that has taken you so unawares?'—The Count did not move from the mother's side; still kneeling, he seized the hem of her dress and kissed it. 'Dearest! Merciful lady! Most honourable!' he whispered, and a tear rolled down his cheek. 'Stand up, Count, stand up!' said the Colonel's lady; 'comfort her; thus we shall all be reconciled, everything will be forgiven and forgotten.' Weeping, the Count rose to his feet. Once again he fell upon his knees before the Marchioness; he gently took her hand, as if it were of gold and could be tarnished by the heat of his own hands. But—'Go! Go! Go!' she cried, rising. 'I had been prepared for a libertine, but not for a —— devil!' Then, shunning him as if he were afflicted by plague, she opened the door of the room and said: 'Call the Commandant!'—'Julietta!' cried her mother in astonishment.

The Marchioness cast a look of deadly savagery first at the Count, then at her mother; her breast was heaving and her face aflame; no Fury could have appeared more terrible. The Commandant and the Forestry Inspector arrived. 'Father,' she cried, even as they were walking through the door, 'I cannot marry this man!' She dipped her hand in a basin of holy water fixed to the door; then, with a wide sweep of her hand, she sprinkled her father, her mother, and her brother and disappeared.

The Commandant, shaken by this grotesque scene, asked what had happened; then, seeing Count F... in the room at this crucial moment, turned deathly pale. His wife took the Count by the hand and said: 'Do not ask; this young man regrets, with all his heart, everything that has happened; give, give your blessing and all will end well.' The Count remained standing as if thunderstruck. The Commandant laid his hand upon the Count's head; his eyelashes trembled and his lips were white as chalk. 'May Heaven's curse vanish from this head!' he cried: 'when do you intend to marry?'—'Tomorrow,' answered the mother on the Count's behalf, for he was unable to utter a word; 'tomorrow —or today, if you wish; for the Count, who has displayed such admirable eagerness to make amends for his misdeed, the very next hour will be the most appropriate.'—'I shall be pleased to see you at 11 o'clock tomorrow in St Augustine's Church,' said the Commandant to the Count; he then withdrew with a bow, called upon his wife and son to go with him to the Marchioness's room, and left the Count alone.

In vain did they attempt to discover from the Marchioness the reason for her strange conduct; she lay ill with a raging fever, simply would not hear of marriage, and requested to be left alone. They asked her why she had suddenly changed her mind and why she found the Count more hateful than another? At this, she gazed at her father blankly, her eyes wide, but made no reply. The Colonel's wife asked whether she had forgotten that she was a mother? To this the Marchioness replied that, in the present circumstances, she was obliged to think of herself more than of the child and, calling all the saints and angels to witness, she once again declared that she would not marry. Her father, believing her to be obviously in a state of overexcitement, insisted that she must keep her word; he then left

her and, after settling all appropriate matters in written form
with the Count, gave all necessary instructions concerning the
wedding. He sent the Count a contract of marriage by which the
latter was to waive all his rights as a husband and, on the other
hand, to agree to all obligations which might be imposed on
him. The Count returned the document, wetted with his tears
and bearing his signature. The following morning, when the
Commandant handed the contract to the Marchioness, her state
of mind was somewhat more composed. Still sitting in her bed,
she read through the contract several times, folded it thoughtfully, and read through it once again; thereupon she declared
that she would attend at St Augustine's Church at 11 o'clock.
She rose from her bed and dressed without saying another word;
then, accompanied by her family, she got into the carriage as the
clock was striking and drove off.

Only at the church entrance was the Count permitted to join
the family. During the ceremony the Marchioness stared ob-
durately at the altar, without sparing so much as a glance for the
man with whom she exchanged rings. When the ceremony was
over the Count offered her his arm; but as soon as they had left
the church again, the Countess bowed to him; the Commandant
asked whether he would have the honour of seeing him again in
his daughter's chambers, whereupon the Count stammered something which no one could understand, doffed his hat to the company, and took his leave of them. He moved into an apartment
in M... where he stayed for several months without even setting
foot in the Commandant's house, where the Countess had remained. It was only thanks to his gentle, respectful, and absolutely exemplary behaviour wherever he happened to meet the
family, that, after the Countess had given birth to a son, he was
invited to the child's christening. Sitting upon her childbed, the
Countess, wrapped in blankets, looked at him only for an instant
as he walked through the door and respectfully greeted her from
a distance. Among the gifts with which the guests bade welcome
to the newborn child, he laid two documents upon the cradle;
after he had left, it was found that one was a deed of gift to the
infant for the sum of 20,000 roubles; the other was a testament,
in which he designated the mother, in the event of his death, as
heiress to his entire fortune. From that day on, at the advocacy

of Madame G..., he was invited frequently; the house was open to him, and soon not an evening passed without his presence there. His heart told him that, on account of the fragile order of the world, he had now been forgiven by everyone, and he began to renew his courtship of the Countess, his wife; after a year had passed she consented a second time, and a second wedding took place, merrier than the first, after which the entire family moved to V.... A whole line of young Russians followed the first. Once, in a happy moment, the Count asked his wife why, on that dreadful 3rd of the month, she had fled from him as if from a devil, since she had seemed prepared for any libertine at all; throwing her arms around his neck, she replied: he would not have seemed like a devil to her at that time if, on the occasion of his first appearance before her, he had not seemed like an angel!

GEORG BÜCHNER

Lenz*

On the 20th of January Lenz crossed through the mountains. The peaks and high-lying mountain slopes in the snow; down into the valleys, grey rock, patches of green, cliffs and pine-trees.

It was cold and wet; the water was streaming down the cliffs and leaping across the path. The branches of the pines drooped heavily into the damp air. Grey clouds moved across the sky, though tightly packed together—then the mist billowed up and spread moist and heavy through the bushes, so sluggish and awkward.

He walked on uncaring, now uphill, now downhill; the path did not interest him. He did not feel any weariness; but at times he found it annoying that he could not walk on his head.

At first he had a driven feeling in his breast, when the cliffs fell away abruptly in that way, when the grey forest trembled below him, when at times the mist swallowed up all shapes and at times again revealed the mighty limbs; he had a feeling of being driven, he searched for something, as if for forgotten dreams, but he found nothing. Everything seemed so small, so close, so wet; he would have liked to set the Earth behind the stove. He could not understand why it took him so long to climb down a hillside, to reach a distant point; he felt he must be able to pace out everything with a few steps. Only sometimes, when the storm hurled the clouds into the valleys and the mist was rising from the forest and the voices swelling on the cliffs, now like distant thunder dying away, now approaching with a mighty roar, with a sound as if trying to sing the earth's praises with their wild jubilation; when the clouds surged forward like wild, whinnying steeds and the sunshine appeared and vanished again between them and drew its flashing sword across the snowfields so that a bright, blinding light cut across the mountain peaks into the valleys; or when the storm drove the clouds downwards, tearing open a pale blue lake and the sound of the wind died away and rose again, humming from deep down in the chasms, from the tips of the pines, like a cradle song and like the sound of bells, and a pale tinge of red crept up in the deep blue of the sky, and tiny clouds drifted by on silver wings; and all the mountain peaks, sharp and clear, glinted and flashed far across the land—then he felt a bursting in his chest, he stood panting, his body bent forward, eyes and mouth opened wide; he felt he must draw the storm into himself and encompass everything within himself; he stretched himself and lay across the Earth, he burrowed his way into the Universe, it was a joy that filled him with pain; or he would stand motionless, laying his head upon the moss and half-closing his eyes; then the entire scene would withdraw far away from him, the Earth would move away below him, to become smaller like a wandering star and vanish into a racing stream whose clear water was flowing beneath him. But these were only brief moments; then he would rise to his feet, cool, calm, and steady, as if a shadow play had passed before him—he was not aware of anything more.

Towards evening he reached the highest point of the mountains, the snowfield, from where the path ran down again into the plain in the west. Reaching the summit, he sat down. It had become calmer as evening drew in; the clouds stood firm and motionless in the sky; as far as the eye could see, there was nothing but mountain peaks from which wide flanks ran down, and all was silent, grey, and gloomy. He felt an awful loneliness; he was alone, quite alone. He attempted to converse with himself, but he could not; he scarcely dared to breathe; the bending of his own feet sounded like thunder beneath him and he had to sit down. In the midst of this nothingness he was seized by a nameless fear; he was in empty space! He forced himself to his feet and raced down the mountainside.

It had grown dark; heaven and earth melted into one. He felt that something was following him, that something dreadful would surely overtake him, something intolerable to mankind, as if madness were pursuing him on horseback.

At last he heard voices; now he could see lights and his heart felt easier. People told him it was still half-an-hour's walk to Waldbach.

He walked through the village. Lights gleamed through the

window-panes and, as he walked past, he looked inside: children at table, old women, girls—quiet, calm faces, all of them: it seemed to him that the light was gleaming from out of their faces; he had a feeling of relief, and soon he was in the vicarage of Waldbach.

They were sitting at table as he entered; his blond curls hung around his pale face, his eyes and mouth were twitching and his clothes were torn.

Oberlin* bade him welcome; he took him for a workman: 'You are welcome, though I don't know who you are.'—'I am a friend of Kaufmann's,* he sends you his regards.' 'What is your name, if I may ask?'—'Lenz.'—'Ha, ha—not the writer, by any chance? Haven't I read a number of plays ascribed to a gentleman of that name?'—'Yes, but please don't judge me by them.'

They continued talking; he was searching for words and speaking rapidly, but in a foment of suspense; gradually he became calmer—the homely room and the calm faces which appeared out of the shadows: the child's clear face, on which all the light seemed to shine, looking up curiously, trustingly; and the face of the mother, who was sitting quiet as an angel back in the shadows. He began to talk, about his home country; he made sketches of the national dress; the family gathered around him, filled with interest; he felt quite at home. His pale, childlike face now smiling, his lively narrative! He became calm; it seemed to him that long-lost figures, long-forgotten faces were appearing out of the shadows again; old songs came to life once more, and he was far, far away.

At last it was time to retire; they accompanied him across the street—the vicarage was too cramped and they gave him a room in the schoolhouse. He went upstairs. It was cold there; a spacious room, empty, with a high bed at the far end. Placing his candle upon the table, he began to walk up and down. He looked back upon the events of the day, how he had come here and where he was now. The room at the vicarage, with its lights and kindly faces, seemed to him a shadow, a dream, and he felt empty, just as he had felt in the mountains; but the emptiness could not be filled at all, the light had gone out, and the darkness swallowed up everything. He was seized by an indefinable fear. Leaping out of bed, he ran through the room, down the stairs, and out in front of the school; but to no avail, darkness everywhere, nothing—he was a dream unto himself. Isolated thoughts rose up in his mind, and he held on tight to them; he felt he must keep repeating the words 'Our Father'. He was no longer able to find himself; a vague instinct urged him to save himself. He stubbed his feet against the stones, he scratched himself with his nails; and the pain began to restore his consciousness. He threw himself into the trough, but the water was not deep, and he merely splashed about.

People appeared; they had heard the noise and they called to him. Oberlin came running. Lenz had recovered once more, he was now fully conscious of his situation, and he felt at ease again. Now he felt ashamed of himself, and sorry, because he had frightened these good people; he told them that he was accustomed to taking cold baths, then he went upstairs again; at last he fell asleep from sheer exhaustion.

The following day things went well with him. Together with Oberlin, he rode on horseback through the valley; wide mountain flanks, running together from a great height to form a narrow, winding valley, which clambered high up the mountains on many sides; huge cliffs, widening towards their base; not much forest, everything shimmering grey and gloomy; to the west you had a view of the country and the mountain chain running due north and south, its peaks standing tremendous, grim or silent, like a twilit dream. Huge masses of light, which sometimes poured out of the valleys like a river of gold, then cloud again, lying upon the highest peak and then drifting slowly down over the forest into the valley or rising and falling in the flashes of sunlight like a silvery, winged ghost; no noise, no movement, no bird, nothing save the blowing of the wind, at times near by, at times far away. And dots, too, black and gloomy, appeared; the skeletons of huts, boards covered with straw. The people, earnest and silent, as if they dared not disturb the peace of their valley, greeted them calmly as they rode past.

The huts were alive with activity; the people thronged around Oberlin, who issued reprimands, gave advice, and offered words of consolation; everywhere, trustful eyes and prayers. They told him of their dreams and premonitions. Then, abruptly, matters of everyday life: paths laid, drains dug, school attendance.

Oberlin was untiring, Lenz his constant companion; at times talking to him, at times working, at other times lost in the contemplation of nature. Everything had a beneficial and calming effect upon him. Often he felt compelled to look Oberlin in the eye, and the enormous feeling of peace which sweeps over us from nature at rest—in the depths of the forest, on warm, moonlit summer nights—seemed to him even closer in this calm gaze, this grave, noble face. Lenz was shy by nature, but he talked, made observations. Oberlin found his conversation very entertaining, and took great pleasure in looking at Lenz's handsome, childlike face.

For Lenz, however, life was tolerable only as long as there was light in the valley; when evening drew near he was overcome by a curious fear, which prompted him to pursue the sun. As his surroundings became more and more bathed in shadow, everything seemed so dreamlike, so repellent; fear arose in him as it does in children who sleep in the dark; he felt as if he were blind. Now the fear was growing; the nightmare of madness sat at his feet: the hopeless idea came to him that everything was but a dream; he clung on to every object. Figures swept past him swiftly, and he pushed his way towards them; but they were shadows; the life drained out of him and his limbs became perfectly rigid. He talked, he sang, he recited pieces from Shakespeare; he reached after everything which, at other times, had made his blood race; he tried everything, but—cold, cold! Then he had an impulse to go out into the open. Once his eyes became accustomed to the darkness, the dim light, diffused by the night, made him feel better; he leapt into the trough, and the harsh effect of the water made him feel better; he even cherished a secret hope that he might become ill—he now made less noise when taking his bath.

Yet the more actively he participated in life, the calmer he became. He helped Oberlin at his work, sketched, read the Bible; old, vanished hopes rose up in him; the New Testament was a great comfort to him [. . .] When Oberlin told him how an unseen hand had held him safe upon the bridge; how, up in the mountains, a light had blinded him; how he had heard a voice, how it had spoken to him in the night; and how God had so completely entered into him that, like a child, he had drawn lots out of his pocket in order to know what he should do: this belief, this eternal heaven here on earth, this existence in God—only now did he begin to understand the Holy Scriptures. How Nature came so close to man, revealing everything in heavenly mysteries; though not in the form of overwhelming majesty, but as something familiar.

One morning he went out of the house. It had snowed during the night; the valley was filled with bright sunshine, but farther off the landscape lay half-veiled in mist. Soon he left the path and climbed a gentle slope beside a pinewood—there were no more footprints to be seen; the sun cut crystals, the snow was light and fluffy, here and there in the snow faint tracks of wild animals leading up into the mountains. The air was perfectly still save for a slight wind, like the sound of a bird gently brushing the snowflakes from its tail. Everything was still, the trees could be seen far off, their white branches trembling like feathers in the deep blue sky. Gradually he began to feel at ease. The gigantic, uniform expanses and contours, which he often felt were speaking to him with mighty voices, were hidden; a comforting feeling of Christmas stole over him; at times, he thought his mother would appear, large as life, from behind a tree and tell him that all this was a present for him. Going downhill, he saw that his shadow was rimmed with radiant rainbow colours; it seemed to him that something had touched his forehead; the being spoke to him.

He came down into the village. Oberlin was in his room; Lenz approached him cheerfully and said that he would like to preach a sermon some time.—'Have you studied theology?'—'Yes!'—'Very well, then; next Sunday.'

Lenz went happily to his room. He thought of a text for his sermon and fell to meditating; and he slept peacefully at nights. Sunday morning arrived, a thaw had set in. Clouds drifting past, blue patches between. The church was on the hillside nearby, on a spur, with the churchyard around it. Lenz was standing on the hill when the churchbell began to ring and the congregation —the women and girls in their solemn, black costumes, each with her white handkerchief folded upon her hymn-book and a sprig of rosemary—coming from all directions, walked up or down the narrow paths between the cliffs. From time to time, sunshine lay over the valley; the mild air moving slowly, the landscape floating in the haze, the sound of distant bells—it seemed as if everything were dissolving into a wave of harmony.

In the little churchyard the snow had disappeared, revealing dark moss under the black crosses; a late rose-bush clung to the churchyard wall, and late flowers peeped from beneath the moss; at times sunshine, then dark again. The service began and the people's voices united in a pure, clear sound; it was as if one were looking into pure, crystal-clear mountain water. The singing died away—Lenz began to speak. He was diffident; under the influence of the music his stiffness had vanished completely, all his sorrow now came alive and settled in his breast. A blissful feeling of utter well-being crept over him. He spoke to the people in simple words; they all shared his pain, and he felt comforted when he was able to bring sleep to eyes tired with weeping and peace to tormented hearts, and send up this dull pain to heaven through this existence racked by earthly wants. When he finished speaking he was more composed—and then the voices began to sing once more:

> May the sacred pains within me
> Let the springs down deep run free;
> May suffering be my profit all,
> Suffering my service to God's call.

The feeling of urgency within him, the music and the pain left him shaken. It seemed to him that the universe was full of wounds; this caused him deep, unspeakable pain. Now another form of existence: god-like, quivering lips bent down to him and clung to his own lips; he went up to his solitary room. He was alone, alone! The brook murmured, streams poured from his eyes, he hunched himself together, his limbs quivered and he felt he must disintegrate, so endless was the voluptuous pleasure of it. At last it dawned upon him: he felt a deep pity for himself, he wept for himself; his head sank upon his breast and he fell asleep. The full moon was in the sky; his curls tumbled over his forehead and his face, his tears clung to his eyelashes and dried upon his cheeks—and so he lay there, alone, all was peaceful and still and cold, and the moon shone the whole night, hanging above the mountains.

Next morning he came downstairs and, with perfect calm, told Oberlin that his mother had appeared to him during the night; she had stepped from the dark churchyard wall wearing a white dress; on her breast she wore a white rose and a red rose; then she had sunk into a corner and the roses had slowly grown over her; he was sure that she was dead; he felt perfectly calm at the knowledge. In reply, Oberlin told Lenz how he had been alone in the fields when his father died, and had heard a voice, by which he knew that his father was dead; and when he arrived home, it was indeed so. This led them to other themes: Oberlin spoke of the mountain dwellers, of girls who could feel the presence of water and metal beneath the earth; of men who, in the mountains, had been seized by and wrestled with a spirit; and he told Lenz how, on one occasion, in the mountains, he had been put into a sort of sleep-walking trance by gazing into a deep, empty mountain pool. Lenz replied that the spirit of the water had come upon him, and that he had then felt something of his own being. He went on: a man of the simplest, most unaffected nature is closest of all to the elemental sense; the more finely developed a man's feeling and spiritual life, the more dulled does this elemental sense become; he himself did not consider it a highly developed condition—it did not display sufficient independence; but he thought it must impart a feeling of infinite joy to be touched by the characteristic life of every form in nature, to have a soul sensitive to stones, metals, water, and plants, to imbibe into oneself, in such a dream-like fashion, every being found in nature, just as the flowers imbibe the air with the waxing and waning of the moon.

He expressed himself in even more detail: how, in all things, there is an ineffable harmony, a sound, a supreme happiness which, among the higher forms of creation—endowed with a greater number of organs—reaches out beyond its own limits, ringing out, resounding and understanding, though as a result, all the more deeply affected; whereas among the lower forms, everything is more repressed, more limited, yet displays a greater degree of inherent calmness. He elaborated upon the theme. Oberlin interrupted his theorizing because it was leading him too far away from his uncomplicated manner. On another occasion, Oberlin showed him some coloured tablets and explained to him the relationship which each colour bears to man; he showed him twelve apostles, each of whom, he said, was represented by a colour. Lenz took up the theme and continued with it; he was afflicted by bad dreams and, like Stilling,* began to read the Apocalypse; and he read the Bible a great deal.

At about this time, Kaufmann and his fiancée came to the Steintal. At first their presence was unpleasant to Lenz; he had made a niche for himself, the little peace and quiet was so enjoyable—and now he was confronted by someone whose coming revived so many memories, with whom he was obliged to talk, someone who was familiar with his circumstances. Oberlin knew nothing of all this; he had accepted Lenz into his house and cared for him; he considered it an act of divine providence that had sent the unhappy man to him, he loved him with all his heart. It was, moreover, important to everyone that he was there; he belonged to them, as if he had always been there; no one asked where he came from and where he was bound.

At the dinner table, Lenz was in a good humour once again; they talked about literature, and here he was in his element. The Idealistic period* was just then beginning; Kaufmann was an ardent supporter of it, but Lenz contradicted him vehemently: 'The poets, who are said to mirror reality, have not the slightest idea of it; nevertheless, they are more bearable than those who try to glorify reality. The dear Lord has certainly made the world as it should be, and we most definitely cannot throw together something better; our sole effort ought to be dedicated to imitating Him a little. In all things, I expect to find—life, the possibility of existence, then I am satisfied; we have no authority to ask whether it is beautiful, or ugly. The feeling that anything that has been created is imbued with life, is stronger than these two sentiments and is the sole criterion in matters of art. It is only seldom, by the way, that we encounter it: we find it in Shakespeare, folk songs are full of its sounds, and we find it sometimes in Goethe; everything else is only fit for burning. The people cannot even draw a dog kennel. They strive for idealistic shapes, but all I have seen of them are wooden dolls. Such Idealism reveals the most shameful contempt for human nature.'—One ought to attempt it sometime, he said, and immerse oneself in the life led by the meanest human creature, and then translate this experience into the convulsive movements, faint signs, and the delicate, almost imperceptible changes of facial expression; he himself had attempted to do so in his works *The Private Tutor* and *The Soldiers*.*—'These are the most prosaic persons under the sun, but the emotional aspect is almost identical in all human beings, save that the outer shell through which it must break out is more or less solid. One need have only eyes and ears for it. Yesterday, as I was walking up the valley, I saw two girls sitting upon a stone; one was putting up her hair and the other was helping her; her golden hair hanging down, and a grave, pale face, yet so young, and her black dress, and the other girl so eager to help.—The most beautiful, touching works of the Old German school* of painting can hardly convey an idea of it. At times, one could wish oneself a Medusa, to be able to turn such a group into stone, and call to the passers-by.—Then they stood up, the lovely group vanished; but as they walked down the valley, between the cliffs, yet another picture ensued.

'The most beautiful pictures, the richest tones, group together and then fall apart. Only one thing remains: an infinite beauty which migrates from one shape to another, forever laid open to view, transformed. Of course, we cannot always capture them and put them into museums or written music, and then summon young and old and let young lads and old men chatter about them and be filled with delight. One must love all human beings in order to penetrate into the inmost soul of each one; one must not consider anyone too mean or too ugly—only then can one understand them; the most nondescript face creates a deeper impression than a mere feeling of beauty, and one can create one's own figures without copying into them external features devoid of life, of muscles, of a pounding, racing pulse.'

Kaufmann objected, saying that, in real life, Lenz would not find any models suitable for a Belvedere Apollo or a Raphael Madonna. 'What of it,' he replied; 'I must admit that such things have the kiss of death for me. When I really make an effort I can certainly respond to them with feeling, but the work is more mine than theirs. Among poets and artists, I prefer the one who can present nature to me in the most realistic manner, so that his work arouses feeling in me; anything else disturbs me. I prefer the Dutch painters to the Italian, they are the only ones whose works are tangible. I know only two paintings, both by Dutch artists, which made the same impression upon me as the New Testament; one—I do not know the artist's name—depicts Christ and the disciples on the road to Emmaus. When you read the description of how the disciples went forth, the whole of Nature is contained in those few words. It is a gloomy, twilit evening, a dull red streak can be seen on the horizon, the road in semi-darkness; a stranger approaches them, they speak to him, and he breaks the bread; then they recognize him by his plain, human manner; and his divinely suffering features speak clearly to them, and they are afraid, for darkness has set in, and they are overcome by an inexplicable feeling; yet it is not a feeling of ghostly terror, but as if a beloved person, now dead, were to come to meet you in the twilight just as he did before; such is the mood of the picture, overshadowed by a mono-chrome, brownish tone, the quiet, gloomy evening. Then a second picture: a woman sitting in her room with her prayer-book in her hand. Everything clean and tidy, Sunday-fashion, sand strewn on the floor, everything cosily clean and warm. The woman has not been able to go to church, and she is performing her devotions at home; the window is open, she is facing the window, and one feels as if the sound of the bells from the village were sweeping across the wide, flat landscape through the window, and the singing of the congregation is echoing from the church close by, and the woman is following the text in her prayer-book.'

He went on speaking in this vein; everyone listened intently, for much of what he said rang true. His face had become red from speaking; one minute smiling, the next grave, he shook his blond curls. He had forgotten himself completely.

After the meal, Kaufmann took him aside. He had received letters from Lenz's father, saying that his son should come home to help him. Kaufmann told Lenz that he was wasting his life here, spending his time uselessly; he ought to set himself a target—and suchlike. 'Go away from here, away?' cried Lenz; 'Home? and go mad there? You know I can't bear it anywhere except here in this region. If I could not climb a mountain once in a while, then come down to the house again, walk through the garden and look in through the window—I should go mad! mad!

Leave me alone, can't you! Let me have a little peace and quiet, now that I am feeling somewhat better! Away? Away? That I don't understand; those two words can ruin the entire world. Every one of us needs something; if he can rest, what more does he need! Always to be striving upwards, struggling, to be eternally throwing away everything that the moment offers us, always going hungry for the sake of eventual satisfaction! To be thirsty when clear streams are flowing across the path ahead! Life is bearable for me now and I want to remain here. Why, why? Simply because I feel well here. What does my father want of me? Can he give me more? Impossible! Leave me alone!' He became vehement; Kaufmann went off leaving Lenz in an ill humour.

The following day Kaufmann decided to leave. He urged Oberlin to accompany him to Switzerland and, prompted by a desire to make the acquaintance of Lavater* in person, whom he had already known for a long time through their correspondence, Oberlin agreed. Because of the necessary preparations, they were obliged to wait a day longer. Lenz was greatly disturbed; in his attempt to free himself from his endless torment, he clutched fearfully at every straw; in isolated moments he felt strongly that he was simply deluding himself; he treated himself like a sick child. There were many thoughts, overwhelming feelings from which he could only free himself with the greatest anxiety; then a boundless force would drive him back to them; he would tremble, his hair all but standing on end, until with the most terrible effort he saw his way through. He sought refuge in a figure which hovered constantly before his eyes, and he sought refuge in Oberlin, whose words and face were infinitely beneficial to him. Whenever he thought of his forthcoming departure he was afraid.

Lenz found the thought of remaining alone in the house uncanny. The weather had turned mild, and he decided to accompany Oberlin into the mountains. On the far side, where the valleys ran into the plain, they parted, and he returned alone. He wandered back and forth through the mountains. Wide expanses stretched down into the valleys; there was little forest, nothing but powerfully defined lines and, beyond, the wide, misty plain; a mighty wind in the air, not a sign of human beings anywhere, save here and there a lonely hut, perched on a slope, where the shepherds lived in summer. He became silent, perhaps almost dreaming; everything seemed to melt into a single line, like a wave rising and falling, between earth and the heavens; it was as if he were lying by an endless ocean which gently rose and fell. Sometimes he sat down; then he walked on again, but slowly, dreamily. He was not seeking a way to go.

It was evening, already dark, when he came to an inhabited hut on the hillside beyond the Steintal valley. The door was closed; he went to the window, through which a shimmer of light could be seen. A lamp illuminated only a single point: the light fell on the pale face of a girl who was lying, her eyes half-open and her lips moving slightly, at the far end of the room. Farther away in the darkness sat an old woman, singing in a grating voice from a hymn-book. After Lenz had been knocking for some time, she opened the door: she was half deaf. She brought him some food and showed him a place to sleep, continuing her singing all the while. The girl had not stirred. Some time later a man entered the cabin: tall and lean, with traces of grey in his hair and wearing a troubled, confused expression. The man approached the girl; she gave a start and became restless. Taking down a bundle of dried herbs from the wall he laid the leaves upon her hand, whereupon she grew calmer and began to sing understandable words in piercing, long drawn-out tones. The man told how he had heard a voice in the mountains which was followed by lightning flashing over the valleys; then the spirit had seized hold of him and he had wrestled with it, as Jacob had done. He fell down on his knees and began to pray fervently in a low voice, whilst the sick girl sang in a slow tone which gently died away. Then he lay down to rest.

Lenz fell asleep, dreaming; then, in his sleep, he heard the ticking of the clock. Through the sounds of the girl's gentle singing and the old woman's voice, the howling of the wind could be heard, now far off, now close by; and the moon, now bright, now clouded over, cast its dream-like, ever-changing light into the room. Once the sounds became louder, the girl was speaking clearly and firmly: she said that there was a church upon the cliffs opposite. Lenz looked up; she was sitting erect at the table, her eyes opened wide, and the moon cast its quiet light upon her features, which seemed to radiate an uncanny brilliance; meanwhile the old woman was singing in her grating voice and, in the midst of this changing and dying light, this talking and singing, Lenz fell at last into a deep sleep.

He awoke early next morning. In the room, lit by the grey dawn, all were asleep; the girl, too, had become calmer. She was lying outstretched, her hands beneath her left cheek; the eerie look had vanished from her features, and she now wore an expression of indescribable suffering. Lenz went to the window and opened it, and the cold morning air struck his face. The hut lay at the end of a deep, narrow valley, which faced east; red rays of light thrust through the grey morning sky into the gloomy valley which lay clad in white mist, and flashed upon the grey rocks, entering the windows of the hut. The man awoke. His eyes turned to a picture on the wall, illuminated by the morning sun, and fixed themselves rigidly upon it; then his lips moved and he began to pray, quietly at first, then more and more loudly. Meanwhile people came into the hut, falling down upon their knees without a word. The girl lay there twitching, the old woman continued her croaking song, talking from time to time with her neighbours.

The people told Lenz that the man had come into the region a long time ago, no one knew from where; he was reputed to be a holy man, they said; was able to see water beneath the earth and summon up spirits, and people made pilgrimages to him. Lenz also learned that he had strayed away from the Steintal valley, and so he set off together with some woodcutters who were heading in that direction. It did him good to have company; for he had an uncanny feeling in the presence of that mighty man, who, Lenz thought, sometimes spoke in frightening tones. He was, moreover, fearful of his own company when alone.

He arrived home again. But the past night had made a tremendous impression on him. The world had revealed itself clearly to him, and he felt within him a moving and pulling towards an abyss into which he was being drawn by an inexorable power. Now he brooded within himself. He ate but little; half the nights were passed in prayer and feverish dreams. He would feel a tremendous force pushing him, then he would be thrown back exhausted; his face was bathed in hot tears. Suddenly he felt strength flowing into him, and he rose from his bed, cold and indifferent; his tears now felt like ice, so that he was obliged to laugh. The higher he forced himself, the deeper down he fell. It all flowed back together. He was shaken by vague memories of his former condition, memories which cast light into the wild chaos of his mind.

During the day he usually remained sitting downstairs in the living-room. Madame Oberlin would walk up and down; he passed his time drawing, painting, reading; seizing every opportunity of distraction, hastening from one to another. In particular he sought the company of Madame Oberlin whenever she was sitting there beside a potted plant growing in the room, her black hymnal in front of her, her youngest child in her lap; he also devoted much of his time to the child. Once, as he was sitting there, he suddenly felt afraid; he sprang to his feet and began walking back and forth. The door half-open—he could hear the maid singing; the words incomprehensible at first, then they came clearly:

> Here in this world I have no joy,
> Only my love—but he's far away.

The song affected him deeply; he almost melted away at the sounds. Madame Oberlin was looking at him. He plucked up his courage—he could not remain silent any longer, he had to speak of it: 'Dear Madame Oberlin, can you tell me: how is the woman whose fate lies so heavily upon my heart?'—'Why, Herr Lenz, I don't know at all.'

He fell silent once more and walked hurriedly back and forth in the room; then he spoke again: 'I want to leave, you see. God knows, you are the only persons among whom I can bear it all, and yet—yet, I must go, to *her*—but I can't, I must not.' Deeply affected, he went out.

Around evening Lenz returned. It was growing dark in the room; he sat down beside Madame Oberlin. 'You see,' he began, 'whenever she walked through the room and sang, as if to herself, and each step was like music—there was such an air of happiness about her and it flowed across into me; I always felt calm whenever I looked at her or whenever she leaned her head against me [. . .] An absolute child; it was as if the world were too wide for her; she would withdraw into herself completely, she would seek the smallest place in the whole house, and there she would sit as if all her happiness were contained in one small point, and then I myself would feel the same: I could have played like a child. Now everything feels so confined, so confined! You know, sometimes I feel as if I were pushing against the sky with my hands; oh, I can't breathe! Often, it's as if I could feel physical pain; here on my left side, in my arm, with which I used to hold her. But I can't visualize her any more; her image always flees away from me and that torments me; only sometimes, when my mind becomes perfectly clear, do I feel well again.'—Later he often spoke to Madame Oberlin on this subject, but mostly in clipped phrases; she was unable to say much in reply, yet it did him good.

Meanwhile his religious torments continued. The colder, the emptier, the more numb he felt inside, the more did he feel an urge to stir up a fire within himself; memories rose up in him, memories of the times when all seethed within him and he lay gasping in the intensity of his emotions. And now everything in him was dead. He despaired of himself; he fell down on his knees, wrang his hands, he stirred up everything within him— but everything was dead, dead! Then he begged God to send him a sign; then he dug deep within himself, fasted, and lay in a trance upon the floor.

On the 3rd of February he heard that a child had died in Fouday; her name was Friederike; the news gripped him like an obsession. Withdrawing to his room, he fasted for a whole day. On the following day he suddenly appeared to Madame Oberlin in the living-room; he had smeared his face with ashes; he asked her to give him an old sack. She was startled; he was given what he asked for. He wrapped the sack around him like someone doing penance and set off for Fouday. The people in the valley were used to him; they told all sorts of strange stories about him. He came to the house where the dead child lay. The people in the house were going about their business, indifferent; they showed him to a room: the child lay, clad in her petticoat, bedded in straw upon a wooden table.

Lenz shuddered as he touched the cold limbs and saw the

glassy, half-open eyes. The child seemed so forsaken, and he felt so alone and lonely. He threw himself over the body. The sight of death filled him with dread, a fierce pain ran through him: these features, this gentle face must fall into decay—he threw himself upon his knees and with all the misery of despair he prayed that God might send him, weak and unhappy as he was, a sign and restore the child to life; then he withdrew completely into himself and concentrated his entire will upon a single point. He sat like this for a long time, absolutely still. Then he rose, took hold of the child's hands and said in a loud, firm voice: 'Arise and walk!'* But the sound echoed unfeelingly from the walls, as if mocking him, and the child's body remained cold. Half-crazed, he flung himself to the floor; then he rushed out and up into the mountains.

Clouds were scudding across the moon; one moment everything lay in darkness, then the clouds would clear to reveal the misty, half-seen landscape in the moonlight. He ran back and forth; a triumphal hymn of hell sounded in his breast. The wind roared like a titan's song. He felt that he could clench a mighty fist towards heaven and pull out God Himself and drag Him through the clouds; he felt he could grind the world between his teeth and spit it into the Creator's face; he cursed and blasphemed. And so he came to the highest point of the mountains, and the vague light spread down to where the white masses of snow lay and the sky was a foolish eye of blue and the moon was sailing dull and stupid in the sky. He could not help laughing aloud, and with the laughter came the atheism which seized him and held him surely and calmly and firmly. He no longer knew what had affected him so intensely shortly before, he was freezing; he thought he would now go to bed, and he walked cold and imperturbable through the uncanny darkness—he felt quite hollow and empty; he had to run and he went to bed.

Next day he was absolutely horrified when he thought of his condition the previous day. He was on the brink of an abyss into which a mad impulse compelled him to look down again and again and to repeat this torment. Then his fear increased and the sin which he had committed against the Holy Spirit revealed itself before him.

A few days later Oberlin returned from Switzerland much

earlier than expected. His arrival filled Lenz with consternation; but he cheered up when Oberlin told him about his friends in Alsace. Oberlin walked back and forth in the room as he spoke, unpacking and setting down various items of luggage. He spoke about Pfeffel,* full of praise for the life of a country pastor. Then he admonished Lenz to follow his father's wishes, to live according to his vocation and to return home. 'Honour thy father and thy mother!' he said, and more in the same vein. At this Lenz became greatly agitated; he sighed deeply, tears streamed from his eyes and he spoke in clipped phrases. 'Yes, but I can't bear it; do you mean to drive me away? Only in you can I find the way to God. But there's no hope for me! I've fallen away, damned for all eternity; I am the Wandering Jew.'* Oberlin told him that this was what Jesus had died for; he should turn to Him fervently and he would partake of His mercy.

Lenz raised his head, wrang his hands, and said: 'Oh! oh! divine consolation—' Suddenly he asked in a friendly manner: 'How is the woman?' Oberlin replied that he did not know at all, but that he was willing to help him and advise him in everything; but Lenz would have to give him details of place, person, and circumstances. Lenz replied in brief, laconic sentences: 'Oh! is she dead? Is she living still? The angel! She loved me—I loved her, she was worthy of my love—Oh! the angel! Damned jealousy, I sacrificed her—she loved another, too—I loved her, she was worthy of my love—oh! dear mother, she loved me too! I am the murderer of you both!' Oberlin replied: perhaps all these persons were still living, perhaps they were happy; whatever the case, if Lenz would turn to God again, God could and would show such love to these persons in answer to Lenz's prayers and tears that the benefit they would receive from him would far outweigh the harm he had caused them. Thereupon Lenz gradually became calmer and at last went back to his painting.

In the afternoon he returned. On his left shoulder he had a piece of fur and in his hand a bundle of willow wands which had been given to Oberlin together with a letter for Lenz. He handed the wands to Oberlin and begged him to whip him. Oberlin took the wands from his hand, kissed him upon the lips several times, and said that these were the only strokes which he had to give him; that he should remain calm and come to terms with God alone; not all the whiplashes in the world would atone for a single one of his sins; Jesus had provided for this and Lenz should turn to Him for help. Lenz went away.

At supper he was, as usual, somewhat steeped in thought. He spoke of many things, but hastily, betraying his fear. Around midnight Oberlin was awakened by a noise. Lenz was running through the yard, shouting 'Friederike!'* in a hard, hollow voice, pronouncing the name quickly, in a confused, despairing tone; then he leapt into the water-trough, plunged around in it, then jumped out and ran up to his room, then down again into the trough—this was repeated several times—at last he became calm. The maids, who slept in the nursery below his room, said that they had often heard, and particularly that night, a droning sound which they could not compare with anything but the sound of pipes. Perhaps it was Lenz, whimpering in an awful, hollow, despairing voice.

Lenz did not appear next morning. At last Oberlin went up to his room and found him lying in bed, calm and still. Oberlin had to question him for a long time before he received an answer; at last Lenz spoke: 'Why, Pastor, the tedium, you understand! the tedium! oh, how tedious! I simply don't know what to say; I've already drawn all sorts of figures on the wall.' Oberlin told him he should turn to God, at which he laughed and said: 'Yes, if I were as fortunate as you, to find such a pleasant pastime, yes, I could occupy my time in that way. Idleness is the cause of everything. For most people pray out of tedium, others fall in love out of tedium, others again are virtuous, still others full of vice, and I am nothing, nothing at all; I haven't even the desire to kill myself: it's simply too tedious!

> O Lord! in the wave of your light,
> In your noontide glowing bright,
> My wakeful eyes have grown so sore.
> Will it never be night once more?'

Oberlin looked at him reluctantly and made to leave. Lenz darted after him and said, with an eerie expression in his eyes: 'You know, something has just occurred to me: if only I could tell whether I am awake or whether I am dreaming; that's very important, you know; we ought to investigate it.'—Then he darted back into bed.

That afternoon Oberlin wished to pay a visit to someone in the vicinity; his wife had already left. Just as he was about to go, there was a knock at the door and Lenz entered the room; his body was bent forward, his head hung down, his face was smeared completely, his coat here and there, with ashes, and he was holding his left arm with his right hand. He asked Oberlin to pull it back into place: he had put it out of joint after throwing himself out of the window; but as no one had seen it happen, he did not intend to tell anyone. Oberlin was shocked but did not say anything; he did as Lenz requested. Then he wrote a letter to Sebastian Scheidecker, the school-master in Bellefosse, asking him to come over and giving him instructions, whereupon he rode away.

The schoolmaster arrived. Lenz had often seen him and had become attached to him. He pretended that he had wished to speak to Oberlin and made as if to leave again. Lenz asked him to stay and they remained together. Lenz proposed that they should take a walk to Fouday. There he visited the grave of the child whom he had tried to recall to life; he kneeled down several times and kissed the earth on the grave; he seemed to be praying, but with an appearance of being entirely confused. Then he plucked a piece from the wreath on the grave as a memento, returned to Waldbach, then went back once more, and Sebastian went with him. Sometimes he walked slowly, complaining of a feeling of great weakness in his limbs, sometimes he walked with a speed that spoke of despair; the landscape frightened him, it was so confined that he was afraid he would run up against its bounds. An indescribable feeling of uneasiness crept over him; at last he began to find his companion a nuisance; he had guessed the man's intentions and was now looking for a means of getting rid of him. Sebastian seemed to give in, though he secretly found a way to inform his brother, so that Lenz now had two guardians instead of one. Resolutely he took them in tow; at last he walked back to Waldbach and, when they arrived near the village, he turned about quick as lightning and ran back towards Fouday swift as a deer with the two men in pursuit of him. While they were searching for him in Fouday, two pedlars came to tell them that a stranger was being held captive in a house—he claimed to be a murderer though he certainly was not. They ran into the house and found this to be true: a young man, frightened by Lenz's violent insistence, had tied him up. They unbound him and brought him safely back to Waldbach, to where Oberlin and his wife had meanwhile returned. Lenz appeared bewildered but, being given an affectionate and friendly reception, regained his spirits; his expression relaxed, he thanked his two companions kindly and gently, and the evening passed without incident. Oberlin requested him urgently not to bathe any more but to remain quietly in bed all night; if he could not sleep, then he should converse with God. Lenz promised to do so and that night kept his promise; the maids heard him praying all night long.

Next morning he appeared at Oberlin's room wearing a cheery expression. After they had spoken of various matters, he said in an exceptionally friendly voice: 'My dear Pastor, the woman I told you about has died, yes, died—the angel!'—'How do you know?'—'Hieroglyphics, hieroglyphics!' whereupon he looked up at the sky and repeated: 'Yes, died—hieroglyphics!' Nothing further was to be got out of him. He sat down and wrote a number of letters, which he then handed to Oberlin, requesting him to add a few lines.

Meanwhile his condition had become worse and worse. All the peace of mind which he had gained from his contact with Oberlin and from the quietness of the valley had disappeared; the world, which he had hoped to put to his own advantage, had a tremendous rift; he felt no hatred, no love, no hope—only a dreadful emptiness and a tormenting anxiety to fill it. He was devoid of emotion. Whatever he did, he did not do consciously, he was compelled by an inner instinct. Whenever he was by himself he felt such awful loneliness that he would talk to himself aloud and shout, then he would stand aghast, and it seemed to him as if an unknown voice had spoken to him. When speaking he would often break off in mid-word, overcome by a nameless fear, having forgotten the end of the sentence; then he thought he must retain the last word he had spoken and repeat it continually, and it was only with a great effort that he managed to overcome this urge. His hosts were deeply shocked when on occasion, sitting with them in a quiet moment talking freely, he would break off abruptly; an inexplicable fear would reveal itself in his features, he would seize the persons next to him desperately by the arm and only gradually recover. If he was alone or reading, it was even worse; his entire train of thought would sometimes remain caught up by a single idea. Whenever he thought of someone unknown to him or imagined him vividly, he felt that he himself was that person; he became totally confused and had a constant compulsion to treat—in his mind—everything around him just as he pleased. It amused him to stand the houses on their heads, to dress and undress the people, and to think up the maddest escapades. Sometimes he felt an irresistible urge to put into action whatever he happened to be thinking of, making dreadful grimaces all the while. On one occasion he was sitting beside Oberlin, and the cat was lying upon the chair opposite. Suddenly his eyes took on a glassy look and he stared at the cat fixedly; then he slid down slowly in his chair and the cat likewise; she seemed hypnotised by his gaze, a dreadful fear seized her and her hackles rose with fright; Lenz, his face hideously distorted, returned her sounds; as if in desperation, the two leapt at each other—then, at last, Madame Oberlin rose in order to separate them. Then he felt deeply ashamed. At night the attacks became more and more terrible; it was only with the greatest effort that he was able to sleep, after having tried to overcome the awful emptiness; then he found himself in a terrifying state between sleeping and waking, he struck against something horrible, ghastly, and madness seized him; he started up, bathed in sweat, shrieking terribly, and only gradually came to his senses again. He was compelled to begin with the simplest things in order to collect himself once more. It was not he himself but a powerful urge of self-preservation that did so; it was as if he were two distinct persons, one of whom was trying to save the other and calling to him; in his worst moods of fear he would tell stories and recite poetry until he recovered.

These attacks also occurred by day and were then even more frightening, for until now the light had kept them away from him. On such occasions he had a feeling of being the only creature in existence, that the world existed only in his imagination, that there was nothing but him; he believed himself eternally damned, believed himself to be Satan, alone with his tormenting fantasies. He would review his life with lightning speed, then he would say: 'Consistent, consistent;' if someone made a remark, however, he would say: 'Inconsistent, inconsistent'—it was the rift caused by hopeless madness, madness in eternity.

The urge to preserve his sanity drove him on; he threw himself into Oberlin's arms and clung to him as if trying to become one with him; Oberlin was the only being who lived for him and through whom life again took on meaning. Oberlin's words gradually brought him to his senses once more; he knelt in front of him, his hands in Oberlin's hands, his face, bathed in cold sweat, pressed against Oberlin's knees, shaking and trembling all over. Oberlin felt an enormous pity for him, and the whole family knelt down and prayed for the poor wretch, whilst the maidservants fled, convinced that he was possessed. When, after a while, he became calmer, his mood resembled the distress of a child: he sobbed and was afflicted by a deep self-pity; yet these were also his happiest moments. Oberlin spoke to him of God. Lenz freed himself gently and looked at him with an expression of unspeakable suffering, and said at last: 'If I were omnipotent, you know, if I were omnipotent, I could not bear to see suffering; I would save people, save them; all I want is rest, rest, just a little rest in order to sleep.' Oberlin said that this was blasphemy. Lenz merely shook his head sadly.

His half-hearted attempts to take his own life, which he undertook constantly, were not really serious. It was less the wish to die—for he saw no peace or hope in death—than an attempt, in moments of the most terrible fear or the dull calm that borders on non-existence, to bring himself to his senses by means of physical pain. The moments in which his mind seemed to concentrate on some mad idea or other were the happiest for him. These did at least provide him with a little rest, and his crazed expression was not as terrible as his fear, thirsting for salvation, the eternal torment of restlessness! Often he would bang his head against the wall or cause himself keen physical pain in some other way.

On the morning of the 8th he remained in bed. Oberlin went upstairs; Lenz lay almost naked upon the bed, in a fit of intense anxiety. Oberlin tried to cover him, but he complained bitterly how heavy everything was, so heavy! he did not believe he could walk, he said; now at last he felt how dreadfully heavy the air was. Oberlin spoke words of encouragement to him. But he remained lying in the same position and remained so for most of the day; nor did he take any food or drink.

Towards evening, Oberlin was called out to a sick person in Bellefosse. The weather was mild and the moon was shining. On his way home he was met by Lenz, who appeared quite reasonable and spoke to Oberlin in a calm, friendly manner. Oberlin requested him not to go too far away and Lenz gave him his word. As he was about to continue on his way he suddenly turned and, walking straight up to Oberlin, said: 'You know, Pastor, if only I didn't have to hear *that* any more, it would help me a great deal.' 'Hear what, my dear fellow?' 'Can't you hear anything? Can't you hear the awful voice that is crying round the whole horizon and is known as "silence"? I hear it all the time, ever since I have been in this silent valley; I can't sleep because of it; yes, Pastor, if only I could sleep again.' And he went on his way, shaking his head.

Oberlin returned to Waldbach and was about to send someone after him when he heard him going upstairs to his room. A moment later, something dropped into the courtyard with such a loud noise that Oberlin thought it impossible it could be the sound of a human being falling. Then the children's maid came, pale as death and trembling like a leaf [. . .]

He sat in the carriage in a mood of cold resignation as they drove west out of the valley. He did not care in the least where they were bringing him. Several times, when the carriage was in danger because of the very bad state of the road, he remained in his seat, perfectly calm. He made the entire journey through the mountains in this condition. Towards evening they reached the Rhine valley, gradually leaving the mountains behind them, which rose like a wave of deep-blue crystal against the red sky; the crimson rays of the evening sun played upon this warm flood, and a shimmering bluish haze lay across the plain at the foot of the mountains. The nearer they came to Strasburg the darker it became; a full moon high in the sky, everything in the distance was dark and only the mountain close by formed a sharp line;

the earth was like a golden goblet with the gold rays of the moon foaming over its rim. Lenz stared quietly out of the window; he felt no foreboding, no urge to do anything; but a dull fear began to grow within him, as their surroundings vanished in the darkness. They had to spend the night at an inn. There again he made several attempts to take his life, but he was watched too carefully for these to succeed.

Next morning—the weather was dull and rainy—they arrived in Strasburg. He appeared perfectly reasonable and spoke to the people. He behaved exactly like the others but there was a dreadful emptiness inside him; he felt no fear and no desire, his existence was a necessary burden to him.—

And so his life went on . . .

ANNETTE VON DROSTE-HÜLSHOFF

The Jew's Beech

A Moral Portrait from the Hills of Westphalia

Where is the hand so gentle, that it might unwind
In truth the threads of the tangled mind,
So sure that it might cast with steady aim
A stone on some poor wretched frame?
Who dares to gauge the pulse of blood so vain,
To weigh each word which still remembered plain,
Once drove tough roots into a youthful breast,
That secret thief of souls who never stops to test?
You happy one, born safe and wrapped in swaddling bands,
Within a well-lit room held firm by pious hands,
The scales not yours to use set down instead,
Let lie the stone—lest it strike the thrower's head!

(Trans. Andrew J. Webber)

Friedrich Mergel, born in the year 1738, was the only son of a
minor smallholder in the village of B. which, tumbledown and
smoky though it may be, captivates the eye of every traveller
with the highly picturesque beauty of its situation in the green
wooded gorge of an important and historically notable range of
hills. The little province in which the village lies was at that time
one of those secluded corners devoid of trade or industry, without military roads, where a strange face still caused a stir and a
journey of thirty miles made even a member of the better class
a Ulysses of his district—in short, a spot such as was frequently
found in Germany, with all the failings and virtues, all the
originality and backwardness which flourish only under such
conditions. Under the influence of extremely simple and often
inadequate laws, the inhabitants' understanding of right and
wrong had to some degree become confused, or rather, in addition to the legal concept of right, a second form of right had
evolved, a right based on public opinion, a right of custom, and

a right of limitations resulting from neglect. The landowners, who held the privilege of minor jurisdiction, punished and rewarded according to their lights, which in most cases were honest; their subjects did what seemed to them to be feasible and compatible with a somewhat flexible conscience; and only to the losers did it sometimes occur to search in dusty old records.

It is difficult to consider that period in an unprejudiced manner —a period which, since its passing, has been either arrogantly criticized or foolishly praised, for anyone who has lived through it is blinded by too many loving memories, and anyone born later is unable to understand it. This much may be said with certainty, however: the outward form was weaker but the core was stronger; offences more frequent, but lack of conscience more uncommon. For a man who acts according to his convictions, however inadequate these may be, can never go completely to the bad, whereas nothing is more deadly to a man's soul than to make demands upon the outer form of justice contrary to his inner feeling for it.

In the little region with which we are concerned here, one particular kind of people, more restless and enterprising than all their neighbours, displayed a far wilder temperament than people elsewhere in similar circumstances. Stealing timber and poaching were events of daily occurrence, and in the frequent brawls every man had to tend his own cracked head. The main wealth of the region consisted of large, prolific woodlands, so that a strict watch was kept over the forests, though less by legal means than by constant new attempts to outdo violence and cunning with the same weapons.

The village of B. had the reputation of being the wiliest, boldest, and most arrogant community in the whole princedom. It is likely that its situation in the midst of proud forests, deep and lonely, had long nourished the innate stubborness of its inhabitants' character; the proximity of a river, which flowed down to the sea bearing covered boats—large enough to transport shipbuilding timber smoothly and safely out of the country—did much to increase the natural boldness of the timber thieves; and the fact that the whole district was crawling with foresters could have only an exhilarating effect in this case, since in the frequent skirmishes the peasants generally had the advantage. On clear moonlit nights, thirty or forty wagons would set out at once accompanied by roughly twice as many men of all ages, from halfgrown lads to the seventy-year old village headman who, like a wise old bellwether, led the wagon train with as much proud assurance as when he took his seat in the courtroom. Those who had remained at home would listen unconcernedly as the creaking and rumbling of the wagon-wheels gradually died away along the forest tracks, and gently drop off to sleep again. Sometimes a young wife or maiden would start up in her sleep, roused by the sound of a gunshot or a faint cry, but no one else paid any heed. Then, at the break of day, the wagon train would return as silently as it had gone, the men's faces glowing like ore in a furnace. Here and there a bandaged head could be seen, though this was of no great consequence; and, a few hours later the district would be buzzing with talk of one or more unlucky foresters who had been carried out of the wood, soundly beaten, blinded with snuff, and incapable of going about their duty for some time.

Such were the surroundings into which Friedrich Mergel was born, in a house with the proud addition of a chimney and mean little glass panes to testify to the aspirations of its erstwhile builder, whilst its dilapidated state revealed the impoverished circumstances of its present owner. The railings which had previously surrounded the yard and garden had been replaced by a neglected fence; the roof leaked, the neighbour's cattle grazed in the pastures; the neighbour's corn grew in the field beside the yard and the garden contained—apart from a few woody rose-bushes, a relic of better days—more weeds than pot-herbs. Much of this decay, admittedly, was due to misfortune, but slovenliness and mismanagement had also played a considerable part. In his bachelor days Friedrich's father, old Hermann Mergel, had been a so-called moderate drinker; that is to say, one who lay in the gutter only on Sundays and feast-days but was as well behaved as any during the rest of the week. Thus, his courtship of a very pretty and well-to-do girl did not meet with any difficulties. The wedding feast was a merry one. Mergel was not very drunk at all, and the bride's parents went home in a cheerful mood that evening; but on the following Sunday the young bride was seen running through the village to her parents' home, screaming and bleeding, and leaving behind all her good clothes and new household effects. This caused a dreadful scandal and greatly angered Mergel, who naturally sought consolation: that afternoon, not a pane of glass in the house was intact, and people saw him lying in front of the door until late at night, now and then lifting a broken-necked bottle to his mouth and cutting his face and hands badly. His young wife remained at her parents' home and, within a short time, pined away and died. Whether Mergel was tormented by remorse or shame—no matter; he seemed more and more in need of his comforter, and it was not long before he, too, could be reckoned among the most degenerate.

The farm went downhill; hired maids ensured that everything went to rack and ruin; and so the years went by. Mergel was and remained a helpless and, in the end, pitiful widower until, suddenly, he once again appeared as a bridegroom. Though this in itself was an unexpected event, the bride's identity did much to increase the general astonishment. Margreth Semmler was a decent, honest woman in her forties; in her youth she had been a village beauty and was now still respected as a very clever, hardworking person; moreover, she was not without money, so that no one was able to understand what had driven her to such a step. We believe the reason lay precisely in her own perfect self-assurance. On the eve of her wedding, she is said to have declared: 'A woman who is ill-treated by her husband is either stupid or incapable; if things should go badly with me, you may all say it is my own fault.' Events proved, unfortunately, that she had overrated her powers. At first, she commanded her husband's respect; whenever he had drunk too much, he would either not come home at all or else creep into the barn; but the burden was too great for him to bear long, and soon he could often be seen staggering across the street into the house; his foul-mouthed shouting would be heard inside and Margreth would hastily close the door and windows. On one such day— and these were no longer confined to Sundays—she was seen running from the house one evening, without bonnet or neckerchief, her hair streaming wildly about her head; she threw herself to the ground by a bed of herbs in the garden and began to grub up the earth with her hands; then she gazed about her in terror, hurriedly plucked a bunch of herbs, and slowly walked towards the house; she did not enter it, however, but went into the barn. People said that this was the first time that Mergel had laid hands upon her, although she never admitted it.

The second year of this unfortunate marriage was—one can hardly say blessed—with a son; Margreth is said to have wept bitterly when they placed the child in her arms. Yet, though the heart under which his mother had borne him had been filled with pain, Friedrich was a healthy, handsome child who grew up tall and strong in the fresh air. His father was very fond of the boy and never came home without bringing him a crust of bread or the like; some even thought that he had become more orderly since the birth of his son; at any rate, the disturbances in the house became less frequent.

Friedrich was now in his ninth year. It was around the Feast of the Three Kings—a bitter, stormy night in winter. Hermann had gone to a wedding and had set out in good time, for the bride's home was three-quarters of a mile away. Although he had promised to be home again that evening, Frau Mergel hardly reckoned on his return, for a heavy snowstorm had arisen after sunset. At about ten o'clock she scraped together the ashes in the hearth and prepared to go to bed. Friedrich was standing beside her, already half-undressed, listening to the howling of the wind and the rattling of the attic windows.

'Mother, isn't father coming tonight?' he asked.—'No, child, tomorrow.' 'But, why not, mother? He promised he would.' 'Heavens, if he were to do everything he promised to do! Come, hurry up and get ready for bed!'

Hardly had they gone to bed when a gale arose, so fierce it seemed it would blow the house away. The bedstead shook, and in the chimney there was a rattling like a hobgoblin.—'Mother, there's a knocking outside!'—'Be quiet, Fritz; it's only the loose board at the gable end, shaken by the wind.'—'No, mother—at the door!'—'The door won't close, the latch is broken. Heavens, go to sleep, now! Don't spoil the little bit of night's rest that I have.'—'But what if father does come?'—His mother turned over abruptly.—'The devil's holding him tight enough!'—'Where is the devil, mother?'—'Just wait, you little nuisance! He's standing at the door, and he'll come and take you away if you're not quiet!'

Friedrich fell silent; he lay listening for a while and then fell asleep. He awoke some hours later. The wind had turned and was now hissing like a serpent through the gap in the window frame by his ear. His shoulder was stiff; he crept deep down under the bedclothes and lay perfectly still, so frightened was he. After a while, he noticed that his mother was awake too. He could hear her weeping and, now and then, she would say: 'Hail Mary!' and 'Pray for us, poor sinners!' The beads of her rosary slipped past his face. Involuntarily he gave a sigh.—'Friedrich, are you awake?'—'Yes, mother.'—'Then say a little prayer, child—you already know half the Lord's Prayer—pray that God may protect us from fire and flood!'

Friedrich began to think about the devil, wondering what he looked like. All this noise and uproar in the house seemed strange to him, and he thought there must be some living creatures both inside and outside the house.—'Mother, listen. I'm sure there are people knocking!'—'Why, no, child; there's not an old board in the whole house that doesn't rattle.'—'Listen! Can't you hear? Someone's calling! Do listen!'

His mother sat upright in the bed; the howling of the storm died down for an instant. The sound of someone knocking at the shutters and the voices of several persons could be plainly heard. 'Margreth! Frau Margreth, hey there, open up!'—Margreth uttered a loud cry: 'They're bringing the swine back again!'

She threw the rosary with a clatter on to the wooden chair and snatched up her clothes. Then she ran to the hearth and, a moment later, Friedrich heard her walking with resolute steps across the threshing floor. Margreth did not come back again; but a great deal of murmuring and unknown voices could be heard in the kitchen. Twice, a stranger came into the room and seemed to be anxiously searching for something. Suddenly a lamp was brought in; two men entered, leading his mother. She was white as a sheet and her eyes were closed. Friedrich thought that she was dead; he set up a dreadful howling, at which some-one boxed his ears, which calmed him down; and now, from the conversation of those present, he began to understand that his father had been found by Uncle Franz Semmler and Hülsmeyer dead in the forest and was now lying in the kitchen.

As soon as Margreth had recovered, her first thought was to

get the strangers out of the house. Her brother remained, however, and Friedrich—who had been ordered to stay in bed under
pain of severe punishment—could hear, all night long, the fire
crackling in the kitchen and a sound as of sweeping and things
being pushed back and forth. They spoke but little and quietly;
yet now and then, the sound of sighing reached Friedrich's ears,
a sound which, young though he was, made his blood run cold.
Once, he clearly heard his uncle say: 'Don't take it to heart,
Margreth; we shall each of us have three masses said for him,
and at Easter, we shall make a pilgrimage to Our Lady of Werl.'

When, two days later, the body was taken away, Margreth sat
by the hearth, hiding her face in her apron. After a few moments, when all was still, she murmured to herself: 'Ten years,
ten crosses. But we bore them together—and now I'm alone!'
Then, in a louder voice: 'Fritz, come here!' Shyly, Friedrich
approached; his mother looked uncanny with her black ribbons
and her distraught features. 'Fritz,' she said, 'are you going to be
a good boy and a joy to me?—Or will you be a wicked boy and
tell lies, or drink and steal?'—'Mother, Hülsmeyer steals!'—
'Hülsmeyer! God forbid! Shall I give you a thrashing? Who has
been telling you such wicked things?'—'He gave Aaron a beating the other day and took six coppers from him.'—'If he took
money from Aaron, then the cursèd Jew must have cheated him
of the money in the first place. He is a respectable, orderly man,
and the Jews are all rogues.'—'But, mother, Brandis also says
that Hülsmeyer steals wood and poaches deer.'—'But, child,
Brandis is a forester!'—'Do the foresters tell lies, mother?'

Margreth was silent for a while, then she said: 'Listen to me,
Fritz. God in Heaven makes the trees grow freely, and the deer
cross from one squire's land to another—they can't belong to
anyone. But that's something you don't understand yet. Now go
to the shed and fetch me some kindling.'

Friedrich had seen his father lying upon the straw—people
said he had looked blue in the face and frightful. But the boy
never spoke of it, and he seemed to dislike thinking of it. His
entire memory of his father had left him with a feeling of tenderness mingled with horror—for nothing is more binding than the
love and care of a being who seems hardened against everything
else; and this feeling grew stronger as the years went by, fostered

by a sense that he was often slighted by others. Throughout his childhood, it hurt him deeply whenever anyone spoke of his dead father in a less than complimentary manner—a sorrow which the neighbours' kindness could not spare him. In those regions, it is common to say of one who has died a violent death that he cannot rest in his grave. Old Mergel had now become 'the ghost of Brede Wood'; once, in the form of a will-o'-the-wisp, he had almost led a drunken man into a water-hole; and when the young cowherds huddled by their fires at night, and the owls were shrieking in the depths of the wood, they would sometimes hear him, quite clearly, shouting in a staccato tone: 'Hear, oh hear, Lizzie dear!'; and one unfranchised woodcutter, who had fallen asleep under the spreading oak tree and been caught by nightfall, had awoken to see his swollen blue face peering through the branches. Friedrich had to listen to many such tales about his father from other boys; then he would weep and hit out on all sides; once he even made to stab someone with his little knife, in return for which he received a cruel beating. Since that time he would drive his mother's cows, all alone, to the far end of the valley, where he was often seen lying in the grass in the same position for hours on end, pulling thyme out of the ground.

Friedrich was twelve years old when his mother was visited by her younger brother, who lived in Brede and had not crossed his sister's doorstep since the day of her foolish marriage. Simon Semmler was a small, thin, restless man with fish eyes bulging from his head and, indeed, a face like a pike's—an uncanny individual, in whose nature deep reticence frequently alternated with equally feigned candour, who would have liked to be considered clever but, instead, had the reputation of being an unpleasant, quarrelsome fellow whom everyone avoided with greater assiduity, the closer he came to the age at which those who are already of limited talents tend to grow more demanding as they grow less competent. Poor Margreth, however, who had no more relatives living, was pleased to see her brother.

'Simon, is it you?' she asked, trembling so much that she had to hold tight to her chair. 'Have you come see how my wretched son and myself are faring?'—Simon looked at her gravely and gave her his hand. 'You've grown old, Margreth!'—Margreth heaved a sigh. 'I've suffered oft and bitterly from misfortunes of all kinds.'—'Yes, my girl—marry late and repent early! Now you're old, and the child is young. There's a right time for everything. But when an old house catches fire, there's no putting it out.'—A flame, red as blood, swept over Margreth's bitter face.

'But I hear the boy's clever and quick-witted,' Simon went on.—'Yes, pretty much, and he's a good boy, too.'—'Hm—there was once a fellow who stole a cow, and his name was Good. But he's a quiet, thoughtful lad, isn't he? Doesn't have anything to do with the other boys?'—'He's a lonely child,' said Margreth, as if talking to herself, 'that's not good.'—Simon laughed loudly. 'Your son's timid, because the others have given him a proper thrashing once or twice. But the boy will pay them back. Hülsmeyer came to see me recently, and he said: "The lad is like a deer."'

What mother does not rejoice to hear her child praised? Poor Margreth had seldom experienced such pleasure; everyone said her son was crafty and furtive. Tears came to her eyes. 'Yes, thank God; he's a well-made boy.'—'What does he look like?' Simon continued.—'He's like you in many ways, Simon.'

Simon laughed. 'Well, he must be a fine fellow, then—I'm getting more handsome every day. They say he's not much of a talker at school. D'you have him tend the cows? That's good, too. What the schoolmaster says isn't even half true. But where does he tend them? In the Telge valley? In Rode Wood? In the Teutoburg Forest? At night and early in the morning, too?'—'All night long; but what do you mean by asking that?'

Simon appeared not to hear the question, and peered round the door. 'Why, here's the young fellow now! The image of his father! He swings his arms just like your late husband. And look at that! The lad really has got my blond hair!'

A secretive, proud smile crept over Margreth's face; her son Friedrich's blond curls and Simon's reddish bristles! Without replying, she broke off a switch from the nearest hedge and walked towards her son, seemingly in order to spur on a reluctant cow, but really in order to whisper a few brief, half-threatening words to him; for she well knew his stubborn nature, and Simon's manner had seemed to her more intimidating today than ever.

But everything went unexpectedly well. Friedrich was neither sullen nor impertinent; on the contrary, he seemed somewhat dull and extremely eager to please his uncle. The result was that Simon, after a half-hour's discussion, proposed a sort of adoption for the lad, by which he would not deprive the mother of her son completely, though he would have the use of the greater part of the lad's time; in return for this, in the end, the old bachelor's inheritance would pass to the boy—who was, of course, entitled to it in any event. Margreth listened patiently as her brother explained to her what a great benefit and, on the other hand, what a small sacrifice the arrangement would mean to her. She knew best of all what a sacrifice it was for a widow in poor health to do without the help of a twelve-year-old lad whom she had already accustomed to take the place of a daughter. But she said nothing and accepted his proposal entirely. She only requested her brother to be strict with the boy, but not harsh.

'He's a good boy,' she said, 'but I am alone, and my child is not like others who had a father's hand to guide them.' Simon nodded knowingly. 'Just leave that to me; we'll get along with each other well enough. And, you know what—let me take the lad with me right now; I have to fetch two sacks of flour from the mill; the smaller one is just right for him, and that way he'll learn to be of help to me. Come on, Fritz, put your clogs on!'— A short time later, Margreth was watching the two as they went off, Simon leading the way, his head butting through the air and the tails of his red coat flying like flames behind him. This gave him pretty much the appearance of a fiery man doing penance under the burden of the sack he has stolen; Friedrich following him, straight and slender for his age, with fine-cut, almost noble features and long blond curls which were better groomed than the rest of his appearance would lead one to expect; otherwise ragged, sun-tanned, with an expression of carelessness and a degree of fierce melancholy in his features. Yet a striking family likeness between the two was plain to see and, as Friedrich slowly followed his guide, his eyes firmly fixed upon him—for it was precisely his uncle's odd appearance which attracted his gaze—you could not help thinking of someone contemplating his future in a magic mirror with distraught attentiveness.

Now they were approaching that part of the Teutoburg Forest

where Brede Wood runs down the hillside and spreads out into a deep, dark valley. Until now, little had been said. Simon seemed lost in thought, the boy's mind was elsewhere, and both were breathing heavily under their loads. All at once Simon asked: 'Do you like brandy?' The boy gave no reply.—'I said, do you like brandy? Does your mother give you some now and then?'—'My mother hasn't any herself,' replied Friedrich.—'So, so, all the better. D'you know the wood there, in front of us?'—'That's Brede Wood.'—'And d'you know what happened there?' Friedrich remained silent. Meanwhile they were coming closer and closer to the gloomy gorge. 'Does your mother still pray so much?' Simon continued. 'Yes—two rosaries every evening.'—'So? And you pray with her?' The boy laughed, half embarrassed, with a sly, sidelong glance.—'My mother says one rosary in the evening, before supper—I'm mostly not yet back again with the cows; and she says the second rosary in bed, and I usually fall asleep.'—'So, so, my friend.'—These last words were spoken under the spreading boughs of a large beech tree which formed a vaulted roof over the entrance to the gorge. It was now quite dark; the first quarter-moon hung in the sky, its pale light only bright enough to impart an alien appearance to anything which it fell upon from time to time through gaps between the branches. Friedrich kept close behind his uncle; he was breathing quickly, and anyone able to distinguish his features would have observed an expression of intense nervousness, though more of fantasy than fear. And so they strode on stoutly, Simon with the resolute step of a seasoned wanderer, Friedrich swaying as if in a dream. It seemed to him as if everything were in motion and that the trees, in the single rays of moonlight, were swaying towards, and then away from one another again. Roots of trees and slippery spots where the rain-water had collected hindered his step; several times he almost fell. Now, some distance away, the darkness seemed to disperse and, soon after, they entered a fairly large clearing. In the clear light of the moon they could see that the woodman's axe had wrought havoc here only a short time ago. Tree-stumps rose everywhere, some several feet above the ground, just as they had proved most convenient for cutting in haste; the villainous work had evidently been suddenly interrupted, for a beech in full leaf lay across the path, its branches stretched high and its leaves, still green, quivering in the night wind. Simon stopped for a moment and viewed the felled tree attentively. In the middle of the clearing stood an old oak, broader than it was tall; a pale ray of moonlight falling through the branches upon its trunk revealed it to be hollow, which had probably caused it to be spared in the general destruction. Now Simon suddenly seized the boy by the arm.

'Friedrich, do you know that tree? That's the broad oak.'— Friedrich flinched and clung tightly to his uncle with cold hands. 'Look,' Simon continued, 'it was here that Uncle Franz and Hülsmeyer found your father after he had gone to the devil, in a drunken state, without penance or the last rites.'—'Uncle, uncle!' panted Friedrich.—'What's the matter with you? Surely you're not afraid? You little devil, you're pinching my arm off! Let go, let go!'—He tried to shake off the lad's grip.—'Your father was a good soul, after all; God won't judge him so harshly. I loved him as if he were my own brother.'—Friedrich let go his uncle's arm; they walked through the remaining stretch of the wood in silence, and then the village of Brede lay before them, with its mud huts and the few brick houses of the better-off inhabitants, including Simon's own house.

It was the following evening, and Margreth had already been sitting working at her distaff for an hour in front of her door, waiting for her son. It was the first night that she had passed without hearing her child's breathing at her side, and Friedrich had still not returned. She was angry and frightened, yet she knew that she had no reason to be either. The clock in the church-tower was striking seven and the cattle were coming home; still he had not come, and so she had to stand up to see to the cows herself. When she came back into the dark kitchen, Friedrich was standing by the hearth; bent forward, he was warming his hands over the coals. The light of the fire was playing upon his features, giving them a ghastly appearance of fleshlessness and fearful twitching. So weirdly transformed did the boy seem that Margreth remained standing in the doorway of the threshing floor.

'Friedrich, how's your uncle?'—The boy murmured a few inaudible words and pressed himself tight against the wall of the fireplace.—'Friedrich, have you forgotten how to speak? Open your mouth, lad! You know I can't hear very well with my right ear.'—The boy raised his voice and began to stammer so badly that now Margreth could not understand a word.—'What's that you say? Master Semmler sends his regards? Off again? Where to? The cows are home already. Damn you, boy, I can't understand you. Wait, let me see whether you've a tongue in your head!'—She stepped forward abruptly. The boy looked up at her with the pitiful eyes of some wretched puppy-dog that is learning to stand guard and, in his fear, he began to stamp his feet and rub his back against the wall of the fireplace.

Margreth stood still and a look of fear came to her eyes. The boy seemed somehow shrunken, and his clothes were not the same; no, that was not her son, and yet—'Friedrich, Friedrich!' she cried. A cupboard door closed with a bang in the bedchamber, and out stepped Friedrich, with a so-called clog fiddle in one hand—an old clog with three or four worn-out violin strings stretched across it—and in the other a bow, fully worthy of the instrument. Thus equipped, he walked straight to his stunted mirror-image, with an attitude of conscious dignity and independence which, in that instant, strongly emphasized the difference between the two boys, otherwise so strangely alike.

'Here, Johannes,' he said, handing him this work of art with a patronizing air, 'here's the fiddle I promised you. My time for playing is over, I have to earn money now.'—Johannes glanced shyly at Margreth once again; slowly he stretched out his hand and firmly grasped the object, then stowed it away almost secretively under the flaps of his shabby jacket.

Margreth remained perfectly still, leaving the children to their own devices. Her thoughts had taken another, most serious turn and she looked nervously from one to the other. The stranger had once again bent forward over the coals with an expression of momentary well-being approaching stupidity; in Friedrich's features, however, hovered a look of sympathy, though clearly more self-interested than good-natured; and his eyes betrayed with almost glass-like clarity—surely for the first time—that expression of unbridled ambition and inclination to boasting which later revealed itself as such a strong motive for most of his actions. His mother's words wrenched him out of a train of thought which was as new to him as it was pleasant. Now she was sitting at her spinning-wheel once more.

'Friedrich,' she said hesitantly, 'tell me—', and then was silent. Friedrich looked up but, as she did not continue, turned once more to his protégé.—'No, listen to me'—and then, in a quiet tone—'What manner of boy is he? What's his name?'— Friedrich replied, just as quietly: 'He's Uncle Simon's swine-herd, bringing a message to Hülsmeyer. My uncle gave me a pair of shoes and a canvas waistcoat, and the boy carried them for me on the way; I promised him my fiddle in return; he's just a poor boy, after all—his name is Johannes.'—'And . . . ?' said Margreth.—'What do you mean, mother?'—'What's his other name?'—'Why, he hasn't any other name—but wait—yes, Niemand, Johannes Niemand.*—He hasn't got a father,' he added in a quieter tone.

Margreth stood up and went into the bedchamber. After a while she came out once more with a hard, grim expression on her face.—'Well, Friedrich,' she said, 'let the lad go, so that he can deliver his message.—Boy, what are you doing, lying there in the ashes? Have you nothing to do at home?'—With a hunted expression, the lad stood upright so quickly that he stumbled over his own arms and legs, and the fiddle almost fell into the fire.—'Wait, Johannes,' said Friedrich, with a touch of pride, 'I'll give you half my bread and butter; it's too much for me, my mother always cuts the bread lengthways.'—'Never mind that,' said Margreth, 'he's going home anyway.'—'Yes, but he won't get anything more to eat; Uncle Simon has supper at seven o'clock.'—Margreth turned to the lad. 'Don't they save anything for you? Tell me—who cares for you?'—'Nobody,' stammered the child. 'Nobody?' she echoed; 'here, take it!' she added abruptly—'your name is Nobody and nobody cares for you! God pity you! Now, off with you! Friedrich, don't you go with him, d'you hear; don't walk through the village together.'—'I'm only going to fetch wood from the shed,' replied Friedrich.— When the two boys had gone, Margreth threw herself on to a chair and clapped her hands together with an expression of deepest sorrow.—'A false oath, a false oath,' she groaned. 'Simon, Simon, will you be able to stand before God's judgement seat?'

Thus she sat for a while, stiffly and with lips tightly pressed together, as if totally lost in thought. Friedrich was standing in front of her; he had already addressed her twice. 'What is it?

What d'you want?' she cried, startled.—'I've brought you some money,' he said, more astonished than frightened.—'Money? Where?' She stirred, and the small coin fell to the ground with a ringing sound. Friedrich picked up the coin.—'Money from Uncle Simon, for helping him with his work. I can earn something for myself, now.'—'Money from Simon? Throw it away, away!—No, give it to the poor. But, no, keep it,' she whispered in a hardly audible voice; 'we are poor ourselves; who knows whether we shan't have to beg ourselves.'—'I'm to go to Uncle Simon again on Monday and help him with the sowing.'—'Go to him again? No, no, never!'—and she caught her son in a fierce embrace.—'Yes,' she added, a stream of tears suddenly running down her sunken cheeks; 'go; he is my only brother, and I mustn't speak ill of him! But always keep God in your thoughts and don't forget to say your prayers every day!'

She laid her face against the wall and wept aloud. Many a hard burden had she borne: the ill-treatment she had received from her husband, then—even harder—his death; and it had been a bitter hour for the widow when she had had to give up the last piece of land to a creditor for his use, and the plough remained untouched in front of the house. But never before had she felt so downhearted; yet, after weeping the whole evening and lying awake all night, she fell to thinking that her brother Simon could not be such a godless man; the boy was certainly not of the same strain, and likenesses did not prove anything. After all, forty years before she herself had lost a little sister, who looked exactly like the itinerant pedlar. One willingly believes anything when one possesses so little and is likely to lose that little by not believing!

From that time on, Friedrich was seldom at home. Simon appeared to have directed all the tender feelings of which he was capable to his nephew; at any rate, he greatly missed Friedrich and often sent him messages whenever some business at home obliged the boy to remain with his mother. Since then, Friedrich seemed almost a different person; his dreamy manner had vanished completely; he became self-assured; he began to take care of his appearance and, soon, to enjoy the reputation of being a good-looking, clever young fellow. His uncle, who could not live without being involved in one project or another, sometimes used to undertake public works which were of quite an important nature, for example, road-building; and Friedrich was everywhere considered one of his best workers and his right-hand man; for, though he had not yet attained his full physical strength, there was hardly anyone who could equal him in endurance. Until then, Margreth had only loved her son; now she began to be proud of him and even to feel a kind of respect for him; for she saw that the young man was developing entirely without her help, without even her advice which, like most people, she considered priceless, and was therefore unable to rate highly enough the capabilities which could dispense with such valuable aid.

In his eighteeenth year Friedrich had already gained a considerable reputation among the young village-folk as the result of a wager, for which he had carried the carcass of a wild boar on his shoulders for two miles without putting it down. But the reflected glory was pretty much the only benefit that Margreth had gained from these favourable circumstances, for Friedrich spent more and more on his appearance and gradually began to find it hard to bear whenever lack of money obliged him to be second-best to someone else in the village. Moreover, he devoted all his strength to earning money elsewhere; at home, however, quite contrary to his reputation, he seemed to find any work of long duration a bore, and preferred instead to undertake a hard but short task which soon enabled him to resume his earlier occupation as a cowherd; this was already unseemly for someone of his age and, on occasion, earned him mockery, but this he was able to ward off by means of a few rough rebukes with his fists. And so it became usual to see him sometimes as the recognized village beau at the head of the young people, at other times as a ragged cowherd dawdling alone and dreamily behind the cows or lying in a forest clearing, seemingly absent-minded and plucking the moss from the trees.

At about this time the sleeping minions of the law were somewhat shaken up by a band of timber thieves who, under the name of Bluejackets, so surpassed their predecessors in cunning and audacity that even the most long-suffering felt that this was going too far. Contrary to normal circumstances, in which the strongest goats in the herd could be pointed out with a finger, in this case, despite all vigilance, it had not been possible until now to identify even a single member of the band. They owed their name to their completely uniform clothing, which made it difficult to recognize them whenever, for example, a forester saw one or two of them disappearing after their fellows into the undergrowth. Like a swarm of voracious caterpillars, they devastated everything; entire stretches of woodland were cut down overnight and immediately transported away, so that next morning nothing was to be seen but chippings and untidy heaps of firewood; the fact that the wheel tracks led never to a village but always from and to the river proved that the thieves worked under the protection (and perhaps with the help) of the shipowners. Clearly there must have been some very cunning spies among the thieves, for the foresters could remain on watch for weeks on end to no avail; but the very first night—whether stormy or moonlit—on which they relaxed their efforts, being overtired, the devastation would begin again. It was strange that the country folk all around seemed to know just as little and be just as anxious as the foresters themselves. In the case of some villages it could be said with certainty that they had nothing to do with the Bluejackets; yet not one could be described as highly suspect since the most suspect of all—the village of B.—had had to be acquitted. This had come about quite by chance: a wedding feast, where almost all the people of this village—as befitted their notorious reputation—had spent the night, whilst at the same time the Bluejackets had carried out one of their most ravaging excursions.

The havoc in the forests was enormous, so that preventive measures were intensified to a previously unknown degree; patrols were on duty day and night; farm-hands and household servants alike were given guns and placed under the orders of the foresters. Yet all these measures were crowned with meagre success and, many a time, the wardens had scarcely left the forest at one end when the Bluejackets entered at the other. All this went on for more than a year, with wardens and Bluejackets, Bluejackets and wardens occupying the terrain alternately, like sun and moon, and never making contact with each other.

It was in July 1756, at three o'clock in the morning; a clear moon was shining in the sky, though its light was already beginning to pale; in the east, a slender yellow streak could already be seen tinging the horizon and closing the entrance of a narrow gorge with a band of gold. Friedrich was lying in the grass in his accustomed manner, whittling at a willow staff and trying to impart the shape of some hulking animal to its gnarled end. He appeared very tired, yawning and, from time to time, laying his head upon a weathered tree-stump, letting his gaze—gloomier than the horizon—wander across the entrance to the gorge, almost overgrown with bushes and seedling trees. Now and then his eyes would light up, assuming their typical glassy gleam, but immediately he would half-close them again, and yawn and stretch as only lazy cowherds may. His dog was lying some distance away near the cows which, with no concern for the forestry laws, were nibbling the tender young tips of the branches just as often as the grass, and snorting in the cool morning air. From time to time, a dull booming crash came from the forest; the sound held only a few seconds, accompanied by a long echo from the hill-sides, and was repeated every five to eight minutes. Friedrich took no notice; only sometimes, when the noise was unusually loud or long-drawn-out, did he raise his head and let his gaze wander slowly over the numerous paths which led into the depths of the valley.

It was already almost daybreak; the birds began to chirp quietly, and one could feel the dew rising from the ground. Friedrich had slid down the side of the tree stump and now, his arms crossed behind his head, he was staring into the rosy light of dawn as it slowly approached. Suddenly he started up: a streak of light flashed across his face, and he listened for a few seconds with his body bent forward like a hunting dog catching a scent borne by the wind. Quickly he put two fingers to his mouth and gave a long, piercing whistle. 'Fidel, you damned creature!'—A stone struck the unsuspecting dog in the flank; roused from his sleep, he snapped at the air around him and then, howling, came limping on three legs to seek comfort in the very direction from which the pain had come. At that instant, the branches of a nearby bush were pushed back with hardly a sound, and out stepped a man in hunting green, with a silver badge on his sleeve and carrying a cocked gun in his hand. His eyes flitted swiftly over the gorge and finally came to rest keenly scrutinizing the lad; then he stepped forward and waved towards the bushes, whereupon seven or eight men gradually appeared, all clothed in similar fashion, with hunting knives in their belts and cocked weapons in their hands.

'Friedrich, what was that?' demanded the man who had first appeared.—'I wish the cur would fall dead on the spot. The cows might eat the ears from my head for all he cares.'—'The rabble have seen us,' said another forester. 'Tomorrow I'll send you off with a stone around your neck,' continued Friedrich and made to kick the dog.—'Friedrich, don't act like a fool! You know me and you know what I mean!'—The words were accompanied by a look which was not slow in having its effect. 'Herr Brandis, think of my mother!'—'I do. Didn't you hear anything in the forest?'—'In the forest?'—The boy glanced quickly at the forester's face.—'Your woodcutters, nothing else.'—'My woodcutters!'

The forester's complexion, dark though it already was, turned a deep reddish brown. 'How many are there, and where are they up to their mischief?'—'Wherever you sent them; I don't know.'—Brandis turned to his companions: 'Go on ahead; I'll be along right away.'

After they had disappeared into the undergrowth, one after another, Brandis stepped directly in front of the boy: 'Friedrich,' he said, in a tone of suppressed anger, 'my patience is at an end; I'd like to beat you like a dog—the whole pack of you aren't worth any more than that. Riffraff—not a tile on the roof can you call your own. You'll soon be reduced to beggary, thank Heaven, and your mother, the old witch, won't get so much as a crust of mouldy bread at my door. But before that, I'll see that both of you land in the doghouse.'

Friedrich desperately seized hold of a branch. He was pale as death and his eyes seemed set to shoot out of their sockets like balls of glass, yet only for a moment. Then the old expression of perfect calm, bordering on limpness, returned. 'Master,' he said firmly, in an almost gentle tone, 'you have said something that you cannot answer for, and perhaps I have, too. Let us set off one against the other; and now I'll tell you what you want to know. If you yourself didn't send the woodcutters, then it must have been the Bluejackets, for not one wagon has come up from the village; I have a clear view of the track, after all, and there were four wagons. I didn't see them, but I heard them driving up the defile.' His voice faltered for an instant. 'Can you truly say that I have ever cut down a tree in your district? Or that I have ever cut down trees elsewhere except on orders? Think well whether you can say so.'

A self-conscious murmur was all the forester's reply—like most rough-natured persons he was quick to regret a mistake. He turned away brusquely and strode towards the bushes.— 'No, master,' called Friedrich, 'if you want to find the other foresters, they went up there past the beech-tree.'—'Past the beech-tree?' said Brandis doubtfully; 'no, they went over there, towards the hollow.'—'I tell you, they went past the beech-tree; Long Heinrich's gun-sling caught on the crooked branch there; I saw it plainly!'

The forester took the way indicated. Friedrich had remained the whole time in his original position; half prone, his arm around a withered branch, he watched without moving as the forester walked away and slipped up the steep, half-overgrown track with the long, cautious strides of his craft, as silently as a fox climbing the ladder of a hen-house. Here and there a branch fell back behind him as he passed; the outline of his figure became fainter and fainter. One last time, something gleamed through the foliage; it was a metal button on his hunting jacket; and then he was gone. While the forester gradually disappeared from view, Friedrich's face had lost its expression of coldness until at length his features seemed to betray uneasiness. Did he perhaps regret not having requested the forester to keep silent about what Friedrich had told him? He walked a few steps and then halted. 'Too late,' he said to himself and reached for his hat. A faint tapping sound came from the bushes, not twenty paces away. It was Brandis, sharpening the flint of his gun. Friedrich listened.—'No!' he said in a determined tone; then he gathered his few belongings together and quickly drove the cattle along the gorge.

Around midday Margreth was sitting at the hearth, making tea. Friedrich had returned home ill, complaining of a severe headache. In reply to her anxious questions, he told her how he had been extremely angry at the forester, and briefly related the entire story just described, with the exception of a few small details which he thought best to keep to himself. Margreth sat silent and gloomy, looking at the boiling water. She was quite accustomed to hearing her son complain at times, but today she found him more out of sorts than ever before. Could it be that he was sickening for something? With a deep sigh, she let fall a block of wood which she had picked up a moment before.

'Mother!' called Friedrich from the bedchamber.—'What is it?'—'Was that a shot?'—'Of course not; I don't know what you mean.'—'I've such a throbbing in my head,' he replied.

Their neighbour came and related in a whisper some unimportant gossip or other; Margreth listened indifferently. Then the woman left.—'Mother!' called Friedrich. Margreth went in to him. 'What was the Hülsmeyer woman saying?'—'Why, nothing at all; lies, nonsense!'—Friedrich sat up in bed.—'About Gretchen Siemers; you know, the old story, there's not a bit of truth in it.'—Friedrich lay down again. 'I'll try to sleep,' he said.

Margreth was sitting by the hearth spinning, and her thoughts were hardly pleasant. The village clock struck half-past eleven; the door opened and in stepped Kapp, the clerk of the court.— 'Good morning, Frau Mergel,' he said; 'could you give me a drink of milk? I've just come from M...'—After Margreth had brought the milk, he asked: 'Where's Friedrich?'—She was just then busy taking down a plate and did not hear the question. He drank slowly, with short sips. Then he spoke. 'Have you heard?' he said; 'Last night the Bluejackets cleared another whole swath of trees in Mast Wood—bare as the palm of my hand!'—'Good heavens!' she replied, indifferently.—'The scoundrels ruin everything,' continued Kapp; 'if only they'd spare the young trees, at least; but young oaks, no thicker than my arm, not even big enough for an oar. It's just as if other people's losses mean as much to them as their own profit!'—'It's a pity!' said Margreth.

The clerk had finished his milk but still did not go. He seemed to have something on his mind. 'Haven't you heard about Brandis?' he asked suddenly.—'No, nothing; he never comes into my house.'—'So, you don't know what has happened to him?'—'What?' asked Margreth eagerly.—'He's dead!'—'Dead!' she exclaimed, 'dead? Merciful God! He went by only this morning, large as life, with his gun over his shoulder!'—'He's dead,' repeated the clerk, staring at her keenly, 'killed by the Bluejackets. His body was brought into the village just a quarter of an hour ago.'

Margreth clapped her hands together.—'God in heaven, have mercy on him! He didn't know what he was doing!'—'Mercy on him?' exclaimed the clerk; 'Mercy on the damned murderer, you mean?' A deep groaning was heard from the bedchamber; Margreth hurried into the room, followed by the clerk. Friedrich was sitting upright in bed, his face pressed into his hands and was moaning like a dying man.—'Friedrich, how do you feel?' asked his mother.—'How do you feel?' repeated Kapp.—'Oh, my chest, my head!' he groaned.—'What's wrong with him?'— 'God knows,' she replied, 'he came back with the cows early at four o'clock, because he felt so ill.—Friedrich, Friedrich, answer me! Shall I run to the doctor?'—'No, no,' he croaked, 'it's only a colic, it will soon be better.'

He lay back once again; his features twitching with pain, then the colour returned to his face. 'Go,' he said in a weak voice, 'I must sleep, then it will pass.'—'Frau Mergel,' said the clerk gravely, 'are you sure that Friedrich came home at four o'clock and didn't go out again?'—She stared at him. 'Ask any child in the street. Go out? I wish to God he could!'—'Didn't he say anything about Brandis?'—'Heavens, yes—that Brandis had berated him in the forest and sneered at us for being poor, the blackguard!—But God forgive me, the man is dead!—Go!' she added angrily, 'have you come here to insult honest people? Go!'—She turned to her son once again; the clerk left the house.—'Friedrich, how do you feel?' she asked. 'Did you hear that? Terrible, terrible! Without confession and absolution!'— 'Mother, mother, for heaven's sake, let me sleep; I can't stand any more!'

Just at that moment Johannes Niemand entered the room; long and thin as a bean-pole, but ragged and timid, just as we saw him five years before. His face was even paler than usual. 'Friedrich,' he stammered, 'you must come to your uncle straight away, he has work for you; straight away.'—Friedrich turned to face the wall.—'I won't come,' he said roughly, 'I'm ill.'—'But you must come,' panted Johannes, 'he said I must bring you with me.'—Friedrich gave a sneering laugh: 'That I'd like to see!'—'Leave him alone,' sighed Margreth, 'he can't come; you can see how it is with him.'—She left the room for several minutes; when she returned, Friedrich was already dressed.— 'What are you thinking of!' she exclaimed, 'You can't go, you mustn't go!'—'What must be, will be,' he answered and immediately went out of the door with Johannes. 'Dear Lord,' Margreth sighed, 'when the children are small, they kick us in the belly, and when they are grown they kick us in the heart!'

The official investigation had already begun; the crime was clear to all, but the evidence regarding the culprit was so slight that, though all the circumstances pointed strongly to the Blue-jackets, no one could venture more than a conjecture. One piece of evidence seemed to offer clarity but, for good reasons, did not appear very hopeful. Owing to the squire's absence, the clerk of the court had been obliged to start the proceedings on his own account. He was sitting at the table; the room was crowded with farmers, some of them having come out of curiosity, whilst from the others it was hoped that some information could be obtained, despite the lack of real witnesses to the crime. Herdsmen who had been watching their herds that same night, labourers who had been working in the fields nearby—all were standing straight and erect, their hands in their pockets, as a tacit sign that they were not willing to be of help. Eight forestry officials were questioned; all gave exactly the same testimony: Brandis, they said, had summoned them to a meeting on the evening of the tenth, since he had evidently heard of an expedition planned by the Bluejackets; but he had only spoken of it in vague terms. At two o'clock in the morning they had set off and encountered many traces of devastation, which had put the head forester in a very evil temper; otherwise all had been quiet. At about four o'clock Brandis had said: 'We've been gulled; let's go home.' As they were walking back around Bremer Hill the wind had changed, and they had clearly heard the sound of felling in Mast Wood; from the quick succession of axe-blows they had concluded that the Bluejackets were at work. For a while they had debated whether it was wise to attack a desperate band of men with such a small force, then, without having come to a definite decision, they had slowly approached the spot where the sounds were coming from. Then came the encounter with Friedrich.

After Brandis had sent them on without orders, they had advanced for a while; but, noticing that the noise in the wood, which was still a fair distance away, had stopped completely, they had halted in order to wait for the head forester. They were annoyed by the delay and, after about ten minutes they had continued on their way until they came to the scene of the devastation. It was all over: there was not a sound in the wood now, and out of twenty trees that had been felled, eight still remained: the rest had already been taken away. They could not understand how this had been done, for there were no wheel-tracks to be seen. Also, because of the dryness of the season and the ground being strewn with pine needles, they had been unable to pick out footprints, although the earth all around was stamped hard. Thinking that it would be of no use to wait for the head forester, they had quickly gone on towards the far side of the wood in the hope of perhaps catching sight of the villains after all. On the way out of the wood one of them had caught the sling of his powderhorn in a blackberry bush and, as he turned around, he had seen something gleaming in the undergrowth; it was the head forester's belt-buckle: they had found him lying behind the brambles, his body stretched out, his right hand clutching the barrel of his gun, the other clenched, and his skull split by an axe.

Such was the testimony of the foresters; now it was the turn of the farmers, though nothing was to be got out of them. Some of them stated that they had still been at home at four o'clock or busy elsewhere, but no one admitted having seen anything. What more could be done? They were all local men, above suspicion, so that the court had to be satisfied with this negative testimony.

Friedrich was called into the courtroom. His manner was in no way different from that which he normally affected, neither nervous nor insolent. The interrogation went on for some considerable time, and the questions, on occasion, were cunningly framed; but he answered all questions frankly and resolutely, and related, more or less truthfully, what had happened between him and the head forester, except for the conclusion, which he thought wiser to keep to himself. His alibi for the time of the murder was easily proved. The forester had been found at the end of Mast Wood, more than three-quarters of an hour's walk from the valley where he had spoken to Friedrich at four o'clock and from where the lad had driven his herd only ten minutes later into the village. Everyone had seen this; all the farmers in the courtroom eagerly testified to it: he had spoken with one, he had nodded to another.

The clerk of the court sat listening, disgruntled and at a loss. Suddenly he reached behind him and presented a gleaming object to Friedrich's eye. 'Whose is this?'—Friedrich leapt three paces backward. 'God in heaven! I thought you were going to break my skull.' His gaze had flitted swiftly over the deadly instrument and seemed to remain fixed for an instant upon a broken splinter in the handle. 'I don't know,' he answered firmly. —It was the axe which they had found buried in the forester's skull.—'Take a good look at it,' said the clerk. Friedrich took the axe in his hand, examined it from one end to the other, and turned it over. Then he said: 'It's an axe like any other,' and placed it impassively upon the table. A bloodstain came into view; he seemed to shudder, but repeated once more in a perfectly firm voice: 'I don't recognize it.' The clerk gave a sigh of displeasure. He himself had no further ideas and had merely made one last attempt to solve the crime by a surprise tactic. Nothing else remained but to conclude the questioning.

For those readers who are perhaps curious as to the outcome of this matter, I must state that the mystery was never solved, although a great deal of effort was made and several more enquiries followed. As a result of the attention that the crime had aroused and the stricter measures undertaken as a result, the Bluejackets seem to have lost their nerve; from that time on they disappeared completely; and, though many a timber thief was caught later, there was never any occasion to connect him with the infamous band. Twenty years later the axe still lay, a useless *corpus delicti*, in the court archives, where it may yet be lying today, spotted with rust. In a work of fiction it would be wrong to abuse the reader's curiosity in such a way; but all this really did happen, and I cannot add anything to, or omit anything from, this tale.

On the following Sunday Friedrich rose very early in order to go to confession. It was the Feast of the Assumption, and the priests had been hearing confessions since before daybreak. He dressed in darkness and left the narrow cubby-hole which he occupied in Simon's house as quietly as possible. His prayer-book, he thought, must be on the window-sill in the kitchen, and he hoped to find it with the help of the pale moonlight; but it was not there. He looked round the room, searching, and gave a start: there in the doorway stood Simon, scantily dressed; his thin figure, his unkempt, tousled hair and his face, pale in the light of the moon, gave him a weirdly altered appearance. Is he sleepwalking? wondered Friedrich, and remained perfectly still. —'Friedrich, where are you off to?' whispered the old man.— 'Is that you, uncle? I mean to go to confession.'—'That's what I thought; well, then, go in God's name, but make your confession like a good Christian.'—'So I shall,' replied Friedrich.— 'Think of the ten commandments: thou shalt not bear witness against thy neighbour.'—'No *false* witness!'—'No, no witness whatsoever; you're wrongly informed; anyone who accuses another in confession receives the sacrament unworthily.'

Both remained silent. Then Friedrich spoke: 'Uncle, why are you telling me this? Your conscience isn't clear; you've lied to me.'—'Lied? So?'—'Where is your axe?'—'My axe? In the threshing room.'—'Have you fitted a new handle to it? Where's the old one?'—'You'll find it by daylight today in the woodshed. Off with you,' he added scornfully, 'I thought you were a man, but you're just an old woman who straight away thinks her house is on fire when her cooking pot begins to smoke. Why,' he went on, 'may my soul perish if I know any more of the matter than the doorpost there. I'd already been home a long while when it happened,' he added.—Friedrich stood motionless, apprehensive and uncertain. What would he not have given to be able to see his uncle's face! but the sky had become overcast as they were whispering.

'Much of the guilt is mine,' sighed Friedrich, 'for having sent him on the wrong path,—although—no, I didn't think of that; no, indeed I didn't. Uncle, I have you to thank for my guilty conscience.'—'Then go and confess!' whispered Simon in a trembling voice; 'commit sacrilege with your bragging and set a spy loose on to honest people—he'll find a way to snatch the little bit of bread from their mouths, even if he has to keep it to himself—go!'—Friedrich remained, hesitating; he heard a slight noise; the clouds parted and the moonlight shone upon the door once more: it was closed. Friedrich did not go to confession that morning.

It is unfortunate that the impression that this incident made on Friedrich vanished only too soon. Who could doubt that Simon did everything to lead his adopted son on to the same path which he himself trod? In Friedrich's nature were traits of character which made this only too easy; thoughtlessness, excitability, and, above all, boundless arrogance which did not shrink from deception and then made every effort, by making the assumed appearance reality, to avoid possible embarrassment. He was not ignoble by nature, but he developed the habit of preferring the inner disgrace to the outer. Suffice it to say that he grew into the habit of cutting a dash whilst his mother lived in want.

This unfortunate change in his character came about over a number of years, during which it was noticed that Margreth became more and more reticent concerning her son, and gradually sank to a level of self-neglect of which no one would previously have thought her capable. She grew timid, negligent, even disorderly, and there were those who believed that she had become weak-minded. Friedrich became all the more rowdy; he did not miss a single kermis or wedding and, since his extreme sense of honour was such that he could not fail to notice the secret disapproval which many felt for him, he was always ready to defy public opinion as well as to lead it in the direction which pleased him. He was outwardly neat, down-to-earth, apparently trusting, yet cunning, boastful, and often rough-mannered; a person whom no one could ever like—least of all his mother—yet thanks to his daring, which people feared, and his maliciousness, which was feared even more, he had achieved a certain degree of pre-eminence in the village, which was all the more respected the more people realized that they did not truly know him, and that they could not predict what he was capable of doing. Only one young fellow in the village, Wilm Hülsmeyer—conscious of his own strength and his favourable circumstances—dared to challenge him; and, since he was more eloquent than Friedrich and, whenever a stinging remark hit home, always knew how to make a joke of it, he was the only one whose company Friedrich did not care for.

Meanwhile four years had passed; it was October 1760; the mild autumn which filled all the granaries with corn and all the cellars with wine had poured its bounty over this region, too; more drunkards were seen, more brawls and foolish japes were heard of, than ever before. Revelling took place everywhere; it became common to scamp work on Mondays; and anyone who had a few thalers to spare wanted a wife as well, who could help him to eat today and starve tomorrow. On one occasion a wedding took place in the village, a grand, first-rate affair at which the guests could expect something more than an out-of-tune fiddle, a glass of brandy, and what good humour they themselves had brought with them. Everyone had been up and doing since an early hour; clothes were being aired at every front door and B. resembled a pedlar's booth the whole day. Many guests from outside B. were expected, so that everyone did his best to uphold the honour of the village.

It was now seven o'clock in the evening, and the revels were at their height; cheering and laughter could be heard everywhere, the humbler dwellings were filled to bursting with blue-, red-, and yellow-clad figures—like rented cattle stalls into which an over-large herd has been driven. On the threshing floor people were dancing, or rather, whoever had managed to secure an area two feet square was turning in circles upon it, trying to make up with his cheers for what he lacked in room for movement. The orchestra was brilliant; a celebrated lady musician took centre-stage, playing the first violin, two dillentantes played the second violin and a large double-bass *ad libitum*; brandy and coffee were there in plenty and all the guests were sweating freely; in short, it was a splendid feast. Friedrich was strutting about like a turkey-cock in his new, sky-blue coat, demonstrating his position as the foremost dandy of the village. And when the squire and his company arrived, too, he was sitting behind the double-bass, bowing the third string vigorously and skilfully.

'Johannes!' he called in an imperious tone; and in came his protégé from the dance floor where he, too, had been swinging his clumsy legs and shouting with glee as best he could. Friedrich handed him the bow, announced his intention with a proud toss of his head, and walked towards the dancers. 'Strike up lively, musicians! Let's have "Papen von Istrup!"' They began to play this favourite dance; Friedrich frisked and sprang before the eyes of his master so that the cows near the threshing floor jerked back their horns, and a rattling of chains and bellowing ran round the stalls. Friedrich's blond head appeared above the others and sank again like a pike turning a somersault in the water; girls shrieked on all sides when, as a sign of his devotion, he flung his long flaxen hair into their faces with a swift shake of his head.

'Enough for now!' he said at last and walked, dripping with sweat, to the refreshments table. 'Long live our gracious squire and his family, and all the noble princes and princesses; and if anyone won't drink to that with me, I'll box his ears so that he can hear the angels sing!'—A loud hurrah was the response to this gallant toast.—Friedrich made a respectful bow.—'Please forgive us, your honours; we're just ignorant farming folk!'— At that instant there was an uproar at the end of the threshing room—shouting, abuse, and laughter all at once. Some children were calling 'Butter thief! Butter thief!' and Johannes Niemand pushed his way, or rather, was pushed to the fore, his head drawn down into his shoulders and trying desperately to reach the door.—'What's the matter? What are you doing with our Johannes?' demanded Friedrich in a peremptory voice.

'You'll know soon enough,' panted an old crone, holding her apron and a duster in her hand.—For shame! Johannes, unhappy wretch, for whom only the poorest was good enough when he was at home, had tried to secure a mere half-pound of butter for the lean times to come; then, forgetting that he had hidden it in his pocket, neatly wrapped in his handkerchief, he had walked over to the kitchen fire, and now, to his shame, the melted butter was running down the tails of his coat.—There was a general uproar, and the girls leapt back for fear of sullying themselves, or pushed the culprit forward. Still others made room for him, out of sympathy as well as prudence. But Friedrich stepped forward: 'You mangy hound!' he shouted, giving his unresisting protégé a few hearty blows in the face, after which he thrust him to the door, sending him on his way with a fierce kick.

He returned despondent; his pride was hurt and the general laughter burned deep into his soul; and though he attempted, with a brave shout of merriment, to regain his good humour, it was of little avail. He was on the point of seeking refuge behind the double-bass once more; but before he did so he decided to produce an eye-opener: he took out his silver pocket-watch, in those days a rare and costly piece of jewellery. 'It's almost ten o'clock,' he said. 'Now, the bridal minuet! I'm going to play.'

'A fine watch!' said the swineherd, thrusting his head forward in respectful curiosity.—'How much did it cost?' called Wilm Hülsmeyer, Friedrich's rival.—'Do you want to pay for it?' asked Friedrich.—'Have you paid for it yourself?' answered Wilm. Friedrich glanced at him arrogantly and reached for his bow in majestic silence.—'Well,' said Hülsmeyer, 'such things have been known before. You know that Franz Ebel had a beautiful watch, too, until Aaron the Jew took it back from him.'— Friedrich made no reply but waved proudly to the first violin, and they began to play with all their might.

Meanwhile, the squire and his company had entered the bridal room, where the bride's neighbours were adorning her with the sign of her new status, the white headband. The girl was weeping bitterly, partly because custom demanded it, partly from genuine anxiety: she was to take charge of a chaotic household under the eyes of a cantankerous old man whom she was also expected to love. He was standing beside her, not a whit like the bridegroom in the Song of Songs,* who 'enters the chamber like the morning sun'.—'That's enough of your weeping,' he said, in an ill-tempered tone: 'remember, it's not you who are making me happy; I am making you happy!'—She raised her eyes humbly to him and seemed to feel that he was right.—The women had finished their task; the young bride had drunk to her husband's health, and the young jokers present had looked through the tripod to see whether the headband was straight; now they pushed their way back to the threshing floor, from where noise and laughter were echoing on and on. Friedrich was no longer there. He had suffered a great, unbearable humiliation: the Jew Aaron—a butcher and, on occasion, second-hand dealer from the next township—had suddenly appeared and, following a short, fruitless discussion with Friedrich, had demanded in a loud voice, in front of everyone, the sum of ten thalers for a watch which he had given him before Easter. Devastated,

Friedrich had left the company. The Jew followed him, crying endlessly: 'Woe is me! Why didn't I listen to sensible folk? Didn't they tell me a hundred times that all you possess you carry upon you, and not a crust of bread in your cupboard!'— The threshing room resounded with laughter; some of the guests had even pushed their way out into the courtyard. 'Seize the Jew! Weigh him against a pig!' some shouted; others, however, had become grave.—'Friedrich was as white as a sheet,' said an old woman; and the crowd parted as the squire's carriage drove into the courtyard.

On the way home, Herr von S. was out of humour, something which happened every time his desire to maintain his popularity moved him to attend celebrations of this kind. He stared in silence out of the carriage, then he said: 'Who on earth are those two?' and pointed to two dark figures running away like ostriches ahead of the carriage. Now they were slinking into the manor house.—'Another pair of happy swine from our own pigsty!' sighed Herr von S. When he arrived home, the entrance was filled with the entire servantry; they were standing around two of the farmhands who were sitting upon the stairs, pale and breathless. They claimed that they had been pursued by old Mergel's ghost as they were returning home through Brede Wood. At first, they said, they had heard the sounds of rustling and crackling on the hillside, then there was a noise in the air as of two sticks being struck together, and suddenly there came a piercing scream and, quite plainly from on high, the words 'Woe is me! my unhappy soul!' One of the two declared that he had seen glowing eyes shining through the branches; and both of them had run for all they were worth.

'Absolute nonsense!' said the squire angrily and went into his chamber to change his clothes. The following morning the fountain in the garden would not work; and it was discovered that someone had disturbed a water-pipe, apparently in order to search for the skull of a horse's skeleton which had been buried there many years before—this was considered a powerful charm against the evil tricks of witches and ghosts. 'Hm,' said the squire, 'what the villains don't steal, the fools will ruin.'

Three days later there was a fearful storm. Though it was midnight, no one in the manor house was in bed. The squire was standing at the window, looking out anxiously into the darkness towards his fields. Leaves and twigs flew past the windowpanes; now and then a tile fell from the roof and shattered upon the cobblestones in the courtyard. 'Dreadful weather!' said Herr von S. His wife looked frightened. 'Is the fire all right?' she said. 'Gretchen, go and see; you'd best put it out properly with water. Come—let us recite the Gospel of St John.' Everyone knelt down, and the mistress of the house began: 'In the beginning was the Word, and the Word was with God, and the Word was God.'—There was a tremendous clap of thunder. Everyone started up in fright and, amidst dreadful shouting and confusion, began to run upstairs.—'Merciful God! Is the house on fire?' exclaimed Frau von S., letting her face sink onto the chair. Then the doors were wrenched open and in rushed the wife of Aaron the Jew, pale as death, her hair hanging wildly about her head and dripping with rain. She cast herself upon her knees in front of the squire. 'Justice!' she cried, 'Justice! My husband has been slain!'; and she fell down in a faint.

It was only too true; the subsequent investigation revealed that the Jew Aaron had been killed by a blow on the temple with a blunt weapon, probably a cudgel, with one single blow. A purple bruise was found on his left temple, but there was no other injury. The testimony of the Jewess and her servant Samuel was as follows: three days before, Aaron had left home in the afternoon in order to buy cattle, saying that he would probably stay the night away from home as he still had some bad debtors in B. and S. to settle with. In that case, he said, he would stay the night at the house of Salomon the butcher in B. When he did not return home the following day, however, his wife had become very anxious and, at last, had set out at three o'clock that afternoon accompanied by her hired hand and their great mastiff. At the house of the Jew Salomon no one knew anything of Aaron; he had not been there at all. Then they had called on all the farmers with whom they knew that Aaron intended to do business. Only two of these had seen him, on the same day on which he had set out. Meanwhile it had become very late. Prompted by a dreadful fear, the woman returned home in the faint hope of finding her husband there. And so they had been taken unawares by the storm in Brede Wood and had sought refuge under a great beech tree standing on the side of the hill; meanwhile the dog had been casting about and searching in a very striking manner and, at last, despite all their calls, had run off into the wood. All at once, by a flash of lightning, the wife sees something white lying in the moss beside her. It is her husband's staff; at almost the same instant the dog bursts out of the undergrowth carrying something in his mouth: her husband's shoe. A short time later, the dead body of the Jew is found in a ditch filled with dry leaves.—Such was the testimony of the servant, supported only in general terms by the wife; her hysterical excitement was now subdued, and she seemed half bewildered or, rather, mindless.—'An eye for an eye, a tooth for a tooth!'— these were the only words which she uttered from time to time.

That same night the gendarmes were summoned in order to arrest Friedrich. There was no need for a warrant, since Herr von S. himself had been witness to a scene which was bound to cast grave suspicion upon him; moreover, there was the business of the ghosts on that same evening, the sound of staves being struck together in Brede Wood, and the scream from on high. Since the clerk of the court was absent just then, Herr von S. himself took all necessary action far more quickly than would usually have been the case. Yet twilight was already approaching before the gendarmes had surrounded poor Margreth's house as noiselessly as possible. The squire himself knocked at the door; hardly a minute passed before it was opened and Margreth, fully dressed, appeared in the doorway. Herr von S. gave a start; she looked so pale and stony-faced that he had hardly recognized her. 'Where is Friedrich?' he asked in an uncertain voice. 'Find him!' she retorted and sat down upon a chair. The squire hesitated for an instant. Then: 'Inside! Inside!' he said harshly, 'what are we waiting for?' They went into Friedrich's room. He was not there, but his bed was still warm. They went up into the attic, down into the cellar, poked around in the straw, looked behind every barrel and even inside the oven; but he was not there. Some went out into the garden, looked behind the fence and up into the apple trees; he was not to be seen.—'Escaped!' said the squire, with very mixed feelings; the sight of the old woman shook him to the core. 'Give me the key to the chest' he said.—Margreth made no reply.—'The key!' repeated the squire, and only now noticed that the key was in the lock. Now the contents of the chest came to view; the fugitive's best Sunday clothes and the shabby clothes of his mother; then two shrouds with black edging, one for a man, the other for a woman. Herr von S. was badly shaken. At the very bottom of the chest lay the silver watch and some documents written in a very clear hand; one of these was signed by a man who stood under grave suspicion of having contact with the timber thieves. Herr von S. took them away for later examination and they left the house; Margreth had not given any further sign of life, save that she was gnawing her lips and blinking without cease.

Arriving back at the manor house, the squire found the clerk of the court, who had returned home the previous evening and claimed to have known nothing of the entire affair, since the squire had not sent for him.—'You always come too late,' said Herr von S. ill-humouredly. 'Wasn't there any old woman in the village to tell your maidservant the story? And why didn't anyone wake you?'—'Well, sir,' replied Kapp, 'it is true that my maid Anne-Marie heard about the affair an hour before I did; but she knew that Your Honour had taken charge of the matter yourself, and also,' he added plaintively, 'that I was dead tired!' —'Fine police!' murmured the squire, 'every old crone in the village knows about it when something is supposed to be kept perfectly secret.' Then he added in a fierce tone: 'The criminal would really have to be a stupid devil to let himself be caught!'

Both were silent for a while. Then: 'My coachman had lost his way in the darkness,' resumed the clerk; 'we halted for more than an hour in the wood; it was dreadful weather, I thought the wind would blow the carriage over. At last the rain stopped and we drove on again, trusting to God, pressing on in the direction of Zeller Meadow; you could not see your hand in front of your face. Then the coachman said: "We'd better not get too close to the quarries!" I myself was worried; I made him halt and struck a light, in order to have some comfort from my pipe at least. All at once we heard the bell ringing, close by and directly beneath us. Your Honour can imagine what a shock that was for me. I leapt from the carriage, for you can trust your own legs but not the horses'. And so I stood there in the mud and rain without moving, until soon, thank God, dawn began to break. And where had we halted? Close to Heerse Cliff, with the church tower of Heerse directly below us. If we had driven another twenty paces, we should have been killed.'—'That was no joke, indeed,' replied the squire, somewhat mollified.

Meanwhile he had looked through the papers which he had brought with him. They were dunning letters concerning borrowed money, most of them from usurers.—'I would never have thought that the Mergels were so deep in debt,' he murmured.—'Yes,' replied Kapp, 'and it will be no small trouble for Frau Margreth, that it must all come to light in this way.'—'My God, she won't be thinking of that now!' With these words the squire rose to his feet and left the room in order to carry out the official post-mortem together with Kapp.—The examination was brief; violent death was proved, the presumed culprit had fled, the grounds for suspecting him were serious, it was true, though not conclusive without his own confession; the fact that he had fled was, of course, extremely suspicious. And so the official enquiry had to be concluded unsuccessfully.

The Jews living in the region displayed deep sympathy for the widow; at no time was her house empty of wailing mourners or people offering advice. Never in living memory had so many Jews been seen together in L. Extremely angered at the murder of their brother, they had spared neither trouble nor expense in order to track down the culprit. Indeed, it is known that one of them, who generally went by the name of Joel the Shark, had offered one of his clients, who owed him several hundred thalers and whom he considered a particularly cunning fellow, to waive the entire debt if he would help him to ensure Mergel's arrest; for there was a general belief among the Jews that the murderer had escaped only with the help of good friends and was probably still hiding in the district. When all this proved of no avail, however, and the court enquiry was declared at an end, a group of the most respected Israelites appeared at the manor house next morning in order to make an offer to the squire. The object of their business was the beech-tree under which Aaron's staff had been found and where the murder had probably been committed.—'Do you want to fell the tree? Now that it's in full leaf?' asked the squire.—'No, Your Honour, it must remain standing in summer and winter, as long as there is a twig left on it.'—'But,

if I have the wood cut down it will harm any new growth.'—
'We don't want to buy it at the normal price,' was the reply.
They offered him two hundred thalers. The business was concluded and all the foresters were given strict orders that the
Jew's beech was on no account to be harmed.—Soon afterwards
some sixty Jews, led by their rabbi, were seen one evening walking to Brede Wood, all of them silent and with downcast eyes.—
They remained in the wood for more than an hour and then
returned just as gravely and solemnly, walking through the village as far as Zeller Meadow, where they separated, each going
his own way. Next morning an inscription cut in the beech-tree
with an axe could be seen:

אם תעבור במקום הזה יפגע בך כאשר אתה עשית לי

And where was Friedrich? Far away, without any doubt, far
enough that he need not fear any more the short arm of such an
ineffective police force. He had vanished completely and was
soon forgotten. His Uncle Simon seldom spoke of him, and then
critically; the Jew's wife sought consolation at last and took
another husband. Only poor Margreth remained unconsoled.

About half a year later the squire was reading some letters
which he had just received, in the presence of the clerk.—
'Strange, strange!' he said. 'Just imagine, Kapp, Mergel might
be innocent of the murder. Listen to what the President of the
Court at P. has just written to me: "le vrai n'est pas toujours
vraisemblable;* I have often had that experience in my calling,
and not least now. D'you know, it may be that your faithful
friend Friedrich Mergel no more killed the Jew than you or I
did? Unfortunately there is no proof, but it is highly probable.
One of the members of the Schlemming band (most of whom,
by the way, we now have behind bars), known by the name of
Ragman Moses, said in his last interrogation that he regretted
nothing so much as having murdered a brother Jew, whom he
had killed in the forest, and had only found six coppers on him
after all. Unfortunately, the interrogation was broken off at midday and, while we were having lunch, the damned dog of a Jew
hanged himself with his own garter. What do you say to that?
Aaron is, of course, a common enough name and so forth."—
What do you say to that?' repeated the squire; 'and why should

that stupid young fellow run off?'—The clerk of the court pondered. 'Well, perhaps because of the timber theft that we were investigating just at that time. Isn't there a saying: "A wicked man runs from his own shadow"? Mergel's conscience was guilty enough without that, in any case.'

With that conclusion, the squire and his clerk put their minds at rest. Friedrich was gone, vanished, and—Johannes Niemand, poor, insignificant Johannes, vanished with him the same day.

A long, long time had passed—twenty-eight years, almost half a lifetime; the squire had meantime grown old and grey, his good-humoured assistant, Kapp, was long since dead and buried. Men, beasts, and plants had come into the world, reached maturity, and passed away; only the manor house still looked down, grey and imposing as ever, upon the huts of the village which, like hectic old folk, always seemed about to fall down and yet remained standing. It was Christmas Eve, the 24th of December 1788. The forest tracks were filled deep with snow, a good twelve feet high, and the keen frosty air had coated the window panes of the heated rooms with ice. It was almost midnight, yet everywhere flickered dim lights from among the dunes of snow, and in every house the people were kneeling, waiting to welcome the beginning of the holy feast of Christmas with prayer, as is the custom in Catholic regions or as, at least, was usual in those times. Then, from Brede Hill, a figure moved slowly down towards the village; the wanderer seemed either very tired or ill, for he was groaning deeply and dragging himself painfully through the snow.

Half-way down the hill he came to a halt, leaning upon his crutch and staring unerringly at the dots of light. Everywhere was so quiet, so cold and dead; one could not help thinking of will-o'-the wisps in a churchyard. Now the clock struck twelve in the tower; the last stroke ebbed away slowly and, in the next house, a gentle singing began and then, swelling louder from house to house, spread throughout the whole village:

> A little holy child
> Is born to us today,
> Born of a virgin mild
> That all rejoice and pray;

And were the child not born,
Then all would be forlorn:
Salvation's ours to tell.
O dearest Jesus mine,
Born as man divine,
Redeem us all from hell!

The man on the hill had fallen to his knees and, in a trembling voice, was trying to join in the singing; but only a loud sobbing was heard and hot, heavy tears fell upon the snow. The second verse began; he started to pray in a low voice; then the third and fourth verses were sung. At last the hymn ended and the lights in the houses began to move. The man dragged himself to his feet and crept slowly down into the village. Panting for breath, he passed several of the houses, then he came to a halt at one house and knocked gently.

'What was that?' said a woman's voice inside the house; 'The door is rattling, but there's no wind blowing.'—He knocked harder: 'For God's sake, let me in—a half-frozen man escaped from Turkish slavery.'—In the kitchen, there was the sound of whispering. 'Go to the inn!' called another voice, 'Five houses farther on!'—'In God's name, let me in! I've no money.' After some hesitation, the door was opened and a man held out a lantern into the darkness. 'Come in,' he said; 'I doubt that you'll cut our throats.'

In the kitchen, as well as the man, were a middle-aged woman, an old grandmother, and five children. The entire company crowded around the stranger and stared at him with shy curiosity. A pitiful figure, indeed! His neck crooked, his back bent, his whole body broken and feeble; long, snow-white hair hung about his face, which bore the twisted expression of long suffering. Without a word, the woman went to the fireplace and laid some fresh twigs upon the fire.—'We can't give you a bed,' she said, 'but I'll put down some clean straw for you here; that will have to do.'—'God bless you!' replied the stranger; 'I'm used to a lot worse.'—The homecomer was recognized as Johannes Niemand, and he himself confirmed that he was the same who had once fled with Friedrich Mergel.

Next day the whole village was talking of the adventures of

the man who had vanished so long ago. Everyone was eager to see the man from Turkey, and people were almost surprised that he still looked like other men. The young people of the village did not remember him, of course, but the old folk still recognized his features easily, pitifully disfigured though he was.

'Johannes, Johannes, how grey you've grown,' said one old woman. 'And how did you come by that crooked neck?'—'From carrying wood and water as a slave,' he replied.—'And what has become of Mergel? I suppose you escaped together?'—'Yes, of course; but I don't know where he is; we lost each other. Pray for him when you think of him,' he added, 'he'll have need of your prayers.'

They asked him why Friedrich had run away, since he had not murdered the Jew after all. 'No?' said Johannes, and listened intently as they told him what the squire had studiously repeated everywhere, in order to remove the stain from Mergel's name.— 'So, 'twas all for nothing,' he murmured thoughtfully, 'so much suffering for nothing!' He sighed deeply and now, in his turn, asked them a great many questions. Simon was long since dead, though he had been absolutely penniless before he died—thanks to lawsuits and bad debtors whom he had not dared to take to law because, it was said, matters were not above board between him and them. Towards the end he had lived by begging and died on a bed of straw in another man's barn. Margreth had lived longer, but her wits had been completely addled. The people of the village had soon grown tired of helping her, for she let everything go to waste that they gave her—as it is usual for people to abandon those who are least able to help themselves, those on whom the support given to them has no lasting effect and who remain for ever in need of help. Yet she had not truly suffered need; the squire's family took good care of her, sent meals to her each day and also ensured that she received a doctor's care when her miserable condition turned to total emaciation. Her house was now occupied by the son of the former swineherd who had so much admired Friedrich's watch that fateful evening.—'All gone, all dead!' sighed Johannes.

That evening, after darkness had set in and the moon was shining, he was seen in the churchyard limping about in the snow. He did not pray at any of the graves, nor did he approach close to any, but seemed to stare at some of them from a distance. That was how the forester Brandis found him—the son of the murdered man—who had been sent by the squire to bring him to the manor house.

As he entered the living-room, Johannes looked shyly around him as if blinded by the light; then at the squire, who was sitting in his armchair, much shrunken, but with clear eyes and wearing his red cap upon his head just as twenty-eight years before; beside him was his wife; she, too, had grown old, very old.

'Now then, Johannes,' said the squire, 'tell me all about your adventures without leaving anything out. Well,' he said, examining him closely through his eye-glass, 'the Turks must have treated you unmercifully!'—Johannes began his tale: how Mergel had called him away from the fireplace at night and told him he must flee with him.—'But, why did the foolish fellow run away after all? You know that he was innocent?'—Johannes looked down at the floor: 'I don't really know; I think it had to do with the timber thieves. Simon had business of all kinds; no one told me anything about it, but I don't believe that everything was as it should be.'—'What did Friedrich say to you?'—'Nothing, except that we had to run away, and that they were after us. And so we fled as far as Heerse; it was still dark and we hid behind the great cross in the churchyard to wait until it grew a bit lighter, because we were worried about the quarries at Zeller Meadow; and after we had been sitting there a while, we suddenly heard a sound of stamping and snorting above us, and we saw long streaks of fire in the sky just above the Heerse church tower. We leapt up and ran in God's name as fast as our legs would carry us, straight on, and when dawn broke, we were indeed on the right way to P.'

Johannes still seemed to shudder at the memory, and the squire thought of Kapp, now gone, and his adventure at Heerse Cliff. 'A strange thing!' he laughed, 'you were so near each other! But go on.'—And Johannes told him how they had gone through P. and across the border without incident. From then on, they had begged their way, as wandering journeymen, as far as Freiburg in Breisgau. 'I had my bread-bag with me,' he said, 'and Friedrich had a small bundle, and so people believed us.' —In Freiburg they had been recruited by the Austrians; the military had not wanted to take him, but Friedrich had insisted. And so he had joined the troop. 'We remained in Freiburg through the winter,' he went on, 'and things went fairly well for us; for me too, for Friedrich often used to jog my memory and help me whenever I made a mistake. In the spring we had to march off to Hungary, and in autumn, the war against the Turks began. I can't say much about that, for I was captured in the very first skirmish and after that I was in Turkish slavery for twenty-six years!'—'God in heaven! How dreadful!' exclaimed Frau von S.—''Twas bad enough; the Turks treat us Christians no better than dogs; the worst thing was that my strength was failing because of the hard toil; and I was growing older but still had to work just as hard as years before.'

He was silent for a while. Then: 'Yes,' he resumed, 'it was more than human strength and patience could stand; I couldn't bear it any longer.—From there I came to a Dutch ship.'—'How did you get there?' asked the squire.—'They fished me out of the water, in the Bosphorus,' replied Johannes. The baron looked at him in surprise and raised a warning finger, but Johannes continued his story. Things had not gone much better for him on the ship. 'Scurvy broke out; anyone who was not badly ill had to work for two, and the rope's end ruled as sternly as the Turkish whip. At last', he concluded, 'we arrived in Holland, in Amsterdam, and they set me free, because I was not fit for anything; the merchant to whom the ship belonged was sorry for me and wanted to employ me as his doorkeeper. But,'—here he shook his head—'instead, I preferred to struggle home by begging.'—'Not the best of plans,' said the squire. Johannes gave a deep sigh. 'Master, I've had to spend my life among Turks and heretics; should I not at least be buried in a Catholic churchyard?'—The squire took out his purse. 'Here, Johannes, take this; go now and come again soon. You must tell me all this again in more detail; it was a little mixed-up today.—You must still be very tired?'—'Very tired,' replied Johannes; 'and', he said, pointing to his forehead, 'I sometimes have such strange thoughts; I can hardly say how it is with me.'—'I know,' said the baron, 'from the old days. Go now! The Hülsmeyers will surely take you in for the night; come back again tomorrow.'

Herr von S. had the deepest sympathy for the poor vagabond;

by the following day it had been decided where he should be lodged; he was to have a meal every day at the manor house, and clothing was also found for him.—'Master,' said Johannes, 'I can do some work, too; I can carve wooden spoons and you can employ me as a messenger.'—Herr von S. shook his head pityingly: 'That wouldn't be of much help.'—'Oh yes, Master, once I am under way—I shan't be quick, but I shall get there in the end; and I shan't think it beneath me, as you might imagine.'— 'Well,' said the baron doubtfully, 'would you like to try? Here's a letter to take to P. There's no great hurry.'

Next day Johannes moved into a small room in the house of a widow who lived in the village. He carved wooden spoons, ate at the manor house, and went on errands for the squire. All in all, things went fairly well for him; the squire's family was most kind, and Herr von S. would often talk at great length with him about Turkey, his service in the Austrian army, and life at sea. 'Johannes could tell a great deal,' he said to his wife, 'if he were not so simple-minded.'—'More deep than simple,' she replied; 'I fear he will lose his wits after all.'—'Heaven forbid!' said the baron; 'He has been a simpleton all his life; simple persons don't go mad.'

After a time, Johannes, who had gone on an errand, remained away far longer than usual. Frau von S. was extremely anxious about him and was on the point of sending out people to look for him when they heard him stalking up the stairs.—'You've been away a long time, Johannes,' she said; 'I thought you had lost your way in Brede Wood.'—'I went through the pine valley.'— 'That's a long way round; why didn't you go through Brede Wood?' He looked up at her gloomily. 'The people told me that the wood had been cut down and there were now so many paths running this way and that, I was afraid I wouldn't find my way out again. I am getting old and muddled,' he added slowly.— 'Didn't you see,' Frau von S. said later to her husband, 'how strange and wandering his eyes looked? I tell you, Ernst, it will come to a bad end.'

Meanwhile September was drawing near. The fields were bare, the leaves were beginning to fall, and many a hectic individual now felt the shears cut through his life-thread. Johannes, too, seemed to be suffering under the influence of the approaching equinox; people who saw him during these days said that he had looked noticeably distraught and had continually talked to himself in a quiet voice, which he did at other times too, though seldom. At last, he failed to come home one evening. People thought that the squire had sent him away on an errand; on the second day, too, he did not return; on the third day the widow became anxious. She went to the manor house and asked after him. 'God forbid,' said the squire; 'I don't know where he could be; call the huntsman, quick, and Wilhelm, the forester's son!— Even if the poor cripple has only fallen into a dry ditch,' he added anxiously, 'he won't be able to get out. Who knows, he might even have broken one of his crooked legs!—Take the dogs with you!' he called to the hunters as they left, 'And search the ditches, above all; and look in the quarries, too!' he added even louder.

Some hours later the huntsmen returned without having found any trace of him. Herr von S. was in a state of great anxiety: 'When I think that someone might be lying there like a stone, unable to help himself! But he might still be alive; a human being can go without food for three days.' He himself went with the searchers; they enquired at all the houses, blew their horns everywhere, shouted, urged on the dogs to search for him—all in vain!—A child had seen him sitting at the edge of Brede Wood, carving a spoon. 'But he cut it right in two,' said the little girl. That had been two days before. In the afternoon a further trace was found: again, it was a child who had noticed him on the other side of the wood, sitting in the bushes with his head resting on his knees, as if he were asleep. That was on the previous day. It seemed as if he had done nothing but roam the whole time around Brede Wood.

'If only the damned undergrowth weren't so thick! No one can get through,' grumbled the squire. They drove the dogs into the young plantation, blew their horns, hallooed and returned home at last in an ill temper after making sure that the dogs had searched the whole wood.—'Don't give up! don't give up!' begged Frau von S.; 'Better a few steps in vain than to miss something.' The baron was almost as afraid as his wife. In his anxiety he even went to Johannes's dwelling, although he was sure that he would not find him there. He had the widow unlock the door of

Johannes's room. The bed was unmade, just as he had left it; there hung his best coat, which the lady of the manor had had made for him out of her husband's old hunting coat; on the table were a bowl, six new wooden spoons, and a box. The squire opened the box; inside were five coppers, neatly wrapped in paper, and four silver waistcoat buttons; these the squire examined carefully. 'A souvenir from Mergel,' he murmured and went out, for the close, cramped little room was quite oppressive. The search continued until they were finally convinced that Johannes was no longer in the district, at least, not living. And so he had vanished a second time; would they find him again, people wondered—perhaps, years later, his bones in a dry ditch? There was little hope of finding him alive once more, and certainly not after twenty-eight years.

One morning, two weeks later, young Brandis was returning home through Brede Wood from an inspection of his territory. It was an unusually hot day for the time of year; the air was quivering, not a bird was singing, and only the ravens were croaking monotonously from the branches, holding their beaks open to the air. Brandis was worn out. One moment he would take off his cap, which was hot from the sun, the next, he would put it on again. It was all equally unbearable, and walking through the knee-high seedlings was hard going. Not a tree was to be seen all around him, save the Jew's beech, and he pushed his way towards it with all his strength, lying down dead-tired upon the shaded moss beneath it. The pleasant coolness spread through his limbs and he closed his eyes. 'Stinking toadstools!' he murmured, half asleep. There is a kind of very rank toadstool in this region which remains standing for only a few days and then falls into decay, spreading an intolerable smell. Brandis thought that he could detect some such unpleasant fellows nearby, and he turned over several times but had no desire to stand up; meanwhile his dog was leaping back and forth, scratching at the trunk of the tree and barking up into it. 'What have you found, Bello? A cat?' he murmured. Half-opening his eyes, he saw the Hebrew inscription; it had very much grown out but was still perfectly recognizable. He closed his eyes again; the dog went on barking and at last laid his cold muzzle on his master's face.—'Leave me alone! What's the matter with you?' As he spoke, lying there upon his back, he looked up into the tree; then he leapt to his feet with one bound and ran off like a madman into the undergrowth. Pale as death he arrived at the manor house: there was a man hanging in the Jew's beech, he said; he had seen the legs hanging just above his face.—'And you didn't cut him down, you idiot?' demanded the baron.—'Master,' panted Brandis, 'if Your Honour had been there, Your Honour would have seen that the man was no longer alive. I thought at first it was the toadstools!' Thereupon the squire summoned his servants in great haste and he himself set out with them.

They arrived beneath the beech-tree. 'I don't see anything,' said Herr von S.—'You must come over here, Master, to this spot!'—And indeed it was true: the squire recognized his own worn-out shoes. 'Heavens, it's Johannes!—Set the ladder up!— So—let him down! Careful, careful, don't drop him!—God, the worms are at him already! Open the noose and the scarf, all the same.' A broad scar came to view; the squire started back.—'My God!' he exclaimed; he bent over the body again, examined the scar very carefully, and remained silent for a while, shaken to the core. Then, turning to the foresters, he said: 'It is not right that the innocent should suffer for the guilty; tell everyone: this man'—and he pointed to the corpse—'was Friedrich Mergel.'— The body was buried in unconsecrated ground.

All this, in the main, actually happened in September of 1789. The Hebrew inscription on the tree means:

'If you approach this place, it will be done unto you as you have done unto me.'

ADALBERT STIFTER

Tourmaline

The tourmaline is dark in colour, and the events which I am going to relate here are very dark, too; they took place in times gone by, just like the events described in the first two tales.* In them we can see, as in a letter bearing sad news, how far a man can go when he dulls the light of his own reason and is no longer able to understand things, ignores the law of his conscience— which leads him unerringly along the way of righteousness— yields completely to the intensity of his pleasures and his pain, loses his step, and falls into circumstances which we are scarcely capable of unravelling.

Many years ago in the city of Vienna, there lived a curious person, just as there are different kinds of people in such large cities who occupy themselves with matters of various kinds. The person with whom we are here concerned was a man of about forty years of age, who lived on the fourth floor of a house on St Petersplatz. A passage, closed off by an iron grille, led to his apartment; a bell cord hung down by the grille and, when it was pulled, an elderly maidservant would appear, open the grille, and escort the visitor to her master. After passing through the grille, you continued along the passage; on the right was a door leading into the kitchen, which was the maid's domain and had only a single window looking out on to the passage; on the left were an iron railing running the whole length of the passage, and the open courtyard. At the end of the passage was the entrance to the apartment. Opening the brown door you entered an ante-room, which was rather dark; here were the large chests containing clothing. The room was also used for meals. The ante-room led into the master's room. This in fact consisted of a very large room and a small adjoining room. All the walls of the large room were completely covered with pictures of famous men. Of the original walls themselves not a piece was still to be seen, not even of the size of a hand. In order that he—or, on occasion, a friend, when one came to visit him—might look at those men whose pictures were close to or directly at floor level, he had had leather-upholstered divans of various heights constructed, fitted with casters. The lowest of these was a hand's breadth in height. You could roll it to any of the men at will, lie down upon it, and regard him. For those pictures higher up on the wall he had rolling step-ladders, their wheels covered with green baize; these ladders could be pushed to any point in the room and, from their steps, different points of observation could be reached. In fact, everything in the room was on rollers, so that it could easily be moved from one point to another in order that the observer should not become confused when looking at the pictures. As far as the fame of the men portrayed was concerned, it was a matter of indifference to the master what sort of occupation they had followed and in what manner they had achieved fame, for almost all possibilities were represented here.

The room also contained a very large grand piano which he was fond of playing, its music-stand heaped with sheets of music. On the shelves there were two violins in cases, which he also used to play. On a table lay a box with two flutes which he would practise on for his own pleasure and in order to perfect his skill. An easel stood by one of the windows together with a box of artist's colours, with which he painted in oil. In the adjoining room was a large writing-desk with many papers lying upon it; here he used to compose poetry and write stories; beside the desk stood a bookshelf, in case he might wish to take down a book and pass the time pleasantly in reading. In the same room stood his bed and, at the far end of the room, was a table at which he used to work with pasteboard, making shelves, boxes, screens, and other handicraft articles.

This man was known to the other people in the house as 'the pensioner'; most people, however, did not know whether he had been given the name because he lived on a pension, or because he worked in a pensions office. But the second supposition could not be correct, for if it had been he would have had to go out to work at definite times of day; as it was, he used to remain at home at varying hours and often the whole day, occupied with the many different activities which he had imposed upon himself. Apart from this, he used to go to the coffee-house to watch the chess-players or walk around in the town observing the various things to be seen there, or again he would join a group at the inn, where some friends of his would meet regularly on certain days of the week. It was therefore clear that he must receive a small pension on which he was able to live in this way.

The man had a most beautiful wife; she was about thirty years old and had borne him a child—a little girl. The wife lived in a room adjoining her husband's; this was as large as her husband's and also had a small room next to it. From the husband's room you could walk into the wife's, but you could also reach the room via a small secret passage from the ante-room, since the four rooms composing the apartment lay in a single line at right angles to the outer corridor. This small passage was highly convenient, for, whenever the husband had friends visiting him, the wife could go into the ante-room without embarrassment or without disturbing the men, and from there pass into the kitchen.

The wife's rooms were furnished to her own taste. The windows of the larger room were hung with dark curtains; there were soft armchairs covered in the same material; there was a large, elegant table, which was always kept free of dust and highly polished, and on the table lay some books or drawings or, on occasion, some other objects. On the window-piers hung mirrors, with narrow tables beneath them; on these stood various beautiful items of silver or porcelain. At one window was a small, most elegant work-table, with beautiful linen, delicate textiles, and other work materials upon it, and in front of the table stood a small chair which fitted into the window niche. Near the second window was an embroidery frame and a chair identical with the first, whilst in front of the narrow sill of the third window stood the writing-desk with its green top, on which lay the writing-case, inkwell, and pens, neatly arranged. Around the desk, in a sort of semicircle, were a number of tall, dark green plants, some bearing broad leaves. The large wall-clock had no chime and ticked so quietly that it could hardly be heard. At the far end of the room was a dresser with glasses in it; it was provided with silk curtains, so that the wife was able to place objects in the compartments and draw the curtains in front of them.

The second, smaller room was fitted out with snow-white

curtains hanging in voluminous folds; near the window stood a table—not for displaying objects of beauty, but for household purposes. In addition there were a large divan and various arm-chairs and stools. The wife's bed, which was white and was concealed by white curtains, stood at the back of the room; close to it was a small bedside table on which were a lamp, a bell, some books, a tinder-box, and some other things. Nearby stood a gilded angel on a pedestal, his wings folded together around his shoulders; he was supporting himself with one hand, the other hand gently stretched out and holding with its fingers the tip of a white curtain which spread outwards and downwards in the form of a tent. On a table beneath this tent was an elegant basket in which lay a white cradle, and in the cradle was the couple's child, the little girl. Often they would stand beside her, looking at her tiny red lips, rosy cheeks, and her little eyes that were tightly closed. And finally there was a large, very beauti-fully painted picture, representing the Blessed Mother and Child, and draped in folds of dark velvet.

The wife was mistress of her own rooms; she bought every-thing that the child needed, and occupied herself by reading, embroidering, managing her household, and so forth. Since she did not maintain a great deal of contact with the outer world, she seldom received visits from other women.

At the time that they were living in St Petersplatz there was another man in Vienna who was very much the talk of the town. He was an actor, a most accomplished performer, and the darl-ing of society in his day. Nowadays many an old man who knew him when he was at his peak goes into raptures when he speaks of him and tells how he used to interpret and play this role or that; such recollections generally conclude with the comment that artists of his calibre do not exist any more and that nothing to be seen in modern times can possibly compare with what the previous generation has seen. Many of us who are now getting old may have known this actor and seen some of his perform-ances, but it is probable that we did not see him at the height of his fame but only after this had already begun to decline, although his brilliance endured for a long time, almost until his old age. This man—Dall was his name—was outstanding in tragic roles, though he also played in other forms of drama—for example, in comedies—with unusual success. Stories are still told of isolated moments during which the audience were positively enthralled, filled with the utmost enthusiasm or dread, so much so that they felt themselves not in the theatre but faced with reality, fearfully awaiting the further course of events. Whenever he played the role of a high-ranking personage, it is said, his performances revealed such dignity and majesty that, since that time, nothing else approaching them has ever been seen upon the stage. A man who was a perfect connoisseur of the theatre once said that Dall did not prepare himself for his performances by pondering them in an abstract manner, or by studying and rehearsing; instead, he would immerse himself in his role, when it matched his own nature, relying upon his own personality, which told him, at the right moment, what he had to do; thus he did not *play* his roles—the performance revealed in them was truly reality. This explains why, when he unconditionally yielded to the situation, he did things which surprised not only himself but also his audience and brought him enormous success. It also explains the fact that, whenever he was unable to project himself into a particular role, he was totally incapable of playing it at all, even badly. For this reason he never accepted such roles and could not be moved to do so by any words of persuasion whatsoever, nor by any arguments, no matter how insistent.

The foregoing also explains Dall's character and mode of living outside the theatre. Extremely good-looking, he was lithe and graceful in his movements, and the way in which he moved was the expression of his quick, lively intellect, which clearly revealed itself in his carriage. He was of a cheerful disposition, took his pleasures where he found them, and was fond of company; no one seeing him sitting before a glass of good wine chatting with a group of friends could possibly believe that this was the same man who, in his splendid performances, could arouse in our souls feelings of the deepest shock, of fear and terror, of joy and delight. But, for the very reason that he was exactly what he represented in his role and found the most appropriate expression for it in his body—for this reason, the feelings which arose in his ardent spirit revealed themselves vividly in his outward appearance, either in his movements, his facial expression, or his voice, carrying all before him. That was why he was the darling of society: he made people come alive and aroused their emotions. He moved in many different levels of society, and from all these he learned to behave in a free and unconcerned manner, but he was in no way a thrall to any of them: just as he allowed himself to be guided by his spirit when on the stage, so did his spirit lead him among people, so that he might live and feel as they did; so, too, did it lead him to Nature, so that he might observe and be conscious of Her; on the other hand, however, it lured him away from people once more when they were unable to provide him with inspiration, and it lured him away from Nature too, when Her gentle voice ceased to excite him and he sought after more dramatic impressions and more profound variety. Thus he lived according to circumstances and abandoned them again, as he wished.

Dall was acquainted with the pensioner, and one could say that in no other point did he display such constancy as in this relationship. No matter where he had just been, he was very fond of going to St Petersplatz; there he would climb the four steps, ring the bell at the iron grille, have the elderly maid open the door to him, and walk through the ante-room into the pensioner's gallery of heroes. There he would sit and chat with the pensioner about the various activities which the latter favoured. Perhaps, indeed, he was so fond of the pensioner's company for the very reason that it revealed so many different facets. It was the arts, above all, which appealed to Dall in all their different forms. And so they would discuss the pensioner's verses; or he would play one of his two violins, or his flute, or play some piece or other upon the grand piano; or they would sit at his easel and discuss the colours of a picture or the lines of a drawing—for in the latter art Dall was highly experienced and was himself a notable artist. And when it came to the pensioner's pasteboard objects, he would advise him on the length and breadth and proportions to be observed.

As for the portraits of famous men affixed to the walls, he would lie down on the lowest divan and proceed to study the bottom row of pictures. The pensioner would then have to tell him all he knew about each of them and, whenever it happened that neither of them knew much about any particular man, save that he was famous, they would take down books and search through them until they found a satisfactory answer. Dall would lie down upon one of the higher divans, then sit upon the next higher one, then he would stand up, and finally he would stand upon one step or another of the ladder. In this way he learned to appreciate the comfort of such divans, so that the pensioner had to have a large armchair with casters made for him, with an upholstered back and comfortable armrests.

Dall was fond of sitting in this armchair whenever he came, and they would chat away pleasantly.

In this way, a considerable time went by.

In the course of time Dall began a love affair with the pensioner's wife. This went on for some while until, at last, the wife became afraid and confessed everything to her husband.

Dall must have got to know of this, or he must have deduced from the wife's behaviour that she would inform her husband of her affair with his friend: he did not come to the apartment any more, although until recently he had visited St Petersplatz more often than he had been accustomed to do in the early days of their friendship.

The pensioner was beside himself with rage; his first thought was to run to Dall's home, to hurl accusations at him, to murder him; but the actor was not to be found in his own home, nor was he appearing at the theatre just at that time, and no one knew where he was. The pensioner made every effort to find Dall; he went to Dall's home every day at various times but never found him there, and people said that Dall had gone away for a short recreational journey. This was known to people of all classes of society in the city; the artist, they said, would soon return to give pleasure to everyone with his brilliant acting ability. The pensioner, however, did not allow himself to be put off, but continued his search for Dall. He looked for him in every part of the city, in public places, in the church, in places of amusement, and in the parks, and he began once again to look for him at his home. But the actor was not to be found anywhere.

The pensioner carried on in this way for some considerable time; then, suddenly, he became very calm. His friends noticed that the mood of restlessness which had recently affected him had disappeared; he was now quiet and thoughtful. He went to his wife and said: it was inevitable that she should have fallen victim to Dall's charms; why had he ever brought Dall to his home!—she had given him her heart, just as he stole the hearts of thousands in one single evening at the theatre.

Even to friends who had heard of the matter in a general way, from vague rumours coursing around the city, he expressed himself either intentionally or unconsciously in such a fashion that they must have suspected in him a mood such as that just described.

Dall, too, though far away from the city, must have heard how matters stood, and he must have known that the pensioner was now his usual quiet self; for, as nothing particular happened and matters seemed to be taking their normal course, Dall returned to the city and was once again to be seen upon the stage.

Then, one day, the pensioner's wife vanished: she had gone out, just as she usually did—and had not come back.

The pensioner had waited, indeed he had waited until late at night; when she did not return, however, he thought that she might have met with an accident; he therefore drove in a hired carriage to all his friends and acquaintances and asked whether they had seen his wife. But no one was able to give him any information. The following day he reported the matter to the authorities, requesting the assistance of various bureaux, whilst he himself made enquiries about all homeless persons or persons found dead. But the authorities could not trace her; she was not among those found dead, nor among those who proved to be homeless.

Then the pensioner thought that Dall might have taken his wife somewhere and was keeping her hidden there. Going to Dall's home, he demanded that the actor should tell him where his wife was and give her back to him. Dall replied he was sorry, but he knew nothing about the pensioner's wife, he had not seen her at all since his last visit to the apartment in St Petersplatz; he himself did not go out a great deal, he said, only to the theatre and back again.

The pensioner returned home.

Some time later he appeared once again at Dall's home, fell on his knees before him, clasping his hands in supplication, and begged the actor to give him back his wife. Once more Dall replied that he knew nothing at all of the pensioner's wife; it was not at his wish that she had gone away, he said; he did not know where she was and therefore could not give her back.

The pensioner went away again.

A few days later he returned once more, knelt down as before and, his hands clasped together, begged Dall to give him back his wife. Dall swore that he did not know where the woman was and that he could not give her back.

The pensioner returned yet again a few days later, behaved as before, and met with the same reply. Thereafter he did not come any more. He dismissed the maid; then he lifted the little child from her bed, took her on his arm, left his dwelling, which he locked behind him, and went away.

Afterwards, whenever friends came to visit him, they were informed by the other people in the house that the pensioner was no longer there and that he must have gone away on a journey; for, they said, he had taken the child with him and had been wearing a coat, although it was summer.

And so the apartment on the fourth floor of the house on St Petersplatz was now empty and the iron grille in the corridor was locked.

Half-a-year passed and the pensioner had still not returned; nor had the rent for the apartment been paid, and so the owner of the house reported the matter to the authorities. A number of the pensioner's friends were summoned and asked whether they knew his whereabouts, but no one knew anything. In time, all those friends were summoned who were known to have been in contact with the pensioner, but not one of them was able to give any information. Acting on the court's advice and, besides, being moved by feelings of kindness towards the pensioner, the owner decided to wait a while and see whether the pensioner would not return of his own will. According to the testimony of the other tenants and the concierge, the pensioner had not had anything whatsoever removed from his apartment; indeed, no one could remember clearly whether or not he had been carrying a bag with him when he left. It was a known fact that there were many valuable objects in the apartment; it was therefore likely that he had merely gone away on a journey, and that something or other had happened to him which had prevented him from returning or sending news of himself, and that he would certainly come back again.

After two years had passed, however, and the pensioner still had not returned or sent any news of himself, an official notice was published in the newspapers ordering him to give a sign of life and to state whether he intended to keep his apartment in St Petersplatz and pay the rent arrears accordingly. If no news was heard of him within a given period, the notice ran, it would be assumed that he had given up the apartment; his possessions would be sold by auction, the arrears would be paid from the proceeds, and any money remaining would be retained for him by the court.

But the period of grace passed by; the pensioner had not returned, nor had any news of him arrived, nor did anyone appear in order to take charge of the apartment.

And so, by order of the court, the apartment was opened.

A locksmith had to be called to open the lock of the iron grille. No elderly maid came to bring the visitors to the ante-room and into the pensioner's room; the kitchen window was no longer clean and shining, but was covered with dust and draped with cobwebs. In the kitchen, everything was as usual; the maid had cleaned every single utensil before she left and put it in its accustomed place; but everything was covered with dust, the wooden tubs had fallen to pieces, and the iron hoops lay around them. The large chests in the ante-room were full of clothes, and a swarm of moths flew up out of the woollens, though the other clothes were undamaged. The wife's clothes, including a number of beautiful silk dresses, were also hanging there. Other chests contained cutlery and the silverware.

When the master's room was opened, everything was just as it had been before. The grand piano stood open, the two violins were also there and the rack for the flutes—save that one flute was missing. A picture, just begun, stood upon the easel, some books and manuscripts lay upon the writing-desk, and the bed was covered with an elegant quilt. The pictures of famous men were likewise coated with dust and had turned yellow in the stuffy air of the room. The divans were standing there, too, but had not been moved around for a long time. In the middle of the room was the large armchair which had been made for Dall.

In the wife's rooms nothing whatsoever had been changed; every piece of furniture was in its accustomed place and the objects were still upon them; but the minor changes which had taken place revealed how different things now were. The heavy curtains, which had always swayed slightly when the windows were open, now hung motionless; the flowers and plants were now shrivelled wisps of brown; the clock which used to tick so quietly now ticked no longer, for the pendulum did not stir, and the clock indicated immutably the same time of day. The linen and other items of handiwork still lay upon the tables, of course, but showed no signs of having been touched, and mourned under a veil of dust. The white curtains in the adjoining room hung down in a multitude of folds, but these were filled with fine dust which trickled out at the slightest touch; the Holy Mother looked down from her portrait, but the red drapery was now grey; the gilded angel still held the tip of the linen tent, but a layer of dust lay upon the linen, and below this was the cradle —in which the child's rosy face was no longer to be seen.

All these items were taken into court custody and carefully recorded in a register. Then they were all stored in two rooms so that they could be checked and guarded more easily; the apartment was then closed once again and officially sealed.

Among the objects found in the apartment, there was nothing which gave any indication of the pensioner's whereabouts or his personal circumstances. Nor was any money found, and it was assumed that he had taken all available cash with him when he left.

A day was fixed for the auction and, when it was over, part of the proceeds was paid to the owner of the house to cover the rent arrears and interest due; the rest of the money was retained for the pensioner by the court. The pictures of famous men were all stripped from the walls. The apartment on the fourth floor of the house in St Petersplatz remained empty, and a notice affixed to the gate of the house announced that the apartment was to let.

In Vienna, the affair had caused a great stir; everyone had—more or less—an idea of the true circumstances and talked about it for a considerable time. Once, a rumour went about that the pensioner was in the Bohemian Forest. There, it was said, he lived in a cave where he kept his daughter hidden; he would leave the cave during the day in order to earn his living, and return in the evening. But then other events took place, as is typical of a great city, where one topic gives way to another; people found other things to talk about and, within a short time, the pensioner and his story were forgotten.

A number of years had passed since the events described above. The following narrative is from a lady friend of mine who knew the actor very well and had learned from his friends the details of the relationship between him and the pensioner's family. She herself had been too young at the time these events had taken place to be much affected by them.

At this point, we shall allow her to tell the story in her own words:

Quite a long time ago, she said, when I had been married only a few years, we lived in a very pleasant, attractive apartment in the suburbs. For my husband, it was only a short way to the city where he went about his official business every day; I myself did not go there very often, having a lot of work to do in my household—in those days my small children kept me very busy, for it gave me a great deal of pleasure to take care of them. Whenever I did have to go to the city, it was only a short walk when the weather was fine, and when the weather was bad, a carriage did not cost very much, after all. For our children, however, the apartment, spacious and airy as it was, and the large garden offered many advantages; and once, when my husband was considering giving up the apartment, a well-known physician, a friend of my husband's, urgently advised him not to do so. Some of the windows of the apartment looked out on to the garden, across other gardens, and, finally, the nearby vine-yards and wooded slopes of the surrounding region. It was here that I spent most of my time with the children. From the front windows you could look out on to the main street of the sub-urbs, straight and wide and splendid, filled with pleasant activity but not too hectic, with shops and stalls, carriages driving up and down, and people walking along it. Our drawing-room was on this side of the apartment, along with another pleasant room and my husband's study. The distance to the city and to the country was the same, and so short that we did not have very far to go.

One very beautiful, mild morning—I think it was about the beginning of spring—when my husband was already in the city and the children at school, I was tempted by the heady air to open the windows in order to ventilate the apartment, taking the opportunity—as is always the case—to do a little dusting, tidy up, and so on. We liked to hear the church bell at the hospital calling people to mass, and I often went across to pray there when I happened to be dressed for church. The sounds of the bell were just ringing through the air when I chanced to be looking out of the window of the loveliest room and shaking out a duster. But apart from the ringing of the bell, something else made an impression on me, something which prompted me to remain at the window a little longer: looking down into the street to see what sort of people were walking by, I noticed an odd couple. A man, rather elderly, judging from the back view which he presented to me, wearing a thin, yellow flannel jacket, pale blue trousers, large shoes, and a small round cap was walking down the street; he was leading a little girl who was dressed as oddly as he was—wearing a brown cape which lay over her shoulders almost like a toga. The girl's head, however, was so large that it would give anyone a dreadful shock to see it, and you could not take your eyes from it. They were both walking fairly quickly, but in such an awkward, clumsy fashion that it was obvious they were not familiar with Vienna and unused to getting around like ordinary people. But despite all his awkwardness and clumsiness, the man took every possible care to guide the girl, to lead her out of the way of the carriages driving past, and ensure that she did not bump into other people. They were just turning on to the path which led to the little church from which the bell was ringing.

My curiosity was aroused; thinking that perhaps the man was taking the girl to mass, I decided to go there too, and say my prayers and, at the same time, I hoped, I would be able to learn more about them or observe them. I dressed quickly, wound a scarf around my neck, put on my hat, and went out. I turned into the narrow lane which led from the main street, walked around the corner of the Army Apothecaries' College, and continued towards the little church, for I had seen them going in that direction; but there was no sign of them. Walking down the lane, I went through the arch at its far end, turned at the corner of the house, and strolled to the church, but could not see them anywhere. Nor did I see them in the church itself, where only a few people were present. I now carried out my devotions as usual, kneeling deep in prayer; then, when mass was over and I was preparing to leave, I looked around me once more, thinking to offer them help if they should need it. But I had been mistaken, they really were not in the church, and so I set off home again.

A considerable time passed after this incident, and I had long forgotten about it when, one beautiful evening, I was returning with my husband from the city. We had been to the Hofburg Theatre and, as it was such a lovely, pleasant evening, we accepted the invitation of a friend who had been to the theatre with us, and spent some time with him and his family before going home. As usual, we talked about the play, arguing about it from all angles; refreshments were served, and it was midnight before we set off home. Our friend offered to lend us his carriage, but we refused with thanks, saying that it would be a pity to ride in a carriage on such a beautiful night, dashing through the open landscape between the city and the suburbs instead of strolling through it at leisure and enjoying its free and clear beauty. Our friends did not remonstrate further and so we set off on foot.

As we walked out through the gate, putting the city behind us, the wide meadow with its many trees lay spread out in front, for it was a truly beautiful moonlit night. Over the broad panorama of the suburbs lay a vast sky, as if cast from a single jewel; not one tiny cloud was to be seen and, high above, the round moon poured forth its light. Strolling past the row of trees that lined the path, we met various people walking alone and several couples, as well. The night air was scented, almost like that in southern climes, and we walked across the meadow and back again a second time, so that at last we were almost the only people there. As we went past the rows of houses in the suburb without meeting anyone else, we noticed that we were not the only persons attracted by this lovely moonlit night, but that the moonbeams had stirred the heart of someone else, too; through the pervading silence, broken only by the sound of our footsteps and the distant song of a nightingale, we heard a curious melody played upon a flute. The music came to us faintly at first, then, as we walked on, it became louder. For a little while we stood still, listening. If it had been music of an ordinary kind, it is likely we would soon have continued on our way again, for it is not unusual in our city to hear music from some house or other, even late at night; but this flute music was so strange that we remained standing somewhat longer. The music was not played skilfully, nor was it botched, either—but what attracted our attention was, that it was different from everything usually termed music and from what we learn as such. The theme was not any melody known to us; probably the musician was simply expressing his own thoughts; and even if they were not his own, still he put so much of himself into his music that they might well be considered his own. The most fascinating thing about it was that, when he had commenced a phrase, tempting the listener's ear to follow him, something else always came instead—something different from what you had expected and what you had a right to expect, so that you always had to start again from the beginning and accompany him—finally revealing a state of confusion that could almost be termed madness. And yet, despite its lack of coherence, there was a mood of sadness, of lament, even something alien in this playing, as if the musician was trying, by unskilled means, to tell the story of his sorrow. It was almost touching.

'Strange thing,' my husband said; 'he seems to have learned to play the flute in an unusual fashion; he begins correctly but doesn't continue in the same way, he plays too quickly, he can't control his breathing—he breathes too fast and then breaks off in mid-air; and yet, his playing has a sort of feeling about it.'

We could not ascertain where the music was coming from. We almost believed that it came from the old Perron house, which was close by; but the house was due to be pulled down, hardly anyone lived in it any more and the music did not sound as if it was coming from an upper window.

After standing there for a short while, we continued on our

way; the strange music faded away behind us until at last we could not hear it at all. Arriving home, we went to bed, thus joining our children, who had already enjoyed more than half their refreshing sleep.

Following this incident, some time passed once again.

Anyone who has been living any length of time in our city will remember the old Perron house; and anyone who has known Vienna for the last fifteen or twenty years will know that the city is changing constantly, and that, despite its age, it is a new city; for the houses are always being renovated in the latest style for residential purposes; ancient, immutable monuments such as St Stephan's Church are too few to be able to impart an overall, characteristic appearance to the city, so that it always seems to be a city of yesterday. The old Perron house stood on the main street of the suburb where we lived, and was not very far at all from our apartment. Furthermore, the house possessed one characteristic with which present-day young residents of the capital are no longer familiar: basement apartments. The windows of such apartments usually looked out directly on to the cobblestones of the street; they were not very large, and were fitted with strong iron bars behind which there was usually a sturdy iron grille as well; if the tenant did not care much about cleanliness, the grille was generally covered with a coating of dried street-mud, giving it a dismal aspect. Moreover, the Perron house was in any case already very old, of gloomy appearance, and bearing adornments which dated back to many years before. Only the narrow side of the house adjoined the street; the side with the larger rooms in it directly bordered a garden. The house had a small gate painted a dark red colour which was now almost black, and studded with a large number of metal nails— though the metal was no longer recognizable because the broad heads of the nails were covered in black. Next to the gate there was a larger door—the entrance—but this had not been used since time immemorial; it was locked, was completely covered with mud and dust, and was secured by two crossbars fitted to the wall with iron clamps.

We had a friend at that time—who has remained our friend ever since—Professor Andorf. He was unmarried, a cheerful, friendly man, intellectually accomplished, warm-hearted and sympathetic, capable of appreciating everything good and beautiful. He frequently came to visit us; together with my husband, he was a member of various learned societies: there, it often happened that someone would read a piece of literature aloud, or they would play music or make pleasant conversation on a variety of topics. Professor Andorf lived in the Perron house; his apartment did not overlook the street, but the courtyard. He had deliberately chosen this apartment because it was very peaceful and thus suitable for his activities—reading, writing, or playing the piano; and although he was a cheery, sociable person, he had selected this particular apartment because it appealed to his artistic inclinations—which expressed themselves in reception rather than production—to observe the gradual process of dilapidation, downfall, and decay, to see how the birds and other creatures gradually took possession of the masonry from which the human tenants had withdrawn. Nothing in the world, he used to say, could fascinate him more than to stand at the window on a rainy day and watch the water dripping from the thistles, coltsfoot, and other plants that grew in the courtyard and to see the dampness creeping down into the ancient stonework.

One day my husband said to me, just as he had put on his coat and was about to leave for his office: 'This book belongs to Professor Andorf. It's a very special book, and it's important to me that it should not get into the wrong hands. Could you please wrap it in paper and seal it, and have someone reliable bring it to the Professor? I didn't have time to take care of it myself, that's why I am asking you.'

He placed the book on my sewing table. I said that I would do as he asked, whereupon he left the house to go to his office.

During the morning, however, it occurred to me that I had to go into the city in any case, and that I would be passing the Perron house; I thought I might take the opportunity of delivering the book, so that there would be no question of it falling into the wrong hands, and I decided to do so. When it was time to leave, I put on my coat and hat, placed the book in my bag, which I used to carry on my arm, and set off. Arriving at the Perron house, I pushed down the handle of the little red gate. I had never been in the house before. The handle turned easily and the little gate opened; but when I stood in the passage behind the gate, I looked round in vain for a room or apartment where I might find a concierge or the like who could give me information. I therefore went on down the passage, but without finding a stairway leading to the upper storeys, and at last came to the courtyard. This was paved with large stones, though some of them were broken. I also saw the plants described by Professor Andorf, which gave him such pleasure with the water dripping from them when it rained; I also saw the grass, rank and untouched, which was growing from every crack in the stones. In the walls surrounding the courtyard there were several gates which may have led to stables or coach-houses; but these gates were never opened—as was obvious from their shrivelled, weatherbeaten, and, in parts, dilapidated appearance, the tall grass growing beneath them, and their rusted hinges. Apart from these, there were three doors, each opening on to a stairway, but the doors had an unwelcoming look about them and the stairways appeared to be unused. Among the windows—some dirty or of a dull bluish sheen, others hidden behind wooden shutters—I saw several with clean panes and fitted with white curtains. These, I concluded, must belong to the Professor's apartment, but I had no idea how to get to it.

Just then I heard the sound of quiet footsteps behind me, and a man's voice, rather cultured and not unpleasant, said: 'Can I help you?'

Turning around, I saw a small man standing behind me, with sparse grey hair and an artless expression. He was not dressed in the true sense of the word: he was wearing only linen trousers and a jacket of the same material, slippers on his feet, and was bareheaded.

'I am looking for Professor Andorf,' I said.

'And what might be your business with Professor Andorf?' he asked; 'Perhaps I can give him something from you or deliver a message?—Professor Andorf is not at home.'

I looked at him more closely. He had a longish face and blue eyes; his features were in no way repulsive.

'I have a book to deliver,' I said, 'which may only be given to him personally. But, as he is not at home, the book can be delivered some other time; my husband can send it here.'

'I am the concierge here,' he said; 'you may leave the book

with me without fear, but if you prefer to give it him yourself, you will find the Professor here every morning until nine o'clock and also, as a rule, between four and six o'clock in the evening.'

I hesitated, uncertain what to do. I looked at him and he said: 'Madam, give me the book; I shall handle it carefully so as not to soil it; I shall not look inside it, but give it to Professor Andorf personally when he comes home.'

I looked at him once again and was struck by the frankness of his manner. Though he had said very little, he was very well-spoken in a way usually found among people of the upper classes; but there was something furtive about his blue eyes which flitted from side to side all the time. I did not have the heart to insult him by some sign of mistrust; opening my bag, I took out the book and gave it to him. I had not wrapped it in paper, having intended to give it to the Professor personally. He noticed this immediately and said, 'I shall wrap the book in paper and put it aside until the Professor comes and then give it to him.'

'Yes, please do,' I replied, after which I left the house.

Scarcely was I back in the street, however, when I began to have misgivings. About twenty paces away from the little red gate, a fruitseller used to sell her wares in front of the wall of the neighbouring house. She sat there every day when the weather was not too inclement, for on ordinary rainy days her goods were protected by a wide awning. I knew her very well and had often bought fruit from her for my children. Now I went to the woman's stall and asked whether she knew the concierge of the Perron house. She replied that she knew him; he was a respectable man who, whenever he went out, was sure to come home again before nightfall. There was nothing at all to be said against him and he lived a quiet, withdrawn life. What was more, she said, the Perron house was due to be renovated; there were not many people living in the house now, and certainly no 'better' people—except Professor Andorf, as I myself knew very well—and in a few years' time no one at all would wish to live there. If Herr Perron were not always away in foreign parts, he would know how matters stood with the house, that it did not bring him much money, and that he would be better advised to have it pulled down and build a new house on the spot.

I bought some fruit from the woman, put it in my bag, and

walked on into the city. But when my husband came home and we were sitting at lunch together, I began to feel pangs of conscience and told him what I had done; in his usual kind and gentle manner, however, he put my mind at rest, saying that I had acted perfectly correctly; he himself, if he had gone there and the same thing had happened, would have done exactly the same. The book would certainly come into the right hands. Nevertheless, the next time the Professor visited us after this incident I asked him whether he had received the book safely, for I had handed it over to the concierge of the Perron house.

'Yes, I received the book,' replied the Professor, 'but I thought you had had that old man bring it to me. I had no idea that we had a concierge in the Perron house and, if we do have one, he must be the quietest concierge in the whole world, for I have never seen or heard the slightest sign of him. I have a key with which I can open the gate whenever I return home so late that it is already closed. I am sorry I was not at home the day you came to the Perron house, by the way—I could have met you and showed you all its peculiarities.'

Following this incident, a long time passed once more until something else happened. One day Alfred, our eldest son, came home from school. He ran madly up the stairs, dashed into the living-room, and exclaimed: 'Mother, I didn't do him any harm, I didn't do him any harm!'

'What's the matter, Alfred?' I asked.

'You know the Perron house, Mother?' he said; 'well, I was walking along the wide pavement past the house when I saw a raven sitting on the paving stones. He wasn't afraid of me and didn't seem able to fly, but walked away from me as I came closer. I bent down and spoke to him, then I reached out for him and he let me catch him. Mother, I didn't do him any harm, I only stroked him. Then I saw an awful big face looking out of a basement window of the Perron house, and it shouted, "Leave go, leave go!"

'I looked at the head; it had staring eyes, was very pale, and was dreadfully big. I let the raven go and stood up and ran straight home. Mother, I didn't do him any harm, really, I only wanted to stroke him.'

'I know, Alfred, I know,' I said. 'Hang up your schoolbag

now and go to the nursery room, and you shall have your lunch. And forget about the raven, he doesn't matter at all.'

He kissed my hand and went into the nursery in a cheerful mood.

My own mood was not so cheerful, however, for I had become very thoughtful. I thought of the strange couple I had seen a long time ago—the couple whom I had followed in the direction of the hospital chapel. On that occasion, too, the girl had had an awful big head, to use Alfred's own words. If the head Alfred saw was the same as the girl's that I had noticed, she must live in a basement room of the Perron house. Now, when I thought of the concierge to whom I had given the book for Professor Andorf, it seemed to me he must have been roughly of the same height and appearance as the man I had seen crossing the street with the girl. In that case, perhaps the concierge was the girl's father.

Once again it occurred to me how well-mannered, how respectful the concierge had been when he had persuaded me to give him the book for Professor Andorf, how careful and well-chosen his speech, giving the impression that he was no ordinary person. At this, my interest in the man was aroused even more, and I determined to make enquiries about the concierge of the Perron house as the opportunity rose and, should he need it, to offer him my help within the limits of the small means at my disposal.

It was in late autumn that Alfred had had his encounter with the raven. During the following winter, which was a very mild one, I often went into the city with my husband. Sometimes we went to visit friends, and at other times we went to the theatre, of which I was very fond at that time. At night, on our way home again, we sometimes heard the strange flute-playing again and we could now hear quite clearly that it came from one of the basement rooms in the Perron house.

It was not easy, however, to find an opportunity of getting to know the concierge of the Perron house. In the first place, I did not wish to appear intrusive, for Professor Andorf was so far from being acquainted with the concierge that he had not even known the house possessed one; in the second place, there was no one who could have introduced me to him as nobody ever visited the house. Thus, part of the winter went by without my being able to realize my intention.

One day I was busy tidying up the more elegant rooms in our apartment. We had given a party the day before, and the rooms were rather disarranged. Then I heard a bustling and commotion from the street below. Opening the window and looking down, I saw a number of people standing at the gate of the Perron house, then I saw several more go to the house and join the first group. I called one of the maids and sent her down into the street to ask what was going on.

After a while, the girl returned and reported that the concierge of the Perron house had killed himself. I at once put on my coat, and went downstairs and across to the Perron house. Not having any wish to speak to the people standing in front of the gate, however, I went to the fruitseller who was sitting at her stall, and asked: 'Whatever has happened? How in the world can a man kill himself?'

'No one has killed himself,' she replied, 'but the concierge of the Perron house has died. A quarter of an hour ago—there was no one walking by this side of the houses—the girl, his daughter, came from the apartment and whispered to me that her father was dead. Then she went back into the house straight away. I called the shoemaker's apprentice over and told him what I had heard; then I told him he should go to the town hall and report what the girl had said to me. The lad must have told the other people on his way and that's why they're already here. But someone from the town hall is bound to come soon—registrar, doctor, coroner, magistrate, or the like.'

Whilst the woman was speaking, even more people had gathered around, but—whether out of respect for the dead person inside or from fear of the strange house itself—not one of them went through the little red gate.

At last the officials from the town clerk's office arrived to investigate the matter.

'It was this woman who told me,' said the apprentice, pointing to the fruitseller.

The fruitseller had to accompany the officials; this she did willingly, after having first spread a large white sheet over her wares. I gave my name to the officials and asked them to take me with them into the apartment, intending to be of help if necessary. They were pleased to agree. The apprentice, having been involved in reporting the matter, was also obliged to accompany them.

As we reached the little gate all the other people pushed towards it as well, but the officials said that no one was permitted to enter the house except themselves and those whom they required to do so. Then two bailiffs from the Department of Public Safety were posted, one at each side of the gate. The little gate was opened, we entered, and the bailiffs took up their positions in the gateway, not allowing anyone else to go through.

Walking down the passage behind the little gate, we came into the courtyard, and from there we went through the entrance which was closed off by the gate. In the side wall of the entrance was a door. After we had opened the door, we went down a flight of steps into the basement: there, we had been told, was the concierge's apartment.

Going down the steps and entering the apartment, we saw that it consisted of only one room. Beside a ladder placed against the wall by the window, we found the old man dead. He was wearing a short coat of yellow flannel cloth and pale blue trousers. When the officials had picked him up and laid him on a bed which appeared to be his, I saw by his features that he was indeed the same man to whom I had given the book. The officials had at first intended to attempt to revive him, but on taking hold of him had realized that he was already cold, and a closer examination showed that he was dead beyond any doubt.

When, then, had he died?

Apart from the man, no one had been in the room except the girl with the huge head. She was sitting on a white, unpainted chair at the far end of the room, observing from a distance what was being done with her father. On a screen in front of another bed, which I took to be the daughter's, was the jackdaw—the bird which Alfred had tried to catch had not been a raven at all. The bird was nodding its head and uttering sounds which, however, were so mutilated as to be unintelligible, and scarcely human in form. On the table, not far away from the girl's chair, lay the flute.

Whilst the men were examining the dead body and trying to arrange it in a dignified position upon the bed, I tried to get the girl to speak, thinking to win her confidence and then take her with me so as to bring her away from these dreary surroundings. I went up to her and spoke to her, in the politest but simplest words possible. To my astonishment, the girl answered me in the purest written language, but what she said was scarcely understandable. Her thoughts were so strange, so completely different from everything encountered in our everyday dealings, that her entire speech could have been considered idiotic if it had not also been, in part, very sensible.

As it happened, I had a few cakes and some fruit in my coat pocket. I took out a small cake and offered it to the girl. She reached out for it and ate it, and the expression of the huge face revealed her obvious pleasure. I took the opportunity of trying to deduce the girl's age from her features; but the unusual shape of the head and the face made it impossible to do so. She might have been sixteen, but she might just as well have been twenty.

I gave her a second cake, then a third, and then several more.

I will repeat the gist of what she said, more or less in our language, for the girl's train of thought would otherwise be impossible to understand; nor would I be able to repeat from memory all these things just as she said them.

I asked her whether she was fond of eating such sweet things when she had them and whether she found them good to eat.

'Yes, good to eat,' she replied; 'give me more.'

'I shall give you more,' I said, 'if you come with me and stay in another room until the night has passed and day comes again. Then I shall bring you back here to your room again. I haven't any more of these sweet things with me now, but there are lots in the room where you are to go with me.'

'I'll go with you,' she said, 'but when day comes, then we'll come back here again.'

'Yes,' I said, 'then we'll come back here to this room.'

I now gave the girl an apple of a better sort, and she ate it with every sign of enjoyment.

Then I asked her whether she had a mother, or whether she had any brothers and sisters living.

She had no mother, she replied, she had always lived alone with her father. She seemed not to understand the expression brothers and sisters at all.

Now I asked her how her father had died.

'He climbed up the ladder that leads up to our window,' she said. 'I don't know what he was going to do; then he fell down and didn't get up again. I waited for him to get well again; but he didn't get well. He was dead. After a day and a night had gone by, I told the woman who always sits there outside, not far from our little gate. Then all the people came.'

I repeated this to the officials, saying I would take the girl with me to my house and look after her for a while myself: the responsible authorities could always find the girl at my home if ever they were to look for her. I also said that I would inform my friends and acquaintances of what had happened, and that we would organize a collection so that the man could be given a decent funeral. To this the men made no objection.

Meanwhile they had finished examining the body. It was found that the poor man, for some reason or other, must have fallen—to all appearances and according to the girl's evidence—from the ladder which was leaning against the window, and injured his neck vertebrae, causing death instantaneously. They explained to me that, by law, a court autopsy would have to be performed and that it was therefore all the more desirable that the girl should be taken away from the apartment. Then the testimonies of the fruitseller and the apprentice were taken down in writing, and they were told that there was no objection to their leaving.

I walked over to the body, which was lying fully dressed upon the bed. The features had hardly changed, and were almost exactly as they had been that morning when the man had stood in front of me in the courtyard of the Perron house and persuaded me to give him the book. The blue eyes were now closed; now that the look of restlessness previously seen in them was concealed by the eyelids, the face even had an expression of gentleness about it. The others seemed to have felt this, too, for they stood around the bed for a moment, looking at the man. At last the apprentice and the fruitseller left the room and I, too, walked away from the bed.

Approaching the girl once more, I said that I would now take her with me, and that she should follow me as she had said she would.

The girl replied that she would indeed go with me and that, when daylight came once more, we should return to the room again.

I said that we would certainly do so.

She now followed me perfectly willingly. We went up the stairs; I took her by the hand and we went across the courtyard, along the passage, and through the little red gate into the street. Here the people were still standing; their numbers even seemed to have increased. A dense throng was gathered around the fruitseller and the apprentice, who were relating what they had seen and heard inside the house. I quickened my step in order to bring myself and the girl away from the throng and to escape from the curious looks and remarks which the sight of the girl's unusually large head had aroused.

Then I took her home with me.

There I gave her a respectable meal, supposing that she had not eaten properly since the previous day. I must have been right, for the girl ate with obvious enjoyment and afterwards seemed considerably refreshed. She later told me that she had eaten all the bread to be found in the room.

In our apartment we had a room overlooking the garden. For a long time this had been the room of our old nursery-maid, who had already been in service with my parents and later looked after my own children, until at last her daughter had married, whereupon she went to live with her and, if need be, to devote herself to her daughter's children, just as she had devoted herself to other people's children for so long. The room had been empty since then, though the furnishings had remained unchanged. I now had the room prepared for the girl. I had a bed made up for her and gave orders for the room to be well heated, then I brought the girl to the room. I had taken good care that she should not be seen by any of the servants, so that she should not be unduly frightened by them staring foolishly or even crying out. For this reason, I myself had brought her the food in the dining-room, where she was waiting, before taking her to her own room, and had ordered that no one was to come into the dining-room.

There was in our family an elderly maidservant who had been with us since our marriage; she was very fond of us and our children, and enjoyed, in a manner of speaking, the privilege of offering an opinion in family matters or other important affairs. I now sent for her, explained to her the circumstances of the girl's presence, and asked her to stay with the girl in her room, to speak to her kindly, to help her, and to make her stay as pleasant as possible. This she promised to do.

I also arranged for linen to be brought, in case the girl should need any, and had cakes and fruit placed in her room, just as I had promised.

I told the girl that I must now leave, having other matters to attend to; that the maid would stay with her, and that I would come again to see how she was.

The girl appeared to understand all this perfectly.

Going to my workroom, I sat down and wrote to a number of friends and acquaintances to request their help.

When my husband came home that evening, I told him everything that had happened and what I had done, and asked him whether this had been correct.

He replied that everything was correct; he agreed with everything and he, too, offered his help. He himself wrote some letters and then sent for a carriage in order to call on a number of friends in person. Returning home late that night, he brought positive assurances with him; and I had received several friendly replies to my letters that very evening. We went to bed content.

Next morning my husband went with me to the basement apartment. The court autopsy had been performed. The cervical vertebra had been crushed, damaging the spinal cord at the most delicate, vital part, thus causing death. The body was already in a coffin, awaiting removal for burial. We reported the man's death to the church in order to arrange for the funeral. While my husband was engaged in making further arrangements, I returned home so as to ensure that the girl should remain there until after the funeral.

She was already awake and fully dressed. She asked to go home; I told her that I did not have time just then, that I had several matters to attend to, but that I would certainly come back after these were completed and that I myself would bring her back to her dwelling. To this she agreed; she was given breakfast, and the maid to whose care I had entrusted her remained with her.

Professor Andorf, who had heard what had happened, arrived. Other friends of ours to whom we had written came to see for themselves. A large number of people had once more assembled at the little gate; most of these were persons of the lower classes who had been drawn by curiosity and a sort of dull sympathy typical of such people; apart from these, passers-by had stopped, as is usual in a large city, had asked what was going on, and, receiving the answer—provided they had the least bit of time to spare—had joined the throng.

Late that afternoon the priest arrived. The dead man was given the last blessing; he was brought to the church, where the customary prayers were said for him, and was then carried to the churchyard. We had arranged for a simple burial so that something from the money we had collected should be left for the girl. After the body had been taken away from the house, all the people who had gathered at the gate went about their business.

I now thought that the time had come to bring the girl to the basement room once again. It was clear to me that I could win her trust only by keeping my promise to the letter, for, among others, it was one of the girl's strange characteristics that she blindly believed whatever she was told. I went to the room overlooking the garden, explained to the girl that I had now finished the business which had prevented me from coming before, and that I would now bring her back to her dwelling. She rose from her chair cheerfully and followed me.

After we had arrived in the basement room, she asked where her father was. I was embarrassed by the question, for I had believed that she knew her father was dead—she herself having said so—and that, not finding him in their dwelling, she must therefore know where he had been taken. And so I replied that she knew her father was dead, that she herself had said that he had not got well again after his fall but was dead, and that he had been buried in accordance with the customs of our religion.

She remained stunned for a while, then she asked: 'Won't he ever come back at all?'

I had not the heart to say no, nor did I have the heart to comfort her by deceiving her, and so I kept to a half-truth.

After a while she asked again: 'Won't he ever come back at all?'

I no longer had the heart to lie to her; instead, I told her that her father was dead, that he would never move again, that he had been placed in the earth like all dead people and that he would rest there in peace.

Then she began to weep bitterly; I tried to comfort her, but my words were of no avail, and she went on weeping until, after a time, she was able to calm herself. When she was a little quieter, I asked her whether she would like to go back to my home with me; I said that I would bring her back here again as soon as she wished. Since the basement room was now empty the girl made almost no demur, and I took her back to the room where she had slept the night before. After a while, we returned to the basement room once again. And so I repeated the process several times in the course of the day, partly in order to keep the girl occupied, partly to get her accustomed to the change in her situation and give her a semblance of freedom, so that she would not think herself coerced and become recalcitrant and unmanageable.

I also gave her things to eat, of the kind which I thought would appeal to her.

Towards evening, when we were in the basement apartment, I suggested that she should again sleep in the room where she had slept the previous night; there, I said, it was warm and there was a comfortable bed; the kindly maidservant was there, too, and an evening meal had been prepared for her.

Yes, she replied, she would go with me if she might take the jackdaw with her.

To this I willingly agreed.

Approaching the bird, she addressed him by various strange-sounding, unintelligible names and made to catch him. The jackdaw cowered down upon the screen and let the girl take him in both hands. She carried the bird out with her, and so we came to the room overlooking the garden. Bidding the girl sit down in a comfortable armchair close to the stove, I called the maid so that she might have company; then I arranged for an evening meal to be served and, tired out with the day's activities, went to my own room.

All the furnishings were locked away in the concierge's dwelling, and the movable items were taken into custody—with one exception: I was given the key to the door of the room, so that I could visit it with the girl, his daughter, from time to time. My husband had been asked whether he would act as the girl's guardian, to which he agreed.

I did not know what we should do with the girl. We therefore decided to keep her with us until all her deceased father's papers and any other possessions had been handed over to my husband; we would then know more about his circumstances and what should best be done with her.

It was very hard to persuade the girl to forget the basement dwelling, for her attachment to it was stubborn to the point of being unfathomable. It was only by frequently visiting the room with her, by talking to her in a kindly way about commonplace matters, and by means of patient care, which did her good, that I was gradually able to get her accustomed to her new room. I gave her decent linen, and had the maid make clothes for her which suited her well, in which she felt comfortable and did not appear so conspicuous. Almost more than anything else, she had a fear of the open air, and whenever I brought her down for a little while to the garden in winter she would stare awkwardly at the leafless branches of the trees. In the first days after her arrival no one came near her except myself and the elderly maidservant; little by little, she grew accustomed to seeing other members of our family, and every one of them had been given strict instructions to treat the girl with kindness, and not to frighten her by openly staring at her.

I now tried to ascertain what schooling she had received. Her vocabulary was well-chosen and good, and her speech well-composed—though her thoughts were often difficult to follow—but she had almost no idea or experience of the simplest form of woman's work. How to wash or clean a duster, or sew two pieces of cloth together—of this she knew nothing at all. Clearly her father must have had such work done outside. On the other hand, she often spoke to the jackdaw, though the words were unintelligible to us; sometimes we would find her singing quietly, and she was able to play a little on her father's flute, which we had had to bring her.

She became very devoted to me, and I persuaded her to tell me about her past. But either she had completely forgotten everything of her past, or the recent events had had such an effect upon her that she could no longer recall it. She told me only things concerning the basement room.

'My father used to go out, taking his flute with him,' she said, 'and often did not come home again until the time the street-lamps were lit. He would bring food in a pot which we would warm in the little stove before eating it. Often, when he was away, I would place wood-shavings on the fire and warm myself some food in a pot which stood on the shelf, for there was some-times a lot of food left over. On another occasion I had nothing but bread to eat. Sometimes he remained at home. He taught me many different things and told me a great deal. He always used to lock the door when he went away. Whenever I asked him what I should do when he was away, he would say: "Describe the moment when I lie dead upon the bier and they bury me." Then, whenever I said: "Father, I have done that so many times," he would reply: "Then describe how your mother is wandering through the world with a broken heart, how she is afraid to come back and, in her despair, takes her own life." And when-ever I said, "Father, I have done that so many times," he would reply: "then describe it again." And when I had finished my task of describing how my father lay dead upon the bier, how my mother wandered through the world and, in despair, took her own life, I would climb the ladder and look out through the wire mesh of the window. I saw the hems of women's dresses passing by, I saw men's boots, I saw skirts trimmed with beautiful lace, or a dog's four feet. But I could not see clearly what went on on the other side of the street.'

I asked the girl where she kept the notes of these tasks, and she replied that her father had saved them and that they had been put aside somewhere. She still had one or two. Thereupon she went to a chest in which she kept her clothes, took from the pocket of a shabby old skirt some pieces of crumpled paper, and gave them to me. I unfolded them. Some were written in ink, others in pencil, and many of the words had been struck out with crosses or other signs. There was not much to be gathered from them.

Then I questioned her about God, the Creation, and other re-ligious matters. She recited by heart the appropriate parts of the catechism, looking around her with her calm, expressionless eyes. I tried to find out whether she had attended religious services at our church and was able to gather that she had often been to church with her father, but that she had never heard music there—or rather, flute-playing, as she expressed it—nor spoken to anyone. I concluded that she could only have attended a simple mass without music.

At last my husband was appointed the girl's guardian, and her father's effects, after being examined and registered by the court, were handed over to him on signature of a receipt. An immediate and thorough examination of the papers revealed that the deceased was none other than the pensioner who had left his dwelling and vanished without trace. The story of the man had been known to us only in general terms and we had forgotten about it a long time ago. But it was now recalled again to memory, details being filled in by a number of people who were familiar with the affair.

So, the girl with the large head and broad features was the same rosy-cheeked child that had once slept beneath the canopy held in the fingers of the gilded angel and draped in folds around the cradle; that same child whose parents had gazed upon it with such joy.

As far as property was concerned, nothing had been found save a few worn-out utensils, some old clothes, and the beds. The only money found was a small bag filled with copper coins. Apart from that, there was nothing.

My husband searched among the papers for information—which must have existed somewhere—about the dead man's financial circumstances; none of the people he questioned could recall that the pensioner had ever occupied an official position at the time he was living in the house on St Petersplatz, or pursued any kind of profession, and yet he had enjoyed a respectable and prosperous existence. He must therefore have had an income from some source or other. But there was not the slightest clue to be found amongst all the documents nor in the tiniest scrap of paper. My husband now sought out all authorities in Vienna who had to do with money or other valuables in any way whatsoever and made enquiries, but was unable to obtain information anywhere. One after another, he called upon company directors, deputy managers, attorneys, and heaven knows who else, but he could not find out anything from any one of them. Finally he resorted to placing a notice in the newspapers regarding the question of the deceased man's property, and requesting anyone having knowledge bearing on the matter to come forward; but no answer was received. The poor girl's inheritance, if any such had existed, had therefore to be considered lost.

The money which had been realized from the sale by auction of the furnishings and other objects left behind by the pensioner in his apartment on St Petersplatz and which, following payment of the arrears to the house-owner, had been retained by the court, was given to my husband in trust for the girl. Thanks to the interest which had accumulated over the years, the amount had grown considerably.

As to how the deceased person had lived and what had befallen him after leaving Vienna, my husband was unable to discover anything certain. After all his efforts to obtain information about the man's life and, in consequence, the whereabouts of the girl's inheritance, he at last learned one thing: that a man whose description corresponded exactly to that of the deceased had often been seen in the suburbs, which were a good distance away from his dwelling; that he had often appeared with his flute at inns, in parks, and in public places, where he had played in return for a modest sum. People used to give him food from their kitchens, which he would carry home in his pot. Whether or not he had played in the neighbourhood of his dwelling, no one could say.

The custodian of the Perron house informed my husband that, at some time—he himself did not know exactly when—the man had been allowed to live in the basement room free of rent in exchange for his services as concierge, although until that time the tenants each had a key to the little red gate, which they still kept. There was, in any case, not much information to be gathered from the custodian since, because of the dilapidated condition of the house, he did not concern himself with it very much, nor was he required to do so by the owner.

One day my husband brought a large bundle of manuscripts to my room and gave them to me. I looked at them, leafed through them, and saw that they were the girl's written exercises and compositions. Afterwards, whenever I had time, I took the trouble to read through the greater part of these manuscripts. What shall I say of them? I would term them poetry, if there had been any line of thought in them, or if a basis or origin or theme could have been identified in them. That the girl understood what death, or wandering about in the world, or taking one's own life out of despair could possibly mean, of this there was no trace whatsoever, although all these themes were the gloomy contents of the writings. Her mode of expression was clear and succinct, the composition of the sentences was good and correct, and the words themselves were elevated, though without meaning.

This experience induced me to read to the girl selections from poets or other writers, pronouncing them with distinct emphasis. The girl listened very attentively. Soon she began to recite such pieces herself and later, in a sort of histrionic performance, she used to proclaim pieces from the best and finest works in our language. But when I went more deeply into the works of literature out of which she had recited, and questioned her regarding their content, meaning, and form, she did not understand what I was asking her. Nor was a single one of the works concerned to be found among her father's effects. It fascinated the girl to recite such pieces, and she devoted herself rapturously to them. We later found that the phrases which she spoke in a low voice to the jackdaw were of a similar nature, and that the melodies which she tried to coax from her father's flute were in the same spirit.

My husband also searched for information about the girl's mother. He had hoped to restore to the girl her closest and natural blood-relation and support and, moreover, to obtain information from the mother with regard to the matter of the inheritance. At first he made careful enquiries to various authorities, and then, with the greatest discretion, he continued his enquiries, partly by contacting individual persons, partly through newspapers; but no matter how carefully these investigations were carried out, no matter how many letters were written, official requests made, and replies received: no information ever arrived from the woman, no one had ever heard anything of her until this day, and she never came back again.

Concerning the girl's earlier life, we never learned anything from what she told us.

We called our family physician, who was a friend of my husband's, and requested him to examine her physically, since the conspicuously large head indicated something unusual. He was of the opinion that such an abnormal growth was caused by living in gloomy, airless dwellings and, perhaps, by her father's own insanity, resulting in a bloated effect and gland disorders. The application of iodine baths, he thought, might perhaps be of valuable help in both cases. Intending in any case to visit my husband's brother in the spring, who lived in the region where the spa was situated, and spend several weeks at his home, I decided to take the girl with me. I hoped that the pure air and the journey would be no less beneficial than the therapy itself. And indeed, after a two-months' stay in the country and the prescribed treatment, her head did become somewhat smaller, and more well-formed, and her features finer, clearer, and more expressive.

We gave the girl lessons in the usual subjects and tried to instruct her in the most indispensable aspects of daily life. We tried to instil in her a taste for women's handiwork of all kinds; and finally, by means of conversation and by reading simple books, but mainly by personal contact, to transform this wild, disjointed, indeed almost uncanny instruction into simple, coherent, and understandable thoughts and impart to her an understanding of the things of this world. How difficult that was may be clear from the fact that it was months before she could bear to see Alfred speaking to the jackdaw, let alone playing with the bird, or on occasion touching her father's flute.

When at last we felt that we could take the risk, we rented a room for her to live in, not far from our house. The landlady looked after the girl; a priest gave her religious instruction, and we very often went across to see her; in this way, she became more gentle and her bodily appearance later improved so that she was able to accept her situation; and, after she became of age, my husband was able to give her the documents relating to the money kept for her by the court and that which had remained after her father's funeral; in the end, she used to make rugs, blankets, and the like for sale, from the proceeds of which, together with the interest from her small inheritance, she was able to live; this was all the more possible since the people, moved by her fate, always gladly bought the articles which she made.——

Such was the woman's story; and the girl lived on in this way in the years that followed.

The great actor is long dead, Professor Andorf is dead, the woman no longer lives in the suburbs, the Perron house no longer exists, and on its site and that of the neighbouring houses now stands a row of splendid residences; and the young people do not know what once stood there, or what happened there.

EDUARD MÖRIKE

Mozart on the Way to Prague

In the autumn of 1787 Mozart, accompanied by his wife, travelled to Prague where he was to present the première of *Don Giovanni*.

On the third day of their journey—the 14th of September—at about eleven o'clock in the morning, the two, both in a pleasant mood, were driving north-west on the far side of Mannhardsberg and the German town of Thaya near Schrems, not much more than thirty hours distance from Vienna, and had soon left the lovely Moravian hills well behind them.

'The vehicle, drawn by three post-horses,' wrote Baroness von T. to her friend, 'was a stately red-and-yellow coach belonging to a certain Frau Volkstett, the wife of General Volkstett, who, it seems, has always been rather vain about her relationship with the Mozart family and the favours she has shown to them.'—Anyone familiar with the taste of the 'eighties will be able to complete for himself the inexact description of the said vehicle with a few details. Both doors of the red-and-yellow carriage are decorated with bouquets of flowers painted in their natural colours, the edges of the doors being finished with narrow gold borders; the paintwork, however, is by no means the high-gloss lacquer favoured by modern Viennese coachmakers; the body, moreover, is not completely ballooned, though shaped with a rather coquettish downward curve; in addition, it has a high canopy with stiff leather curtains which at present are drawn back.

With regard to the dress of the two passengers, so much may be said: out of consideration for his new court dress now packed in the trunk, the husband's modest attire has been selected by Constanze, his wife; with his rather faded blue waistcoat he is wearing his usual brown surcoat which boasts a row of large buttons fashioned in such a way that a layer of reddish gilt shimmers through their star-patterned woven texture; black silk hose, stockings, and shoes with gilded buckles complete the picture. Because of the heat, which is most unusual for the time of year, he has taken off his surcoat half-an-hour ago and is now sitting bareheaded and in his shirt-sleeves, chatting merrily. Madame Mozart is wearing a comfortable travelling costume with white and light-green stripes; the abundance of her beautiful light-brown curls, half-loosened, has fallen over her neck and shoulders; never in all her life have they been spoiled by powder, whilst her husband's thick hair, worn in a plait, is today powdered even more carelessly than usual.

They had driven at a comfortable pace up a gently rising hill amidst fertile fields interspersed from time to time with spacious woodland, and had now arrived at the edge of the wood.

'How many woods,' said Mozart, 'have we already gone through today, yesterday, and the day before? I didn't pay any attention to them, let alone think of setting a foot in them. Let's step down here for once, darling, and pluck some of those pretty bluebells standing over there in the shadow. Your horses, good driver, can rest for a little while.'

As they rose from their seats, a minor mishap came to light, which landed the maestro in a quarrel. Thanks to his carelessness, a bottle of costly perfume had opened and spilled its contents unnoticed into their clothing and the upholstery. 'I might have realized,' she complained; 'there's been such a strong smell for a long time. Oh dear, a whole vial of real *Rosée d'Aurore* spilt! I'd been hoarding it like gold.'—'Why, you little scatterbrain,' he replied, by way of consolation, 'don't you see? That way alone, your divine smelling-schnaps was of some use to us. At first we were sitting in an oven and all your fanning was of no use at all, but then the whole carriage seemed to have cooled down, so to speak; you put it down to the few drops that I had spilled on my jabot; that revived us and the conversation went on in lively fashion, instead of us letting our heads hang down like sheep in a butcher's cart—and this blessing will remain with us the whole of the way. But now, just let us quickly poke two Viennese noses into the green wilderness here!'

Arm in arm they stepped over the wayside ditch and immediately entered the dimness of the pine trees which, very soon transformed into darkness, was only now and again blindingly pierced by a ray of sunlight shining upon the velvet mossy floor.

The sudden change from the baking heat outside to the refreshing coolness within might have been dangerous for the unthinking husband had it not been for his companion's watchfulness: with difficulty she forced upon him the item of clothing which she had been holding in readiness.—'Heavens, how splendid!' he exclaimed, looking up at the tall tree-trunks; 'it makes you think you were in church. I feel as if I had never been in a forest, and only now do I realize what a whole crowd of trees is. They weren't planted by human hand, they all sprang up by themselves and are standing here like this just because it is pleasant to live and work together. You know, when I was a child, I travelled through half Europe; I've seen the Alps and the ocean, the greatest and most beautiful things ever created; and now, quite by chance, here I stand like a simpleton in a perfectly ordinary pine forest on the Bohemian border, amazed and ravished that such things exist, not just *una finzione di poeti*,* like their nymphs, fauns, and so forth, nor a theatre backdrop— no, a forest that has grown up out of the ground, nurtured by moisture and the sun's warmth and light. Here the stag, with his curious crooked antlers on his forehead, is at home, the comical squirrel, the wood grouse, the jay.'—Bending down, he broke off a mushroom and extolled the splendid bright red colour of the cap, the delicate whitish gills on the underside; then he stuffed pine cones of various kinds into his pocket.

'Anyone would think,' said his wife, 'you hadn't looked even twenty yards into the Prater* where such rarities are certainly to be seen as well.'

'The Prater! Good Lord!—How can you even mention the name here! With all those coaches, imperial sabres, robes and fans, music, and every spectacle in the whole world, who could see anything else? And even the trees there, though there are so many of them, I don't know—beech-nuts and acorns strewn on the ground look more like the twin brothers of the thousands of corks lying beneath them. The wood reeks of wine-cellars and sauces at a distance of two hours away.'

'That's the limit,' she exclaimed—'coming from a man who enjoys nothing so much as eating broiled chicken in the Prater!'

When they were seated in the carriage once more and the road, after running on the level for some distance, was gradually dropping to a point where a smiling landscape extended to the farthest hills, our maestro, after remaining silent for a while, began again: 'The earth is truly beautiful, and no one can be blamed for wanting to remain on it as long as possible. Thank God, I feel as fit and well as ever and prepared for a thousand deeds, all to be performed immediately one after another as soon as my new work is completed and performed. How many beautiful and remarkable things are out there in the world and here at home, that I do not know at all—marvels of nature, of science, the arts, and useful occupations. That grimy charcoal-burner's lad over there beside his fire can tell you just as much as I can, in absolute detail, about lots of things; and I feel an urge and a desire to take a look at various things that have simply nothing to do with what directly concerns me.'

'A few days ago,' she replied, 'I came across your old pocket diary for '85; and at the back you had put down three or four NB's. The first one read: Mid-October, casting the great lions in the Imperial Foundry; the second one, underlined twice: Visit Professor Gattner! Who's he?'

'Oh, yes, I know—the friendly old gentleman from the observatory who invites me there from time to time. I've been wanting for a long time to look at the moon and the little man in it, with you. Now there's a huge telescope up there; they say the moon appears like an enormous disc where you can see mountains, valleys, and gorges close enough to touch, and also, from the side away from the sun, the shadow cast by the mountains. For two years now I've been meaning to go there, but never got round to it—shame on me, wretch that I am!'

'Well,' she said, 'the moon won't run away from us. There's a lot of things that we can catch up on.'

After a pause, he went on: 'And isn't it the same with everything? Ugh, I hate to think of the things we fail to do, and put off and leave undone!—Not to mention our duty to God and man—I mean, simple enjoyment and the little innocent pleasures we see every day before our eyes.'

Madame Mozart either could not or would not divert him from the direction in which his volatile emotions were leading him more and more, and regretfully, she could only agree with him wholeheartedly as he continued with growing enthusiasm:

'Was I ever able to take pleasure in my children for a full hour at a time? It's something I do by halves and always *en passant*. Letting the boys ride horseback on my knee, dashing through the room with them for two minutes, and then shaking them off again—finished! I can't recall that we ever went off for a day out in the country together, at Easter or Whitsun, in a garden or forest or meadow, just ourselves, having fun with the children and playing flower games, until we ourselves were like children again. And meanwhile, life walks and runs and gallops on—God in Heaven, it's enough to make you break out in a cold sweat when you really think about it!'

The self-accusation expressed here had unexpectedly led to an extremely serious discussion between the two, conducted with every manifestation of trust and affection. We shall not repeat it here in detail, preferring rather to give a general view of the circumstances which constituted in part, explicitly and directly, the content, and in part, only the conscious background of the discussion.

Here, first of all, we are obliged to face the painful fact that this person, of fiery temperament and unbelievably sensitive to every possible stimulus and to the highest level attainable by an aware spirit—though he had during the brief span of his life experienced, enjoyed, and achieved a great deal by his own efforts —was nevertheless deprived of a lasting feeling of satisfaction with himself throughout his life.

Anyone who does not wish to seek the causes of this phenomenon more deeply than they probably lie, will at first find them simply in those—apparently—ineradicably acquired weaknesses which, not quite without reason, we are so fond of connecting by a sort of necessary link with everything we admire about Mozart.

His needs were very many and his liking for social pleasures in particular extremely great. Honoured and sought after as an incomparable genius by the most distinguished families of the town, he seldom or never refused invitations to banquets, soirées, or gaming parties. At the same time, he fulfilled his own duties of hospitality within the circle of his close friends. A long-established musical evening at his home on a Sunday, an informal lunch at his well-provided table with a few friends and acquaintances two or three times a week—these were things he would not have done without. Sometimes, much to his wife's dismay, he would bring his guests from the street straight into the house without giving her any warning; people of very different classes: music-lovers, colleagues, singers, and poets. The idle sponger, whose only merits were a permanent merry mood, wit and humour—namely, of the coarser type—was just as much in demand as the keen-witted connoisseur and the expert performer. Mozart, however, was in the habit of seeking relaxation mainly away from his own home. He could be found almost any day after lunch playing billiards in the coffee house and, many an evening, in the tavern. He was very fond of driving and riding in company through the countryside; an accomplished dancer, he used to attend dances and masked balls and very much liked to visit village festivals several times a year, especially the open air festival of St Brigitte's Kirmes, where he used to appear as a masked pierrot.

Such pleasures as these, sometimes loud and lively, sometimes attuned to a quieter mood, were calculated to provide the necessary relaxation for his long-stressed soul after immense expenditures of energy; nor did such pleasures fail to impart to his soul—via the mysterious ways in which the genius unconsciously plays his game—the delicate volatile impressions which nourish it from time to time. Regrettably, however, at such times, because he always tried to drain the last drop of pleasure out of every moment, he did not show any consideration either for his intelligence, his duty to preserve his health, or his duty towards his family. Whether spending his time in enjoyment or creatively, Mozart had equally little sense of moderation and of objectives. Part of the night was always devoted to composition. Early in the morning he would revise his work of the night before, often remaining in bed for a long while. Then, from ten o'clock onwards, he would set out on his round of private lessons—either on foot or in a carriage sent to fetch him—which generally accounted for several hours of the afternoon.

'We really slave away at it,' he himself writes on one occasion to a patron, 'and it is often hard not to lose patience. As a qualified cembalist and music professor, one burdens oneself with a dozen pupils and, again and again, takes on a new one without

knowing whether he has any talent, as long as he pays his fees
per marca.* Any mustachioed Hungarian officer from the Corps
of Engineers, driven by some demon to study bass and counter-
point without any good reason, is welcome; the most arrogant
petty countess who receives me—like Master Coquerel the hair-
dresser—with a crimson face if, just once, I do not knock at her
door punctually, etc.' And when, tired out by these and other
professional obligations, appearances at academies, rehearsals,
and so forth, he yearned for a respite, his weary nerves were
often permitted an apparent tonic only in the form of new dis-
tractions. Unperceived by anyone, his health became under-
mined; a mood of melancholy which returned again and again,
if it was not the result of, was certainly nourished by this very
weakness and thus his premonition of an early death, which in
the end always dogged his heels, was inevitably fulfilled. Grief
of every kind and degree, not excluding the emotion of regret,
was something to which he was accustomed as a piquant spice
accompanying every pleasure. And yet we know that these pains
flowed pure and cleansed into that deep well which, fed through
a hundred golden pipes, and releasing an inexhaustible range of
melodies, poured out every torment and every delight that dwells
in the human breast.

The harmful effects of Mozart's way of life were most evident
in his domestic situation. The accusation that he indulged in
foolish, ill-considered squandering is not far from the truth;
it was closely bound up with one of his most admirable traits
of character. If someone in dire straits came to him to borrow
money or ask him to stand guarantor, he had generally already
taken it for granted that Mozart would not ask for any pledge or
surety; that would indeed have become him as little as it would
a child. He preferred most of all to lend the money without
further ceremony and always with smiling generosity, especially
when he considered himself affluent just at that time.

It must be admitted, however, that the financial means neces-
sitated by such expenditure, in addition to the normal housekeeping costs, were out of all proportion to his income. The
money obtained from theatrical productions and concerts, from
publishers and pupils, together with his annuity from the Emperor, was even less sufficient, for the public's taste was still far

removed from clearly declaring itself in favour of Mozart's music; the latter's pure beauty, depth, and richness was in general disconcerting compared with the easily digestible type of music previously popular. Admittedly the people of Vienna had not been able to hear their fill of *Belmonte and Constance**—thanks to the popular elements of the work—but on the other hand, some years later *Figaro*—and certainly not only thanks to the intrigues of the theatre director—had been an unexpected, miserable failure compared with the pleasant but far inferior work *Cosa Rara;** that same *Figaro* which, immediately afterwards, the more educated or less prejudiced people of Prague received with such enthusiasm that the maestro, grateful and deeply moved, decided to write his next great opera especially for them.—Despite the influence of his enemies, and although the time was unfavourable, Mozart, with a little more care and shrewdness, could still have made a respectable profit from his art; as it was, he came off badly even with those productions where the common majority cheered him nightly. Be that as it may, everything— fate, his character, and his own faults—combined to prevent him—unique a talent as he was—from prospering.

It is easy for us to realize how unpleasant the situation of a housewife must have been under such circumstances, provided she understood her task. Constanze, although herself young and vivacious, and—as the daughter of a musician—a most artistic person, being moreover accustomed from childhood to privation, revealed every intention of preventing disaster at the start, of putting a stop to mistakes and compensating large-scale losses by means of thriftiness on a small scale. It was, perhaps, only with regard to the latter point that she lacked the necessary skill and long experience. She was in charge of the finances and kept the books; every demand for payment, every dunning letter, and everything of a disagreeable nature went to her directly without exception. It is certain that, at times, she was up to her neck in unpleasantness, especially when, in addition to such distress, privation, painful embarrassment, and fear of public dishonour, she had to contend with her husband's moods of depression in which he used to remain for days on end, completely inactive, not receptive to any attempts to console him; sighing and complaining either at his wife's side or sitting wordlessly in a corner, eternally preoccupied with the one melancholy thought of death that ran on like an endless spiral. But she seldom lost her good humour; her clear gaze generally found, even if only for a short time, help and advice. For the most part, however, there was little or no improvement. Even if she succeeded by means of seriousness and humour, cajolery and flattery, in persuading him to take afternoon tea beside her, to enjoy his supper at home with the family without going out again afterwards—what did she achieve by it? At times, suddenly moved and affected by his wife's tearful eyes, he would curse a bad habit of his in all honesty, and promise to do the right thing, even more than she demanded of him—but it was all in vain—he would suddenly find himself back in his old rut once more. One was tempted to believe that it was not in his power to act otherwise and that this way of life which, to our way of thinking, was completely different from that which is right and good for all men, imposed by force upon him, must yet have lifted this extraordinary individual to greater heights.

Constanze, however, always hoped that things would change for the better, as far as this was possible through an external influence: namely, by means of a thorough improvement in their economic situation, which, she thought, with her husband's growing fame, could not fail to come about. Once the continued pressure from this direction—which was palpable to him, too, sometimes more, sometimes less insistently—was removed, once he could follow his true vocation without distraction, instead of sacrificing half his time and strength simply to earning money, and when at last he could once again experience increasing pleasure of body and mind, pleasure which he would no longer hunt for but would enjoy with an incomparably better conscience— then, she thought, his entire condition must soon become more relaxed, more natural, more peaceful. At times she even considered moving away from the district, for his absolute preference for Vienna—where, she was convinced, no real benefit was to be gained for him—could after all, she believed, be overcome. The next decisive contribution to realizing her hopes and wishes, however, she expected from the success of the new opera, which was the reason for this journey.

Well over half of the composition was completed. Close friends of Mozart, competent to give an opinion, who, as witnesses to the birth of this extraordinary work, must have had sufficient understanding of its nature and power, spoke of it everywhere in such tones that even many of his enemies could expect that, in less than six months, this *Don Giovanni* would have shaken the entire musical world from one end of Germany to the other, turned it upside down, and taken it by storm. The well-meaning opinions of other critics, however, who, judging by musical standards of the day, hardly expected a swift and overall success, were more reserved and cautious. The maestro himself secretly shared their doubts, which were only too well founded.

Constanze, for her part, as is the way with women when their feelings are once aroused and who, moreover, spurred on by the zeal of a fully justified wish, from then on allow themselves to be deceived by later doubts much less often than men, stuck firmly to her faith in him and just now, in the carriage, once again had occasion to defend it. This she did, in her bright, happy manner, with double enthusiasm, for her husband's humour during the course of the previous conversation, which could not lead to any result and in consequence broke off in a most unsatisfying way, had already worsened noticeably. Now, with the same degree of cheerfulness, she tediously explained to her husband how she intended, after their return home, to use the hundred ducats which had been agreed upon with the theatre director in Prague as the price for the musical score, to pay off the most pressing debts and other items, and how, with their budget, she hoped to hold out through the coming winter well enough until the spring.

'That Herr Bondini of yours will make his killing with the new opera, believe me; and if he's half the man of honour you always claim him to be, he'll afterwards give you a decent little percentage of the proceeds that the theatres pay him for the copies; if not, well, we still have other opportunities to look forward to, thank heaven—and a thousand times more dependable. I've got all sorts of ideas.'

'Let's hear them, then!'

'Well, not long ago, a little bird told me that the King of Prussia is looking for a Kapellmeister.'*

'Oho!'

'General Director of Music, I meant to say. Just let me indulge my fantasy a little. It's a weakness I have from my mother.'

'Go on! the madder, the better.'

'No, it's all perfectly down-to-earth.—For a start, just suppose: in about a year from now—'

'The Pope will take a marriage vow—'

'Be quiet, idiot! I said, in a year's time, around St Aegidius's Day, there mustn't be an Imperial Court Composer named Wolf Mozart to be found in all the length and breadth of Vienna.'

'You'll be sorry you said that!'

'I can just imagine our old friends gossiping about us and what they shall have to tell each other.'

'For instance?'

'For instance, our fanciful old friend Volkstett, shortly after nine o'clock in the morning, sailing across the Kohlmarkt in her fiery morning-visit trot. She has been away for three months— the long journey to her brother-in-law in Saxony, her daily topic of conversation ever since we've known her, has finally taken place; she's been back again since yesterday evening and now, absolutely overflowing—bursting with the joy of travel and impatience to see her friends and all the most interesting news— straight off to the Colonel's lady with it! Up the stairs, knocking at the door and not waiting for a "Come in!"; just imagine for yourself the jubilation and the embracing on both sides!—"My dear, dear, friend," she will say after a few preliminaries, "I've brought you a mountain of kind regards—I wonder if you can guess from whom? I haven't come straight from Stendal, I made a slight detour over to the left, towards Brandenburg."—"What! Is that true? . . . You went to Berlin? And visited the Mozarts?"— "Ten wonderful days!"—"Oh, my dear, sweet Frau Volkstett, tell me, describe it to me! How are our dear young friends? Do they still like it there as much as they did at first? I find it fantastic, incredible, even today, and now all the more so, since you have come here directly from him—Mozart as a Berliner! How does he behave? How does he look?"—"Oh, him! You should just see him. This summer the King sent him to take the waters at Carlsbad. When did his beloved Emperor Joseph ever think of such a thing? Both of them had only just returned to Berlin when I arrived. He was brimming over with life and good health, he's round and plump and lively as quicksilver; you can see the happiness and contentment in his eyes."'

Now the speaker, in her assumed role, began to describe the new situation in the most vivid colours. Starting from his apartments in the Boulevard Unter den Linden,* from his garden and country house and on to the brilliant scenes of his public appearances and the more intimate court circles, where he had to accompany the Queen on the piano—with her description, everything became present, became reality. She invented entire conversations, the most wonderful anecdotes; indeed, she seemed more at home in the royal capital, in Potsdam and in Sanssouci* than in Château Schönbrunn and the Imperial castle. Roguishly, she tricked out our hero's personage with a whole row of completely new fatherly attributes which had blossomed on the solid foundation of his life in Prussia, and under the influence of which the said Frau Volkstett had noticed in him the onset of real miserliness (which became him in a most charming manner) as a most splendid phenomenon and proof of how extremes sometimes converge. 'Yes, just imagine, he has his fixed salary of 3,000 thalers and for what? For conducting a chamber concert once a week and the Grand Opera twice a week!—Oh, my dear friend, I saw our dear little golden man, in the midst of his wonderful orchestra, which he himself has trained and which adores him! Sat with Madame Mozart in her box, diagonally opposite the highest nobility! And what was written on the note, here you are—I brought it with me for you—there's a little souvenir from myself and the Mozarts wrapped up in it— see here, read it—there it is, printed in huge letters!'—'Good heavens, what is it?' *Tarar!*—'Yes, indeed, my dear friend— amazing what can happen! Two years ago, when Mozart wrote *Don Giovanni* and that nasty, venomous wasp Salieri was trying in secret to repeat, at first on his own territory, the triumph which he had enjoyed in Paris with his composition and to present to our worthy public, so fond of grouse and of *Cosa Rara*, a sort of falcon—and when he and his henchmen were already whispering together and plotting to adapt *Don Giovanni*, all plucked to pieces just like *Figaro* once before, neither dead nor alive, for the theatre—well, then, you know, I made a vow: when that infamous work is performed, I shan't go to see it, not for anything in the world! And I kept my word. When everyone else was running and jostling—and you, too, with them, my dear—I remained sitting by my stove, took my cat upon my lap, and ate my biscuits; and afterwards as well. But now, just imagine, Mozart conducting *Tarar* in the Berlin Opera, the work of his deadly enemy!—"You must go and see it!" he exclaimed, in the very first quarter-of-an-hour, "if only to be able to tell the people of Vienna whether I let a hair of young Absolom's head be harmed. I only wish he was here himself, the green-eyed monster, he should see that I've no need to mess up someone else's work, so that I can always remain as I am!"'

'Brava! bravissima!' cried Mozart in a loud voice; taking his little wife by the ears, he kissed, hugged, and tickled her so heartily that this horseplay, adorned with coloured soap-bubbles of a dream future, which regrettably was never to be fulfilled, not even in the most modest degree, finally ended in high spirits, noise, and laughter.

Meanwhile they had descended into the valley some time ago and were approaching a village which they had already noticed from up above. Directly behind it, on the smiling plain, lay a small château of modern appearance, the residence of a Count Schinzberg. They decided to feed the horses, take a rest, and have lunch in the village. The inn at which they stopped lay in an isolated position on the street at the end of the village, and from it an avenue of poplars not six hundred paces long led to the château garden.

After they had got down from the carriage, Mozart, as usual, left the business of ordering the meal to his wife. Meanwhile he ordered a glass of wine for himself to be served in the neighbouring room, whilst Constanze, after taking a drink of cold water, asked only for a quiet corner where she might sleep for a little while. A maid led her upstairs and her husband followed, singing and whistling merrily to himself. Here, in a spotless, white-painted room, hastily aired, were some pieces of old but elegant furniture—doubtless spirited here in days gone by from the Count's chambers—and a small, clean bed with a painted canopy hung on slender, green-lacquered posts, the silk curtains long ago replaced by others of a more commonplace material. Constanze made herself comfortable; he promised to wake her in good time and she locked the door behind him, whereupon he went off in search of some entertainment in the tap-room. Here, however, not a soul was to be found, with the exception of the landlord and, since the latter's conversation was as little to the guest's taste as his wine, Mozart expressed his inclination to take a stroll to the château garden until lunch was ready. Respectable strangers were freely admitted to the garden, he was told, and in any case, the family were away from home today.

He set off, and in a little while had walked the short distance to the garden gate, which was open, and slowly climbed a steep track lined with lime trees. At the end of this track, on the left-hand side, he suddenly saw the château close in front of him. It was built in the Italian style and painted in a light colour, with a double stairway extending forward; some statues in the customary fashion representing gods and goddesses, together with a balustrade, adorned the slate roof.

Crossing between two large, luxuriant flower terraces, our maestro walked towards that part of the garden overgrown with bushes; skirting a few beautiful, dark groups of pine trees, he turned his steps towards some tortuously twisted paths, gradually nearing the less thickly grown areas, following the loud splashing of a fountain which he came upon at once.

The wide, elegant oval basin was surrounded by a carefully tended group of orange trees in tubs, interspersed with laurel and oleander bushes, the whole encircled by a path of soft sand adjoined by a narrow trelliswork bower. This offered the most peaceful resting-place imaginable; in front of the bench stood a small table, and here Mozart sat down before the entrance.

With his ear listening contentedly to the splashing of the water and his gaze fixed upon a mid-sized orange tree which stood alone outside the row of other trees, directly beside him and full of the most beautiful fruits, our friend was carried back by this vision of the south to a charming memory from his childhood. With a thoughtful smile, he reached out to the nearest fruit, as if to feel its splendid roundness and juicy coolness in the hollow of his hand. Yet this scene from his youth, which rose up once more in his mind's eye, was closely bound up with a long-vanished musical reminiscence in whose vague traces he indulged dreamily for a while. Now his eyes are gleaming, wandering here and there, and his attention is struck by a thought which straight away he eagerly seizes upon. Without thinking, he has taken hold of the orange for the second time, it falls from the branch and remains lying in his hand. He sees it, yet he does not see it; indeed, he is so lost in thoughts of an artistic nature that, rolling the sweet-smelling fruit under his nose without cease, silently humming between his lips the beginning, then the middle part of a melody, he at last draws out, as if by instinct, an enamelled case from a side pocket of his coat; from it he takes a small knife with a silver handle and slowly slices through the yellow orb from top to bottom. Some vague, distant feeling of thirst may, perhaps, have prompted this action, but his aroused senses are content to breathe in the delicious fragrance. For some minutes he stares at the two inner surfaces, joins them together gently, very gently, then separates them again and places them together a second time.

Just then he hears the sound of footsteps close by; he gives a start and suddenly becomes conscious of where he is and what he has done. Though already on the point of concealing the orange, he stops, either out of pride or because it is too late to do so. A tall, broad-shouldered man in livery, the estate gardener, was standing in front of him. The man had obviously seen his last stealthy movement and now remained silent for a few seconds, shocked. Equally speechless, Mozart seemed glued to his seat; half-laughing, he looked the man in the face with his blue eyes, plainly blushing yet rather boldly and unflinchingly; then—what to an observer would have appeared extremely funny —with a sort of defiantly courageous deliberation, he placed the apparently unharmed orange on the middle of the table.

'Begging your pardon,' began the gardener, studying with barely concealed displeasure the stranger's scarcely impressive attire, 'I don't know who—'

'Kapellmeister Mozart, from Vienna.'

'No doubt you are known at the château?'

'I'm a stranger here, passing through. Is His Lordship at home?'

'No.'

'And his lady?'

'Her Ladyship is busy and not to be disturbed.'

Mozart rose to his feet and made as if to go.

'With your permission, sir—what do you mean by coming here and helping yourself just like that?'

'What!' exclaimed Mozart, 'helping myself? Damn it, d'ye think I wanted to steal the thing and gobble it up?'

'I believe my own eyes, sir. These fruits have all been counted and I am responsible for them. The tree is intended by His Lordship for a banquet and is to be taken away immediately. I won't let you leave here until I have reported the matter and you yourself have explained to me how it happened.'

'Very well, then, I shall wait here. You may depend on it!'

The gardener looked around hesitantly and Mozart, thinking that perhaps the man was only out for a tip, reached into his pocket only to realize that he had not a penny on him.

Then, indeed, two labourers came along, loaded the tree on to a board, and carried it away. Meanwhile our maestro had taken out his wallet from which he extracted a sheet of white paper and, whilst the gardener was standing there without moving an inch, he wrote in pencil the following:

'Madam: Here I linger, unhappy wretch that I am, in your Paradise, like Adam of old after he had tasted the apple. The misfortune has already happened, and I cannot even put the blame upon a faithful Eve who, just at this moment, beguiled by the Graces and Cupids of a canopy bed at the inn, is enjoying the most innocent sleep. Only command me and I shall attend in person to confess to Your Ladyship my awful crime, incomprehensible even to myself. Bowing my head in sincere shame, I am, Madam,
Your most humble and obedient servant
W. A. Mozart
on the way to Prague.'

He handed the note, rather clumsily folded, to the waiting gardener, at the same time giving him appropriate instructions.

Hardly had the ogre disappeared when a vehicle was heard rumbling into the courtyard on the farther side of the château. It was the Count, bringing his niece and her fiancé, a rich young baron, from the neighbouring estate. The young man's mother had not left her house for years and so the engagement had been celebrated today at her home; now it was to be marked by a merry party attended by a number of relatives here at the château, Eugenie's second home ever since her childhood, where she had lived like a daughter of the family.

The Countess, together with her son Max, the lieutenant, had driven home somewhat earlier in order to make various arrangements. Now the château was bustling with activity everywhere, in every corridor and on every stairway, and it was only with great difficulty that the gardener was at last able to hand the note to Her Ladyship in the ante-chamber. She did not open it immediately, however, but hurried on busily without really paying attention to what the messenger was saying. He waited and waited, but she did not return. Members of the household staff ran past him one after the other—servants, ladies-in-waiting, footmen; he asked where His Lordship was—he is changing his clothes, came the reply; then he sought and found the young Count Max in his chamber; the latter, however, was deeply engaged in conversation with the Baron, and cut off the gardener in mid-speech, as if afraid that the man wished to report something or ask something which was still to be kept secret: 'I'll come immediately—go on, now!' But the gardener remained waiting for a good while until at last both father and son appeared at the same time and received the awful news.

'Why, that's damnable!' exclaimed the Count—a fat, good-natured person, though somewhat quick-tempered; 'That really beats everything! A musician from Vienna, you say? Probably some rascal who wanders about earning just his travelling expenses and takes anything he can find, eh?'

'Begging Your Honour's pardon, but he does not seem quite that type. I think he is not quite right in the head; he is very arrogant, too. Moser, he said his name was. He is still waiting down there for a reply; I told Franz to stay there and keep an eye on him.'

'What good will that do now that it's happened, damn it! Even if I have the idiot thrown into a cell, the damage can't be made good now. I've told you a thousand times, the front gate must remain closed at all times. The whole thing could have been prevented if you had carried out your duties at the proper time.'

At that moment, the Countess hurried in from the adjoining room, holding the note unfolded in her hand and smiling excitedly. 'D'you know who is down in the village?' she exclaimed. 'For heaven's sake:—read the letter—Mozart, the composer, from Vienna! Someone must go immediately and ask him to come to the château—I'm only afraid he might have left already! Whatever will he think of me! Velten, I hope you were polite to him? What happened, anyway?'

'Happened?' echoed her husband: even the possibility of a visit from a famous man could not entirely soften his anger on the spot; 'The madman has plucked one of the nine oranges from the tree intended for Eugenie—the monster! It's taken the edge off our fun completely, and Max can forget about his poem straight away.'

'Oh, no, not at all!' said the lady energetically. 'The gap can be filled easily, just leave it to me. Now, off you go, both of you, and welcome the worthy man, in as friendly and flattering a manner as you possibly can. He mustn't travel any farther today if we can prevent it. If you don't find him in the garden, look for him at the inn and bring him here, with his wife. Fate could not have bestowed on us a finer gift or a more wonderful surprise for Eugenie on this day.'

'Exactly!' replied Max, 'that was my first thought, too. Come, Papa, quickly. And', he added, as they hurried towards the stairs, 'don't worry about the poem. The ninth Muse won't go short; on the contrary, I shall gain a great advantage from the mishap.'—'Impossible.'—'No, not at all.'—'Well, if that is the case—I take your word for it, mind!—let's show the awkward fellow every possible honour.'

While this was taking place at the château, our semi-prisoner —little concerned about the outcome of the matter—had been occupying himself for a considerable time writing. When no one appeared, however, he began walking nervously back and forth; then an urgent message came from the inn informing him that lunch had been ready for a long time and that he should come back immediately, as the postillion was in a hurry. Picking up his belongings, he was just about to leave without more ado when the two gentlemen appeared in front of the bower.

The Count greeted him heartily in his loud voice, almost like an old acquaintance. Without giving Mozart the slightest opportunity of apologizing, he immediately expressed his desire to welcome the Mozarts, that afternoon and evening at least, in his family circle. 'My dear maestro,' he declared, 'you are so far from being a stranger to us that the name of Mozart can hardly be uttered anywhere else more often and with more enthusiasm than here. My niece sings and plays; she spends almost the whole day at the piano, knows your works by heart, and has a tremendous desire to see you once at closer quarters than she was able to do last winter at one of your concerts. We shall shortly be going to Vienna for a few weeks, and our relatives there have promised her an invitation to the house of Prince Gallizin where you are often to be found. But now you are travelling to Prague and will not be returning so soon; and heaven only knows whether the road back will lead you here again—so, make today and tomorrow a day of rest! We shall send back the carriage immediately—and please allow me to arrange for your further travel.'

The composer, who in such cases readily sacrificed ten times more to friendship or pleasure than was necessary on this occasion, did not long stop to consider; he gladly agreed to spend half the day there; however, he said, they must continue their journey as early as possible next morning. Count Max requested the honour of bringing Madame Mozart from the inn and making all necessary arrangements there. The young man set off; a carriage was to follow him directly.

Incidentally, we would like to mention here that the young man had inherited from his parents a cheerful nature, bound up with a talent and liking for the fine arts, and, though lacking a true inclination for the military profession, had nevertheless highly distinguished himself as an officer by his ability and his excellent manners. He was well versed in French literature and, at a time when German poetry carried little weight among the higher classes of society, had won for himself praise and honour with his uncommon talent for writing poetry in his mother tongue, inspired by such worthy examples as Hagedorn, Götz,* and others. As we have already seen, this day was a particularly happy occasion for making use of his gifts.

He found Madame Mozart sitting at the table—which was

already laid, and where she had already had a plate of soup served to her—chatting with the innkeeper's daughter. She was far too accustomed to unusual incidents and spontaneous pranks on the part of her husband to be more disturbed than was fitting by the arrival of the young officer and his request. Calmly and efficiently, with unfeigned amusement, she made all necessary arrangements without omitting anything. Luggage was repacked, bills were paid, the postillion was dismissed; she herself got ready without being over-anxious about her dress and drove off cheerfully to the château with her companion, not suspecting the strange circumstances which had brought her husband there.

He, in the meantime, was already feeling as comfortable as could be, and was enjoying himself very much indeed. After a little while Eugenie and her fiancé appeared. She was a very beautiful, vivacious woman; blonde, her slim figure sumptuously clad in a dress of shimmering, carmine-red silk trimmed with exquisite lace, her forehead adorned by a white band with precious pearls. Her fiancé, the Baron, was only a little older than herself; he was of a frank, gentle nature and seemed worthy of her in every respect.

The conversation was led off at first by the master of the house himself, who was in excellent humour—perhaps a little too animatedly, thanks to his rather loud manner of talking, well spiced with jokes and anecdotes of all kinds. Refreshments were served, to which our maestro helped himself heartily without any hesitation.

Someone had opened the grand piano; *The Marriage of Figaro* lay open on the music-stand and the young lady, accompanied by the Baron, began to sing Susanna's aria from the garden scene, in which we breathe the spirit of sweet passion in streams, like the heady air of a summer evening. For the space of two breaths, the delicate pink of Eugenie's cheeks turned the palest white; but at the very first sound that issued sweetly from her lips, every trammel of bashfulness fell from her breast. She stood smiling and confident, borne on the high wave of harmony and perfectly exhilarated by the feeling of this moment, perhaps the only one of its kind throughout her entire life.

Mozart was clearly surprised. When she had finished, he walked across to her and said, with typical unaffected sincerity:

'My dear child, what can I say here, where you must feel like the glorious sun that is flattered most of all when everyone is basking in its light! Such singing as this makes the soul as blissful as a baby in its bath; it laughs with wonder and cannot imagine anything finer in all the world. And—believe me—even in Vienna, it's not every day one is able to hear one's work sung in such style, so fine, so warm, so pure and so perfect.'—With these words he took her hand and kissed it devotedly. Eugenie was moved by his kindness and sincerity no less than by the courtly words with which he praised her talent; she was overcome by that irresistible emotion that resembles a slight feeling of giddiness, and her eyes suddenly filled with tears.

Just then Madame Mozart entered the room immediately followed by some new guests, who had been expected: a baronial family—close relatives of the Count—from the neighbourhood. They were accompanied by their daughter Franziska, who had been one of Eugenie's dearest friends ever since childhood and was completely at home here.

After greetings, embraces, and congratulations had been exchanged on all sides and the two guests from Vienna introduced to the company, Mozart took his place at the grand piano. He played part of a concerto of his own composition which Eugenie was learning at the time.

In a small circle like this one, the effect of such a performance is of course different from a similar performance given in public, by reason of the enormous pleasure born of the direct contact with the artist himself and his genius, within the familiar walls of one's own home.

It was one of those brilliant pieces whose pure beauty freely places itself at the service of elegance though in such a way that, in a manner of speaking, it is only shrouded in these more convenient, playful forms, hidden behind a throng of dazzling lights, but reveals its true nobility in every gesture and pours out an extravagance of glorious emotion.

The Countess remarked that most listeners, perhaps not even excepting Eugenie, despite the keenest attention and most solemn silence maintained during such a delightful performance, were nevertheless 'torn 'twixt eye and ear'—whilst carefully observing the composer, his erect, almost rigid posture, his good-humoured features, and the circular movements of these small hands, it was certainly not easy to resist the onrush of thoughts concerning the wondrous man which assailed one from all sides.

After the maestro had risen to his feet, the Count turned to Madame Mozart, saying: 'How easy it is for kings and emperors when they wish to pay a connoisseur's compliment to a famous artist, something which not everyone can do. Whatever they say, every word proceeding from their mouths is unique and extraordinary. There is nothing they cannot permit themselves. How simple it is, for instance, standing right behind your husband's chair, to pat him, modest fellow that he is, on the shoulder after the final chord of a brilliant fantasia and to say: "My dear Mozart, you're a devil of a fellow!" The words are hardly spoken when a murmur runs round the hall with the speed of a forest fire: "What did he say to him?" "He said, 'you're a devil of a fellow.'" And everyone present who plays the violin and the flute and composes music, is beside himself on hearing this *one* solitary phrase; in a word, this is the grandiose style, the familiar style of an emperor, the inimitable style which I have always envied the Josephs and Friedrichs; and never more than today, when I must totally despair of happening to find a single piece of any other intellectual coinage in any of my pockets.'

The mischievous manner in which he uttered these remarks always hit the right note and never failed to provoke laughter.

Now, following the invitation of their gracious hostess, the company entered the festively adorned dining-room where they were met by the scent of the floral decorations and by cooler air—a welcome stimulus to the appetite.

The people now took their places, which had been allocated with some forethought, the distinguished guest seating himself opposite the engaged couple. His neighbour on one side was a small, elderly lady—a maiden aunt of Franziska's; on his other side sat the charming young niece herself, who quickly impressed him with her wit and vivacity. Madame Constanze was seated between the host and her friendly guide, the lieutenant; the other guests took their places, so that there were now eleven people—a motley selection—at the table, the bottom of which remained unoccupied. In the middle of the table stood two very large porcelain centre-pieces adorned with painted figures which supported wide bowls filled with fresh fruits and flowers. The walls of the hall were richly festooned with decorations. What was on the table or followed little by little seemed to promise a prolonged banquet. Exquisite wines from deepest red to pale gold—whose merry sparkle generally graces only the second half of a feast—gleamed from the dining-table from amidst terrines and platters and from the serving-table in the background.

Until now the conversation had proceeded in all directions, contributions coming merrily from all sides at once. The Count, however, had at the start made several veiled references to Mozart's escapade in the garden, and was now hinting at it more and more pointedly and humorously, so that some of the guests smiled in a mysterious fashion whilst others racked their brains in vain, wondering what he meant, and our friend finally came out with the truth.

'I wish to confess,' he began, 'in what manner I had the honour of becoming acquainted with this noble family. My own role is not the most worthy one and, instead of sitting here now enjoying lunch, I came very close to landing in a remote cell in the château, with an empty stomach, looking at the cobwebs on the wall.'

'Well,' exclaimed Madame Mozart, 'it seems I'm about to hear a pretty story, indeed!'

Now he described in detail, first of all, how he had left his wife at the 'White Horse,' his walk in the park, the misadventure in the garden-bower, and his disagreement with the garden police, in brief, more or less what we already know—all this he related with the greatest innocence and much to the delight of his listeners. They could hardly stop laughing; even Eugenie, reserved as she was, joined in the merriment and positively shook with laughter.

'Well,' he continued, 'in the words of the proverb: he who has the highest score, mocking laughter can ignore! I *did* gain a little profit from the affair, as you shall see. But, above all, you will see how it came about that a childish old fool could so easily forget himself. There was a childhood memory involved in it, too.

'In the spring of 1770, as a thirteen-year-old boy, I travelled to Italy with my father. We were driving from Rome to Naples. I had played at the Conservatory on two occasions and several times elsewhere. We were shown many acts of kindness by the nobility and the clergy, in particular by a priest who attached himself to us; he considered himself a connoisseur and, moreover, was a man of some importance at court. The day before our departure, he took us, together with a number of other gentlemen, to a royal garden, the Villa Reale, situated near the splendid road that runs by the sea. Here a troupe of Sicilian *commedianti* was performing; they called themselves the *figli di Nettuno** in addition to several other fine-sounding names. Together with many noble guests, including the lovely young Queen Caroline and the two young princesses, we sat upon a long row of benches in the shade of a low, covered gallery resembling a tent, the waves splashing against its walls below. Directly ahead of us was Vesuvius, whilst on the left shimmered a lovely, gently winding coastline.

'The first part of the performance was over; this had taken place upon the dry deck of a sort of raft, which had nothing remarkable about it, floating upon the water; the second, and most beautiful part, however, consisted of interludes performed by boatmen, swimmers, and divers, and has always remained clearly engraved in my memory in every detail.

'Two frail, very lightly built craft now approached from opposite directions; both appeared to be out on a pleasure cruise. One, somewhat larger than the other, was fitted out with a half-canopy and, in addition to the banks of oars, with a slender mast and a sail; its paintwork was splendid, its prow lacquered with gold. Five handsome youths, scantily clad—their arms, breasts, and legs apparently naked—busied themselves at times at the oars, at other times dallying with five pretty girls, their sweethearts. One of the girls, sitting at the midpoint of the canopy plaiting wreaths of flowers, stood out among all the rest by reason of her beauty, her stature, and her dress. Her companions were willing handmaidens to her; they spread a sheet of cloth above her to protect her from the sun and offered her flowers from their baskets. At her feet sat a girl playing the flute, its clear tones underlying the others' song. She, too—a radiant beauty—was not without a protector; but the two behaved rather indifferently towards each other, and the lover, I thought, was almost boorish.

'Meanwhile the other, more modest craft had come closer; in this one only young men were to be seen. Whereas the young men in the larger boat were clad in bright red, these wore sea-green. They started in surprise at seeing the lovely maidens, then waved to them and made known their desire for closer acquaintance. Thereupon the boldest girl took a rose from her bosom and held it mischievously above her head, as if asking whether such gifts would be welcomed, to which all the young men in the other boat replied with unequivocal gestures. The red-clad young men bore a grim, scornful look but were unable to do anything when several of the girls agreed to throw the poor devils something to still their hunger and thirst at least. On the deck stood a basket filled with oranges; these were probably only yellow balls painted so as to resemble the fruit. And now began an enchanting spectacle, accompanied by music from the orchestra on the shore.

'One of the maidens made the first move, lightly throwing a few oranges across; these were caught with equal dexterity and soon flew back again; so it went on and on and, as more and more girls joined in, the oranges went hurtling back and forth in dozens at an ever-increasing tempo. The lovely girl in the middle of the group took no part in the battle, save that she watched, highly enraptured, from her stool. Our admiration for the skill displayed on both sides knew no bounds. The two boats revolved slowly around each other at a distance of about thirty paces; now, they faced each other flank to flank, now diagonally; about twenty-four balls were constantly flying through the air, though such was the confusion, you would have thought that there were far more. At times, a regular cross-fire developed; often they would rise and fall in a high arc; hardly ever did the one or the other miss its mark, they seemed to fall of their own accord into the open hands, drawn by some magnetic power of attraction.

'Though all this was a pleasant distraction for the eye, the melodies, too, fell sweetly upon the air: Sicilian folk music, dances, *saltarelli*, *canzoni a ballo**—an entire medley lightly linked together like a garland of flowers. The younger princess, a lovely, unaffected creature of about my own age, nodded her head gracefully in time to the music; I can still see her smile and her long eyelashes to this very day.

'Now, if you will allow me, I shall briefly describe the ensuing *scherzo*, although it has nothing to do with my own escapade! A prettier sight can hardly be imagined. While the skirmish gradually drew to an end (only a few missiles now being exchanged) and the girls collected their golden apples and brought them back to the basket, a youth on the other boat had picked up a wide green woven net, as if in play, and held it for a short time under the water; now he pulled it in again and, to the astonishment of all, there was a large fish, shimmering blue, green, and gold, inside it. Those nearby leapt to the net to draw out the fish, but it slipped out of their hands as if it were really alive and fell into the water. The whole thing was a trick intended to deceive the red-clad youths and lure them away from their boat; they, however, though enchanted by this wonder, as soon as they saw that the fish would not submerge but instead was disporting itself on the surface all the time, did not stop to think for a moment but leapt into the sea. The green-clad youths followed their example, so that now twelve well-built, expert swimmers could be seen trying to capture the fleeing creature, sometimes bobbing around upon the waves, sometimes vanishing for several minutes beneath them, now here, now there, now appearing between someone's legs, then again between someone's breast and chin. Suddenly, while the reds were concentrated most feverishly upon the chase, the rival group perceived their advantage and, quick as lightning, clambered on to the enemy boat, to the loud screams of the girls who had been left in sole command. The noblest lad, with a physique like Mercury, ran, beaming with pleasure, to the loveliest girl, took her in his arms, and kissed her; she, far from joining in the screams of her companions, threw her arms passionately around the neck of the young man, who was well known to her. The group which had been tricked now returned in haste but was driven off with oars and other weapons. Their helpless fury, the girls' screams of fear, the violent resistance offered by some, their begging and pleading, almost drowned by the other sounds, the sound of the water and of the music (which had suddenly assumed another character)—all this was beautiful beyond the power of description, and the spectators broke out in a storm of applause.

'At that moment the sail, which until then had been loosely

tied up, now unfurled, and from it appeared a rosy cherub with silver wings, armed with bow, arrows, and quiver; gracefully he hovered in mid-air above the yardarm. Now all the oars were wielded vigorously; the sail billowed out: but the presence of the god and his hasty gestures seemed to drive the craft forward with even greater power; the swimmers following it, almost out of breath—one of them holding the golden fish in his left hand above his head—very soon gave up hope and, overcome by exhaustion, were compelled to seek refuge on the deserted ship. The green-clad youths meanwhile reached a small peninsula overgrown with bushes, where a stately ship manned by an armed crew was lying in ambush. Faced by this menace, the little group put up a white flag to show that they were ready to parley. Encouraged by a similar signal from the opposing side, they too set course for the peninsula, and soon we saw all the girls (save one, who at her own wish remained behind) merrily boarding their own ship together with their sweethearts. And with that, the spectacle was at an end.'

A pause ensued, during which everyone expressed praise of the foregoing narrative. 'It seems to me,' whispered Eugenie to the Baron, her eyes shining, 'that we have just been listening to a pictorial symphony from beginning to end and a perfect reflection of the Mozart spirit itself in all its merriness, as well. Don't you think I am right? And isn't the entire beauty of *Figaro* bound up in it?'

Her fiancé was just about to repeat her remarks to the composer when Mozart continued:

'It's now seventeen years since I last saw Italy. Which of us who has once been there—especially Naples—does not think of it for the rest of his life? But I have hardly ever recalled again that last beautiful evening in the Bay of Naples as vividly as I did today in your garden. When I closed my eyes, the entire heavenly region lay spread out before me, distinct, bright, and clear, banishing the last veil of mist! Sea and strand, mountain and city, the motley crowd of people near the shore and then, that wonderful spectacle of the oranges, all mingled together! I thought I heard the same music once again and, deep inside me, an entire cavalcade of joyful melodies, composed by myself and others, passed by, willy-nilly, each one giving way to the next.

Then, by chance, I hear a dance melody which I have never heard before, in six-eight time.—Hold on, I thought, what's going on here? That's a damned pretty piece of music! I take a closer look. By Heaven, that's Masetto exactly, that's Zerlina!'* —He laughed in the direction of Madame Mozart, who immediately knew what he meant.

'It's simply this,' he continued. 'In the first act, there was a small, light part still unfinished—duet and chorus at a country wedding feast. Now, two months ago, when I intended to complete this part in chronological order, I could not think of a suitable piece straight away. A simple, childish melody brimming over with merriment, a fresh corsage of flowers with a ribbon pinned to a girl's bodice—that's what was needed. But nothing at all can be achieved by force and such minor problems often solve themselves, and so I passed over it and hardly reverted to it in the course of the major work. Then today in the carriage, just before we drove into the village, the thought of this text flashed through my mind; nothing further evolved, at least not that I know of. Anyway, about an hour later in the bower near the fountain, I hit upon a motif, better and more appropriate than I would ever have found at any other time or in any other way. We sometimes have particular experiences in the arts, but such a phenomenon has never happened to me before. Because a melody which fits the text like a second skin—but I mustn't anticipate, we are not that far advanced yet: the bird had only put his head out of the egg and so I immediately began to peel him out of the shell completely. In my mind's eye I could vividly picture Zerlina's dance and, strangely enough, the smiling landscape around the Bay of Naples came into it too. I could hear the alternating voices of the bridal pair, and the girls and young men in the chorus.'

At this point, Mozart cheerfully sang the opening lines of the song:*

> Giovinette, che fatte all'amore, che fatte all'amore,
> Non lasciate, che passi l'età, che passi l'età, che passi l'età!
> Se nel seno vi bulica il core, vi bulica il core,
> Il remedio vedete lo quà! La la la! La la la!
> Che piacer, che piacer che sarà!
>   Ah la la! Ah la la, etc.

'In the meantime my hands had committed the heinous crime. Nemesis was already lurking near the hedge and now made its appearance in the form of that dreadful man in his blue, gold-braided coat. Even if Vesuvius had erupted on that divine evening by the sea, covering and burying spectators and actors and the entire splendour of Naples with a rain of black ashes—by Heaven, the disaster could not have been more unexpected or more terrible for me. That devil! I don't believe I have ever felt such dread. A face that seemed cast in bronze—somewhat resembling that cruel Roman emperor Tiberius. Well, I thought, after he had gone, if the servant looks like that, Heaven knows what His Grace himself will look like! But to be honest, I was already very much counting upon the protection of the ladies, and not without good reason, for Stanzel here—my little wife—who is rather inquisitive by nature, had got the fat landlady at the inn to tell her the most interesting details about all the members of this distinguished family in my presence; I was standing nearby and so I heard—'

At this point Madame Mozart could not refrain from interrupting him to assure him in no uncertain terms that, on the contrary, *he* had been asking the questions; this led to a lively argument between the two which caused a great deal of laughter. 'Be that as it may,' he said; 'to cut a long story short, I was able to hear something about a dear foster-daughter—the fiancée, very beautiful, who was kindness itself and had the voice of an angel. *Per Dio!* I thought to myself, that will help you out of your scrape. Sit down this moment, write a little song as best you can, explain the truth about your stupid prank, and it will be a great joke. No sooner said than done. I had enough time to spare, and managed to find a clean little sheet of green, lined paper—And here is the result! I now place it in these lovely hands—an impromptu marriage song, if you will accept it as such.'

With this he handed a sheet of music in his neatest hand-writing to Eugenie across the table; but her uncle's hand was too quick for her—snatching it away, he exclaimed, 'Just be patient a moment, my dear!'

He waved his hand; the folding doors of the salon were opened wide and several footmen appeared. Carefully and without a sound they carried the ominous orange tree into the hall and set it down on a bench at the far end of the table; and two small, slender myrtle trees were placed left and right of it. A label attached to the stem of the orange tree proclaimed it the property of the fiancée; but in front, on a bed of moss, was a porcelain dish covered with a serviette; when the serviette was removed, a sliced orange was revealed, beside which the uncle, with a mischievous look, placed the maestro's manuscript, giving rise to general amusement which continued for a long time.

'I quite believe Eugenie doesn't even realize what is in front of her!' said the Countess. 'Really, she doesn't recognize her old favourite any more with its new blossoms and fruits!'

The young lady looked in amazement and disbelief, first at the tree, then at her uncle. 'It's not possible,' she said. 'I know for certain that there was no means of curing it.'

'So,' her uncle replied, 'you think that someone has found a substitute? That would be a fine thing! No, no—just look here— I must do exactly as they do in the comedies, where sons or brothers who were believed dead identify themselves by their scars and birthmarks. Look at this outgrowth here! And this crack running crosswise, you must have noticed them a hundred times. Well, is it your tree or isn't it?'—She could not doubt it any longer; her astonishment, her emotion, and her joy were indescribable.

As far as the family was concerned, this tree was linked with the memory—going back over more than a hundred years—of a distinguished woman, who well deserves to be briefly mentioned here.

The grandfather of Eugenie's uncle, famous for his diplomatic achievements in the Vienna government, had enjoyed the confidence and trust of two regents in succession. In his own family, too, he was no less fortunate in being married to an excellent lady, Renate Leonore. Having lived for several periods of time in France, she frequently came into contact with the brilliant court of Louis XIV and the most influential men and women of this remarkable epoch.

Despite her wholehearted participation in that continued exchange of intellectual pleasures, she never denied, either in word or deed, her innate German honesty and moral firmness which are unmistakably imprinted in the Countess's striking features as revealed in her portrait, which still exists. Thanks to this same mentality, she exercised a strangely naïve form of opposition in the society of the time, and her surviving correspondence strongly reveals the frankness and boldness—whether concerning religion, literature, politics, or any other subject—with which this unique woman was capable of defending her sound principles and viewpoints, and of attacking the weaknesses of society, without drawing its anger upon herself in the least degree. Her keen interest in everyone to be met at the house of Ninon de Lenclos, the veritable focus of the finest intellectual activity, was such as to be perfectly adapted to the exalted friendship which she shared with one of the noblest ladies of that time—Madame de Sévigné. Besides many a witty note from Chapelle* addressed to her, scribbled in the poet's own handwriting on sheets with silver-flowered margins, the letters of Madame de Sévigné and her daughter, written in the most loving terms to their good friend from Austria, were found in an ebony casket of the grandmother's after her death.

It was from Madame de Sévigné, too, that she received one day during a banquet at the Trianon the orange branch, in bloom, on the garden terrace. She immediately planted it in a pot, trusting to luck, and later, after it had successfully taken root, took it with her to Germany.

Under her care, the little tree gradually grew in size for a good twenty-five years and was later tended with the most loving care by her children and grandchildren. In addition to its intrinsic worth, it was a living symbol of the intellectual charm of an almost deified epoch, in which today, admittedly, we can find little that is worthy of praise and which already bore within itself the seeds of an ominous future whose world-shattering beginning lay not very far ahead of the period of our harmless narrative.

Eugenie bestowed a great amount of affection upon this heritage of her great-grandmother; so that her uncle often remarked that it would some day belong to her alone. It was therefore all the more painful for the young lady when, in the spring of the previous year, during her absence from the château, the tree had begun to fail; its leaves turned yellow and many of the branches died. Since no particular reason could be found for this and every remedy was without effect, the gardener soon gave up the struggle, although botanically speaking it could easily have lived to be two or three times older. The Count, however, following the advice of a neighbour who was an expert in this field, arranged for the tree to be treated by a particularly mysterious method frequently used by country-folk; this was carried out in a room reserved for the purpose and in absolute secrecy, and his hopes of one day surprising his beloved niece by presenting her old friend now filled with new vitality and fertility were fulfilled beyond all expectations. Suppressing his impatience, and not without anxiety that the fruits—many of which were already fully ripe—would not remain on the branches for so long, he postponed the joyful occasion by several weeks until today's celebration; and it can now easily be imagined with what feelings the kindly gentleman was obliged to see this happiness spoiled at the last moment by a perfect stranger.

Even before lunch, the lieutenant had found both time and opportunity to polish up his poetic contribution to the handing-over ceremony, and to adapt his verses—which perhaps were in any case too grave in tone—to the circumstances by changing the conclusion. Taking out his sheet of paper, he rose from his chair, turned towards his cousin, and began to read. The gist of his verses, in brief, was as follows:

A seedling of the famous tree of the Hesperides which, long ago, on an island in the west, had grown in Juno's garden as a wedding gift to her from Mother Earth, watched over by the three nymphs of music, has always wished and hoped for a similiar destiny itself, for the custom of presenting such a tree to a beautiful bride had been brought among mortals by the gods a long time before.

At last, after waiting long and in vain, the maiden on whom the seedling may dare to cast its gaze seems to have been found. She is kindly disposed towards it and often sits beside it. But the laurel bush of poetic renown, the seedling's proud neighbour at the edge of the fountain, has aroused its jealousy by threatening to steal the artistic maiden's desire and understanding for man's love. In vain does the myrtle try to comfort the seedling, teaching it patience by her own example; but finally, the maiden's continued absence increases the seedling's bitterness so that, after a short illness, it dies.

Summer witnesses the return of the maiden, her heart now happily transformed. The village, the château, the garden—all bid her welcome with a thousand tokens of joy. Roses and lilies, gleaming brightly, turn up their heads to her, charmed yet abashed; bushes and trees wave to her, wishing her happiness; but for *one*—alas, the noblest of all—she has come too late. Its crown is withered, her fingers stroke the lifeless stem and the brittle tips of its branches. It sees and knows its fair gardener no more. How she weeps, pouring out her tender sorrow!

From far away, Apollo hears his daughter's lament. Entering upon the scene, he looks upon her sorrow, sharing her grief. Then he touches the tree with his all-healing hands; it trembles, the dried-up sap swells mightily in the bark, fresh young leaves appear and, here and there, white blossoms burst out in ambrosial abundance. Even more—for what is beyond the power of the gods?—lovely, round fruits appear, three times three (the number of the nine sisters); they grow and grow, their young greenness visibly turning to the colour of gold. Phoebus—so ended the verse—

> Phoebus swiftly counts the harvest,
> Gloating o'er such splendour bright,
> And his mouth begins to water,
> Scarcely has he caught a sight.
>
> With a smile, the god of music
> Takes the juiciest as his price:
> 'Now let's share it, lovely maiden,
> Leaving Cupid—just this slice!'

This was followed by a storm of applause, and the guests readily forgave the poet for the grotesque ending, by which the impression created by the whole work, so truly filled with feeling, was totally revoked.

Franziska's merry wit had been stimulated more than once, sometimes by the host, sometimes by Mozart; now, as if suddenly reminded of something, she quickly scurried away and returned with an English sepia engraving of large dimensions which hung in a glazed frame, almost unnoticed, in a room far away.

'I have often heard it said,' she exclaimed, setting down the picture at the end of the table, 'and it must be true—that there is nothing new under the sun! Here is a scene from the Golden Age—and have we not seen it ourselves only today? I hope Apollo will recognize himself in this situation.'

'Excellent!' cried Max triumphantly. 'There we see him, the handsome god, just as he is leaning pensively over the sacred fountain. And what is more—there, look, an old satyr among the bushes in the background, eavesdropping on him! One could swear that Apollo is at this moment recalling a long-forgotten Arcadian dance taught to him as a child by old Chiron on the zither.'

'Of course! Exactly!' seconded Franziska, who was standing behind Mozart. 'And,' she continued, addressing him, 'do you see the branch, laden with fruit, bending towards the god?'

'You're quite right; it's the olive tree that is dedicated to him.'

'Not at all! they are the most gorgeous oranges! Any moment now, he will pluck one out of sheer absent-mindedness.'

'No, no,' exclaimed Mozart; 'any moment now, he will seal those roguish lips with a thousand kisses.' Thereupon he seized her by the arm and swore he would not release her until she offered him her lips—which she did without much demur.

'Max!' said the Countess, 'please explain for us what it says here below the picture!'

'Those are verses from a famous ode by Horace. The poet Ramler in Berlin gave us a superb German translation of the poem only a short time ago. It's absolutely marvellous. *This* part in particular is wonderful:

> —here, who on his shoulder
> Bears a bow that does not lie unused!
>
> Who dwells in the green grove of his native Delos
> And upon Patara's shaded shore,
> Who dips the golden locks of his head
> Into the waves of the Castalian sea.*

'Beautiful! Simply beautiful!' said the Count; 'except that it needs explaining here and there. For example, "who . . . bears a bow that does not lie unused" means quite simply, he was at all times a most accomplished violinist. But what I was about to say, my dear Mozart: you are sowing the seeds of discord between two tender hearts.'

'I sincerely hope not—in what way?'

'Eugenie is envious of her friend—and has every reason to be so.'

'Aha, so you have already spotted my weakness. But what does her fiancé have to say about it?'

'I'll turn a blind eye once or twice.'

'Very well; we shall take the next opportunity. Have no fear, Baron, there's no danger, as long as Apollo here does not lend me his visage and his long golden hair. I only wish he would! He would receive in exchange Mozart's plait, with its most splendid ribbon, on the spot.'

'Then Apollo had better see to it that he may decently dip his new French coiffure into the Castalian waves in future!' laughed Franziska.

This and similar witticisms only served to heighten the jolly, carefree mood more and more. The men gradually began to feel the effect of the wine, and a great many toasts were drunk. Mozart began, according to his custom, to speak in verse, in which he was matched by the lieutenant; nor was the Count far behind, for on several occasions he succeeded splendidly in following their example. But matters of this kind are not appropriate for such a narrative and ought not even to be repeated, for the very quality that makes them irresistible where they happen —the heightened merriment, the brilliance, the jovial humour of personal expression in looks and words—is missing.

The old maiden aunt proposed a toast in the maestro's honour, which foretold a whole row of immortal masterpieces from his pen. '*A la bonne heure!** I'll drink to that!' exclaimed Mozart, touching glasses vigorously with her. Thereupon the Count, with a powerful, assured intonation, began to sing a verse born of his own inspiration:

Count
May the gods the strength increase
That he needs for each fine piece,

  Max (continuing)
Of which neither old da Ponte,
No, nor Schikaneder mighty,*

Mozart
Nor their composer, Lord, I fear
Have, as yet, the first idea.

Count
May he live to hear the lot,
That rascally Italian sot.
That to see I'd really care,
Our Signor Bonbonnière!*

Max
Good, one hundred years of cares—

Mozart
I'll grant to him, his goods and wares—

All (con forza)
If yet the Devil deigns to spare
Our Monsieur Bonbonnière!

Stimulated by the Count's pleasure in singing, the trio—this product of chance—after repeating the last four lines, went on into a so-called final canon, and the maiden aunt possessed sufficient self-confidence or humour to assist by adding her own cracked soprano with flourishes of all kinds. Afterwards, Mozart promised to prepare a complete version specially for all the guests, a promise which he later fulfilled following his return to Vienna.

Eugenie had already secretly learned by heart her treasure from the bower of Tiberius; now everyone clamoured to hear the duet sung by herself and the composer, and her uncle was pleased to show off his voice once more in the chorus. And so the whole party rose from the table and hurried to the piano in the large adjoining room.

Entirely charmed though the company was by the lovely duet, its content rapidly led on to that pinnacle of social enjoyment in which the music itself no longer counts: first of all, our friend gave the signal by leaping up from the piano and, walking over to Franziska, invited her to join him in a gliding waltz, whilst Max very willingly took up his violin. At this, the host lost no time in inviting Madame Mozart to dance. In a flash, all the movable furniture had been taken away by a troupe of diligent servants in order to make more room. One after another, all had to take their turn, and the maiden aunt was not in the least put out when the gallant lieutenant invited her to join him in a minuet, which made her feel years younger. Finally, when Mozart had the last dance with Eugenie, he claimed his right, already assured, to her lovely lips in the most charming possible manner.

Evening had now drawn in and the sun was going down. Only now was it really pleasant out of doors, so that the Countess proposed to the ladies that they should refresh themselves a little in the garden. The Count, on the other hand, invited the gentlemen to the billiard room, knowing that Mozart was very fond of the game. The company therefore split into two groups; we, for our part, shall now follow the ladies into the garden.

After walking slowly up and down the path several times, they climbed a round hill, half-surrounded by fields of tall grapevines, which offered a good view of the open countryside, the village, and the highway. The last rays of the autumn sun were gleaming crimson through the vine-leaves.

'Wouldn't it be nice if we were to sit here,' said the Countess, 'and Madame Mozart were to tell us something of herself and her husband?'

Constanze was perfectly willing, and the whole group made themselves very comfortable on the chairs, which were arranged in a circle.

'I would like to tell you something which you ought to have heard in any case, because it is the subject of a little joke which I am planning. I intend to give Countess Eugenie, in happy memory of this day, a small present of a very special kind. There is so little that is fashionable or luxurious about it that only the story behind it can make it interesting.'

'What can it be, Eugenie?' said Franziska. 'The inkwell of a famous man, at least!'

'Not far wrong! You shall see the treasure within the hour; it's in my travelling chest. Now I shall begin; but with your permission, I must go back in time a little.

'Last winter I was very anxious about Mozart's state of health; he was sometimes very irritable and often depressed, with a tendency to fever. At times, when in company, he was merry, often more than was natural; but at home he was usually sunk in melancholy, sighing and complaining. The physician recommended diet, Pyrmont water, and exercise away from the city.

But the patient paid little attention to this good advice, for a cure of that kind was a nuisance and time-consuming and ran quite contrary to his daily routine. Then the doctor gave him a thorough dressing-down, and he was obliged to listen to a long lecture about the nature of human blood and the corpuscles in it, about breathing and phlogiston*—things he had never dreamt of before; how eating, drinking, and digestion are part of Nature's plan—something which, until then, Mozart knew as much about as his five-year-old son. The lesson really made a deep impression upon him. The doctor had not been gone half-an-hour when I found my husband in his room, with a thoughtful but cheerful expression, studying a walking-stick which he had looked for and found in a cupboard full of old odds and ends; I had not thought he would even remember it. It had once belonged to my father, a fine stick with a long handle made of lapis lazuli. Mozart was never to be seen with a stick in his hand, and I could not help laughing.

'"There, you see," he exclaimed, "I'm in the process of taking the cure completely. I shall drink the water, take exercise in the open air every day and make use of the stick. A number of things have just occurred to me. It's not without good reason, I thought, that other people, men with both feet on the ground, could never be without their walking-sticks. Our neighbour, the Commercial Councillor, never goes across the street to visit his crony without his stick. Professional men, public servants, government officials, shopkeepers and their customers—when they go for a walk with their families outside the city, every one of them takes his honest, decent walking-stick with him. And I've often noticed on Stephansplatz* a quarter-of-an-hour before the sermon and before mass, respectable citizens standing here and there in groups talking: you can see perfectly how all their unsung virtues, their industry and sense of propriety, composure and contentment lean upon those sturdy walking-sticks and use them as a support. In short—there must be a blessing and particular consolation in this old-fashioned and rather tasteless custom. Believe it or not, as you wish; I can hardly wait to walk for the first time together with this good friend across the bridge to the race track! We already know each other a little and I hope that our relationship is sealed for ever."

'The relationship was of short duration: the third time the two went out together, his companion did not come back again. Another was procured and was true to him somewhat longer; in any case, I put it down to Mozart's liking for sticks that he followed the doctor's orders very passably for three weeks. And with good results; hardly ever did we see him so fresh, so wide-awake, and so even-tempered. But a short time later he kicked over the traces once again and, as a result, I had my problems with him every day. That was when he went to a musical soirée—though it was already late and he was tired after a hard day's work—simply to oblige a few inquisitive visitors to the city; just for an hour, he said, and promised me on his word of honour; but those are the occasions when people most often take advantage of his good nature, after he has only just taken his place at the piano full of eagerness; there he sits like the little man in a Montgolfier balloon floating six miles above the ground, so high that you cannot hear the bells ringing. I sent the servant there twice in the middle of the night, but it was no use—he could not get through to his master, who finally came home at three in the morning. I decided to go into a real sulk for the whole day.'

Here Madame Mozart omitted a number of incidents. The reader should know that it was not unlikely that a young singer, Signora Malerbi, whom Constanze had good reason to dislike, would attend the soirée in question. This person, a native of Rome, had been engaged by the Vienna Opera on Mozart's recommendation; and there was no doubt that her powers of co-quetry had played no small part in winning the maestro's favour. Some even claimed that she had bewitched him for months on end and kept his ardour aglow upon her grill. Whether this was completely true or grossly exaggerated—the fact is that she afterwards showed herself impertinent and ungrateful and even indulged in mocking remarks about her benefactor. Thus it was quite typical of her that she once described him to one of her more fortunate admirers simply as 'un piccolo grifo raso' (a little shaved snout). This description, worthy of Circe herself, was all the more cruel because—it must be admitted—it contained a tiny grain of truth, after all.

On the way home from the soirée (at which, as it happened, Signora Malerbi had not appeared) a friend of Mozart's, made merry by the wine, was indiscreet enough to repeat the malicious remark to the maestro. This annoyed him considerably, since he saw it, in fact, as the first indisputable proof of his protégée's heartlessness. He was so angry that he did not even notice at first the frosty reception he received at his wife's bedside. He repeated the story of the insult in a single breath; and we may infer from such honesty that his feelings of guilt were very small. She almost expressed sympathy for him; she deliberately kept it to herself, however, not wishing to make it too easy for him. When he awoke from a deep sleep, shortly after noon, he found that his wife had gone out with their two small sons, leaving the table neatly laid for him alone.

It had always been the case that few things could make Mozart so unhappy as when the relationship between himself and his better half was unpleasant and unharmonious. And yet—if only he had known of the other anxiety she had had to bear for several days now!—one of the most serious, indeed, though it had always been her custom to delay revealing it to him for as long as possible. Her housekeeping money had been spent almost entirely and she had no prospects of further funds in the near future. Though he was completely unaware of this domestic problem, his heart was weighed down with a feeling of helplessness and frustration. He had no appetite and no desire to stay at home; he dressed quickly with only one aim—to escape from the oppressive air of the house. Taking a small sheet of paper, he wrote a few lines in Italian: 'You really have paid me back, and I deserve it. Please forgive me and smile once more when I come home again. Believe me, I'm so down in the dumps that I almost feel like becoming a Carthusian or a Trappist.' Then he picked up his hat, though not his stick—that belonged to another epoch.

Having until now assumed Madame Constanze's role in telling this tale, we may as well proceed a little further.

After leaving his dwelling near the market hall, our good friend turned right at the Arsenal and strolled in a leisurely fashion (it was a warm, somewhat cloudy summer afternoon), lost in thought, across the courtyard, as it was called, past the Presbytery of Our Lady and on towards the Schottentor. Here he turned left, climbing to the Mölkerbastei, and thus avoided being spoken to by several acquaintances who were just entering the city. Here he enjoyed the splendid view across the green plain of the glacis and the suburbs towards Kahlenberg and the Styrian Alps to the south, but only briefly, although the sentry pacing back and forth without a sound beside the cannon did not disturb him. Nature's peaceful beauty around him conflicted with his inner feelings. With a sigh, he continued his walk across the Esplanade and on through the Alser suburb without any particular destination in mind.

At the far end of the Währinger Gasse was a tavern with a skittle alley. The owner, a master ropemaker, was well known to the neighbours and other citizens whose business led them past, on account of his good merchandise and the excellence of his wines. The clattering of skittles could be heard, although, with only a dozen customers present at the most, there was not much activity. Moved by an almost unconscious impulse to lose himself among ordinary simple folk, the composer went inside. Here he sat down at one of the tables in the scanty shadow of some trees beside a Viennese Inspector of Wells and two other worthy citizens. He ordered a glass of wine and joined heartily in their conversation, which was of a very commonplace kind, from time to time walking about or watching the game in the skittle alley.

Not far from the skittle alley, at the side of the house, was the ropemaker's shop, open to the street. This was a narrow room filled to bursting with wares; in addition to products of the rope-making trade, all kinds of wooden articles for the kitchen, wine-cellar and agricultural use, as well as fish oil and axle grease, and small quantities of seeds, dill, and caraway, were for sale, standing on the floor or hanging from the walls. The waitress, a girl whose task it was to look after the shop as well as wait on the guests, was dealing with a peasant who, holding his small son by the hand, had come to make some purchases—a fruit measure, a brush, and a whip. Selecting an article from among many others, he would examine it, put it to one side, pick up a second, then a third, and then come back doubtfully to the first one. This went on with no end in sight. The girl went away several times to serve guests; then she returned, sparing no effort to help him with his choice and make it easier for him, though not saying too much.

Mozart, sitting on a small bench by the skittle alley, was watching and listening to all of this with enjoyment. Pleased though he was by the girl's capable, knowledgeable manner and the calm, serious expression of her attractive features, his interest was even more aroused by the peasant who, though he had gone away perfectly satisfied, still gave Mozart much food for thought. He had put himself absolutely in the man's position, had felt how carefully this bit of business had been completed, how anxiously and conscientiously he had weighed up the prices, though the difference was a matter of a few coppers. And then he imagined the man coming home to his wife and proudly telling her about his purchases while the children wait expectantly for the sack to be opened, to see whether there is something in it for them—but his wife hurries away to bring him a bite to eat and a cool drink of home-made cider for which he has been saving up his entire appetite!

'Who else could be as happy as this peasant, so independent of his fellow men! reliant only upon Nature and her blessings, however hard-earned these may be!

'Though I have been put to a different trade—my art—which, after all, I would not change for any other in the world—why am I obliged to live under conditions totally different from such an innocent, simple existence as his? If I had a small farm, a little house in a village in pleasant surroundings, I would awake to new life again! Working hard at my composition all morning, spending the rest of the time with the family; planting trees, inspecting the fields, picking the apples and pears with the children in autumn; now and then travelling to the city to hear a concert and, from time to time, a visit from a friend or two— what happiness that would be! Oh, well, who can say how things will turn out?'

Walking over to the counter he spoke a few friendly words to the girl and began to examine her wares carefully. Because of the direct relationship between most of the articles and his idyllic flight of fancy a moment before, he was attracted by the cleanness, the brightness, the smoothness, even the smell of the various wooden items. Suddenly he had the idea of buying a number of articles for his wife which, he thought, would please her and prove useful. He directed his attention first of all to the gardening tools; just a year ago, at his suggestion, Constanze had rented a small plot of land in front of the Kärntner Tor where she had grown a few vegetables; a large new rake, a small rake, and a spade, he thought, would serve the purpose to begin with. He then picked up some other utensils, and it says much for his sense of economy that, after a moment of reflection, he decided against a butter tub—though reluctantly—which had very much appealed to him; on the other hand, a tall receptacle intended for a variety of purposes, fitted with a lid and a prettily carved handle, caught his fancy. It was made of narrow staves of two different kinds of wood, alternately light and dark, wider at the bottom than at the top and skilfully caulked inside. An attractive selection of wooden spoons, rolling pins, chopping blocks, and platters of various sizes, as well as a salt box of very simple construction for hanging on the wall, were clearly ideal for kitchen use.

Finally he examined a large cudgel with a leather-bound grip and well studded with round brass nails. Seeing that this strange customer seemed somewhat tempted by this last item, too, the girl remarked with a smile that it was hardly a thing to be carried by a gentleman. 'You're quite right, my child,' he replied; 'I have an idea they are carried by butchers when travelling. Away with it! I don't want it. But all the other things that we have set aside, you may bring to my house today or tomorrow.' He gave her his name and address, then went back to finish his glass at his table where, of the original three guests, only one, a tinsmith, was sitting.

'The waitress is having a good day today,' said the man; 'her cousin gives her a penny from every guilder of the profits from the shop.'

Mozart's pleasure in his purchases was now twofold, but his interest in the girl was soon to become even greater: when she was close by once again, the tinsmith called out to her: 'How are things, Creszenz? How's your locksmith friend? Will he soon be running his own business?'

'Heavens, no!' she exclaimed as she hurried past; 'That's still way off in the clouds, I should think.'

'She's a good girl,' said the tinsmith. 'Kept house for her stepfather for a long time and took care of him when he was ill, and after he died it came out that he'd gone through all her money; since then, she's been working for her cousin here, and she manages everything: in the shop, in the tavern, and looks after the children. She's courting a craftsman, a decent young fellow, and she'd like to marry him, the sooner the better; but there's a problem.'

'What sort of problem? I suppose he hasn't any money?'

'Both of them have saved something, but it's not nearly enough. Now's there's half a house and a workshop coming up for auction shortly, and it would be an easy matter for the ropemaker to lend them what they need to make up the purchase price, but of course he doesn't like the idea of letting the girl go. He's got some good friends on the Council and in the guild, and so now the locksmith is running into difficulties everywhere.'

'Damnation!' cried Mozart, so violently that the other was startled and looked around to see if anyone was listening. 'And there's no one man enough to speak up and say the right thing? Or hold his fist under the master's nose? Blackguards, the lot of them! Just you wait, we'll catch you yet!'

The tinsmith sat there as if on hot coals. Clumsily he tried to tone down what he had said; indeed he almost revoked it completely. But Mozart would not listen to him. 'Shame on you for talking like that! It's always the same with rogues like you, the moment you have to stand up for something worthwhile.'

With this remark he turned his back on the lily-livered fellow without bidding him goodbye. The waitress was very busy attending to some new guests, but as he walked past her he whispered: 'Come early tomorrow; my regards to your sweetheart, and I hope things will turn out well for you both.' She started in surprise and had neither time nor presence of mind enough to thank him.

More quickly than usual—for the incident had stirred his blood—he walked back the way he had come, as far as the glacis; here he slowed his pace and, turning from his accustomed path, strolled around the embankments in a wide semicircle. His thoughts centering entirely upon the poor lovers, he mentally ran through an entire row of friends and patrons who might be able to help in one way or another.

However, he still required some further details from the girl before being able to take any action, and he therefore decided to wait until he had obtained them; now, his heart and mind running ahead of his feet, he was already, in his thoughts, at home with his wife.

He was looking forward with a feeling of certainty to a friendly —indeed joyful—welcome, kiss, and embrace at the threshhold, and as he turned into the Kärntner Tor his yearning impelled him to double his pace. He has not gone far when the postman calls to him and gives him a small but heavy packet addressed, he sees immediately, in a clear, honest handwriting. He goes with the postman into the nearest shop to sign for the packet; back in the street once more, he cannot wait until he arrives home and, breaking the seal, he devours the letter, half-walking, half-standing still.

'I was sitting at my sewing table,' said Madame Mozart, continuing her narrative, 'when I heard my husband coming up the stairs and asking the servant where I was. His voice and his step seemed somehow more confident and more determined than I had expected and—to tell the truth—more than I liked. First he went to his room, but then he came straight away to me. "Good evening!" he said; I replied quietly, without looking up from my work. After pacing up and down the room in silence a few times he took down the fly-swatter from behind the door—this accompanied by a few forced yawns—which he had never thought to do before—murmuring to himself: "I wonder where all these flies have come from!"—then he began swatting here and there as vigorously as he possibly could. This had always been the most unpleasant noise possible as far as he was concerned, which I must never dare to make in his presence. Strange, I thought, how some things seem quite different to people—especially to men—when they themselves are doing them! I had not, by the way, noticed many flies at all. His odd behaviour really annoyed me. "Six at *one* blow!" he exclaimed; "Shall I show you?" No answer. Then he placed something on my sewing cushion, so that I could not help seeing it without even taking my eyes from my work. It was nothing worse than a small pile of gold coins, as many ducats as you can hold between finger and thumb. He continued his tomfoolery behind my back, striking a blow now and again and murmuring to himself: "Nasty, worthless, shameless creatures! I'd just like to know what they are good for!—Bang!—Obviously just for the purpose of being swatted!—Bang!—Well, I may say I'm rather good at that.—A study of natural history teaches us about the amazing powers of reproduction of these creatures.—Bang, bang!—In my house we always get rid of them right away. Ah, *maledette! disperate!*—Here's another twenty of them. Would you like them?"—He came towards me and did the same as before. Until then I had managed, with an effort, to stop laughing, but now I couldn't do so any longer; I burst out laughing, he threw his arms around me, and we both laughed and giggled like idiots.

'"But where did you get the money?" I ask, while he is shaking the rest of it out of the packet.—"From Prince Esterhazy!* Through Haydn. Just read the letter." I read as follows:

'Eisenstadt, etc. My dear friend! His Highness, my most gracious lord, has instructed me, to my great pleasure, to send you the enclosed sum of sixty ducats. We recently performed your quartets* again and His Highness was almost more impressed and taken by them than on the occasion of the first performance three months ago. The Prince remarked to me (I must repeat it word for word): "When Mozart dedicated this work to you, he intended to honour only you, but it will do him no harm at all if I, too, see it as a compliment to myself. Tell him, I think almost as highly of his genius as you yourself—he cannot hope for more, even if he were to live forever!"—Amen, I say! Are you satisfied?

'P.S. A word in your loving wife's ear: make sure that the words of thanks are not put off too long. It would be best of all if he were to thank the Prince personally. We must not lose such a favourable wind in our sails.

'"You angel! Heavenly creature!" exclaimed Mozart again and again, and it is hard to say what pleased him most: the letter, or the Prince's words of praise, or the money. As far as I am concerned—well, to be honest, it was the money that was most welcome to me. We celebrated a very merry evening together.

'With regard to the incident in the suburbs, I did not hear anything that day nor in the days that followed; the whole week went by, but Crescenz did not appear and my husband soon forgot about the matter amidst a whole pile of business matters. One Sunday evening we had visitors: Captain Wesselt, Count Hardegg, and some other gentlemen were playing music. During a pause I am called out of the room—and there it is! I go back in and ask: "Did you order a collection of household implements in the Alser?" "Good heavens, yes! I suppose a girl brought them? Let her come in."——And so, in she came with a friendly smile and a full basket on her arm and rakes and spades in her hands; she apologized for the delay, said she had forgotten the name of the street and found the way here only that day. Mozart took the articles from her one after the other and immediately handed them over to me with every satisfaction. I thanked him kindly, being very pleased with everything, though I did not understand why he had bought the gardening implements. "Why," he said, "for your little allotment by the river, of course."——"Good Lord, we gave that up long ago, because the water always caused so much damage, and because nothing came of it anyway. I told you, and you made no objection."——"What! So the asparagus we had this spring—" "—always came from the market."——"Well, well," he said, "if only I had known! I complimented you on the asparagus out of pure kindness, because I really felt sorry for you with your gardening; they had all the delicacy of quills."

'The gentlemen were most amused to hear of the incident and I had to make a present of a few unwanted articles to some of them as a souvenir. But then Mozart began to question the girl about her marriage plans and encouraged her to speak without any fear, for, he said, what they intended to do for her and her sweetheart would be done quietly, without serious consequences and without interference from anyone; and she replied so modestly, so deferentially and nicely that she completely won the hearts of all present, and at last they let her go after promising her every help and support.

'"We must help these people!" said the captain. "Interference from the guild is the least problem of all; I know someone in the guild who will soon put a stop to that. The important thing is a donation for the house, furniture, and so forth. How would it be if we were to announce a concert for friends to be held in the

Trattner Hall, price of admission to be 'ad lib'?" The proposal met with everyone's approval. One of the gentlemen picked up the salt tub and said: "Someone should begin the concert with an elegant speech recounting the story of Herr Mozart's purchases and explaining his philanthropic intentions; and this beautiful salt tub should be placed on a table as a collecting box, with the two rakes crosswise behind it as a decoration."

'This was not done, in fact; but the concert did take place; it brought in a respectable sum of money, and various donations followed so that the happy couple had money to spare and all the other difficulties were quickly disposed of. The Duscheks in Prague—our best friends there, we stay at their home—heard about the story, and Frau Duschek, a pleasant, kind-hearted woman, asked to have one of the articles for curiosity's sake, and so I set aside the most suitable item for her and took it with me the next time we visited them. Now that we have meantime unexpectedly made the acquaintance of a new lover of art, who is on the point of setting up her own home and surely would not refuse a simple household utensil selected by Mozart, I shall halve my gifts: you have the choice between a beautifully carved chocolate whisk and the notorious salt cellar, which the artist has embellished with an elegant tulip. I would recommend the latter absolutely; salt, a noble substance, is as far as I know a symbol of homeliness and hospitality, and we would like to add to it our very best wishes for you both.'

Thus Madame Mozart. The reader can imagine with what gratitude and merriment all this was received by the ladies. The laughter broke out anew when, shortly afterwards, the articles were shown to the gentlemen upstairs and that example of patriarchal simplicity formally handed over, for which the uncle promised no lesser a place in the silver cupboard of its new owner and her future children than that occupied by the Florentine master* in the Ambras collection.

It was now almost eight o'clock and time for tea. Soon, however, our maestro was urgently reminded of the promise he had given in the afternoon, namely, to give the guests a foretaste of the 'Fire of Hell', which was under lock and key, though fortunately not too deep inside the chest. He was ready to do so without hesitation. Without spending much time in explaining the plot, he opened the libretto and soon the candles were burning upon the piano.

We would be pleased if the reader could experience at least something of that curious feeling aroused by a single, interrupted chord of music which falls upon our ears when we are walking past a window—it cannot come from anywhere else—which strikes us like an electric shock, bringing us to a halt as if frozen; something of that pleasurable apprehension that we feel in the theatre when we are seated in front of the curtain while the orchestra is tuning up. Is it not so? When, at the opening of any noble work of tragedy—whether it be *Macbeth* or *Oedipus* or whatever—a breath of eternal beauty hovers in the air, where would we feel this to a greater degree than here, or even to the same degree? Man wishes and at the same time fears to be driven out of his normal self, he feels that the infinite will touch him, squeezing his breast as if it would stretch it open and violently pull the spirit to it. Added to this is the awe which one feels when confronted by a perfect work of art; the idea of being permitted and able to enjoy a divine miracle, to assimilate it into oneself, arouses a sort of emotion, even of pride, perhaps the purest and happiest we are capable of feeling.

The guests on that particular evening, however, who were now to hear for the first time a work of music which has been ours from the time of our youth, were in a position totally different from ours and—apart from the enviable good fortune of having the work performed for them personally by the author himself—by no means as favourable as ours, since no one could have understood it entirely and completely, and, from more than one point of view, could not have done so even if the work could have been performed entire and unabridged.

Out of a total of eighteen completed pieces, the composer probably did not play even half (in the report on which our story is based, only the final piece in this series, the sextet, is expressly mentioned)—it seems that he gave them in the form of a free selection, played only on the piano, singing now and then as the mood and opportunity arose. As for the lady, the report only mentions that she sang two arias. Since her voice is said to have been as powerful as it was sweet, we may imagine the first aria to have been that of Donna Anna ('You know the traitor'), and the other, one of the two sung by Zerlina.

In terms of intellect, insight, and taste, Eugenie and her fiancé were, to be precise, the only listeners of the kind the maestro preferred, the former even more so than the latter. Both were seated at the very back of the room; the young lady as motionless as a statue and carried away by the music so much that, even in the shorter intervals, during which the other guests modestly displayed their appreciation or involuntarily expressed their inner feelings by an exclamation of admiration, she was unable to reply in full to her fiancé's remarks.

After Mozart had finished his performance with the effusively beautiful sextet and the conversation gradually revived, he seemed to be listening with particular interest and goodwill to some isolated remarks made by the Baron. The talk was mainly about the conclusion of the opera and of the performance provisionally fixed for the beginning of November; and when someone remarked that certain sections of the finale might constitute a tremendous challenge, the maestro smiled somewhat reservedly; Constanze, however, said to the Countess, so that he too was bound to hear her: 'He still has something up his sleeve, which he makes a great secret of—even to me.'

'You're forgetting yourself, my sweet,' he replied, 'in mentioning that now; what if I suddenly had an urge to begin again? And to tell the truth, I'm itching to do so.'

'Leporello!'* shouted the Count, leaping merrily to his feet and waving to a footman. 'Wine! Sillery,* three bottles!'

'No, no! That's enough now—my squire has had all the wine he's going to drink today.'

'To his health, then—and to each his own!'

'Heavens, what have I done!' wailed Constanze, looking at the clock, 'It will soon be eleven, and we must leave early in the morning—however shall we do it?'

'You can't do it, dear lady—you simply can't do it.'

'Sometimes,' Mozart began, 'things can turn out very strangely. What will my dear Stanzl say when she learns that the very piece she is now about to hear was born at just this time of night, and before the start of an intended journey just as now?'

'Is that true? When? I'm sure it must have been three weeks ago when you were about to go to Eisenstadt?'

'Exactly! And it happened like this: I came home from a dinner at Richters', after ten o'clock—you were already fast asleep. I wanted to go to bed earlier than usual, as I had promised, so as to rise early and step straight into the carriage. Veit had lighted the candles on my writing desk as usual and I was putting on my dressing-gown mechanically, when I thought of taking a quick look at my last piece of composition. But what a mishap! A curse on women's useless interference! You had put everything away, packed the manuscripts—I had to take them with me, the Prince wanted to see a sample of the opus—I searched, growled, and grumbled—all to no avail! Just then, my eye falls upon a sealed envelope: from the priest,* judging by the dreadful handwriting of the address—yes, indeed! sending me the revised remainder of his libretto, which I hadn't expected to see before the end of the month. I immediately sit down, filled with curiosity, and begin to read—I am overjoyed to see how well the odd fellow understands what I want. Everything was much simpler, more compressed and yet fuller. Both the churchyard scene and the finale, up to the hero's death, had been improved in every way. (O excellent poet, I thought, you shall not go without thanks for having summoned up heaven and hell for a second time!) Now, I am not in the habit of anticipating when I am composing, no matter how tempting it may be; that is a bad habit which can cause a lot of problems. But there are exceptions to this: briefly, the scene near the statue of the governor on horseback, the threat suddenly coming from the grave of the murdered man and interrupting the laughter of the nocturnal reveller in a horrible fashion, had already occurred to me. I struck a chord and felt that I had knocked at the right gate, with the entire host of terrors assembled behind it which are to be released at the finale. At first an adagio emerged—D minor, only four beats, followed by a second phrase with five beats—I flatter myself it will be something extraordinary on the stage when the voice is accompanied by the loudest brass instruments. Now you shall hear it as well as it can be done here on the piano.'

Without further ado he snuffed out the candles in the two

candelabra beside him, and that dreadful chorus, 'Your laughter will cease before the day dawns!' resounded through the deathly silence of the room. The sounds of silver trumpets fall as if from distant stars, ice cold, cutting through the blue night and freezing the blood and marrow.

'Who is there? Answer!' calls Don Giovanni. Then the music begins again, in a monotone as before, commanding the dastardly youth to leave the dead in peace.

After the last vibration of these ominous chords had died away Mozart continued: 'Now, of course, there was no question of my stopping. When once the ice breaks at only *one* spot on the shore, the ice shatters over the entire lake, resounding to the most distant corner of it. Involuntarily I picked up the same thread again further on, at Don Giovanni's supper, after Donna Elvira has just left and the ghost appears following the invitation.—Now listen!'

And now the entire, long, dreadful dialogue followed, which sweeps even the most hardened listener to the limits of human imagination, indeed, beyond them, where we see and hear the supernatural and, within our hearts, feel ourselves thrown helplessly back and forth from one extreme to the other.

Though far estranged from human speech, the dead man's immortal voice forces itself to speak once more. When, soon after the first dreadful greeting, when the spirit spurns the earthly food that is offered to him, with what strange eeriness does his voice range unevenly up and down the steps of an air-woven ladder! He demands atonement, to be decided swiftly: he has but little time left; long, long, long is the road he must travel! And when Don Giovanni in a mood of monstrous stubbornness defies the laws of eternity, struggling helplessly against the growing onslaught of the powers of hell, twisting and turning, and finally falls to his doom though still displaying a sublime power in every gesture—who, among those listening, does not shudder in heart and soul with fear and pleasure both? It is a feeling akin to that experienced when watching awestruck the tremendous spectacle of an indomitable natural force or the burning of a splendid ship. Unwillingly we feel at one, so to speak, with this blind majesty, sharing its agony and overcome with grief during the sweeping moments of its self-destruction.

The composer had now finished. No one dared at first to break the universal silence.

At last the Countess spoke in a voice still choked with emotion. 'Tell us,' she said, 'tell us, I beg you, something of your feelings as you laid down your pen that night.'

He looked up at her amiably as if recalled from a peaceful reverie, then quickly recollecting himself he said, partly to the lady, partly to his wife: 'Well, of course, my head was spinning at the end. I had completed this despairing debate, up to the ghosts' chorus, in one single frenzy, beside the open window, and after a short pause I rose from my chair to go to your chamber so that we might chat a little and my heated blood cool down. Then a curious thought struck me, causing me to stop in the middle of the room.' (At this point he looked down for two or three seconds and, when he continued, a slight tremor, hardly noticeable, could be detected in his voice.) 'I said to myself: if you were to die tonight and leave the work unfinished at this point—could you lie in peace in your grave? I stared at the wick of the candle I was holding and the mountains of melted wax. For a moment a flash of pain ran through me at the idea; then I went on thinking: if, sooner or later, another, perhaps some Italian or other, were to be given the work to complete and find everything, from the introduction up to No. 17, with the exception of *one* piece, all neatly arranged—ripe, healthy fruit fallen into the deep grass, so that he need only to pick it up—the middle part of the finale might make him a little apprehensive— and then, if unexpectedly he were to find this great portion here that had been set aside—*then* indeed he might well laugh up his sleeve! Perhaps he would be tempted to usurp the honour that was rightly mine. If so he would certainly burn his fingers; I have a few good friends who know the marks of my work and would ensure that what is mine should be ascribed to me.— Now I went back to my desk, thanking God with my eyes turned to heaven and, dear wife, thanking your guardian angel, who held his hands so gently over your face for so long that you slept on like a dormouse, entirely unable to call to me. When at last I came to you and you asked me what time it was, I simply lied to you, making you a few hours younger than you were, for it was almost four o'clock. So now you will understand why you could not get me out of bed at six and why the coachman had to be sent home again and told to come the following day instead.'

'Of course!' replied Constanze, 'But the clever fellow need not flatter himself that others were so stupid as not to notice anything! So there was truly no need for you to keep your head-start a secret from me!'

'That was not the reason!'

'Yes, I know—for the time being, you didn't want your treasure known.'

'I am only pleased,' said their good-natured host, 'that we shall not have to disappoint a noble Vienna coachman tomorrow, if Herr Mozart simply cannot get out of bed. It always hurts a coachman to hear "Hans, unharness the horses again!"'

This indirect appeal to the Mozarts to stay longer—with which the other voices heartily concurred—was cause for the two travellers to argue most convincingly that this was not possible; but both sides gladly agreed that they should not set out too early and that all should partake of a pleasant breakfast together.

The company stood about in groups for a while, chatting with one another. Mozart looked around in search of someone, evidently Eugenie; but as she was not there just at that moment, he addressed the question he had intended for her directly to Franziska, who was standing near him. 'What do you think of our *Don Giovanni* on the whole? What sort of future would you prophecy for it?'

'On behalf of my cousin,' she replied laughing, 'I shall answer as best I can. My own foolish opinion is, that if the whole world does not madly applaud *Don Giovanni*, then God in Heaven will close the lid of His music box—for a long time, I mean—and give mankind to understand—' 'And give mankind,' broke in her uncle, correcting her, 'a set of bagpipes and so deaden people's hearts that they shall henceforth worship Baal.'

'God forbid!' laughed Mozart. 'Anyway, in the course of the next sixty or seventy years, long after I am gone, many a false prophet will arise.'

Now Eugenie joined them together with Max and the Baron; the conversation spontaneously revived anew, turning once more to important, serious topics, so that, before the company broke up, the composer was able to hear many a pleasing, appropriate remark which flattered his hopes.

It was long after midnight when the party dispersed; no one realized until then how much he or she needed sleep.

At ten o'clock next morning—the weather being just as fine as the day before—a handsome travelling carriage, packed with the belongings of the guests from Vienna, was seen waiting in the courtyard of the château. The Count, standing with Mozart in front of the carriage just before the horses were led out, asked Mozart how he liked the vehicle.

'Very much—it looks extremely comfortable to me.'

'Very well, then—do me the pleasure of keeping it as a souvenir of me.'

'What? Are you serious?'

'Why not?'

'By all the saints in Heaven!—Constanze!' he shouted up to the window, where she was looking out with the other ladies. 'The carriage is to belong to me! In future, you'll be riding in your own carriage!'

After embracing his smiling benefactor, he walked around his new possession inspecting it from all sides; then he opened the door, sprang into the carriage, and called from inside it: 'I feel as rich and elegant as the Chevalier Gluck* himself! The people in Vienna will have eyes like saucers!'—'I hope,' said the Count, 'that we shall see your carriage again on your return from Prague, festooned with wreaths all over!'

Shortly after this last merry scene, the much-praised carriage with the departing couple finally moved off, driving towards the highway at a swift trot. The Count had them driven as far as Wittingau, where they would hire post-horses.

Whenever amiable, excellent people bring life into our homes for a time by their very presence, quickly stimulating us anew with the fresh wind of their intellect and letting us feel in the highest degree the pleasure of bestowing hospitality, their departure always leaves us with an unpleasant feeling of dullness for the remainder of the day at least, in so far as we are then left entirely to our own devices.

In the case of the people at the château, the latter eventuality did not occur. Franziska's parents and the maiden aunt also departed a short time later, but Franziska herself, Eugenie's fiancé, and Max, in any case, remained behind. Eugenie, with whom we are mainly concerned here, for that wonderful experience had affected her more than all the other persons present—Eugenie, one might think, could not possibly lack for anything or know the meaning of sadness; the pure happiness she found in her dearly beloved fiancé, now formally confirmed, was bound to banish every other emotion, or rather, the noblest and most glorious feeling which could touch her heart could not but melt into one with that divine, unbounded happiness. And that would surely have happened if she had been capable of nothing more than enjoying his mere presence yesterday and today and now recalling it with pure pleasure. The evening before, however, listening to Madame Mozart's stories, she had been touched by a sneaking fear for him, whose kindly image she so adored; later, the whole time that Mozart was playing, this apprehension hovered behind that entire feeling of unutterable captivation, creeping through the eerie dread inspired by the music and remaining in the depths of her consciousness; moreover, she was astonished and shaken by what he himself had said from time to time on this theme. She felt so sure, so absolutely sure, that this man would swiftly and inevitably be consumed in his own fire, that he could only be a short-lived phenomenon on this earth because it could not, in truth, bear the bounty which would otherwise stream from him.

These thoughts and many others besides ran through her mind after she had gone to bed that night, whilst the echo of *Don Giovanni* long afterwards sounded dimly through her inner ear. Only as dawn was approaching did she at last, weary, fall asleep.

The three ladies had now taken their places in the garden with their needlework, where they were joined by the gentlemen. The conversation naturally turned first of all to Mozart, and Eugenie did not conceal her apprehensions. These were not in the least shared by any of the company, though the Baron understood perfectly. In a relaxed hour, when everyone is in a happy convivial mood, people are accustomed to reject as vigorously as possible every thought of disaster which does not directly concern them. The most plausible, amusing counter-arguments were offered, particularly by her uncle, and Eugenie willingly listened to them all. In a short time she almost believed that she had been too pessimistic.

A few moments later, she walked through the large salon upstairs, which had just been cleaned and tidied; through the green damask curtains, now drawn, a soft, dim light filtered into the room and, in a mood of melancholy, she remained standing in front of the piano. She felt as if she were dreaming when she thought who had been sitting at the piano only a few hours ago. For a long time, lost in thought, she gazed at the keys which he had been the last to touch, then she quietly closed the lid and, after locking it, took out the key, anxious to ensure that no other hand should open it again so soon. As she was leaving the room, she casually put back some song-books in their accustomed place; an old sheet of paper fell from one of them: a copy of a Bohemian folk song which Franziska and she herself had sometimes sung before. She picked it up and could not help feeling saddened as she did so; in a mood such as hers at that moment, the merest chance is easily taken for an oracle. But, however she might interpret it, its content, as she read through the simple verses once more, brought hot tears to her eyes.

> A fir tree growing in the forest—
> Who knows where?
> A rose bush—in what garden,
> Who can say?
> Both are they chosen—
> Think on it, o soul—
> To take root on thy grave
> And there to grow.
>
> Two black horses grazing
> In the meadow,
> Now to the town they return
> At a merry trot.
> Slowly shall they walk
> Drawing thy body cold;
> Perhaps, yes, perhaps even
> Before the shoes on their hooves
> That I see glinting
> Are cast away!

GOTTFRIED KELLER

*Clothes Make the Man**

On a bleak day in November, a poor tailor was wandering along
the highway towards Goldach, a small, prosperous town only a
few hours distant from Seldwyla. He had nothing in his pocket
save a thimble which, for lack of a coin of any kind, he kept
turning between his fingers whenever he put his hands in his
trouser pockets because of the cold, and the constant turning
and rubbing was very painful to his fingers. Owing to the business failure of his employer, a master tailor in Seldwyla, he had
lost both his work and wages, so that he had been obliged to
leave the town. He had not eaten anything for breakfast except
a few snowflakes which had flown into his mouth, and had even
less idea where even the smallest midday crust of bread was to
come from. He found it very hard to beg, indeed he found it
quite impossible, for over his black Sunday suit—his only one—
he wore a wide, dark grey cloak trimmed with black velvet,
which lent its wearer a noble, romantic aspect; while his long
black hair and his moustache were carefully groomed and his
features pale but pleasing.

This appearance had become second nature to him, though
his intentions were neither wicked nor deceitful; on the contrary, he was content to be left alone and be allowed to do his
work in peace and quiet; but he would have starved rather than
be parted from his cloak and his Polish fur cap—which, too, he
wore with great dignity.

For these reasons, he was able to work only in large towns
where his appearance was not so conspicuous; but when he was
travelling and had no savings, his plight was a sorry one. Whenever he approached a house, the people would look at him in
astonishment and curiosity, expecting anything from him except
that he would beg; and since, moreover, he did not have the gift
of eloquence, the words would stick in his throat, so that he was

a martyr to his cloak and suffered hunger as black as its velvet lining.

Climbing a hill, tired and heavy-hearted, he came upon a travelling carriage. It was a comfortable, brand-new vehicle which a nobleman's coachman had taken delivery of in Basle and was now bringing to his master, a foreign count living somewhere in the east of Switzerland, in a castle which he had rented or bought. The carriage was fitted with all kinds of devices for carrying luggage, so that it appeared to be heavily loaded although it was completely empty. Because of the steep hill, the coachman was walking beside his horses. When they reached the top of the hill, he climbed back on to his seat and asked the tailor whether he would not like to get into the empty carriage, for it was just beginning to rain, and he had seen at a glance that the traveller was struggling along, down-hearted and weary.

The tailor accepted with modest thanks and, after he had taken his place, the carriage moved off swiftly and, in less than an hour, thundered majestically through the arched gate of Goldach. The stately vehicle halted abruptly in front of the first inn, which bore the name 'At the Sign of the Scales'. Immediately, the hotel servant tugged at the bell so fiercely that the cord almost snapped. The innkeeper and all his staff came rushing downstairs and pulled open the carriage door; children and neighbours had already surrounded the splendid vehicle, curious to see what kind of kernel would emerge from such an extraordinary shell; when, at last, the bewildered tailor jumped out, pale and handsome in his cloak and gazing in melancholy fashion at the ground, they thought him at least a mysterious prince or the son of a count. The gap between the carriage and the gateway of the inn was narrow, and the way was in any case blocked by the host of spectators; perhaps he lacked presence of mind or the courage to push through the crowd and go on his way—whatever the reason, he did not do so, but allowed himself to be led, without a will of his own, into the house and up the stairs, only becoming aware of this strange new situation when he found himself in a comfortable dining-room, where willing hands removed his distinguished cloak.

'Would the gentleman care to dine?' he was asked; 'Dinner has just been prepared and will be served immediately.'

Without waiting to hear his reply, the landlord rushed into the kitchen. 'Saints alive!' he cried, 'we've nothing but beef and the leg of mutton! I mustn't cut the partridge pasty; that's for the evening guests and I've promised it to them. It's always the same! The only day when we're not expecting a strange guest and there's nothing for him, a gentleman like that has to come! And the coachman has a coat-of-arms on his buttons, and the carriage is fit for a duke! And the young man is so genteel, he won't even open his mouth!'

The cook, however, remained perfectly calm. 'There's no need to upset yourself, master!' she said; 'Just go right in and serve the pasty and don't worry—he won't eat it all! The evening guests shall have the pasty cut into portions; we shall be sure to get six portions out of it!'

'Six portions? You're forgetting that the gentlemen are used to eating their fill,' replied the landlord; but the cook, not in the least perturbed, went on: 'That they shall! We'll have a dozen cutlets brought over—we need them for the noble gentleman in any case—and what he leaves over, I shall cut into small pieces and mix into the pasty; just you leave that to me!'

'Cook,' said the worthy landlord in a grave tone, 'I've told you before: that sort of thing can't be done in this town, nor in this house either. We are honest and respectable folk and we know what is right and proper!'

'Bless the mark, yes, yes!' exclaimed the cook, shaken out of her initial calm at last; 'If a body doesn't know how to help himself, then he'll ruin everything! Here are two snipe that I've just bought from the huntsman—they can be added to the pasty for that matter! Those gourmets won't complain about a partridge pasty that's been helped along with snipe! And we have the trout, too: I put the largest one into boiling water just as that strange carriage arrived, and the broth is simmering in the little pan, too; so, we have a fish, the beef, the vegetables with the cutlets, the roast mutton, and the pasty; just give me the key, so that we can fetch out the preserved fruits and the dessert! And I think you might give me the key with every confidence, master, so that we don't have to run after you everywhere, and get into a terrible muddle so often!'

'My dear cook! you mustn't take it so badly—but I had to

promise my poor wife on her deathbed that I would always keep the keys myself: I keep them as a matter of principle, and not from any lack of trust. Here are the cucumbers, here are the cherries, here are the pears, and here are the apricots; but we mustn't serve up the old pastries again; Lise had better run to the confectioner's right away and bring fresh cakes—three plate-fuls; and if he has a good gâteau, then she should bring that, too!'

'But, master! you can't charge all that to the one guest; that won't do, with the best will in the world!'

'That doesn't matter; it's a question of honour! It won't ruin me; no, but, if a noble gentleman travels through our town, he shall be able to say he found a good meal waiting for him, even though he came unexpected and in the depths of winter! No one must be able to say of me what they say of the innkeepers in Seldwyla, who gobble up all the best food themselves and serve up the bones to their guests! So, off to work now; make haste, the lot of you!'

While all these elaborate preparations were going on, the tailor was in a most unpleasant state of anxiety; for the table was laid with gleaming cutlery and, though he was half-starved and, until a short time before, had been yearning for food, he was now fearfully desirous of escaping from the threatening meal. Plucking up courage at last, he wrapped his cloak around him, put on his cap, and left the dining-room in search of the way out. In his confusion, however, and the house being very large, he could not find the stairs immediately, so that the waiter, who was prowling around nervously, thought that the guest was in search of a particular convenience, and said: 'If you will permit me, sir, I shall be pleased to show you the way!' Whereupon he led him down a long corridor which did not come to an end until they reached a beautifully painted door bearing an inscription in fine lettering.

Without a word of contradiction, the man in the cloak entered the room meek as a lamb and carefully closed the door behind him. With a bitter sigh he leaned against the wall, wishing with all his heart that he might once more enjoy the golden freedom of the highway which now, despite the inclement weather, seemed to him the greatest good fortune.

But now, by remaining a while in the closed room, he ensnared himself in the first lie of his own making, thus stepping on to the downhill path of wickedness.

Meanwhile the landlord, who had seen him walking to the said locality wearing his cloak, was shouting: 'The gentleman is freezing! Heat up the dining-room! Where's Lise, where's Anna? Throw a basketful of wood into the stove, quick, and add a few handfuls of shavings to make a blaze. Damnation!—Are guests supposed to sit down to dine wearing their cloaks at "The Scales"!'

When the tailor wandered back once more down the long corridor, as melancholy as some ghost haunting an ancestral castle, the landlord accompanied him into that accursed dining-hall again with a hundred compliments, rubbing his hands unctuously. There he was immediately conducted to the table; his chair was pushed into place and, as the smell of the nourishing soup—the like of which he had not smelled for a long time—completely robbed him of his will-power, he sank philosophically into the chair and straight away dipped the heavy spoon into the gold-brown broth. While he revived his weary spirits in deep silence, he was waited upon with calm and respectful quietness.

At last his plate was empty and the landlord, seeing how much he had enjoyed the soup, politely urged him to take another spoonful, declaring that it would do him good in such raw weather.

Next the trout, garnished with green herbs, was served, and the landlord placed a fine piece of the fish upon his plate. In his awkwardness, however, the worried tailor did not venture to use the gleaming knife, but, instead, picked timidly and nervously at the fish with the silver fork. Seeing this, the cook, who had peered in at the door in order to catch a glimpse of the noble gentleman, said to those standing near her: 'Praise be to God! He knows how to eat a fine fish; he doesn't hack at the tender flesh with a knife, as if he was about to slaughter a calf; he's a man of noble family—I'd take my oath on it, if it weren't forbidden! How melancholy and handsome he is! For sure, he's in love with some poor young lady that they won't let him marry. Oh yes, the fine folk have their worries too!'

Meanwhile the landlord had noticed that the guest was not

drinking anything. 'The gentleman does not like the table wine,' he said deferentially; 'perhaps he would care for a glass of good claret, which I can thoroughly recommend?'

Now the tailor committed the second error of his own making, by saying yes instead of no, simply out of obedience; and the landlord himself went straight away down into the cellar to fetch a bottle of excellent wine; for it was of great importance to him that people should say, one could eat and drink well in the town. When the guest, moved by a guilty conscience, began to drink the wine in tiny sips, the landlord ran joyfully into the kitchen, clicking his tongue. 'The Devil take me!' he exclaimed; 'He knows what's right and proper; he's savouring my good wine on his tongue, as one puts a gold ducat on the scales!'

'Praise be to God!' said the cook; 'I said all along that he knows what's right and proper!'

And so the meal continued, though very slowly, for the poor tailor ate and drank most nervously and hesitantly, and the landlord left the food long enough upon the table and let him take his time. But what the guest had eaten and drunk until then was hardly worth mentioning; now, however, his hunger, which had been whetted so fiercely the whole time, began to overcome his fear; and when the partridge pasty appeared the tailor's mood changed immediately and a feeling of determination rose within him: 'There's nothing I can do about it!' he said to himself, his body warmed and his spirits raised by another drop of wine; 'I'd be a pretty fool to accept the shame and disgrace that will follow, without having eaten my fill beforehand. I'd better enjoy myself while there's still time. This little mountain of food that they have piled up here might well be the last meal I shall have; I'll make the best of it whatever happens! What is once inside me, no king can take away from me!'

No sooner said than done; with the courage of despair, he fell upon the delicious pasty and did not think of stopping, so that it had half-vanished within less than five minutes, and the outlook for the evening guests began to appear very grim indeed. Meat, truffles, dumplings, top and bottom—he devoured everything without regard for anyone, his only thought being to fill his belly before the approaching doom overtook him; he drank the wine in copious draughts, and pushed great pieces of bread into his mouth; in short, it was a process of transfer as hasty as when, before an oncoming storm, the hay from the nearby meadow is heaved straight from the fork into the barn. The landlord ran into the kitchen once again: 'Cook! He's eating up the pasty, though he's hardly touched the roast beef! And he's drinking the claret half a glass at a time!'

'A health to him!' said the cook; 'Just let him carry on; he knows what a partridge is! If he'd been just a common fellow, he'd have kept to the roast!'

'That's what *I* say,' said the landlord; 'it doesn't look very elegant, I admit, but when I was away from home learning the trade, the only people I saw eating like that were prebendaries and generals!'

Meanwhile the coachman had had the horses fed and had eaten a hearty meal in the room reserved for servants. Time was now pressing and he ordered the horses to be harnessed again. The inn servants were no longer able to contain their curiosity, and now, before it was too late, asked the lordly coachman bluntly who his master was, and what his name. 'Why,' said the coachman—a roguish, crafty fellow—'has he not yet told you himself?'

'No,' came the reply. '*That* I can believe,' he commented, 'he doesn't speak much the whole day; well, his name is Count Strapinski! He'll be staying here today and perhaps a few days longer: he ordered me to drive on ahead with the carriage.'

The coachman permitted himself this malicious joke in order to revenge himself on the tailor who, as he thought, had disappeared into the inn without turning his head or without bidding him a word of thanks or farewell, and was now acting the noble gentleman. Then, carrying his practical joke to the extreme, he climbed up on to the carriage without asking for the bill either for himself or for the horses and, cracking his whip, drove out of the town. This was considered perfectly in order and was put down to the worthy tailor's account.

As it happened, however, the name of the tailor—a native of Silesia—really was Strapinski, Wenzel Strapinski; perhaps it was coincidence, or perhaps the tailor had taken out his journeyman's book while in the carriage and forgotten it, so that the coachman had kept it. Whatever the reason: when the landlord, beaming with pleasure and rubbing his hands, approached him and asked whether Count Strapinski would like a glass of old Tokay wine or a glass of champagne with the dessert, and announced that his rooms were just being prepared for him, poor Strapinski turned pale, became confused as before, and made no reply at all.

'Very interesting!' growled the landlord to himself, whereupon he rushed down into the cellar again, where, from a special rack, he took not only a bottle of Tokay but also a Bocksbeutel* and, in addition, tucked a bottle of champagne under his arm. Within a short time, Strapinski saw a small forest of wineglasses in front of him, from the midst of which the champagne cup rose like a poplar tree. A whole host, gleaming, tinkling, and fragrant—a strange sight indeed; yet it was even more strange to see how the poor but elegant man reached, not at all clumsily, into the little forest and, seeing the landlord pour a few drops of red wine into his champagne, poured a few drops of Tokay into his own. Meanwhile, the town clerk and the notary had arrived to take coffee and play their daily round of cards; they were shortly afterwards followed by the elder son of the firm of Häberlin and Co., the younger son of the firm of Pütschli-Nievergelt,* and Herr Melchior Böhni, the bookkeeper of a large spinning-mill; but, instead of beginning their game, all the gentlemen walked in a wide circle around the Polish count, their hands stuck into their back pockets, winking and smiling secretively, for they were members of respectable firms and, though they remained at home all their lives, they had friends and relatives all over the world and therefore believed that they themselves knew the world well enough.

So this was supposed to be a Polish count? They had seen the carriage from their office windows, of course; yet it was not clear whether the landlord was serving the count, or the count the landlord; but the landlord had not done anything foolish until now; on the contrary, he was known to be quite a clever fellow; and so the inquisitive gentlemen walked around the stranger in ever-dwindling circles until at last they sat down in a friendly fashion at the same table, cunningly inviting themselves to the drinking session quite spontaneously, simply by throwing dice for one of the bottles of wine.

They did not drink too much, however, for it was still early in the evening; instead, they contented themselves with a sip of excellent coffee and offering the Pole—as they already secretly called him—some good tobacco, so that he might better get a whiff of what manner of company he was keeping.

'May I offer Your Lordship a good cigar?' asked one of the company; 'I got it straight from my brother in Cuba!'

'Polish gentlemen are fond of a good cigarette, too; this is real Smyrna tobacco, sent to me by my partner,' said another, pushing a red silk pouch towards him.

'This one from Damascus is better, Your Lordship,' said a third, 'our chief clerk there personally obtained it for me.'

The fourth pushed forward a huge brute of a cigar, exclaiming: 'If you would like something quite special, then try this planter's cigar from Virginia, home-grown, home-rolled, and not to be had for love nor money!'

Strapinski smiled a bitter-sweet smile but said not a word, and was soon wreathed in delicate clouds of aromatic smoke gently tinged with the silver light of the emerging sun. In less than a quarter-of-an-hour the clouds had vanished from the sky and a beautiful autumn afternoon revealed itself; the company thought they should take advantage of the fine weather, realizing that there might not be many more such days that year; and they decided to drive out and visit the cheery District Councillor on his estate (who had pressed his grapes only a few days before) and taste his new wine, the red 'sparkler'. Pütschli-Nievergelt Jr. sent for his hunting-brake, and soon his pair of dapple greys were stamping the cobblestones in front of the inn. The land-lord himself had his own horses harnessed, too; and the count was cordially invited to join the party and see something of the region.

The wine had animated his wits and he quickly considered that this would offer him the best opportunity of slipping away unseen and continuing his journey; let these foolish, intrusive gentlemen suffer for it! He therefore accepted the invitation with a few polite words and, together with young Pütschli, climbed into the hunting-brake.

By a further chance, it happened that the tailor had, as a young lad in his native village, been employed for a time by the local squire and then completed his military service with the Hussars, so that he knew how to handle horses well enough. And so, when his companion politely asked whether, perhaps, he might like to drive, he immediately seized the reins and whip and drove in true cavalry style at a fast trot through the gate and on to the highway; the gentlemen looked at one another and whispered: 'It's true; he really is a nobleman!'

Half-an-hour later they arrived at the Councillor's estate. Strapinski drove up in a splendid semicircle, pulling the mettle-some steeds smartly to a halt; all the visitors leapt out of the carriages and the Councillor came to welcome them and led the party into the house. In no time at all, half-a-dozen carafes filled with sparkling, strawberry-coloured new wine were standing on the table. The lively, fizzing beverage was first tasted, praised, and then subjected to a merry attack, whilst the master spread the news that there was a noble count in the house, a Pole, and ordered a more elegant meal to be prepared.

Meanwhile the company had divided into two groups in order to catch up on their game; for in this part of the country it is impossible for men to come together without sitting down to a game of cards, probably because of an innate urge to be active. Strapinski, who for a number of reasons had been obliged to refrain from taking part in the game, was invited to take part as a spectator; this they considered in any event desirable, being used to demonstrating such a deal of intelligence and presence of mind during their play. He had to take his place between the two groups, and they now made every effort to play skilfully and cleverly whilst entertaining the guest at the same time. And so he sat there like some ailing prince whose courtiers are perform-ing an enjoyable play before him commenting on the ways of the world. They explained to him the most important coups and twists and turns, and when one group had to concentrate its entire attention upon the game, the other would continue the conversation with the tailor with all the more animation. The most suitable topics, they thought, were horses, hunting, and similar matters; Strapinski knew best of all about such things, for he had only to recall the hackneyed remarks which he had heard in the past from officers and members of the landed gentry, and which had very much amused him even in those days. Though he now made use of these remarks only sparingly, with a certain modesty and always with a melancholy smile, the effect he achieved was all the greater; and whenever two or three of the gentlemen rose from the table and went aside, they would say: 'He's a perfect young nobleman!'

Only Melchior Böhni, the bookkeeper—a born Doubting Thomas—rubbed his hands in glee, saying to himself: 'I can see it coming: there's going to be an *éclat* once again in Goldach; in fact, in a manner of speaking, it's already underway! And high time, too, it's already been two years since the last one! What curiously pricked fingers the fellow has! Perhaps he got them at the uprisings in Praga or Ostrolenka!* Well, I'll take good care not to disturb the course of events!'

Both card games were now at an end, and the gentlemen's thirst for the sparkling wine was stilled; instead, they preferred to cool themselves a little with the Councillor's old wines which were now being served, though the cooling process was of a somewhat passionate nature: a game of hazard was immediately proposed for all present in order not to relapse into dreary idleness. The cards were shuffled, everyone put in a Brabant thaler—though, when it came to Strapinski's turn, he could not very well place his thimble upon the table. 'I don't have such a coin,' he said, blushing; but immediately, Melchior Böhni, who had been observing him, put down the money for him without anyone paying attention; for they were all much too contented to suspect that anyone in the world could possibly be without money. Next moment the entire stake money was pushed over to the tailor, who had won the game; in his confusion, he left the money where it was, and Böhni placed Strapinski's stake for the second game—which was won by another player—as well as for the third. But the fourth and fifth games were won by the Pole, who was gradually waking up and beginning to understand the game. Now, by remaining silent and keeping calm, he played with ever-changing luck; once, his funds dwindled to a single thaler, which he was obliged to stake; then he won again and, at last, when everyone had had enough of playing, he was in possession of several louis d'or—more than he had ever owned in his life— which, seeing the other players put away their money, he, too, put into his pocket, though he feared that it was all a dream.

Böhni, who had been watching him keenly the whole time, had almost seen through him by now and thought: 'The Devil take me if *he* drives in a coach-and-four!'

At the same time, however, Böhni noted that the mysterious stranger did not display any greed as far as the money was concerned, and that he had conducted himself in a most modest and sensible manner; he therefore did not harbour any resentment towards him, but instead determined to let matters take their course.

Before supper, everyone went out for a stroll in the open air; Count Strapinski, however, collecting his thoughts, considered that it was now the right moment for a discreet departure. He was now in possession of respectable travelling funds and determined that, after reaching the next town, he would pay the landlord of 'The Scales' for the dinner which had been forced upon him. Folding his cloak around him in a picturesque fashion and pulling his fur cap down over his eyes, he walked slowly back and forth in the evening sunlight under a row of tall acacia trees, contemplating the delightful countryside or, rather, spying out the road he intended to take. With his worried brow, his elegant but melancholy moustache, his shining black hair, his dark eyes, and his cloak billowing in furls around him, he cut a most dashing figure; the evening sun and the sighing of the trees above him heightened the impression, so that the company watched him from a distance with benevolence and keen attention. Gradually he began to draw farther and farther away from the house and slipped through a clump of bushes behind which a path ran past. Seeing that he was now hidden from the eyes of the company, he was just about to walk with a firm step into the field when, suddenly, the Councillor and his daughter Nettchen* came around a corner towards him. Nettchen was a pretty girl of glorious appearance, rather too fashionably dressed, and wearing a lavish display of jewellery.

'We've been looking for you, Count!' exclaimed the Councillor; 'First of all, so that I might introduce you to my daughter; secondly, to ask you to do us the honour of taking a little supper with us; the other gentlemen are already in the house.'

The wanderer quickly doffed his cap and, blushing deeply, made a series of respectful, even timid, bows; for the situation had changed: a young lady had entered upon the scene. But his awkwardness and exaggerated respectfulness did not detract from him in the lady's eyes; on the contrary, the shyness, modesty, and courtesy of such an elegant and interesting young nobleman seemed to her somehow touching, not to say charming. It's plain to see, she thought, the nobler a person, the more modest and unspoiled he is; take note, young gallants of Goldach, you who hardly raise your hats to young girls!

She greeted the knight in the sweetest possible manner; blushing charmingly, she spoke to him quickly and hastily about a myriad of things, as is usual with comfortable provincial girls who wish to make an impression upon a stranger. Strapinski's manner, however, changed almost immediately; whilst he had previously made no effort whatsoever to slip into the role which had been thrust upon him, he now began involuntarily to speak more gracefully, mixing scraps of Polish generously in his speech; in a word, the tailor's blood, stirred by the young woman's proximity, began to leap and carry its rider away.

At the supper table he was given the place of honour beside the daughter of the house; for her mother was no longer living. His mood became melancholy once more when he thought that he must now return to the town together with the others or else break out and flee into the night, and when, too, he thought how fleeting was the good fortune that he was now enjoying. At the same time, he was fully conscious of this fortune and said to himself from the start: Well, for once in your life you will count for something and have the honour of having sat beside such a lofty creature.

It was, indeed, no small matter to see a hand gleaming beside him, with three or four tinkling bracelets upon it and, with every fleeting sidelong glance, to see an audaciously and charmingly coiffured head, a sweet blush, and eyelashes fluttering widely. For, whatever he might do or not do, she interpreted everything as being exceptional and noble, and even his clumsiness seemed a lovable and unusual form of unaffectedness to the young lady, who at other times could talk for hours on end about breaches of etiquette. Everyone was in a good humour, so that some of the guests sang songs which were popular in the 'thirties. They requested the count to sing a Polish song. The

wine had overcome his shyness at last, though not his anxiety;
he had once worked for several weeks in Poland and knew some
words of Polish; he even knew a Polish folk song by heart, like
a parrot, without knowing its meaning. And so he sang in noble
manner and in a voice, more timid than loud, which trembled as
if with secret sorrow, in Polish:

> One hundred thousand swine in pig-pens
> From the Vistula to the Desna,
> And that filthy sow, Kathinka,
> Walks in muck up to her knees!
>
> One hundred thousand oxen bellowing
> In Poland's meadows green and fair,
> And Kathinka, oh Kathinka,
> Thinks that I'm in love with her!

'Bravo, bravo!' cried all the gentlemen, clapping their hands, and
Nettchen, charmed, said: 'A national song is always so beautiful!' Fortunately, no one asked for the song to be translated.

The peak of enjoyment having thus been reached, the party
now dispersed; the tailor was wrapped up once more and carefully brought back to Goldach, after first having had to promise
that he would not leave the region without saying goodbye.
Arriving at the inn again, the company partook of a last glass of
punch, but Strapinski was exhausted and asked to be shown to
bed. The landlord himself conducted him to his room; but he
scarcely noticed how splendid it was, though he was accustomed
only to sleeping in humble lodgings. He was standing in the
middle of the room on a beautiful carpet, without a single one of
his belongings, when the landlord suddenly realized that the
Count's baggage was missing and clapped his hand to his forehead. Then he ran out of the room and rang the bell to summon
the waiter and servants; after exchanging a few words with them,
he returned and announced: 'It's true, Your Lordship, they have
forgotten to unload your baggage. Even the essentials are missing!'

'Even the small package that was inside the carriage?' asked
Strapinski anxiously, thinking of the small bundle, no larger than
his hand, which he had left upon the seat, and which contained
a handkerchief, a hairbrush, a comb, a small jar of pomade, and
a stick of moustache wax.

'That's missing, too—there's not a thing here,' said the worthy landlord in dismay, supposing that the package contained something very important. 'We must send the coachman an express message,' he exclaimed eagerly; 'I shall arrange for it!'

But the Count, equally dismayed, seized him by the arm; 'No, no,' he said, in an agitated voice, 'you mustn't! They must lose all trace of me for a while,' he added, himself embarrassed by this untruth.

Astonished, the landlord went to the other guests, who were still drinking their punch, told them what had happened, and concluded by declaring that the Count was doubtless the victim of political or family persecution; for many Poles and other fugitives were being expelled from the country just at that time because of violent conspiracies; others were under observation by foreign agents trying to ensnare them.

Strapinski, however, slept well that night and, waking late next morning, he saw, first of all, the landlord's elegant Sunday peignoir hung over a chair, and then a small table with toilet articles of all kinds. Then a procession of waiting servants appeared, bringing baskets and trunks filled with fine linen, with clothes, with cigars, with books, with boots, with shoes, with spurs, with riding whips, with furs, with caps, with hats, with socks, with stockings, with tobacco pipes, with flutes, and with violins; these had been sent by his friends of the previous day, with the fervent request that he should make use of them as the need arose. Since they were obliged to spend their mornings at their places of business, they announced their visits for after lunch.

These people were not in the least ridiculous or foolish, but prudent men of business, cunning rather than stupid; but, living as they did in a well-ordered little town, where they sometimes found life boring, they were always eager for a change, a particular event, or an occurrence into which they flung themselves without hesitation. The coach-and-four, the emergence of the stranger, his midday meal, and the coachman's statement were such simple and natural matters that the people of Goldach, who were not in the habit of wasting time with useless suspicions, constructed an event upon them as on a foundation of solid rock.

When Strapinski saw the stock of goods that was piling up in front of him, his first reaction was to reach into his pocket to see whether he was awake or dreaming. If, he thought, his thimble was still there in its accustomed isolation, he must be dreaming. But, no; the thimble was nestling comfortably among the money which he had won, rubbing amiably against the thalers; and so its lord and master submitted to circumstances once again and left his room to go down into the street in order to see the town where everything was going so well for him. There, in the kitchen doorway, the cook was standing; she made him a deep curtsey and stared after him with new-found benevolence; other retainers were standing in the hallway and at the door, all holding their caps in their hands, and Strapinski walked out, graciously but modestly, pulling his cloak demurely about him. Destiny, it seemed, was making him greater with every minute.

He looked at the town with far different eyes than he would have done had he been looking for work there. It consisted mostly of attractive, solidly built houses, all adorned with painted or stone symbols and all bearing a name. These names clearly displayed the customs of the different centuries. The Middle Ages were reflected in the oldest houses, or in the new houses built to replace them, which retained the old names from the days of the warrior-burgomasters and the fairy-tales; names such as: The Sword, The Iron Helmet, The Breastplate, The Crossbow, The Blue Shield, The Swiss Rapier, The Knight, The Flintstone, The Turk, The Sea Monster, The Golden Dragon, The Linden, The Pilgrim's Staff, The Water Sprite, The Bird of Paradise, The Pomegranate Tree, The Camel, The Unicorn, and so forth. The Age of Enlightenment and Philanthropy was clearly to be seen in the moral terms which gleamed in beautiful gold letters above the doors of the houses, such as: Harmony, Honesty, Old Independence, New Independence, Civil Virtue a, Civil Virtue b, Trust, Charity, Hope, We Shall Meet Again 1 and 2, Happiness, Inner Righteousness, Outer Righteousness, The National Wellbeing (a neat little house in which, behind a canary cage covered with cress, a friendly old lady in a white peaked bonnet was sitting and reeling yarn), The Constitution (here lived a cooper, who diligently and with a great deal of clatter fitted hoops to small pails and casks and hammered without cease); one house bore the macabre name of Death!—a bleached skeleton stretched between the windows from the eaves to the ground; this was the house of the Justice of the Peace. In the house named Patience lived the debt collector, a half-starved, wretched creature, for in this town no one remained in debt to anyone.

Finally there were the newest houses, proclaiming in their melodious names the poetry of the factory-owners, the bankers, the carriers, and their imitators: Rose Vale, Morning Vale, Sunny Hill, Violet Castle, Garden of Youth, Happiness Hill, Henrietta Vale, Camelia, Wilhelmina Castle, etc. To knowledgeable persons, the valleys and castles combined with women's names were always a sign of a respectable dowry.

At every street corner was an old tower with a splendid clock, a many-coloured roof, and an elegantly gilded weathercock. The towers were tended with loving care, for the people of Goldach took pleasure in past and present and behaved accordingly. All this splendour was encircled by the old town wall which, though no longer serving any purpose, was nevertheless maintained as an embellishment—thickly overgrown with old ivy, it formed a wreath of evergreen around the little town.

All this provoked a feeling of wonder in him; he thought himself transported to another planet. For, as he read the inscriptions on the houses, the like of which he had never seen before, he believed that they referred to the particular secrets and ways of life of the houses themselves, and that, behind each door, everything was exactly in accordance with the inscription outside, so that he had chanced upon a sort of moral Utopia. Thus he was inclined to believe that the curious reception which he had been given was connected with this system, so that, for example, the symbol of 'The Scales', where he was residing, signified that an unjust fate was there weighed in the balance and made good, and that, on occasion, a wandering tailor would thus be made a count.

During the course of his walk he arrived at the town gate and, as he looked out across the open fields, the dutiful thought that he ought to continue on his way without staying any longer occurred to him for the last time. The sun was shining; the road was good and firm, not too dry and not too wet—simply made for wandering. And he was provided with travelling funds, so that he could stop off at a decent inn whenever he chose, and nothing appeared to stand in his way.

There he stood at a real crossroads, like the youth* at the parting of the ways; from the circle of linden trees which surrounded the town, homely columns of smoke were rising; the golden orbs of the towers gleamed enticingly from the treetops; there, happiness, pleasure, and indebtedness and a mysterious destiny beckoned to him; but far away across the fields shone freedom; work, sacrifice, poverty, and uncertainty awaited him there, but, at the same time, a clear conscience and a peaceful way of life; as he became aware of this, he made to turn off determinedly into the fields when, at that same moment, a vehicle swiftly approached. It was the young lady of the previous day, her blue veil fluttering, quite alone in a neat little carriage drawn by a handsome horse, driving towards the town. In his surprise, he had no sooner doffed his cap and was holding it humbly before his breast when the girl, blushing, made a quick but very friendly bow and, urging the horse to a gallop, drove off at a great pace.

Involuntarily, Strapinski made a complete about-face and walked back confidently to the town. That very same day, mounted on the finest horse in town, he was galloping at the head of an entire company of riders along the avenue surrounding the green-clad town wall, and the leaves falling from the linden trees danced about his transfigured head like golden rain.

Now the spirit had taken possession of him. With every day that passed he changed more and more, like a rainbow that, before one's very eyes, becomes brighter and brighter in the light of the emerging sun. He learned in hours, in seconds, what others cannot learn in years, for it had lain hidden within him like the colours in a drop of rain. Keenly he observed the manners of his hosts and, even while he was observing, he was reshaping them into something new and unknown; most of all, he tried to overhear what they thought of him and what image they had formed of him. He then moulded this impression in accordance with his own taste—to the pleasurable amusement of some, who liked to see something new, and to the admiration of others, particularly the women, who thirsted after edifying stimulation.

And so he quickly became the hero of a charming novel, on which he worked lovingly and together with the people of the town, but the main element of which was still its mystery.

Despite all this, Strapinski experienced something which, in his previous state of ignorance, he had never known before: one sleepless night after another, and, to his shame, it must be emphasized that it was just as much fear of being ignominiously revealed as a poor tailor, as his honest conscience, which kept him awake at night. His innate need to cut a graceful, impressive figure, if only in the choice of his attire, had led him into this conflict and was the cause of this fear; his conscience was only strong enough to nourish constantly his resolution to find a plausible reason for departure, when the occasion arose, and then—by means of lotteries and similar methods—to acquire the necessary funds to repay, from far, far away, everything of which he had cheated the hospitable people of Goldach. He ordered lottery tickets at more or less modest stakes from all the towns which organized lotteries or where lottery agencies were established, and the resulting correspondence and the letters which were delivered to him were in turn interpreted as evidence of his good connections and acquaintances.

More than once he had won a few guilders, which he immediately invested again in the purchase of further lottery tickets, when, one day, he received a considerable sum of money from an agent—who, however, termed himself a banker—in another town; this money was sufficient for him to realize his plans for rescue. By now, he was no longer astonished by his luck, which seemed to come of its own accord, but he felt comforted—and greatly relieved as far as the landlord of 'The Scales' was concerned, for whom he had a great affection on account of the excellent meals which he served. But instead of putting an end to matters, paying his debts completely, and leaving, he thought of pleading a short business journey and then, afterwards, sending a message from some large city, saying that his implacable destiny made it impossible for him ever to return; it was his wish, however, to pay his debts and leave people with a kind memory of him, and to resume his trade as a tailor with more luck and prudence than before, or to look around for some other respectable means of earning his bread. Of course, he would have much preferred to remain in Goldach as a master tailor, and now possessed the financial means with which to build up a modest existence; but it was clear that he could live here only as a count.

Thanks to the obvious liking and affection which the lovely Nettchen displayed to him on every occasion, a number of stories were already in circulation: he had even noticed that the young lady was sometimes referrred to as 'the countess'. How could he possibly draw her into such a situation? How could he deceive fate in such an infamous manner—fate, which had elevated him to such heights—and so disgrace himself?

From his lottery agent—alias banker—he had received a cheque, which he cashed at a bank in Goldach; this enhanced even more the favourable opinions which prevailed concerning his person and his circumstances, for the solid business folk of Goldach had not the slightest suspicion of his lottery dealings. That same day, Strapinski went to an elegant ball to which he had been invited. He arrived simply dressed in a suit of deep black, and immediately announced to the other guests as they greeted him, that he was obliged to leave the town.

Within ten minutes, the entire assembly had heard the news. Nettchen, whose eyes Strapinski had been trying to catch, seemed to avoid his look as if petrified; she flushed and turned pale alternately. Then she danced with a number of young men in succession, sat down again distractedly and breathing quickly, and with a curt bow refused an invitation to dance from the Pole, who had at last approached her, without looking at him.

In a strange mood of agitation and anxiety he left the ball-room; wrapping himself in his splendid cloak, he began to walk back and forth in the garden, his curls fluttering about his head. It now became clear to him that, in fact, it was only because of her that he had remained in the town so long; that the vague hope of coming close to her again excited him unconsciously, but that the whole thing was absolutely and hopelessly impossible.

As he strode back and forth, he heard the sound of quick footsteps behind him, light but nervous. Nettchen walked past him. Judging from a few words which she called out, she seemed to be looking for her carriage, though it was on the other side of the house; on this side there was nothing but winter cabbages and rose bushes—the latter wrapped up against the winter and sleeping the sleep of the just. Then she came back and, as he stood in front of her, his heart pounding and his arms stretched out imploringly towards her, she simply threw her arms around his neck and began to weep bitterly. He covered her glowing cheeks with his dark, perfumed curls, and his cloak encircled the girl's stately, slender, snow-white figure like black eagle's wings: a truly splendid picture which seemed to bear its justification entirely within itself.

Entangled in such an adventure, Strapinski lost his common sense but won the happiness which often falls into the lap of the ignorant. That same evening, during the drive home, Nettchen told her father that no one but the count would be her husband; the young man himself appeared early next morning, pleasantly shy and melancholy as ever, to ask her father for her hand in marriage; and her father made the following speech:

'So, the foolish girl's destiny and desire have been fulfilled! Even as a schoolgirl, she never ceased to declare that she would only marry an Italian or a Pole, a famous pianist or the captain of a band of robbers with beautiful curls—and now, see what has come of it! She has refused all serious offers of marriage from local gentlemen; just recently, I had to send Melchior Böhni away—a capable, hard-working fellow, he'll do well for himself—and she made awful game of him because he has a reddish beard and takes snuff from a silver snuff-box. And now, thank heaven, a Polish count has arrived from out of the blue! Take the silly goose, Count, and send her back to me if she freezes in that Poland of yours, or if she's unhappy and cries! How charmed her poor, dead mother would be to see that the spoiled child has become a countess!'

Now everywhere was alive with activity; the engagement was to be celebrated soon, in a few days time, for the Councillor declared that his future son-in-law must not let marriage matters interfere with his business and travelling plans, but must expedite the latter by the completion of the former.

On the occasion of the engagement, Strapinski brought presents which cost him half the money he possessed; the remaining half went on a banquet which he intended to give for his fiancée. It was carnival time; beautiful, belatedly snowy weather, with not a cloud in the sky. The country roads were transformed into the most splendid sleigh trails, something which happens seldom and then not for long; Herr von Strapinski, therefore, arranged a sleigh-ride, to be followed by a ball at an excellent restaurant very popular for such occasions, situated upon a plateau with the most wonderful view; this was some two hours' journey away, exactly half-way between Goldach and Seldwyla.

It so happened that Herr Melchior Böhni had business to attend to in Seldwyla and had driven there in a light sleigh, smoking one of his best cigars, a few days before the banquet was to take place; it also happened that the people of Seldwyla arranged a sleigh-ride to the same place on the same day as the people of Goldach, with fancy dress and masks.

And so, around midday, the Goldach sleigh party set off through the streets of the town, with bells jingling, posthorns blaring, and whips cracking, and went out through the town gate; and the symbols on the ancient houses looked down in astonishment. Strapinski was sitting with his fiancée in the first sleigh, clad in a Polish greatcoat of green velvet, adorned with braid and thickly trimmed and lined with fur. Nettchen was wrapped entirely in white furs, whilst a blue veil protected her face from the cold air and the blinding sun. Some unexpected occurrence had prevented the Councillor from taking part, but it was his sleigh, drawn by his horses, in which they were riding; the sleigh was embellished by a gilded female figure in front of them, representing Fortuna, this being the name of the Councillor's town residence.

Behind them drove fifteen or sixteen other sleighs, with a lady and gentleman in each, all of them finely dressed and laughing merrily, but not a single pair was so fine and handsome as the engaged couple. Just as ocean-going ships bear figureheads, so did each sleigh bear the symbol of the house to which it belonged, so that the townsfolk called out: 'Look! here comes Courage! Isn't Diligence beautiful! Improvability seems to have a new coat of paint and Thrift seems newly gilded! Oh, here come Jacob's Well and the Pool of Bethesda!' In the 'Pool of Bethesda,' a modest one-horse sleigh at the end of the procession, sat Melchior Böhni, quietly enjoying himself. In front of him, as the figurehead of his sleigh, was a statue of the man who had waited thirty years* at the said pool to be healed. And so the fleet sailed on in the sunshine and soon reached the top of the hill shimmering from afar, close to their destination. As they arrived, the sound of merry music came from the opposite side.

Out of a forest of fragrant trees tipped with hoarfrost burst a jumble of motley colours and figures to form a procession of sleighs of bizarre appearance, at first silhouetted against the blue sky high up at the white edge of the field, then gliding down into the middle of the field. For the most part, they seemed to be large, agricultural transport sleighs, fastened together in pairs to form supports for curious structures and displays. On the foremost vehicle towered a huge figure representing the goddess Fortuna, who seemed to be flying away into the ether. This was a gigantic straw doll covered with glittering gold tinsel, its robes of gauze fluttering in the breeze. On the second vehicle, however, stood an equally gigantic he-goat, black and grim, running after Fortuna with its horns lowered. This was followed by a strange contraption which revealed itself as a fifteen-foot-high smoothing-iron; then came an enormous pair of snapping scissors —opened and closed by means of a cord—which seemed to consider the sky an expanse of blue silk material for a waistcoat. Other common allusions to the tailoring trade followed, and at the foot of all these figures was the colourfully dressed Seldwyla group, laughing and singing loudly, sitting on the spacious sleighs, each of which was drawn by four horses.

As both processions drew up simultaneously on the forecourt of the restaurant, a noisy scene with a jostling mass of people and horses ensued. The ladies and gentlemen from Goldach were surprised and astonished by this bizarre encounter; the people of the Seldwyla party, however, were amiable and friendly in a modest fashion. Their foremost sleigh with the figure of Fortuna bore the motto: 'Man makes clothes', and it turned out that the entire company represented people in the tailoring trade from every nation and from every period of history. In a manner of speaking, it was a historical–ethnographical pageant of tailors, and concluded with the complementary reversal of the original: 'Clothes make the man!' For, in the last sleigh, which bore this title, were sitting—the product of practitioners of the sewing trade of all kinds, both heathen and Christian—venerable emperors and kings, councillors and general staff officers, prelates and abbesses, all displaying the greatest dignity.

Skilfully transforming itself from a confused crowd into an orderly group, this world of tailors politely allowed the ladies and gentlemen from Goldach, led by the engaged couple, to enter the house, whereupon they themselves occupied the ground-floor rooms which had been reserved for them, whilst the people from Goldach swept up the wide staircase to the large banqueting hall. His Lordship's party thought this most becoming behaviour, and their surprise turned to merriment and approving smiles at the Seldwyla group's irrepressible good humour; only the count himself harboured dark forebodings which were not at all to his liking, though in the present partiality of his heart he did not feel any definite suspicion, and had not even noticed where the people came from. Melchior Böhni, who had carefully disposed of his 'Pool of Bethesda', was sitting close to Strapinski, watching attentively; in a voice loud enough for Strapinski to hear, he named a completely different town as the starting-point of the masked pageant.

Soon both parties, each in its own storey, were seated at the laid tables and began to talk merrily and to make jokes in expectation of further pleasures.

These heralded their approach for the people from Goldach, too, as they walked across to the ballroom in pairs, where the musicians were already tuning their violins. Then, however, as they were all standing in a circle and just about to line up, a delegation from the Seldwyla group appeared, with the friendly request and offer to come to the ladies and gentlemen of Goldach and entertain them with a display of dancing. Such an offer could not very well be refused; everyone looked forward to being royally entertained by the merry people from Seldwyla and so, following the directions of the said delegation, they seated themselves in a large semicircle, in the midst of which Strapinski and Nettchen shone like princely stars.

And now, one after another, the various groups of tailors entered the scene. In a graceful charade, each group depicted the phrase 'Man makes clothes' and its reversed form: first of all, the group seemed to be busily preparing some elegant garment,

such as a prince's cloak, a priest's gown, or the like; this was
then put on to some needy person who, thus suddenly transformed, would pull himself erect with supreme dignity and
proceed to walk about solemnly in time to the music. Animal
fables, too, were depicted in the sense of the reversed motto: a
huge crow appeared, which dressed itself up in peacock's feathers and hopped around cawing; a wolf, which made itself a
sheepskin coat; and finally a donkey, wearing a fearsome lion's
skin made of tow, which it had heroically draped over itself like
a Carbonari coat.*

All these players withdrew after the completion of their performances, so that the semicircle of the Goldach party gradually
became a large circle of spectators, the inner part of which at last
became empty. At that moment the music turned to a grave,
melancholy air, whilst at the same time a final apparition stepped
into the circle of people, whose eyes were fixed upon it without
exception. It was a slim young man in a dark cloak, with beautiful dark hair and a Polish cap; none other than Count Strapinski,
just as he had wandered along the road that day in November
and climbed into that fateful carriage.

The entire assembly looked at the figure in tense silence; after
pacing around to the music in a solemn, melancholy way, the
young man walked to the middle of the circle, spread his cloak
upon the floor, and sat down upon it tailor fashion and then
began to unpack a bundle. He took out a count's robe, almost
finished; it was exactly like the robe which Strapinski was wearing at that moment; with great haste and skill, he sewed tassles
and braids on to the robe and ironed it in proper style, testing
the seemingly hot iron with his wetted fingers. Then he rose
slowly to his feet, took off his threadbare coat, and put on the
splendid garment; he took out a small mirror, combed his hair,
and straightened his clothing, standing there at last as the living
image of the Count. The music suddenly became fast and lively;
the man wrapped his belongings in his old cloak and threw the
bundle over the heads of the onlookers to the far end of the hall,
as if desirous of casting off his past for ever. Then he walked
into the circle, a proud man of the world, with stately dance
steps, here and there bowing graciously to the onlookers until
he came to the engaged couple. Suddenly looking the Pole, who

was completely amazed, straight in the eyes, he remained standing motionless as a pillar in front of him whilst, at the same time, the music stopped as if to a pre-arranged signal and a dreadful silence fell, like a soundless flash of lightning.

'Well, well, well!' he exclaimed, in a voice that could be heard far away, stretching out his hand to the wretched Strapinski, 'if it isn't my Silesian friend, the prize Pole! The one who left his work and ran off on me, when he thought, just because business went slack a little, that I was finished. But I'm glad to see that you're doing so well and celebrating carnival so merrily here. Are you working in Goldach?'

As he spoke, he held out his hand to the Count, who was sitting pale and smiling; without a will of his own, the Count grasped the hand as if it were a glowing bar of iron, whilst his doppelgänger called: 'Come here, my friends—here's our meek little tailor, who looks like the Angel Raphael and was such a favourite with our servant girls—and with the pastor's daughter, too, though admittedly she's a bit cracked!'

Now all the people from Seldwyla approached, crowding around Strapinski and his former master and warmly shaking Strapinski's hand, so that he quivered and trembled upon his chair. At the same time, the music struck up once again with a lively march; as soon as they had passed the engaged couple, the people from Seldwyla lined up to leave, and marched out of the hall with a well-rehearsed chorus of diabolical laughter; and the people from Goldach, to whom Böhni had explained the meaning of the miracle as quick as lightning, jostled together and mingled with the people from Seldwyla, so that a great tumult ensued.

When the noise finally died down, the hall was almost empty; a few people were standing near the walls, whispering to each other in embarrassment; two or three young ladies remained at a distance from Nettchen, uncertain whether to approach her or not.

The two sat motionless upon their chairs, however, silent and lonely, like an Egyptian royal couple of stone; one could almost feel the boundless, glowing desert sand.

White as marble, Nettchen slowly turned her head towards her fiancé and looked at him from the side in a strange manner.

Slowly, he then rose to his feet and walked away with leaden steps, his gaze turned to the ground, while great tears ran from his eyes.

He walked through the groups of people from Goldach and Seldwyla, who were crowding on the stairs, like a dead man stealing away as a ghost from a fair, and, strangely enough, they let him pass as if it were so, moving quietly out of his way without laughing or hurling abuse after him. He passed through the sleighs and horses from Goldach, too, which were assembled ready for departure, whilst the people from Seldwyla were still making merry in their rooms; unconsciously, with only one thought, namely, never to return to Goldach, he wandered along that same road to Seldwyla by which he had come several months before. Soon he vanished in the darkness of the forest through which the road passed. He was bareheaded, for his Polish cap had been left, together with his gloves, upon the window-sill of the ballroom, and so he strode on, his head bent down and his freezing hands hidden under his folded arms, whilst he gradually collected his thoughts, and certain things became apparent to him. The first clear feeling of which he became conscious was one of abysmal shame, as if he had truly been a man of rank and position and had now fallen into disgrace because of some fateful misfortune. But this feeling then gave way to a consciousness of having suffered an injustice; until his glorious arrival in that accursed town, he had never been guilty of any misdemeanour whatsoever; as far as he could think back into his childhood, he could not recall ever having been punished or scolded for lying or deceiving, and now he had become a fraud, because the foolish vanity of the world had descended upon him in an unguarded—and, so to speak, defenceless—moment and made him its playmate. He felt like a child who has been persuaded by a wicked companion to steal the chalice from an altar; now he hated and despised himself, yet he wept for himself and for having so miserably gone astray.

When a prince seizes possession of a country and people; when a priest pronounces without conviction the teaching of his church, but consumes with dignity the fruits of his benefice; when an arrogant professor possesses and enjoys the honours and advantages of a high teaching post without having the slightest understanding of the worth of his science or furthering it in the slightest degree; when an untalented artist succeeds in becoming fashionable by means of careless actions and empty tricks, stealing the bread and fame that rightly belong to true endeavour; or when a swindler, who has inherited or deviously acquired the name of a great merchant family, through his stupidity and lack of conscience robs thousands of their savings and nest-eggs —persons such as this do not weep for themselves, but rather rejoice at their own well-being and are not for one single day without amusing company and good friends.

But our tailor wept bitterly for himself; that is to say, he began to weep suddenly as his thoughts, passing along the heavy chain upon which they now hung, unconsciously reverted to his abandoned fiancée only to double up in shame in the dust before her unseen form. In *one* bright ray of light, the misery and humiliation revealed to him his lost happiness, making him—who had been a poor fool vaguely in love—now a rejected lover. He stretched out his arms to the coldly glittering stars above and tottered, rather than walked, along the road; he stood still once again and shook his head, when suddenly he became aware of a red glow upon the snow and, at the same time, the sound of sleigh-bells and laughter. It was the people from Seldwyla driving home by torch-light. Just as the foremost horses were drawing close to him, he pulled himself together, took a mighty leap over the edge of the road, and cowered down under the nearest trees. The merry procession passed by and, at last, the sounds died away in the dark distance, no one having noticed the fugitive; but he, after remaining motionless and listening for a good while, overwhelmed by the cold and by the fiery drink he had just consumed and his anger at his own crass stupidity, stretched out his limbs and fell asleep in the crackling snow, whilst an icy breath of wind began to blow from the east.

Meanwhile, Nettchen too rose from her lonely chair. She had watched her lover with some degree of attention as he left the hall; she remained motionless for more than an hour before rising to her feet, then she began to sob bitterly and walked helplessly towards the door. There she was joined by two friends who murmured words of dubious consolation to her; and she requested them to bring her coat, scarves, hat, and so forth, in which she wrapped herself without saying a word, roughly drying her eyes with her veil. Anyone weeping, however, is almost always compelled to blow his nose, so that Nettchen was obliged to take out her handkerchief and give a fierce blow, whereupon she looked around her with a proud, angry expression. Her gaze fell upon Melchior Böhni, who now approached deferentially, smiling in a friendly manner, and pointed out to her that she would need a driver and companion to bring her home to her father's house. He would leave the 'Pool of Bethesda' here at the inn, he said, and instead drive the 'Fortuna' with the much-respected, unhappy young lady safely back to Goldach.

Without a word of reply, she walked on with firm steps out into the courtyard, where her sleigh—now one of the last—with the impatient, well-fed horses, was standing ready. Quickly taking her seat in the sleigh, she seized the reins and whip and, whilst the unwitting Böhni, with joyful eagerness, was searching for a gratuity for the groom, who had been holding the horses, she suddenly urged on the horses and drove out on to the highway with leaps and bounds, which soon gave way to a steady, lively gallop.

She did not make for home, however, but drove towards the Seldwyla road. Only when the nimble vehicle had disappeared from view did Herr Böhni realize it had gone, and he ran off in the direction of Goldach shouting: 'Hey!' and calling to Nettchen to stop; then, running back to the inn for his own sleigh, he dashed off in pursuit of the beautiful girl as she fled away—whom, however, he believed to have been carried off by her runaway horses—until he reached the gate of the excited town, where everyone was already talking about the scandal.

Why Nettchen took that road—whether in a state of confusion or deliberately—cannot be said with certainty. Two circumstances may cast a little light upon the question: first, for some strange reason, Strapinski's gloves and fur cap, which had been lying on the window-sill behind the couple's chairs, were now beside Nettchen in the sleigh; when and how she had picked up these articles, no one had seen, and she herself did not know; it had happened as if in a dream. She was not yet aware that both cap and gloves were lying beside her. Then she said to herself aloud, more than once: 'I must have a word or two with him, just a word or two!'

Both these facts seem to show that it was not pure chance alone which was guiding these fiery steeds. It was curious, too, as the 'Fortuna' entered the wooded section of the road on which the bright full moon was shining, how Nettchen shortened the reins and made the horses slacken their pace, so that they were now moving at almost only a trot, whilst their driver kept her sad yet keen eyes fixed upon the road, without ignoring the slightest noticeable object either left or right.

Yet at the same time, her soul was lamed as if by a deep, dull, unhappy forgetfulness. What are life and happiness? What do they depend upon? What manner of beings are we ourselves, that can be made happy or unhappy by a foolish carnival deception? What have we done wrong, that a joyful, trusting affection should bring us shame and hopelessness in return? Who sends us such foolish figures of deceit to intrude upon our destiny with deadly effect, whilst they themselves fade away like inane soap bubbles?

Such questions as these—more in the manner of a dream than of concrete thoughts—were drifting through Nettchen's mind when, suddenly, her eyes were caught by a long dark object at the roadside, contrasting sharply with the moonlit snow. It was Wenzel, his dark hair mingling with the shadows of the trees, whilst his slender figure lay stretched out clearly visible in the light of the moon.

Involuntarily, she pulled the horses to a halt, and a deep silence fell upon the forest. She stared fixedly at the dark figure, until it became almost unmistakable to her keen eye; fastening the reins, she stepped down from the sleigh, stroking the horses for a moment to calm them and then, carefully and without a sound, approached the apparition.

Yes, it was he. Even against the shadowy snow, the dark green velvet of his coat seemed elegant and noble; his slender body and supple limbs in their fine, close-fitting attire—all this, though he lay there rigid, on the brink of ruin, totally withdrawn, all this proclaimed: Clothes make the man!

As the abandoned maiden bent closer over him and now recognized him beyond any doubt, she realized, too, that his life was in danger; indeed, she feared that he might already be frozen to death. Without a thought she seized one of his hands, which felt cold and lifeless. Forgetting everything else, she shook the poor wretch and shouted his Christian name into his ear: 'Wenzel! Wenzel!' In vain: he did not stir, but only breathed weakly and hopelessly. She fell upon him, ran her hand over his face and, in her fear, hit him several times on the bloodless tip of his nose. Then, inspired by a happy thought, she took handfuls of snow and rubbed his nose and face and fingers energetically as long as she could until the unfortunate young man began to recover, awoke once more, and slowly sat up.

Looking around him, he saw his rescuer standing in front of him. She had thrown back her veil, and Wenzel recognized every trait of her pale face as she looked at him with wide eyes.

He threw himself down before her, kissed the hem of her cloak, and cried: 'Forgive me! Forgive me!'

'Come, stranger!' she said in a suppressed, trembling voice, 'I want to speak with you and bring you away from here!'

She made a sign to him to get into the sleigh, and he obeyed; giving him the cap and gloves as involuntarily as she had taken them with her, she picked up the reins and whip and drove away.

On the other side of the forest, not far from the road, was a farmhouse; here lived the farmer's wife, whose husband had died but a short time before. Nettchen was the godmother of one of her children, and the Councillor, Nettchen's father, was her landlord. Only recently the woman had been to visit them, to wish Nettchen happiness and to obtain advice on various matters; but, at this late hour, she could not yet have known what had happened.

Nettchen now drove to this farmhouse; turning off the road, she stopped in front of the house with a loud crack of the whip. There was still light to be seen behind the small windows, for the widow was still up and working, whilst the children and servants had been asleep for a good while. She opened the window and looked out in surprise. 'It's only me; it's us,' called Nettchen. 'We lost our way on the new road up there, which I've never driven on before. Make us a pot of coffee, good neighbour, and let us in for a while before we drive on!'

The farmer's wife hurried to open the door, highly pleased, for she had recognized Nettchen immediately and was overjoyed yet diffident to see the great man, the foreign count. To her mind, the happiness and glamour of this world had crossed her threshold in the shape of these two persons; the good woman was spurred by vague hopes of gaining some small part of this, some modest share for herself or for her children, which made her eager to be of service to the young gentlefolk. Quickly, she woke a servant lad to tend the horses and had soon prepared a pot of hot coffee, which she now brought into the shadowy little room where Wenzel and Nettchen were sitting facing each other, with a dimly flickering lamp on the table between them.

Wenzel was sitting with his head in his hands, not daring to look up. Nettchen leaned back in her chair, keeping her eyes firmly closed; her lovely mouth, too, was closed, with a bitter expression, so that it was clear that she was not asleep.

After the woman had placed the coffee upon the table, Nettchen rose quickly and whispered to her: 'Leave us alone for a quarter-of-an-hour, dear neighbour, and go back to bed; we have had a quarrel; and we must talk matters out tonight, having a good opportunity to do so here!'

'I understand; you're quite right!' said the woman, leaving them alone.

'Drink this,' said Nettchen, who had sat down again, 'it will do you good.' She herself took nothing. Wenzel Strapinski, trembling slightly, sat up and drank a cup of coffee, more out of obedience than for the sake of refreshing himself. Now, he looked at her, too, and as their eyes met and Nettchen looked at his questioningly, she shook her head, then asked: 'Who are you? What do you want of me?'

'I am not what I seem,' he replied sadly, 'I am a poor fool, but I shall put everything to rights and make amends to you; I shall not live much longer!' He spoke these words with such determination and so free from any trace of pretence that Nettchen's eyes blazed imperceptibly. But she repeated: 'I want to know who you really are, where you come from and where you are bound?'

'It all happened exactly as I shall tell you now,' he replied; and he told her who he was, and what had happened to him following his arrival in Goldach. In particular, he declared that he had often intended to flee, but in the end had been prevented from doing so by her appearance on the scene, as if in an enchanted dream.

More than once, Nettchen was tempted to laugh, but the seriousness of her situation was too great for the laughter to burst forth. Rather, she went on with her questioning: 'And where did you intend to go with me, what did you intend to do?' 'I hardly know myself,' he replied, 'I had hopes that other strange and lucky events would come along; and at times I thought of death, namely that I would end my life after I—'

Here Wenzel faltered, and his pale face turned crimson.

'Go on!' said Nettchen, and she herself turned pale whilst her heart began to pound strangely.

Wenzel's eyes blazed and widened. 'Yes,' he cried, 'now I see plainly and clearly what would have happened! I would have gone with you out into the wide world, and after a few brief days of happiness with you, I would have confessed my deception to you and then taken my own life. You would have returned to your father, where you would have been in good hands and easily forgotten me. No one would have needed to know; I would have vanished without trace.—Instead of being sick all my life with longing for a worthy existence, for a kindly heart, for love,' he continued wistfully, 'I would have been elevated and happy for an instant, far above all those who are neither happy nor unhappy, but never wish to die! Oh, if only you had left me lying in the icy snow, I would have fallen asleep so quietly!'

Once again he had fallen silent and was now staring ahead, lost in gloomy thought.

Nettchen's thumping heart, which had been aroused by Wenzel's words, had now calmed down a little and, after watching him quietly for a while, she said: 'Have you ever played such tricks or similar tricks before, and deceived people who had never done you any harm?'

'I have asked myself the same question in this bitter night, but I cannot recall that I was ever a liar! Never have I embarked upon or experienced such an adventure! In the days when I felt an inclination to be or to appear something respectable, when I was still practically a child, I overcame myself, and gave up a chance of happiness that seemed promised to me!'

'What was that?' asked Nettchen.

'Before she married, my mother was in the service of a neighbouring landowner—the lady of the manor—and had travelled with her and visited great cities. And so she had acquired finer manners than the other women in our village, and she was somewhat vain, too, for she always dressed herself and me, her only child, more tastefully and elegantly than was usual for our class. My father, a poor schoolmaster, died when I was very young, and we were so dreadfully poor that there was no chance of us ever achieving the happiness my mother was so fond of dreaming about. Instead, she had to work hard in order to feed us, and as a result, had to give up what she loved most—better manners and better clothing. When I was about sixteen, the lady of the manor, who was now a widow, announced unexpectedly that she intended to move for good, with her household, to the capital; my mother, she said, should let me go with her; it would be a pity for me to become a day-labourer or farmhand in the village; she wished to have me learn a finer occupation, whatever I wished, and I could live in her house meanwhile and perform light services of one kind or another. That seemed the most wonderful thing that could possibly happen to us. And so everything was arranged accordingly, until my mother began to be sad and pensive; and suddenly, one day, she begged me, weeping, not to leave her, but to stay with her in poverty; she would not live to grow old, she said, and I would certainly achieve success even after she was dead. Deeply saddened, I reported this to the lady, who came and remonstrated with my mother; but then my mother became most excited and exclaimed time and again, she would not allow anyone to steal her child from her; no one who knew him—'

Here Strapinski broke off once again and was unable to continue. Nettchen asked: 'What did your mother say: no one who knew him . . . ? Why don't you continue?'

Wenzel blushed and replied: 'She said something strange, which I did not rightly understand, something that I have not felt again since then; she said, no one who knew the child could bear to be parted from him, by which she no doubt meant that

I was a good-natured boy, or something like that. In a word, she was so upset that I refused the lady's offer despite all her persuasion and remained with my mother—she loved me twice as much for it, and begged my forgiveness a thousand times for having stood in the way of my happiness. But when the time came for me to learn a trade, it became clear that there was not much I could do except to go as an apprentice to the village tailor. I didn't want to, but my mother wept so much that I gave in to her. And that is the whole story.'

Nettchen asked why he had left his mother after all; and Wenzel replied:

'I was called up for military service. They sent me to the Hussars; and I was quite a handsome Red Hussar, though perhaps the most stupid in the whole regiment, at any rate the quietest. After serving for a year, I was finally able to obtain a few weeks leave and hurried home to see my dear mother, but she had just died. And so, when my term of service was over, I set off alone into the world and finally met my miserable fate here.'

Nettchen smiled as he thus lamented, looking at him attentively meanwhile. Then there was silence in the room for a while; all at once, a thought seemed to occur to her.

'As you were always so well thought of and well-liked,' she said suddenly, but in a hesitant, pointed tone, 'you have no doubt had your share of love affairs and so on, and certainly more than one poor woman on your conscience—not to speak of myself?'

'Heavens,' said Wenzel, blushing deep crimson, 'before I met you, I had never so much as touched a girl's fingertips, except—'

'Well?' said Nettchen.

'Well,' he continued, 'the same lady who wanted to take me with her and have me trained had a child, a girl of seven or eight—a strange, impulsive child, yet she was as good as gold and as lovely as an angel. I often had to be her servant and protector, and she had grown accustomed to me. I had to take her regularly to the vicarage, which was some distance away, where she took lessons from the old pastor, and bring her home again. And often I had to go out with her into the fields when no one else was able to go with her. And then, as I was bringing her home for the last time across the fields in the evening sun, she began to talk of their approaching departure, and declared that I must go with them instead, and asked whether I would not do so. I said it was out of the question. But the child kept on begging me to stay, entreating me urgently, hanging on to my arm and dragging me back, as children often do, so that, without thinking, I pulled myself free rather roughly. The girl then bowed her head, trying in her embarrassment and sadness to hold back her tears, that were now flowing freely, but she could hardly restrain her sobbing. I was much affected and tried to comfort the child; but then she became angry and turned away and we parted on bad terms. I have never forgotten that lovely child since then, and I have always remained fond of her, though I never heard from her again.'

Suddenly the speaker, now in a fit of mild agitation, broke off as if frightened and stared at his companion, his face turning pale.

'Well,' said Nettchen in a strange tone, and she, too, turned pale; 'why are you looking at me like that?'

Wenzel stretched out his arm, pointed at her with his finger as if seeing a ghost, and exclaimed: 'I've seen that once before. Whenever the child was in a rage, the pretty hair above her forehead and on her temples would rise a little—just like yours now—so that you could see it move, and so it was in the fields, in the evening sunlight, when I last saw her.'

And it was true. Nettchen's curls above her forehead and at her temples had trembled slightly, just as if a breath of wind had brushed her face.

Mother Nature, always somewhat coquettish, had employed one of her mysteries in this case in order to put an end to this difficult situation.

After a brief silence, Nettchen rose, her breast beginning to heave, walked around the table towards the young man, and threw her arms about his neck. 'I shan't leave you! You are mine, and I shall stand by you in spite of everyone.'

And so she now truly celebrated her engagement with heart and soul; she accepted her destiny amid sweet passion and thus remained true to him.

Yet she was by no means so foolish as not to attempt to guide this destiny a little; quickly and boldly she made up her mind anew. Turning to Wenzel, who, now that his luck had changed again, was lost in dreams, she said:

'And now we shall drive straight to Seldwyla and show the people there, who thought to destroy us, that they have brought us together and only made us all the more happy.'

The doughty Wenzel could not understand this. He much rather wished to move on to some far-off unfamiliar region and to live there, unknown and romantically, in peaceful happiness, as he put it.

But Nettchen exclaimed: 'No more story-book romancing! I want to declare myself for you just as you are, a poor journey-man, and to be your wife here, where my home is, despite all these proud, sneering people. We shall go to Seldwyla and, with hard work and intelligence, we shall make them dependent upon us—those same people who sneered at us.'

No sooner said than done. Nettchen called the farmer's wife, and Wenzel, who was beginning to feel at home in his new situation, rewarded her; then they went on their way. This time Wenzel was holding the reins and Nettchen was leaning con-tentedly against him as if he were a church pillar. For free will is the stuff of heaven; Nettchen had come of age only three days before and was able to follow her own wishes.

Reaching Seldwyla, they stopped in front of the 'Rainbow Inn', where a number of people from the sleigh-ride were still sitting over a glass of wine. As soon as they entered the taproom, a murmur ran like lightning through the company: 'Ha, there's an elopement for you! We've really set off a fine affair!'

Without turning his head, Wenzel walked through the com-pany with his fiancée; after she had disappeared into her room, he went off to the 'Wild Man', another respectable inn, and strode proudly past the other members of the Seldwyla sleigh party who were there; asking for a room, he went inside and left them to their bewildered discussions, because of which they felt obliged to drink themselves into a most unpleasant headache.

In the town of Goldach, too, the word 'elopement!' was mak-ing the rounds like wildfire. Very early next morning, the 'Pool of Bethesda' made its way to Seldwyla, carrying the agitated

Böhni and Nettchen's dismayed father. Such was their haste that they almost drove through Seldwyla without stopping; just in time, they saw the 'Fortuna' standing safe and sound in front of the inn, and consoled themselves with the thought that the fine horses, at least, could not be far away. When their supposition was confirmed, and they heard that Nettchen had arrived, and where she was staying, they had their own horses unharnessed, whereupon they, too, went into the 'Rainbow'.

Some little time elapsed, however, before Nettchen sent word to ask her father to come to her room in order to speak to her there alone. People said, moreover, that she had already sent for the best lawyer in the town, who would be arriving during the course of the morning. Somewhat heavy-hearted, the Councillor went upstairs to his daughter; he was considering how he might best lead back the reckless girl from her path of aberration, and was prepared to find her in a desperate mood.

But Nettchen met him calmly and with quiet determination. In a voice filled with emotion, she thanked her father for all the love and kindness he had shown her, and then declared firmly: first, she did not wish to live in Goldach any longer after what had happened, not for the next few years, at least; second, she wished to have the inheritance, a considerable one, which was due to her from her mother, and which her father had long been keeping for the event of her marriage; third, she wished to marry Wenzel Strapinski—on this point, she was adamant; fourth, she intended to live with him in Seldwyla and there help him set up a prosperous business; and, fifth and last, she said, everything would turn out well; for she was convinced that he was a good man and would make her happy.

The Councillor began his campaign by reminding Nettchen that she knew how much he had wished to be able to place her fortune in her hands, the sooner the better, in order to provide her with the foundations of true happiness. But then he went on, with all the anxiety that had filled him since he had first heard of the dreadful catastrophe, to explain the impossibility of the relationship which she desired to preserve; finally, he revealed the potent means by which alone this difficult problem could be resolved in a worthy manner: none other than Herr Melchior Böhni who, immediately and on his own personal guarantee, was prepared to put an end to the whole business and, with his own unimpeachable name, to protect and uphold her honour before the whole world.

Hearing the word 'honour', however, his daughter grew most excited. It was exactly her honour, she exclaimed, which demanded she should *not* marry Herr Böhni, for she could not abide him, but on the contrary, that she should remain true to the poor stranger, to whom she had given her word and of whom she was so fond!

Now followed a fruitless argument, the result of which was that the steadfast maiden finally burst into tears.

Then, at nearly the same time, Wenzel and Böhni, who had met on the stairs, stormed into the room, almost provoking a scene of great confusion. At that moment the lawyer, who was well known to the Councillor, arrived and strongly recommended everyone to remain calm and sensible. After the matter had been explained to him in a few brief words, he ordered that Wenzel should go back to the 'Wild Man', and remain there quietly; further, that Herr Böhni, too, should leave without interfering in the affair; Nettchen, for her part, was to observe all the forms of civility befitting her station until the whole affair was concluded; and her father should refrain from exercising any kind of coercion whatsoever, since his daughter's personal liberty was legally beyond any doubt.

Thus, for several hours, an armistice was concluded and all persons concerned were separated. The lawyer had spread the word in the town to the effect that a considerable sum of money might be coming to Seldwyla as a result of the affair, and a great tumult ensued. The mood of the people of Seldwyla suddenly changed in favour of the tailor and his fiancée, and they determined to protect the lovers with their own blood and to stand up for personal rights and liberty in their town. And so, when a rumour arose that the maiden from Goldach was to be taken back by force, they banded together, posted armed sentries and guards of honour in front of the 'Rainbow' and the 'Wild Man', and thus embarked with enormous gusto upon one of their greatest adventures—a notable continuation of that of the previous day.

Dismayed and angered, the Councillor despatched his ally Böhni to Goldach to summon help. Böhni set off at a gallop;

next day, a company of men together with an impressive police force rode over from Goldach in support of the Councillor; and it seemed that Seldwyla was to become a latter-day Troy. The two groups faced each other threateningly; the town drummer was already tightening his drum and struck it several times with his right-hand drumstick. Then some high-ranking officials, both clerics and laymen, appeared; negotiations took place on all sides and it was agreed—since, encouraged by the people of Seldwyla, Nettchen stood firm and Wenzel would not allow himself to be intimidated—to have the marriage bans officially published after all necessary documents had been procured, and to investigate whether any legal objections, and if so, which, might be raised in the meantime and with what results.

Since Nettchen was fully of age, no objections could be raised except with regard to the dubious person of the bogus Count Wenzel Strapinski.

The lawyer, however, who was now acting for Wenzel and Nettchen, discovered that there was not the slightest blemish on the young stranger's reputation, either in his home village or during his previous travels; on the contrary, only favourable and well-disposed reports about him were received from all sides.

With regard to the events in Goldach, the lawyer was able to prove that Wenzel had, in fact, never claimed to be a count, but that this rank had been forcibly conferred upon him by others; that on all pieces of documentary evidence he had signed his name as Wenzel Strapinski without any supplementary title, so that he had committed no misdemeanour save that he had accepted a foolish hospitality which would never have been accorded to him had he not arrived in that carriage, and the coachman not permitted himself that ill-considered joke.

And so the war ended with a wedding, on the occasion of which the people of Seldwyla made a tremendous noise shooting off their so-called 'cat's heads'—much to the annoyance of the people of Goldach, who could hear the firing of the cannon very well, since the west wind was blowing. The Councillor gave Nettchen her entire inheritance, and she declared that Wenzel must now become a notable merchant-tailor and 'cloth-master' in Seldwyla—for there, a draper was still known as a 'cloth-master', an ironmonger as an 'iron-master', and so forth.

And so it was, too—though in quite a different way than the people of Seldwyla had expected. He was modest, thrifty, and hard-working in his business and clever at extending his activities. He made their waistcoats of violet or blue-and-white checked velvet, their swallow-tail coats with golden buttons, and their cloaks lined with crimson, for all of which they ran up debts with him—though never for long. For in order to obtain new, even more elegant clothes which he ordered or made for them, they were obliged to pay for their previous orders first, so that they used to complain among themselves that he was squeezing them to their very marrow.

With all this he became round and imposing, so that there was hardly anything of the romantic dreamer about him any more; he became more experienced and clever in business from year to year; and, together with his father-in-law, the Councillor, with whom he soon became reconciled, he engaged in such skilful speculations that his fortune doubled, and after ten or twelve years, together with the same number of children, which Nettchen —his Strapinska—had borne in the meantime, and with Nettchen herself, he moved back to Goldach, where he became a respected man.

But in Seldwyla he did not leave so much as a penny behind —either out of ingratitude or revenge.

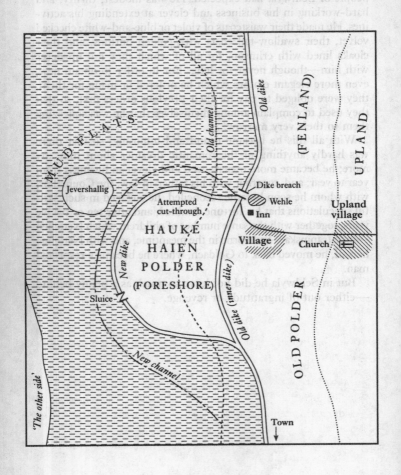

1964   The White Horse Rider

THEODOR STORM
The White Horse Rider

The events which I intend to relate came to my knowledge a good half-century ago in the house of my great-grandmother, the old wife of Senator Feddersen, as I sat by her armchair and busied myself reading a blue-bound volume of magazines; I can no longer recall whether the magazine in question was the *Leipziger* or *Pappe's Hamburg Digest*. I can still feel—like a shiver —the gentle hand of the old lady (she was over eighty) as, from time to time, it slipped caressingly over her great-grandchild's hair. Both she and those days are long since buried; my later attempts to find those magazines have been in vain, and I can therefore no more guarantee the truth of the events than I could vouch for them if someone were to deny them; yet I can assure the reader this much: that I have never forgotten them since that time, though they have not been revived in me by any external circumstance whatsoever.

It was in the third decade of this century—began the magazine narrator—one afternoon in October, as I was riding along a dike in North Friesland during a heavy storm. For more than an hour now, I had had on my left the dismal fenland, already abandoned by all the cattle, and on my right and in most uncomfortable proximity, the mudflats of the North Sea; from the dike I should have been able to see the *halligen** and other islands, yet I could see nothing but the yellow-grey waves beating ceaselessly against the dike with a noise like angry bellowing and, at times, spraying me and my horse with dirty foam; beyond them, a dreary twilight, in which sky and land could not be told apart, for the half-moon which was now high in the sky was most of the time concealed by dark, scudding clouds. It was icy cold; my frozen hands could hardly hold the reins, and I could not blame the crows and gulls which, cawing and screaming without cease, let themselves be driven inland by the storm.

Night was now drawing in, and I was already no longer able to see my horse's hooves clearly; I had not met a single soul; I could hear nothing but the cries of the birds, as they almost brushed me or my trusty mare with their long wings, and the roar of the wind and waves. I cannot deny that, now and then, I longed for a safe roof over my head.

It was now the third day of such weather, and I had allowed a favourite relative of mine to detain me for an unduly long time on his farm, which was situated in one of the more northerly districts. But today I could not bear it any longer; I had business in the town, which even now was certainly a few hours ride to the south and, despite all the powers of persuasion of my cousin and his dear wife, despite the delicious home-grown Perinette and Grand Richard apples still to be tasted, I had ridden away that afternoon. 'Just wait till you reach the sea,' he had called after me even from the front door, 'you'll turn back; your room will be waiting for you!'

And indeed, for an instant, as a black bank of cloud cloaked me in pitch darkness whilst the howling squalls of wind sought to thrust me and my mare from the dike, a thought flashed through my head: 'Don't be a fool! Turn back and join your friends in their cosy nest.' But then I realized that the way back was surely even longer than the way ahead of me; and so I trotted on, drawing up the collar of my cloak around my ears.

Now, however, something was coming towards me on the dike; I could not hear anything, but when the half-moon cast its bare light I thought I could make out, more and more clearly, a dark figure; and soon, as it came closer, I saw it, sitting upon a horse, a lean, long-legged white horse; a black cloak was fluttering around the rider's shoulders and, as the figure raced by, two burning eyes stared at me from a pale face.

Who was it? What could he want?—And now it occurred to me that I had not heard any sound of hooves, nor the panting breath of the horse, though both horse and rider had passed close by me!

I rode on, still thinking about the incident, but I had not long to think before the figure passed me once again from behind; it seemed to me that the flying cloak brushed against me and, just as before, the apparition had galloped past without a sound.

Then I saw it farther and farther ahead of me; then I thought I saw its shadow suddenly go down the landward side of the dike.

With some reluctance I followed. As I reached the spot, I saw in the polder* below, hard by the dike, the glinting water of a large *Wehle*—such is the name given here to the pits which are washed out of the land by the storm floods and generally remain as small but deep pools.

The surface of the water was remarkably placid, even allowing for the sheltering dike; the rider could not have disturbed it; I saw no more of him. But I saw something else, a sight which I greeted joyfully: ahead of me, from the polder below, a multitude of scattered lights was shining towards me; they appeared to come from those long, low Frisian houses standing singly upon high earthen mounds; directly in front of me, however, half-way up the inner dike, stood a large house of the same type; on the south side, to the right of the front door, there were lights at all the windows; behind these I could see people and, despite the storm, thought that I could hear their voices. My horse, of its own accord, had trotted down the dike path which brought me up to the door of the house. I saw that it was an inn, for, in front of the windows, I noticed the 'hitching rails'—beams supported by two uprights and fitted with large iron rings for tethering the cattle and horses which stopped here.

I tied my own horse to one of these rings, entrusting the animal to the care of the groom who came towards me as I walked through the entrance. 'Is there a meeting going on?' I asked, for the sound of voices and the chinking of glasses was plainly to be heard from the taproom door.

'Aye, summat o' th' sort,' answered the groom in Plattdeutsch*—I learned later that this, besides Frisian, had been common here for over a hundred years—'t' daik reeve un' 'is deppities un' sum o' t' other fowk wut 'as ter do with it. It's abaht th' flood!'

As I entered the room, I saw about a dozen men sitting at a table alongside the windows; on the table was a punch bowl, which appeared to be under the supervision of a very portly gentleman.

I greeted the company and asked leave to sit at their table, which was readily granted. 'You're keeping watch here, I see!'

said I, turning to the portly gentleman; 'It's nasty weather out-side; the dikes will be in danger!'

'True,' he replied, 'but we on the eastern side believe that we're out of danger now; only the other side isn't safe; the dikes there are still mostly of the old type; our main dike was im-proved during the last century.—It got too cold for us out there just now,' he went on, 'and I suppose it was the same with you, but we have to wait here for a few hours yet; we've trustworthy men out there to report to us.' And before I could give my order to the landlord, a steaming glass had been pushed towards me.

I soon learned that my friendly neighbour was the dike reeve; we had got into conversation and I had started to tell him about my strange encounter upon the dike. He pricked up his ears, and I suddenly noticed that, all around us, the conversation had died away. 'The White Horse Rider!' shouted one of the com-pany, and a shudder of fear ran through his companions.

The dike reeve had risen to his feet. 'No need for you to be afraid,' he said across the table; 'it isn't meant for us alone; in the year '17 it was meant for those on the other side; they'd better be prepared for anything!'

Now a shudder ran through me: 'Your pardon!' I said, 'What was that about the White Horse Rider?'

Some distance away behind the stove, bent over somewhat, sat a small, thin man in a threadbare black coat; one shoulder ap-peared a little misshapen. He had not contributed a single word to the others' conversation, but his eyes, still framed by dark eyelashes despite his thinning grey hair, showed unmistakeably that he was not sitting here with the intention of sleeping.

The dike reeve stretched out his hand towards him. 'Our schoolmaster,' he said, raising his voice, 'will best be able to tell you the story; only in his own way, of course, and not as faith-fully as my old housekeeper Antje Vollmers would.'

'You're joking, dike reeve!'—the schoolmaster's somewhat ailing voice came from behind the stove—'The very idea of comparing that stupid shrew of yours with me!'

'Yes, indeed, schoolmaster,' replied the dike reeve, 'but they say that such stories are best kept by shrews.'

'Of course!' said the little man; 'we are not quite in agreement on this point,' and a superior smile glided across his fine-cut features as he spoke.

'As you can see,' the dike reeve whispered in my ear, 'he's still somewhat proud; he once studied theology as a young man and remained stuck here in his birthplace as schoolmaster only because of an engagement that went wrong.'

The latter had meanwhile emerged from his niche behind the stove and seated himself beside me at the long table. 'Tell us, tell us, schoolmaster,' called a few of the younger members of the company.

'Indeed I shall, gladly' said the old man, turning to me, 'but there is a good deal of superstition in the tale, and it's quite an art to tell the tale without it.'

'I must ask you not to leave it out,' I replied; 'you can trust me to separate the wheat from the chaff myself!' The old man looked at me with an understanding smile.

Very well, then! he said. In the middle of the last century, or rather, to be precise, before and after that time, there lived here a dike reeve who understood more about dikes and drainage matters than is usual for a farmer and landowner; yet this was hardly sufficient, for he had read only little of what the learned experts had written on these subjects; he had conceived his ideas entirely by himself, though admittedly ever since childhood. You will surely have heard, sir, that the Frisians are born calculators, and you will surely have heard tell of our countryman Hans Mommsen* of Fahretoft, who was only a farmer and yet was skilled in making boussoles, maritime clocks, telescopes, and organs. Well, the father of this man who later became dike reeve had something of Hans Mommsen about him, if only very little. He had a few fields in which he used to grow rapeseed and beans, and kept a cow; in autumn and spring he would sometimes carry out surveying and, in winter, when the north-west wind was blowing outside and rattling at his shutters, he would sit in his room working at his drawing board. The boy was usually sitting there too, and would look across his ABC book or his Bible at his father as he measured and calculated and ran his hand through his blond hair. One evening the boy asked his father why something which he had just written had to be just so and could not be anything else, and proceeded to offer his own opinion on the matter. But his father, not knowing the answer, shook his head and replied: 'That I can't tell you; it *is* so, that's enough, and you're quite mistaken. If you want to know more, go up to the attic tomorrow and look in the chest for a book written by a man called Euclid; that will give you the answer!'

— —Next morning the boy ran up to the attic and had soon found the book, for there were not many books in the house at all; but his father laughed when the boy laid it on the table before him. It was a Dutch version of Euclid, and neither of them understood Dutch, even though it is half German. 'Yes, yes,' he said, 'the book belonged to my father, he understood it; isn't there a German version there?'

The son, who was a lad of few words, looked at his father calmly and said only: 'May I keep it? There isn't a German version.'

When the old man nodded, he brought out a second little book, torn and battered. 'This one, too?' he asked.

'Keep them both!' said Tede Haien; 'they won't help you much, mind.'

But the second book was a small Dutch grammar; winter was by no means at an end, and so, when at last the gooseberry plants in their garden blossomed once again, the book had helped the lad so much that he could understand the Euclid, which was very popular in those days, almost entirely.

I am well aware, sir (said the narrator, breaking off his tale), that the same is told of Hans Mommsen too; but this story of Hauke Haien—that was the boy's name—had been told here in this region before Mommsen was born. You know very well, it only needs a greater man to come along and everything is attributed to him that his predecessors are said to have done, whether in earnest or in jest.

When the old man saw that his son was interested neither in cows nor sheep, and hardly noticed when the beanstalks were flowering, which gladdens the heart of every true man of the fenland, and when, too, he considered that the little farm could no doubt survive if run by a farmer and his son, but not by a half-educated man and a farm-hand—furthermore that he himself had not got anywhere in life—he sent his grown lad to the dike, where he had to cart earth with other labourers from Easter till Martinmas. 'That will cure him of Euclid,' the old man said to himself.

And the lad carted earth; but he carried his Euclid in his pocket at all times and, whenever the labourers were eating their breakfast or midday meal, he would sit on an upturned wheel-barrow with the book in his hand. And when, in autumn, the flood tides were rising higher and, many a time, work had to stop, he did not go home with the others but remained sitting on the sloping seaward side of the dike, his hands clasped upon his knees, watching for hours on end the grey waves of the North Sea beating higher and higher against the grassy mound of the dike; only when his shoes had been drenched and the foam was flying in his face would he retreat a few feet higher and remain seated once more. He heard neither the splashing of the waters nor the screaming of the gulls and other seabirds flying around him or over him, almost brushing him with their wings, their black eyes gleaming into his own; nor did he see the night spreading before him over the wide, wild, watery waste; all he saw was the surging edge of the water which, at flood-tide, would beat savagely again and again upon the same spot, wash-ing away before his eyes the grassy wall of the steep dike.

After staring long at the sight, he would nod his head slowly or, without lifting his gaze, trace with his hand a smooth line in the air, as if he meant to give the dike a more gentle slope. When it became so dark that all earthly things had vanished from his sight and only the sound of the flood-tide was thundering in his ears, he would rise to his feet and trot home, almost soaked to the skin.

One evening, as he came home in this way and entered the room where his father was cleaning his surveying instruments, the old man rounded on him: 'What are you up to out there? You might have been drowned; the water is tearing at the dike today.'

Hauke looked at him defiantly.

—'D'you hear me? I said, you might have been drowned.'

'Yes,' replied Hauke, 'but I wasn't.'

'No,' countered the old man after a while and looked him in the face as if elsewhere in thought; 'not this time.'

'But,' Hauke went on, 'our dikes are worthless!'

—'What's that you say, lad?'

'The dikes, I say!'

—'What about the dikes?'

'They're no good, father!' replied Hauke.

The old man laughed in his face. 'How, then, lad? I suppose you're the boy wonder from Lübeck!'*

But the boy would not be put off. 'The seaward side is too steep,' he said; 'if things go just as they already have more than once, we could drown here even behind the dike!'

The old man drew his chewing tobacco from his pocket, twisted off a quid, and pushed it into his mouth. 'And how many barrowloads have you carted today?' he asked in a vexed tone; for he could clearly see that even the work on the dike had not been able to spoil the lad's taste for mental work.

'Don't know, father,' he replied, ''bout the same number as the others; maybe half-a-dozen more; but—the dikes ought to be built different!'

'Well,' said the old man, and he laughed—'maybe you can get to be dike reeve; then build them different!'

'Yes, father,' replied the lad.

The old man looked at him and swallowed once or twice; then he left the room, not knowing how to answer the lad.

Even when work on the dike finished at the end of October, the walk north to the sea still afforded Hauke Haien the best amusement; he looked forward to All Souls' Day (which, as we say, is a day of sorrow for Friesland)—at about which time the autumn equinoctial storms generally rage—as the children today look forward to Christmas. Whenever a spring tide was in the offing, you could be sure that he would be lying far out on the dike, utterly alone, despite storm and weather; and when the gulls were shrieking, and the waves pounding against the dike and tearing down great divots of turf into the sea as they rolled back, Hauke's angry laughter might have been heard. 'You can't do anything right,' he would shout into the tumult, 'just as men can't do anything right!' At last, often in darkness, he would turn away from the endless waste and return home, trotting along the dike until his tall figure reached the low door of his father's reed-thatched house and slipped through it into the little room.

Sometimes he had brought a handful of clay with him; then he would sit down beside the old man, who let him do as he wished now, and by the light of the slender tallow candle he would fashion model dikes of all types; placing them in a shallow bowl with water, he would try to reproduce the washing-out effect of the waves; or he would pick up his slate and sketch the seaward profile of the dike, as he believed it should be built.

It did not occur to him to keep company with those who had gone to school with him; they, for their part, did not seem to care much for the dreamer. When winter had come around once again and the frost had settled, he would wander even farther to a point where he had never been before, far out on the dike, until the ice-covered surface of the mud-flats stretched before him farther than the eye could see.

In February, during a long spell of frosty weather, some bodies were found washed up; they had lain on the frozen mud-flats near the open sea. A young woman, who had been present when they were brought into the village, stood chattering in front of old Haien. 'Don't imagine that they looked like human beings,' she cried, 'no—they were like sea monsters! Great heads, like that,' and she held her spread hands wide apart; 'black as pitch and smooth as fresh-baked bread! And the crabs had been nibbling at them, and the children shrieked when they saw them!'

This was nothing new to old Haien: 'They'll have been drifting in the sea since November,' he said calmly.

Hauke was standing beside him, silent; but, as soon as he could he slipped away to the dike; whether he intended to look for more drowned bodies, or whether he was lured by the horror that surely still lingered over the place, none can say. On and on he went, until he was standing alone in the wilderness, where only the winds were blowing over the dike, where nothing was to be heard save the plaintive cries of the great birds swiftly streaking past; on his left, the bare, wide fenland; on the other side, the endless shore with its mud-flats now shimmering with the ice; it was as if the whole world lay beneath a film of white death.

Hauke remained standing up on the dike, his keen eyes scanning all around; but there were no more bodies to be seen; only where the unseen streams in the mud-flats forced their way beneath was the ice layer rising and falling in wavering lines.

He ran home; but one evening, soon afterwards, he was out there once again. The ice which had covered the spot was now split, and it was as if clouds of smoke were rising from the cracks; all over the mud-flats there spread a tracery of mist and vapour, mingling eerily with the evening twilight. Hauke looked towards it with staring eyes; dark figures were walking back and forth in the mist, they seemed to him as tall as human beings. Dignified, but with strange, frightening gestures; he could see them far away, with long necks and long noses, promenading back and forth by the reeking cracks in the ice. Suddenly they began to leap up and down in an uncanny manner, like madmen, the tall figures jumping over the smaller ones, the smaller ones bumping into the taller ones; then they fell apart from one another and lost every semblance of shape.

'What are they doing? Are they the spirits of the drowned men?' thought Hauke. 'Hallo!' he shouted in a loud voice into the night; but the distant figures paid no heed to his cry and continued their strange capering.

Then the dreadful Norwegian sea ghosts, about which an old sea captain had once told him, came into his mind—each with a broken tussock of sea grass on its neck instead of a face; yet he did not flee, but dug the heels of his boots firmly into the clay of the dike and stared at the clownish antics which were still going on before his eyes in the deepening twilight. 'Have you come to plague us, too?' he called in a harsh voice; 'You shan't frighten me away!'

Only when darkness lay everywhere did he set off for home with slow, stiff strides; yet behind him, he thought he heard a sound as of beating wings and echoing cries. He did not look back; but neither did he quicken his pace and he did not arrive home until a late hour; yet he never spoke a word about his experience to his father nor to anyone else. It was not until many years after that he took his daughter, a weak-minded creature with whom the good Lord later burdened him, to the dike at the same time of day and year, and the same scene is said to have taken place out there on the mud-flats on that occasion, too; but he told her that she need not be afraid; it was only the grey herons and the crows which appeared so huge and dreadful in the fog: they were catching fish through the open cracks in the ice.

'God knows, sir,' the schoolmaster broke off, 'there are many things on earth which can bewilder an honest Christian; but Hauke was neither a fool nor an idiot.'

Since I made no reply, he was about to continue; but a sudden stir broke out among the other guests who, until then, had been listening in silence, merely filling the low room with thicker clouds of tobacco smoke; first singly, then almost to a man, they turned towards the window. Outside—clearly visible through the uncurtained windows—the clouds were being driven by the storm, light and darkness were chasing each other in a frenzy; but it seemed to me, too, that I had seen the gaunt rider on his white horse careering by.

'Wait a moment, schoolmaster!' said the dike reeve quietly.

'You needn't be afraid, dike reeve!' replied the little story-teller, 'I haven't spoken evil of him, nor have I cause to do so,' and he looked up at him with his small, canny eyes.

'Yes, yes,' said the dike reeve, 'just fill your glass again.' And after this had been done and the listeners, most of them wearing a rather troubled look, had turned to him once again, the school-master continued his tale:

And so Hauke grew up to be a tall, lean young fellow, solitary and, preferably, with only the wind and waves and images of loneliness for company. More than a year had passed since his confirmation when things suddenly took a different turn with him; the reason for this was the old white Angora tomcat which had once been brought back for old Trin' Jans by her son, who later lost his life, from a voyage to Spain. Trin' lived in a small cottage a good way out on the dike and, whenever the old woman was busy in her house, this monstrous tomcat used to sit in front of the door, blinking at the summer sunshine and the lapwings darting overhead. Whenever Hauke walked by, the cat would mew at him and Hauke would nod to the cat; each knew what to make of the other.

Now it was spring, and Hauke, as was his custom, often used to lie out on the dike—farther down the slope and closer to the water, amidst sea lavender and the sweet-scented wormwood—lying in the sunlight, which was already strong. The day before, on the upland, he had filled his pockets with pebbles and, when the mud-flats were laid bare by the ebb-tide and the little grey stilt plovers swept shrieking over his head, he suddenly snatched a stone and threw it at the birds. He had practised this ever since he was a child and generally managed to hit a bird, which then remained lying in the mud; but invariably it fell beyond reach; Hauke had often thought of taking the tomcat with him and training him to retrieve the prey, like a hunting dog. But here and there were firm patches or sandbanks and, in such cases, he would run out to the spot and fetch his prey himself. If, on his return, the tomcat was still sitting before the door, the animal would yowl with unmistakable rapacity until Hauke finally threw him one of the birds he had bagged.

On this day, walking home with his jacket over his shoulder, he was carrying only a single bird, of a kind unknown to him but with a plumage like shining silk and metal, and the cat mewed at him as usual when it saw him coming. But on this occasion Hauke was not willing to give up his prey—it may have been a kingfisher—and remained unmoved by the animal's greed. 'Turns apiece!' he cried, 'my turn today, yours tomorrow; this is no catfood!' But the tomcat came slinking cautiously towards him; Hauke stood and looked at him, with the bird hanging in his hand, and the tomcat remained motionless with his paw outstretched. But it appeared that Hauke did not know his friend very well; for just as he had turned his back on the animal and was about to walk on, he felt his booty torn from his hand with a jerk and, at the same time, a sharp claw sank into his flesh. A fit of rage, like that of a beast of prey, came over the young man; he whirled round in a fury and straight away seized the robber by the neck. Holding the great beast in the air with his fist, he choked it until its eyes bulged out of its coarse fur, without heeding the powerful hind claws which were lacerating his arm. 'Oho!' he shouted, seizing the cat even more firmly, 'let's see which of us can hold out longer!'

Suddenly the big cat's hind legs fell down limply and Hauke walked back a few paces and threw it against the wall of the old woman's cottage. The cat did not stir and Hauke turned and resumed his way home.

But the Angora tomcat was the apple of his mistress's eye; he was her companion and the only thing which her son, the seaman, had left her after he had met his sudden death here on the coast, while helping his mother to catch shrimps during a storm. Hauke had hardly gone a hundred paces, mopping the blood from his wounds with a kerchief, when, from the cottage behind him, a howling and wailing assailed his ears. He turned and saw the old woman lying upon the ground in front of the cottage, her grey hair streaming in the wind around her red headscarf: 'Dead!' she screamed, 'dead!' and she raised her skinny arm threateningly towards him. 'Curse you! You've killed him, you worthless beachcomber; you weren't fit to brush his tail!' She threw herself over the animal and, with her apron, tenderly wiped away the blood that was still running out of its nose and mouth; then she began her wailing once again.

'Have you finished?' shouted Hauke, 'Then I'll tell you this: I'll get you a cat that's content with mouse's and rat's blood!'

With this he continued on his way, not seeming to care any more about the matter. But the dead cat must have troubled his thoughts for, when he reached the houses, he walked past his father's house and the others and carried on a long way to the south towards the town dike.

Meanwhile Trin' Jans, too, was wandering along the dike in the same direction, carrying in her arms a burden wrapped in an old, blue-checked pillowcase, which she clasped carefully as if it were a child; her grey hair was fluttering in the mild spring breeze. 'What's that you're carrying, Trina?' asked a farmer whom she met on her way. 'More than your house and home,' the old woman replied; and she hurried on. As she came near to old Haien's house down below, she descended the path which ran obliquely down the side of the dike to the houses.

Old Tede Haien was standing at his door contemplating the weather. 'Well, Trin'!' he greeted her as she stood puffing before him and stuck her crook into the ground, 'What have you got there in your sack?'

'First let me come in, Tede Haien! then you shall see!' and she looked at him with a strange gleam in her eyes.

'Come in, then!' said the old man. What did he care about the stupid creature's eyes!

When they were both inside, she went on: 'Take that old tobacco box and the writing things off the table— —what is it you're always writing, anyway?— —well; and now wipe it clean!'

The old man, who was becoming rather intrigued, did as she wished; then she took the blue pillowcase by both ends and shook out the body of the big tomcat on to the table. 'There you are!' she cried; 'your son Hauke killed him!' With this she began to weep bitterly; she stroked the dead animal's thick fur, arranged its paws, lowered her long nose to its head, and whispered unintelligible words of affection into its ears.

Tede Haien watched her; 'So,' he said, 'Hauke killed him?' He did not know how to deal with the weeping woman.

The old woman nodded grimly: 'Yes, yes; as God is my judge, he did it!' and with her hand, crippled with gout, she wiped the tears from her eyes. 'I've no child, no living soul more!' she wept. 'And you know, too, that when All Souls' comes, us old folks' feet are cold in bed at night and, instead of sleeping, we hear the Nor'wester rattling at the shutters. I don't like to hear it, Tede Haien, it comes from the spot where my son was dragged down in the quicksand.'

Tede Haien nodded, and the old woman stroked the dead cat's fur. 'But,' she went on, 'in winter, when I used to sit at my spinning-wheel, he would sit beside me, purring, and look at me with his green eyes. And when I was cold and crept into bed— why, in no time at all, he would jump up on to the bed and lie on my freezing feet, and we would sleep as warm as if I still had my young darling in bed with me!' As if seeking confirmation, she looked with her gleaming eyes at the old man standing beside her at the table.

But the old man replied in a pensive tone: 'I know what we'll do, Trin' Jans,' and he went to his coffer and took out a silver coin from the drawer.—'You say that Hauke killed your cat, and I know that you are not a liar; here's a Christian IV crown for you; buy yourself a tanned lambskin for your cold feet! And the next time our cat has kittens, you may choose the biggest for yourself; altogether, that ought to make up for a sorry old Angora tomcat. Now take the creature away and bring it to the knacker in the town, for all I care, and not a word to anyone that it's been lying on my respectable table!'

Whilst he was talking, the old woman had already seized the crown and put it into a small pouch which she carried under her dress; then she pushed the tomcat back into the pillowcase, wiped the bloodstains from the table with her apron, and stalked out of the door. 'Don't go forgetting the young tomcat for me!' she called over her shoulder.

— —Some time later, as old Haien was walking back and forth in the cramped little room, Hauke came in and threw the brightly coloured bird on to the table; but, seeing the bloodstain which was still visible on the white-scoured table-top, he asked casually: 'What's that?'

His father came to a halt: 'That's blood that was spilt by you!'

The lad flushed hotly: 'Has Trin' Jans been here with her tomcat, then?'

The old man nodded: 'Why did you kill him?'

Hauke bared his bloody arm. 'That's why,' he said; 'he'd snatched the bird from me!'

The old man made no reply to this, but resumed walking back and forth for a time; then he came to a halt in front of his son and looked down at him for a moment as if elsewhere in his thoughts. Then he said: 'I've settled the matter of the cat; but— see here, Hauke, this cottage is too small; there's no room here for two masters—it's time now for you to find a place of service!'

'Yes, father,' replied Hauke, 'I've thought the same myself.'

'Why?' asked the old man.

—'Well, a man becomes filled with fury if he can't let it out on a respectable piece of work.'

'So?' said the old man, 'And that's why you killed the Angora cat? It could easily get even worse than that!'

—'You may be right, father; but the dike reeve has dismissed his second man; that's work that I could do!'

The old man recommenced walking back and forth, squirting out the brown tobacco juice as he did so. 'The dike reeve is a fool, he hasn't the brains of a louse! He's dike reeve only because his father and grandfather were dike reeves before him, and

because of his twenty-nine fields. When Martinmas comes and
the accounts for the dikes and sluices have to be settled, he feeds
the schoolmaster with roast goose and mead and wheat cakes;
and he sits there nodding while the schoolmaster runs down the
columns of figures with his quill and says: "Yes, indeed, schoolmaster, the Lord has given you talent! How clever you are
at reckoning!" But if it happens that the schoolmaster can't or
won't help him, then he has to do it himself, and sits and writes
and crosses out again, and that great stupid head of his gets hot
and red, and his eyes bulge like marbles as if the little bit of
sense he has were trying to get out.'

The lad was standing directly in front of his father, surprised
that he should speak this way; for he had never heard such
remarks from the old man. 'Yes, God help him!' he said, 'He is
stupid, indeed; but his daughter Elke—she's clever at reckoning!'

The old man glanced at him sharply. 'Ahoi, Hauke,' he exclaimed, 'what do you know about Elke Volkerts?'

—'Nothing, father; the schoolmaster told me; that's all'

The old man made no reply, but only thrust his wad of
tobacco thoughtfully from one cheek to the other.

'And you think', he said then, 'that you'll be able to help with
the reckoning, too?'

'Oh, yes, father, I think I shall,' answered Hauke, and his
mouth twitched gravely.

The old man shook his head; 'Well, all right, then; go and try
your luck!'

'Thank you, father!' said Hauke and went up to his sleeping-
quarters in the attic; here he sat down upon the edge of the bed
and wondered why his father had questioned him about Elke
Volkerts. He knew her, of course, the slim, eighteen-year-old
girl with the slender, bronzed face and the dark eyebrows which
met above the defiant eyes and delicate nose; but until now he
had hardly spoken a word to her; now, when he went to speak
to old Tede Volkerts, he intended to have a closer look at her
and see what kind of girl she was. He would go straight away, so
that no one else should obtain the position before him; the evening was almost past. And so he put on his Sunday jacket and his
best boots and set off confidently.

—The dike reeve's long house was visible from afar because of the high mound on which it stood and, in particular, because of the tallest tree in the village, a mighty ash; the grandfather of the present incumbent, the first dike reeve in the family, had planted an ash-tree here on the east side of the front door when he was a young man, but the first two saplings had died and so, on the morning of his wedding day, he had planted this, the third ash, which even now, with its crown of leaves growing wider and wider, was sighing, as if over bygone times, in the wind which blew here without cease.

After a while Hauke's tall, lanky figure clambered up the high mound, on the sides of which turnips and cabbage were growing; reaching the top, he saw the dike reeve's daughter standing near the low front door. One rather thin arm hung limply by her side, the hand of the other seemed to be reaching behind her for one of the two iron rings which were fixed to the wall, one on each side of the door, so that anyone riding up to the house could tether his horse. The girl appeared to be looking out across the dike towards the sea, where, in the quiet evening, the sun was just going down below the water line, turning the girl's bronzed skin to gold with its last rays.

Hauke walked a little more slowly up the mound, thinking to himself: 'She doesn't look so bad, and that's a fact!' Then he had reached the top. 'Good evening!' he said, walking towards her; 'What is it you're looking at with those big eyes of yours, Miss Elke?'

'Something that happens here every evening, but isn't to be seen here every evening.' She let the ring fall from her hand, so that it struck the wall with a clinking sound. 'What brings you here, Hauke Haien?' she asked.

'Something I hope won't displease you,' he replied. 'Your father has dismissed his second man, and I thought I might go into your family's service.'

She looked him up and down: 'You're still a little scrawny, Hauke!' she said; 'But we're better served by two keen eyes than two strong arms!' She looked at him almost darkly as she spoke, but Hauke withstood her gaze stoutly. 'Come on, then,' she went on; 'the master's in the living-room; let's go in!'

The following day Tede Haien and his son entered the dike reeve's spacious living-room; the walls were covered with glazed tiles on which, here a ship under full sail or an angler on a river-bank, or there a cow lying crouched in front of a farmhouse, could gladden the eye of the beholder; this stout wall-covering was interrupted by a great console-bed, its doors now closed, and a wall cabinet, its two glass doors revealing porcelain and silverware of all kinds; beside the door to the adjoining reception room was a Dutch striking clock let into the wall behind a glass window.

The master of the house, a heavy, somewhat apoplectic man, was sitting in his armchair on a brightly coloured woollen cushion at the end of the scoured table. His hands folded over his paunch, he was staring contentedly with his round eyes at the carcass of a fat duck; a knife and fork lay on the plate before him.

'Good day, dike reeve!' said Haien, and the man thus addressed slowly turned his head and eyes towards him.

'It's you, is it, Tede?' he replied, and the fat duck on which he had just dined was evident in his voice; 'Sit down; you're a long way off!'

'I'm coming, dike reeve,' said Tede Haien, sitting down at right angles to the other on the bench running along the wall. 'I hear you had trouble with your second man and came to an agreement with my son that he should take his place?'

The dike reeve nodded. 'Yes, Tede—but what do you mean by "trouble"? We fenland folk have a remedy against that, thank Heaven!' and he picked up the knife in front of him and tapped the carcass of the unfortunate duck with it almost caressingly. 'That was my favourite bird,' he added, laughing comfortably, 'it used to eat out of my hand!'

'I thought', said old Haien, ignoring this last remark, 'the rogue had caused mischief in the cowshed.'

'Mischief? Yes, Tede; to be sure, mischief aplenty! The fat buffoon hadn't watered the calves; he was lying blind drunk in the hay-loft, and the animals were crying all night with thirst, so that I had to stay in bed till midday to catch up on my sleep; a farm can't survive like that!'

'No, dike reeve; but there's no danger of that happening with my lad.'

Hauke was standing with his hands in his pockets by the door-post, his head set back, studying the window frames opposite.

The dike reeve raised his eyes to Hauke and nodded across to him. 'No, no, Tede,' he said, and nodded to the old man, too; 'Your lad Hauke won't disturb my night's sleep; the school-master's told me already: Hauke would rather sit at his slate than over a glass of brandy.'

Hauke paid no attention to these words of praise, for Elke had entered the room and removed the remnants of the meal from the table with her nimble hands, and her dark eyes ran swiftly over him. Then his gaze fell upon her too. 'By God in Heaven,' he said to himself, 'she doesn't look so bad here either!'

The girl had left the room again. 'You know, Tede,' began the dike reeve once more, 'the Lord didn't bless me with a son!'

'Yes, dike reeve; but you shouldn't let it trouble you,' answered Haien, 'for they say that a family's wits become addled in the third generation; we all know that your grandfather was a man who defended his country!'

After pondering this remark, the dike reeve looked quite bewildered: 'What do you mean by that, Tede Haien?' he said, sitting upright in his armchair, 'I *am* in the third generation!'

'Oh, yes, indeed! No offence, dike reeve, it's only a saying!' And Tede Haien looked at the old dignitary with rather malignant eyes.

But the dike reeve began again unconcernedly: 'You shouldn't swallow such stupid old wives' tales, Tede Haien; you don't know my daughter yet, she can calculate me into a corner! What I mean to say is, your lad Hauke will be able to learn a lot, not only outdoors but here in my house with quill and pencil, too, that will stand him in good stead!'

'Yes, yes, dike reeve, that he will; you're absolutely right there!' said old Haien, whereupon he began to negotiate into the contract of service a few more privileges which his son had not thought of on the previous evening. Thus, in addition to his linen shirts in autumn, Hauke was to receive eight pairs of woollen stockings as a supplement to his wage; old Haien himself wanted to have the lad to help him with his own work for eight days in the spring; and a number of similar benefits. But

the dike reeve agreed to everything; Hauke Haien seemed to be
the ideal second man for him.

— —'God help you, lad,' said the old man just as they had
left the house, 'if he's the man to explain the world to you!'

But Hauke calmly replied: 'Never mind, father; everything
will turn out alright.'

Nor had Hauke been very much mistaken; the longer he remained in this house, the clearer the world (or what for him
represented the world) became to him; perhaps even more so,
the less a superior insight came to his aid and the more dependent he was upon his own strength, with which he had always
been able to help himself. There was one person in the house,
however, who did not seem to take to him, namely Ole Peters,
the first man—a hard worker with the gift of the gab. The previous second man—a stocky but lazy, dull-witted fellow whom
he had been able to saddle with a cask of oats without complaint
and push around to his heart's content—had been more to his
liking. He was not able to get at Hauke, who was even more
quiet-natured yet far surpassing him in intelligence, in the same
way; Hauke had such an odd way of looking at him. Yet he was
cunning enough to choose tasks for Hauke which might have
been harmful to his still-unsteeled body; and whenever Peters
said, 'You should have seen that fat oaf, he managed it with no
trouble!' Hauke would set to with all his strength and finish the
job, though with difficulty. It was fortunate for him that Elke,
either by herself or through her father's agency, was able to
prevent this most of the time. One might well ask what it is that
sometimes unites persons who are complete strangers to each
other; here, perhaps, it was the fact that they were both born
calculators and that the girl could not bear to see a kindred spirit
ruined by slavish toil.

Nor did the discord between the first man and second man
improve in winter, when the various dike accounts came in for
review after Martinmas.

It was an evening in May, though the weather was typical of
November; inside the house the roaring of the surf outside, behind the dike, could be heard. 'Hey, Hauke!' called the dike reeve,
'come inside; now you shall show whether or not you can reckon!'

'Maister,' replied Hauke—as the people here address their masters—'I have to feed the young cattle first!'

'Elke!' called the dike reeve, 'where are you, Elke! Go and tell Ole that he's to feed the young cattle; Hauke must see to the accounts!'

Elke hurried into the cowshed and gave the message to the first man, who was busy hanging the harness which had been used during the day back in its place.

Ole dashed a bridle against the post near which he was working, as if intent on smashing it to pieces: 'To hell with the damned pen-pusher!'

Elke was able to hear the words just before she closed the stable door again.

'Well?' asked her father, as she entered the room once more.

'Ole was just going to do it,' said his daughter, biting her lip somewhat, and sat down facing Hauke on a roughly carved wooden chair, such as people in those days used to make themselves on winter evenings at home. She had taken a white stocking with a pattern of red birds from a drawer and was now continuing with her knitting; the long-legged creatures on the stocking were probably intended to represent herons or storks. Hauke sat opposite her, absorbed in his calculations; the dike reeve himself was taking his ease in his armchair, blinking sleepily at Hauke's quill; as was customary in the dike reeve's house, two tallow candles were burning on the table, and the shutters in front of the two leaded windows had been closed from outside and barred from within, so that the wind could now rage as it pleased. Now and then Hauke would look up from his work and cast a glance at the bird stockings or the girl's calm, slender face.

Suddenly a loud snore came from the armchair, and the two young people exchanged a quick glance and smile; then the breathing gradually became quieter; they were now able to chat a little, though Hauke scarcely knew what to say.

When she held up her knitting, however, revealing the birds in their entire length, he whispered across the table: 'Where did you learn that, Elke?'

'Learn what?' asked the girl.

—'How to knit birds,' said Hauke.

'That? From Trin' Jans, who lives out on the dike; she can

do all sorts of things; she used to be in service here with my grandfather.'

'But that must have been before you were born?' asked Hauke.

'I should think so; but she often came to the house afterwards.'

'Does she like birds, then?' asked Hauke; 'I thought she only liked cats!'

Elke shook her head; 'Yes, she raises ducks and sells them; but last spring, after you had killed the Angora cat, the rats got into her pen at the back; now she wants to build herself another one in front of the house.'

'So,' said Hauke, whistling lightly through his teeth, 'that's why she dragged stones and clay over from the upland! But then the pen will jut out into the track! Does she have permission?'

'I don't know,' replied Elke. But Hauke had spoken the last word in such a loud tone that the dike reeve started up from his sleep. 'What permission? he asked, looking almost fiercely from one to the other. 'What's that about permission?'

After Hauke had explained the matter to him, however, he slapped him on the shoulder, laughing. 'Oh, no; the track is wide enough; God help the dike reeve if he has to worry about the duck-pens as well!'

Hauke was hurt that he was considered to blame for the old woman and her young ducks falling to the mercy of the rats, and he made no protest. 'But maister,' he began again, 'a rap on the knuckles would be a good thing for some people, and if you don't want to rap *their* knuckles, then do it to the dike agent who's supposed to enforce the dike laws!'

'What? What's that you're saying, lad?' The dike reeve sat bolt upright, and Elke set down her decorative stocking and turned to listen.

'Yes, maister,' Hauke went on; 'you've already carried out the spring dike-inspection, but Peter Jansen still hasn't cleared the weeds from his section, even now; and in summer the gold-finches will be merrily playing around the red thistle flowers again. And right next to it, I don't know who it belongs to, there's a great pit in the dike, on the outside; when the weather is fine it's always full of little children who roll around in it; but—God save us if there's a flood!'

The old dike reeve's eyes had become bigger and bigger.

'And then—', Hauke went on.

'What else, lad?' asked the dike reeve, 'Haven't you finished yet?' and it sounded as if his second man's remarks had already been too much for him.

'Well, then, maister,' Hauke continued, 'you know that fat Vollina, the daughter of your dike agent Harders, who always brings her father's horses from the fields—when she's sitting atop the old brown mare, holding on with nothing but her fat legs, gee up! off she goes up the dike embankment at a slant.'

Only now did Hauke notice that Elke had turned her intelligent eyes upon him and was gently shaking her head.

He fell silent, but the sound of the old man's fist striking the table resounded in his ears; 'I hope the lightning strikes her!' shouted the old man, and Hauke almost trembled at the bear-like roar which suddenly broke forth. 'A fine! Make a note that the fat creature's to be fined, Hauke. The wench snapped up three young ducks from me last summer! Yes, yes, make a note of it,' he repeated, as Hauke hesitated; 'I fancy it was even four of them!'

'Why, father,' said Elke, 'wasn't it the adder that stole the ducks?'

'A huge adder!' shouted the old man with a snort; 'I can tell the difference between that fat Vollina and an adder! No, no, four ducks, Hauke—as for the other things you were babbling about—the Dike Superintendant and myself, after having had breakfast together here in my house, rode past those weeds and that pit of yours in the spring and we didn't see them. But you two', and he nodded meaningfully once or twice to Hauke and his daughter, 'can thank heaven that you're not dike reeve! A man has only two eyes though he could well do with a hundred. — —Just pick up the bills for the reinforcement works, Hauke, and check them; those fellows are often slovenly with their adding up!'

Then he leaned back in his armchair again, shifted his massive body once or twice, and soon fell into a carefree slumber.

This sort of thing recurred on many an evening. Hauke had sharp eyes and, whenever he was sitting together with the dike reeve and his daughter, he did not fail to call the old man's attention to some offence or other of commission or omission connected with the dikes; and since the dike reeve could not always turn a blind eye, the dike administration took on a more businesslike aspect almost unnoticed; and those who, previously, had dawdled on in their old, sinful way and now felt themselves unexpectedly rapped on the knuckles for their blameworthy or idle behaviour, looked about them in irritation and bewilderment to see where the blows had come from. And Ole, the first man, made sure to spread the revelation as far as possible and, by this means, to arouse ill-feeling among these persons against Hauke and his father, who of course had to share the guilt; the others, however—those who were not affected or were genuinely concerned that matters should proceed correctly—laughed and were pleased to observe that the lad had made the old man get a move on for once. 'It's only a pity', they said, 'the rascal doesn't own the right amount of land, otherwise, some day, he'd make a dike reeve like those in the old days; but his father's few acres wouldn't be enough!'

When, the following autumn, the Dike Superintendent came to carry out his inspection, he measured old Tede Volkerts from head to toe while the old man was urging him to have breakfast. 'Well, indeed, dike reeve,' he said, 'I think you really are ten years younger; you've roused me properly with all your suggestions this time; I just wonder how we're going to get through them all today!'

'We will, Superintendent, we will,' replied the old man, grinning; 'the roast goose will give us strength! Yes, thank heaven, I'm still fit and lively.' He glanced round the room to make sure that Hauke was not there; then he added with calm dignity: 'And if it please God, I hope I can perform my duty in peace for a few more years yet.'

'Well, my dear dike reeve,' his superior replied, rising to his feet, 'let's drink to that!'

Elke, who had served breakfast, left the room with a quiet smile just as the glasses were ringing. Then she took a pail of left-overs from the kitchen and went through the stable to throw it to the poultry in front of the outer door. Hauke Haien was in the stable, forking hay into the racks for the cows, which had already had to be brought back because of the heavy storm.

Seeing the girl approaching, he stuck his fork into the floor. 'Well, Elke?' he said.

She halted and nodded to him: 'Yes, Hauke—you should have been inside just now!'

'You think so? Why, Elke?'

'The Dike Superintendant praised the master.'

'The master? What has that to do with me?'

'No, I mean that he praised the dike reeve!'

The young man's face flushed a deep crimson: 'I know very well what you're getting at!' he said.

'You needn't blush, Hauke—it was really *you* that the Superintendant was praising!'

Hauke looked at her with a faint smile. 'And you, too, Elke,' he said.

But she shook her head. 'No, Hauke. When I was the only one helping him, we didn't receive any praise. I can only count, after all; but you see everything out there that the dike reeve really ought to see himself; you've cut me out!'

'I didn't mean to do that—to you, least of all,' said Hauke diffidently, pushing a cow's head aside. 'Get on with you, Rosie, no need to eat the hayfork, you shall have all you want!'

'Don't think that I'm envious, Hauke,' said the girl, after reflecting for a moment; 'it's men's business, after all!'

At this, Hauke held out his hand towards her. 'Elke, give me your hand on it!'

A deep crimson flush ran over the girl's face up to her dark eyebrows. 'Why? I'm no liar!' she cried.

Hauke made to reply, but she had already left the stable, and he remained standing with his fork in his hand, hearing only the ducks and hens outside quacking and clucking around her.

In January of Hauke's third year of service a winter festival was to be held: 'ice bowling', as it is called in these parts. The coastal winds had dropped, and a prolonged frost had covered all the ditches between the fields with a firm, level crystal layer, so that the patchwork landscape now formed a wide field for throwing the small, lead-filled wooden balls with which the players aimed at the goal. Day in, day out, a light north-easterly breeze was blowing; everything was as it should be for the festival; the people from the upland village to the east, who had won the game the previous year, had been challenged and had accepted; nine throwers had been selected by each side; the judge and the referees had also been chosen. The latter, whose task it was to argue the matter whenever a dubious throw had led to disagreement, were always men who knew how to present their case in the best possible light, preferably young fellows who, apart from good common sense, also possessed the gift of the gab. This category included, first and foremost, Ole Peters, the dike reeve's first man. 'Just you throw like the very devil,' he would say, 'and I'll take care of the jabbering!'

It was on the eve of the festival; in the parlour of the village inn, in the upland, a number of players had assembled in order to decide upon the admission of a few late applicants to the team. Hauke Haien was one of these late-comers; he had not wanted to apply at first, though perfectly aware that he had a well-trained arm; but he was afraid of being turned down by Ole Peters, who held an honorary position among the organizers of the game; he wished to avoid the indignity. But Elke had succeeded in changing his mind at the last minute; 'He won't dare, Hauke,' she had said; 'he's the son of a day-labourer; *your* father owns horses and cattle and he's the cleverest man in the village, as well!'

'But, what if he does it all the same?'

Half-smiling, she looked at him with her dark eyes. 'Then,' she said, 'then he'll be sent off with a flea in his ear if he hopes to dance with his master's daughter this evening!'—Whereupon Hauke had bravely nodded his consent.

Now the young men who still wished to take part in the game were standing in front of the village inn, freezing and stamping their feet and looking up at the spire of the rock-built church-tower which stood next to the inn. The pastor's pigeons, which fed in the village fields during the summer, were just now returning from the farmhouses and barns, where they had been searching for grains of corn, and vanished beneath the shingles of the tower behind which they had their nests; in the west, a red sky was glowing above the sea.

'It'll be fine tomorrow,' said one of the young fellows and began walking quickly back and forth, 'but cold! cold!' A second lad, seeing that there were no more pigeons flying, entered the inn and stood listening near the door of the parlour, from which a babble of lively conversation was pouring; the dike reeve's second man had come and stood beside him. 'Listen, Hauke,' said the lad, 'now they're shouting about you!'; and from inside the parlour Ole Peters's grating voice could be clearly heard: 'Boys and underlings don't belong in the game!'

'Come,' whispered the other and tried to draw Hauke by his sleeve towards the parlour door; 'now you can hear how highly they think of you!'

But Hauke pulled himself free and went out in front of the inn again. 'They didn't lock us out so that we should hear it!' he called back.

In front of the inn the third applicant was standing. 'I'm afraid I won't have any luck,' he called to Hauke; 'I'm hardly eighteen; I only hope they don't ask for my christening certificate! But you, Hauke—your first man will speak out for you!'

'Yes, *out!*' growled Hauke, kicking a stone across the street, 'but not *in!*'

The noise in the parlour grew louder; then, gradually, silence ensued; those standing outside could once again hear the light north-east wind which was blowing against the church spire above. The eavesdropper appeared once more. 'Who did they choose?' asked the eighteen-year-old.

'Him!' replied the other, pointing to Hauke; 'Ole Peters was for putting him with the boys, but all the others shouted him down. "And his father owns land and cattle," said Jesse Hansen. "Yes, land," shouted Ole Peters, "so much that you could cart it off in thirteen barrows!"—Last to speak was Ole Hensen: "Pipe down there!" he shouted; "I'll explain it to you: just tell me, who is the foremost man in the village?" They were all silent at first and seemed to be thinking it over; then a voice said: "The dike reeve, of course!" And all the others shouted: "Right, the dike reeve!"—"And *who* is the dike reeve?" shouted Ole Hensen again; "but think about it!"——Then one of them began to laugh quietly, and then another, until there was nothing else to be heard but laughing. "Very well, then, choose him," said Ole Hensen; "you wouldn't turn the dike reeve from the door!" I think they're still laughing; but Ole Peters's voice wasn't to be heard any more!' the lad concluded his report.

At almost that same moment, the parlour door was torn open and loud cries of 'Hauke! Hauke Haien!' rang out merrily into the cold night.

Then Hauke trotted into the inn but was unable to hear who, after all, was the dike reeve; and no one ever knew what thoughts were churning in his head.

— —Some time later, as he was approaching his master's house, he saw Elke standing by the gate at the bottom of the track, and the moon was shining upon the pasture covered by the endless white of the frost. 'You still here, Elke?' he asked.

She merely nodded. Then she said: 'What happened? Did he dare to vote against you?'

—'Why shouldn't he!'

'Well?'

—'Why, Elke—tomorrow I can join the game!'

'Good night, Hauke!' And she hurried up the mound and vanished into the house.

Slowly he followed her.

The next afternoon, on the wide pasture which ran to the east along the landward side of the dike, a dense throng of people could be seen, now motionless, now—after a wooden ball had flown twice out of their midst over the ground now cleared of frost by the sun—gradually moving on and down from the long, low houses behind them; the ice-bowling teams in the middle of the throng, surrounded by old and young, who either lived in these houses or had their dwellings or lodgings in the upland; the older men in long coats, puffing thoughtfully at their short pipes; the women wearing shawls and jackets, some also holding children by the hand or carrying them in their arms. From the frozen ditches, across which the crowd was gradually advancing, the pale light of the afternoon sun glittered through the sharp tips of the reeds; it was freezing hard, but the game went on without cease, and all eyes followed the flying ball at each throw, for on it depended the honour of the day for the entire village. Each referee carried an iron-tipped staff—the village referee, a white staff; the upland referee, a black staff; where the ball had come to a stop, the staff was stuck into the frozen ground, either to the accompaniment of silent approval or the scornful laughter of the opposing team, depending upon the skill of the throw; and the player whose ball first reached the goal had won the game for his team.

The people spoke but little; only when a player made an excellent throw was a shout from the young men or women to be heard; or one of the old men would take his pipe out of his mouth and tap the player on the shoulder with it while murmuring a few words of approval: 'That was a fine throw, said Zachary, and threw his wife out of the hatch!' or: 'That's how your father used to throw; God comfort him in eternity!' or whatever else they considered to be a compliment.

Hauke had been unlucky with his first throw; just as he was swinging back his arm in order to hurl the ball, a cloud which had previously hidden the sun had moved on, and the sun's rays struck him full in the eyes; the throw was too short, the ball fell into a ditch and stuck fast in a sheet of ice.

'Doesn't count! doesn't count! Hauke, throw again!' shouted his team-mates.

But the upland referee leapt to the attack: 'Of course it counts; a throw is a throw!'

'Ole! Ole Peters!' shouted the young fenlanders. 'Where's Ole? Where the devil is he?'

But Ole was already there. 'No need to shout! Is Hauke in a pinch? I thought so!'

—'Not a bit! Hauke has to throw again; now show what you can do with that mouth of yours!'

'That I shall!' cried Ole; he walked over to the upland referee and poured out a volley of nonsense. But the cutting remarks and sharp words that generally laced his speech were missing on this occasion. The girl with the questioning eyebrows stood beside him, looking at him keenly with fierce, angry eyes; but she could not speak—the women were not entitled to voice an opinion regarding the game.

'You're talking nonsense,' cried the other referee, 'because talking sense won't suit your purpose! Sun, moon, and stars are the same for all of us, they're always in the sky; it was a bad throw and all bad throws count!'

They argued with each other in this vein for a while; but in
the end the judge's decision was that Hauke could not repeat his
throw.

'Forward!' shouted the upland team, and their referee pulled
his black staff out of the ground; the number of the next thrower
was called out; he stepped forward and hurled the ball. As the
dike reeve's first man went to observe the throw, he had to walk
past Elke Volkerts: 'For whose sake did you leave your wits at
home today?' she murmured.

He looked at her almost angrily and all trace of merriment
had vanished from his broad features. 'For your sake,' he said,
'for you've forgotten *your* wits, too!'

'Away with you! I know you, Ole Peters!' the girl replied,
standing erect; but he turned his head away, pretending not to
have heard.

The game and, with it, the white and the black staves, moved
on. When it was Hauke's turn to throw again, his ball flew such
a distance that the goal—a large, whitewashed barrel—came
into clear view. He was now a well-made young fellow and had
practised the arts of throwing and mathematics every day of his
boyhood. 'Oho, Hauke!' cried a voice from the throng, 'that was
worthy of the Archangel Michael himself!' An old woman carrying cakes and brandy pushed her way through the crowd towards him; filling a glass, she offered it to him. 'Come,' she said;
'let bygones be bygones; you've done better today than when
you killed my cat.' As he looked at her, he recognized her as
Trin' Jans. 'Thank you,' he said, 'but I shan't drink.' He reached
into his pocket and pressed a freshly minted mark piece into her
hand: 'Take that and drink the glass yourself; now we've let
bygones be bygones!'

'You're right, Hauke,' answered the old woman, obeying;
'you're right; that's better for an old woman like me.'

'How are you making out with your ducks?' he called after
her as she walked on with her basket; but she only shook her
head without turning round and waved her old hands in the air.
'Not at all, Hauke, not at all; there's too many rats in those
ditches of yours; God save me, a body has to earn her bread some
other way!' And with this, she pushed her way into the throng
and began to offer her brandy and honey-cakes for sale again.

The sun had sunk below the dike at last; in its stead, a pur-
plish red shimmer was rising into the sky; from time to time
black crows would fly overhead and, for a moment, they seemed
to be of gold; evening was drawing in. But in the fields the dark
throng was moving farther and farther away from the black,
already distant houses towards the barrel; an especially skilful
throw ought now to be able to reach it. The fenland team was
now playing; it was Hauke's turn to throw.

The whitewashed barrel gleamed brightly amid the broad
evening shadows now falling from the dike over the flat fields.
'Ye'll be leaving it to us this time!' called one of the upland
group, for play was in deadly earnest; they were at least ten feet
in the lead.

Hauke's lean figure was just stepping out of the throng; the
grey eyes in the long Frisian face looked ahead to the barrel; the
ball lay in his hand, which hung by his side.

At that moment, he heard Ole Peters's grating voice directly
by his ear. 'The bird's a bit too big for your liking, eh? Maybe
we should put a grey pot in its place?'

Hauke turned and looked at him steadily. 'I'm throwing for
the fenland!' he said. 'Whose side are you on?'

'The same as you, I think; you're throwing for Elke Volkerts!'

'Move aside!' shouted Hauke and took up his stance again.
But Ole pushed his head even closer to Hauke. Suddenly, before
Hauke himself was able to react, a hand seized the obtrusive
fellow and jerked him backwards so that he stumbled against his
laughing comrades. It was not a large hand, for, as Hauke quickly
turned his head, he saw Elke Volkerts beside him straightening
her sleeve, and her dark eyebrows stood out angrily in her flushed
face.

Then a strength like steel flowed into Hauke's arm; he leaned
forward a little, hefting the ball in his hand a few times; then
he swung back his arm, a deathly silence fell over both groups;
all eyes followed the flying ball, and a rushing sound was heard
as it cut through the air; suddenly, already far away from the
starting-point, it was lost from view behind the wings of a silver
gull which approached from the dike uttering its cry; and at the
same time, they heard it strike against the barrel in the distance.
'Hurrah for Hauke!' shouted the fenland group, and the crowd

noisily took up the cry: 'Hauke! Hauke Haien has won the game!'

But it was only one particular hand that Hauke, closely surrounded as he was by the crowd, had reached out for! And when they again called, 'What are you waiting for, Hauke? The ball is in the barrel!' he merely nodded without moving from the spot; only when he felt the small hand firmly grasping his own did he speak: 'You may be right; I think I've won, too!'

Then the entire throng streamed back, and Elke and Hauke became separated and were borne along by the crowd on the path to the inn which turned at the mound of the dike reeve's house and led to the upland. But here they both slipped free of the surging crowd and, while Elke went to her chamber, Hauke remained standing on the mound in front of the stable door, watching the dark procession gradually wandering uphill to the inn, where a room had been prepared for the dancers. Darkness slowly spread over the entire area; the silence deepened around him, and only the cattle in the stable behind him could be heard moving; from the upland, he fancied he could already hear the piping of the clarinets from the inn. Then he heard the rustle of a dress around the corner of the house and the sound of firm, short steps walking down the footpath which ran through the fields up to the upland. Now, even in the darkness, he could see the figure walking away, and he recognized it as Elke; she, too, was going to the dance at the inn. The blood rushed to his face; should he not go after her and walk to the inn with her? But Hauke was no ladies' man; and he remained standing, pondering the question, until she had vanished from his sight in the darkness.

Once the danger of overtaking her was past, he himself took the same path, until he had reached the inn beside the church, where the shouting and chattering of the people crowding in front of the house and in the entrance and the shrill tones of the violins and clarinets deafened him and made his head spin. Unnoticed, he pushed his way into the 'assembly room'; it was not large and was so full that one could hardly see a step in front. Without a word to anyone he went and stood by the doorpost and looked into the seething throng; the people seemed like fools to him; nor had he to worry that someone might still be thinking about that afternoon's battle or who had won the game only an hour before; each had eyes only for his sweetheart and was turning circles with her to the music. His eyes were searching for one person only, and at last—there! She was dancing with her cousin, the young dike agent; but already she had vanished from his sight and he could see only other girls from the fenland and the upland who were of no interest to him. Then the clarinets and violins stopped abruptly and the dance was over, to be followed immediately by another. A thought flashed suddenly into Hauke's head: would Elke keep her word? Or would she dance past him with Ole Peters? He almost cried out aloud at the thought; but then— —what did he expect, after all? But she did not appear to be taking part in this dance at all; at last this one, too, came to an end, and then another—a two-step, a dance which had only just become fashionable here—followed. The music began like a fury, the young fellows rushed towards the girls, and the lights on the walls of the room flickered. Hauke almost strained his neck trying to pick out the dancers; and there, in the third pair, was Ole Peters; but where was his partner? A broad young fellow from the fenland was standing in front of her, hiding her face from Hauke's view! But the dance went on madly, and Ole and his partner spun out of the row. 'Vollina! Vollina Harders!' exclaimed Hauke almost aloud and straight away sighed with relief. But where was Elke? Did she not have a partner, or had she refused all invitations because she had not wanted to dance with Ole?—And the music stopped once again and a new dance began; yet still he could not see Elke anywhere! Then Ole appeared, still holding his plump Vollina in his arms. 'Well, well,' murmured Hauke, 'old Jesse Harders with his twelve acres will soon be having to retire!—But where's Elke?'

He left his place by the doorpost and pushed his way farther into the room; suddenly he found himself in front of her, sitting with a friend, an older woman, in a corner. 'Hauke!' she cried, raising her slender face to his; 'You here? I didn't see you dancing.'

'I wasn't dancing,' he replied.

—'Why not, Hauke?' Half rising from her seat, she added: 'Do you want to dance with me? I didn't do Ole Peters the honour; he won't be back!'

But Hauke made no move to do so. 'Thank you, Elke,' he

said, 'but I'm not good enough; they might laugh at you; and then . . .' He broke off abruptly and only looked at her tenderly with his grey eyes, as if compelled to let them say the rest.

'What do you mean, Hauke?' she asked quietly.

—'I mean, Elke, the day couldn't be finer for me than it already has been.'

'Yes,' she said, 'you won the game.'

'Elke!' he admonished her almost inaudibly.

She flushed hotly. 'Go on with you!' she said; 'What are you trying to say?' and she dropped her gaze.

Just then her friend was swept away to dance by a young fellow, and Hauke spoke in a louder voice: 'Elke, I thought I had won something better than that!'

She looked down at the floor for a few moments; then, slowly, she raised her gaze, and her eyes, filled with the quiet strength of her being, met his with a look which flowed through him like summer air. 'Do as your heart tells you, Hauke!' she said; 'Surely we know each other well enough by now!'

Elke danced no more that evening and, on their way home, they walked hand in hand; from high in the heavens, the stars glittered above the silent fenland; a light east wind was blowing, bringing bitter cold; but the two young people walked on without much in the way of scarves or cloaks, as if spring had suddenly arrived.

Hauke had thought of something, the appropriate use of which still lay in an indefinite future, but with which he intended to hold a quiet celebration. And so, the following Sunday, he went to the town and called on old Andersen, the goldsmith, and ordered a broad gold ring. 'Show me your finger, so that I can take your measure!' said the old man, taking hold of Hauke's ring-finger. 'Well,' he said, 'it's not as thick as is usual with you people!' But Hauke said: 'Measure my little finger instead!' and held it out to the old man.

The goldsmith looked at him, somewhat surprised; but what did he care for the strange ideas of these country lads! 'We'll find something among the girls' rings!' he said, and the blood rushed hotly into Hauke's face. But the small gold ring fitted his little finger; he took it hastily and paid for it with shining silver;

then, his heart pounding, he put the ring into his waistcoat pocket as if performing a solemn act. From then on, he carried it there always, uneasily yet with pride, as if the waistcoat pocket were there only for the purpose of carrying the ring.

He carried the ring in his pocket for years; indeed, the ring later had to take up its abode in a new waistcoat pocket; the occasion for its liberation had not yet arisen. Of course, the fleeting idea had occurred to him to speak straight out to his master; after all, his father was long-established in the region too! When he became calmer, however, he realized that the dike reeve would only have laughed at his servant. And so he and the dike reeve's daughter went on living side by side; she, too, in maidenly silence, yet both as if they were always walking hand in hand.

A year after the winter festival Ole Peters had left his master's service and married Vollina Harders; Hauke had been right: old Harders had gone into retirement and now, instead of his plump daughter, his cheery son-in-law rode the brown mare into the fields and, it was said, always rode back up the dike. Hauke was now first man and a younger lad had taken his former position; at first the dike reeve had not been willing to promote him: 'He's better as second man!' he had grumbled; 'I need him here at my books.' But Elke had remonstrated with him: 'Then Hauke will leave too, father!' At this the old man had become apprehensive, and Hauke had been promoted first man, though he continued to help with the duties of the dike reeve as before.

After a further year had gone by he began saying to Elke that he was worried about his father, and that the few days in summer on which the master allowed him to work for his father were no longer sufficient; work had become drudgery for the old man, he said, and he could not bear to see it any longer. It was an evening in summer; the two were standing in the twilight beneath the great ash tree in front of the door. The girl looked up in silence at the branches of the tree for a while; then she replied: 'I didn't want to say anything, Hauke; I thought you yourself would be sure to make the right decision.'

'Then I must leave your house,' he said, 'and I won't be able to come back.'

Both were silent for a while, looking into the glow of the

evening sun as it sank into the sea beyond the dike. 'I must tell you this,' she said, 'I called on your father only this morning and found him asleep in his armchair; his drawing pen in his hand, the drawing board with a half-finished drawing in front of him on the table—then he woke up and talked to me for a quarter of an hour or so with an effort, and as I was about to leave, he held me back by the hand, so timidly, as if he was afraid that it was for the last time; but . . .'

'But what, Elke?' prompted Hauke, as she hesitated to go on.

A few tears ran down the girl's cheeks. 'I was only thinking of my own father,' she said; 'believe me, it will be hard for him to let you go.' And as if she herself had to summon up courage to say the word, she added: 'I often have a feeling that he's preparing for his deathbed.'

Hauke made no reply; suddenly he had a feeling as if the ring had moved in his pocket; but even before he had suppressed his annoyance at this involuntary animation, Elke went on: 'No, don't be angry, Hauke! I'm sure you won't leave us, whatever happens!'

He seized her hand ardently, and she did not withdraw it. The two young people remained standing together in the gathering darkness for a while, then their hands slipped apart and they went their separate ways.—A gust of wind arose, rushing through the leaves of the ash tree and rattling the shutters at the front of the house; but by and by night fell, and silence lay over the endless plain.

With Elke's help, Hauke was released from the old dike reeve's service, although he had not given notice in good time, and two new servants were now in the house. A few months later Tede Haien died; but before his death, he called his son to his bedside. 'Sit down beside me, my boy,' said the old man in a weak voice, 'close to me! You needn't be afraid; the one by me is only the dark angel of the Lord come to summon me.'

Appalled, Hauke sat down close to the gloomy console-bed: 'Speak, father, say what you have to say!'

'Yes, my boy, something else,' whispered the old man, stretching out his hands over the bed cover. 'When you entered the dike reeve's service, still only a boy, you had an idea of becoming dike reeve yourself some day. The idea took hold of me and

I, too, began to think that you were the right man for the task. But your inheritance was too small for such an office—I've lived carefully while you were in service, thinking to increase it.'

Hauke seized his father's hands fiercely, and the old man tried to sit up in order to see him. 'Yes, my boy,' he said, 'the document's there in the top drawer of the coffer. You know that old Antje Wohlers had a field of two-and-a-half acres; but, old and crippled as she was, she couldn't live on the rent alone; and so, at Martinmas each year, I used to give the poor woman a certain sum of money—sometimes more, when I had it—and in return she made the field over to me; it's all legally settled.— — Now she is on her deathbed, too; the sickness of the fenland, cancer, has hold of her; you won't have to pay her any more!'

He closed his eyes for a while; then he went on: 'It's not much; but you'll have more than you were used to when you were here with me. May it serve you in this earthly life!'

And while Hauke was thanking him, he fell asleep. There was nothing more left for him to do; a few days later, the dark angel of the Lord had closed the old man's eyes for ever, and Hauke came into his inheritance.

— —On the day after the burial, Elke came to the house. 'Thank you for looking in, Elke!' said Hauke, by way of greeting.

'I'm not looking in,' she replied, 'I want to tidy up a little, so that you can live in an orderly home! Your father was too busy calculating and drawing to bother much about keeping house, and death causes confusion, too; I want to bring a little life back into the house for you.'

He looked at her with his grey, trusting eyes: 'Yes,' he said, 'tidy things up! I'd rather have it like that, too.'

Then she began to put the house in order: the drawing board, which still lay there, was dusted clean and carried up to the attic, drawing pens, pencil, and chalk carefully locked away in a drawer of the coffer; then the young servant girl was called in and, with her help, all the furniture in the room was moved into another, better position, so that the room now seemed to have become bigger and brighter. 'Only we women know how to do that!' said Elke, smiling, and Hauke, despite his grief, had watched with happiness in his eyes and, where needed, helped them with the work himself.

As twilight drew near—it was early in September—and everything was as she had wanted it for him, she took his hand and nodded to him with her dark eyes: 'Now come and have supper with us; I had to promise my father to bring you with me; and when you go home again, you can enter your house easy in your mind.'

As they entered the dike reeve's spacious living-room, where the shutters were already closed and the two candles burning on the table, the old man made to rise from his armchair; but then, his heavy body falling back, he called instead to his former servant: 'Good, Hauke, good that you come to visit your old friends. But come closer, come closer!' And when Hauke had stepped over to his armchair, the old man took his hand in his own plump hands. 'Well, my boy,' he said, 'you may rest easy now; for we all have to die, and your father was one of the best!— Elke, go and bring in the roast; we must take some refreshment! There's a lot of work for us to do, Hauke! The autumn inspection drawing near; the bills for dike and sluice repairs tremendous; the recent damage to the dike by the west polder—it makes my head spin, but yours is a good deal younger, thank heaven; you're a good lad, Hauke!'

Following this long speech, with which the old man had poured out all his troubles, he fell back into his armchair and blinked longingly towards the door, through which Elke was just entering the room, carrying the meat dish. Hauke stood beside him, smiling. 'Now then, sit down,' said the dike reeve, 'and let's not waste time; it doesn't taste good when it's cold!'

And Hauke took his place at the table; it seemed to him perfectly natural to share the work of Elke's father. And when the autumn inspection came round and the year was a few months older, he had indeed completed the best part of the work.'

The narrator stopped and looked around him. The cry of a gull was heard through the window and outside, from the entrance, came a sound of trampling, as if someone was stamping the clay from his heavy boots.

The dike reeve and his deputies turned their heads towards the taproom door. 'What is it?' called the dike reeve.

A stout man wearing a sou'wester had entered the room. 'Master,' he said, 'we've seen it, Hans Nickels and me: the White Horse rider sprang into the pit!'

'Where did you see it?' asked the dike reeve.

—'There's only the one pit; in Jansen's field, where the Hauke Haien Polder begins.'

'Did you only see it once?'

—'Only once; it was nought but a shadow, but that doesn't mean it was the first time!'

The dike reeve had risen to his feet. 'Excuse me,' he said, turning to me, 'we must go out and see where the disaster may strike!' Then he went out through the door together with the messenger; the company, too, rose and followed him.

I remained sitting with the schoolmaster in the great, bare room; through the uncurtained windows, which were now no longer concealed by the backs of the guests who had been sitting in front of them, I could see outside clearly, and the storm lashing the dark clouds across the sky.

The old man was still sitting in his place, a condescending, almost pitying smile playing upon his lips. 'It's too empty here now,' he said; 'may I invite you to my room? I live here at the inn; and believe me, I know the weather here at the dike, we've nothing to fear.'

I accepted thankfully, for I, too, had begun to shiver, and, taking a candle, we climbed the stairs to an attic room, also facing west, but with its windows now concealed by dark woollen curtains. On a bookshelf I saw a modest library, next to which were the portraits of two old teachers; a large armchair stood in front of a table. 'Make yourself comfortable,' said my friendly host and threw a few pieces of peat into the little stove, still glowing, on which a tin kettle was standing. 'Won't be long now! It'll soon be boiling, and then I'll make us a glass of grog; that will liven you up!'

'I've no need of that,' I said; 'I don't feel sleepy when I'm accompanying your friend Hauke on his journey through life!'

—'D'you think so?' and he nodded across to me with his canny eyes, after I was seated comfortably in his armchair. 'Now then, where were we?— —Oh yes, I know! Well then:

Hauke had come into his inheritance and, as old Antje Wohlers, too, had died of her illness, her land had increased his. But since the death, or rather, the last words of his father, something had ripened within him, the seed of which he had been carrying within him since his boyhood; he repeated it to himself time and time again: that he was the right man when the time came to choose a new dike reeve. That was it; his father, who must have known, who, after all, had been the cleverest man in the village, had added these words to his inheritance as a final gift; Antje Wohler's land, which he also owed to his father, was to form the first step to these lofty heights! For, of course, even though this land belonged to him—a dike reeve had to be able to prove ownership of other landed property!— —But his father had been thrifty during the lonely years and, by means of what he had saved had become the owner of the new property; *he* could do that, too; he could do even more; his father's strer.gth had already been exhausted, but he could perform even the hardest work for many years yet!— —Of course, even if he could achieve prosperity in this way, nevertheless, as a result of the severity and harshness which he had brought to his old master's administration, he had won no friendship among the people of the village; and Ole Peters, his old rival, had recently come into an inheritance and was on the way to becoming a well-to-do man! A procession of faces passed before his mind's eye, all of them looking at him vindictively, and he was seized by a feeling of ill-will towards them; he stretched out his arms as if to seize them— for they wished to depose him from an office for which he alone, of all of them, was competent.—These thoughts refused to leave him, but returned time and time again, so that, beside honesty and love, over-ambition and hatred began to grow in his young heart. But these latter feelings he buried deep inside him; not even Elke suspected.

—In the new year a wedding took place; the bride was a relative of the Haiens, and both Hauke and Elke were among the guests; indeed, it happened that, through the absence of a close relative, they found themselves placed together at the wedding banquet. Only a smile, fleeting over their faces, betrayed the pleasure they felt. But on this day Elke sat impassively amid the sounds of talk and the chinking of glasses.

'Is something the matter?' asked Hauke.

—'No, nothing; it's just that there are too many people here.'

'But you look so sad!'

She shook her head and they both were silent.

Then a feeling as if he were jealous of her silence swept through him and, stealthily, he took hold of her hand beneath the hanging folds of the tablecloth; her hand did not flinch, but trustingly clasped his own. Had she been seized by a feeling of abandonment, obliged, as she was, to see her father's frail figure each day?—Hauke refused to entertain the thought, but his breathing now came to a standstill as he drew the gold ring from his pocket. 'Will you keep it on?' he asked, trembling, as he slipped it on to the ring-finger of her slender hand.

Opposite them at the table sat the pastor's wife; suddenly she laid down her fork and turned to her neighbour. 'Heavens!' she cried, 'the girl's as pale as death!'

But soon the blood came back into Elke's cheeks. 'Can you wait, Hauke?' she asked quietly.

The canny young Frisian reflected for some moments. 'For what?' he asked.

—'You know very well; I don't have to tell you.'

'You're right,' he said; 'yes, Elke, I can wait—as long as there's an end in sight!'

'Oh God, only too close, I'm afraid! Don't say such things, Hauke; you're talking of my father's death!' She placed the other hand upon her breast: 'Until then,' she said, 'I shall wear the ring here; you needn't be afraid you shall have it back as long as I live!'

Then they smiled, and their hands gripped each other so tightly that, on any other occasion, the girl would certainly have cried out.

Meanwhile, the pastor's wife had incessantly been watching Elke's eyes, which were now glowing like dark coals beneath the lace brim of her gold-brocade cap. Because of the increasing murmur at the table, however, she had not understood a word; nor did she turn to her neighbour again, for it was not her habit to disturb a budding marriage—and it seemed to her that that was the case here—if only for the sake of her husband's marriage fee, for here the prospects were likewise budding.

Elke's premonition had become reality; one morning after Easter the dike reeve Tede Volkerts had been found dead in his bed; it was plainly written on his face that his death had been a peaceful one. In the last few months he had frequently complained that he was tired of living; his favourite dish, roast beef, even his ducks, had no longer appealed to him.

And now a great funeral celebration was held in the village. On the upland, on the west side of the burial ground by the church, was a grave with a wrought-iron railing; leaning against a weeping ash stood a broad, blue-grey tombstone, bearing an engraved likeness of Death with grinning jaws, and beneath it, in large capitals, was the following inscription:

> This 'yar be Death, as flings dahn all,
> Houds poet un' doctor alaike in thrall.
> T'cliver man's nah goan tuh rest—
> God grant he'll live amaung th'blest.

It was the burial place of the former dike reeve, Volkert Tedsen; now a fresh grave had been dug, in which his son, the late dike reeve Tede Volkerts, was to be laid to rest. Now, already, the funeral procession was approaching from the fenland, a line of wagons from all the villages in the parish; the heavy coffin lay in the foremost wagon, which the two gleaming horses from the dike reeve's stable were already drawing up the sandy track to the upland; the horses' tails and manes were fluttering in the keen spring wind. The burial ground surrounding the church was filled to the walls with people; even on the stone gateway, boys were sitting with small children in their arms, all of them eager to see the burial.

In the house down in the fenland, Elke had prepared the funeral banquet in the living-room and the reception room; bottles of old wine stood beside the covers, and at the places laid for the Dike Superintendant—he, too, had not failed to appear on this day—and for the Pastor, stood a bottle of special vintage. After all the preparations had been made, she walked through the stable and out of the yard door without meeting anyone on the way: the farm-hands were taking part in the funeral procession with two wagons. Here she stopped, her mourning-dress fluttering in the spring breeze, and saw the last vehicles drawing up to the church in the village yonder. After a while there was a bustling of activity, which seemed to be followed by a deathly silence. Elke clasped her hands; now they would be lowering the coffin into the grave. 'And to dust thou shalt return!' Involuntarily, she quietly repeated the words, as if she had been able to hear them from far away; then her eyes filled with tears; her hands, which she had clasped over her breast, fell to her lap. 'Our Father, Who art in Heaven!' she prayed fervently. And after the Lord's Prayer had ended, she stood motionless for a long, long time, she, who was now the mistress of this great fenland farmstead; and thoughts of life and death began to struggle within her.

A distant rumbling roused her from her reverie. Opening her eyes, she saw once again one wagon after another driving quickly down from the upland and approaching her house. She straightened up, gazed out keenly at the scene once more, and then went back the way she had come, through the stable into the rooms solemnly decked out for the occasion. Here, too, no one was to be seen; only the sound of the maids working in the kitchen could be heard through the wall. The banquet tables stood quiet and lonely; the pier-glass between the windows was covered with white cloths;* so, too, the brass knobs on the stove; not a thing gleamed in the room. Elke saw that the doors of the console-bed, in which her father had slept his last sleep, were open; she walked to the bed and closed them tightly; as if unthinkingly, she read the motto written upon them in gold letters between roses and carnations:

> A hard day's wark un' meeterly dun
> Brings sartin slape tull anywun.

That was from her grandfather's time!—She glanced towards the wall cupboard; it was almost empty, but through the glass doors she could see the cut-glass goblet which her father, as he had been fond of telling, had won as a prize in a ring-spearing contest in his youth. She took out the goblet and placed it by the Dike Superintendant's cover. Then she walked to the window, for she could already hear the wagons driving up the mound; one after another, they stopped in front of the house and the guests were now jumping from their seats to the ground, more cheerful than when they had first come. Chatting and rubbing their hands, they crowded into the room; and soon they were taking their places at the banquet tables on which the dishes of food were steaming appetizingly; the Dike Superintendent was sitting in the reception room with the Pastor; and the sounds of loud conversation ran along the table as if Death had never cast his dreadful silence over this house. Without a word, with eyes only for her guests, Elke made her rounds of the tables, accompanied by her maids, to ensure that everything at the banquet was as it should be. And Hauke Haien, too, sat in the living-room next to Ole Peters and some other small landholders.

After the meal was over, white clay pipes were brought and lighted, and Elke was busy once again offering cups of coffee to the guests; there was no sparing of coffee on this day either. In the living-room the Dike Superintendent stood at the desk of the late dike reeve, engaged in conversation with the Pastor and the white-haired dike agent, Jewe Manners. 'That's all very well, gentlemen,' said the former, 'we've buried the old dike reeve with full honours, but where are we going to get a new one? I think, Manners, you will have to take on this duty!'

The old man removed his black satin cap from his white hair, smiling: 'Superintendent,' he said, 'the game would be too short; when the late Tede Volkerts became dike reeve, I was made dike agent, and have been for forty years now!'

'That's no drawback, Manners; you know the business all the better and won't have any difficulty with it!'

But the old man shook his head. 'No, no, Your Honour, just leave me where I am, and I shall carry on like that for a few more years!'

The Pastor came to his aid: 'Why not appoint the man who has, in reality, been performing the duty in the last few years?'

The Dike Superintendent looked at him: 'I don't follow you, Pastor!'

But the Pastor pointed into the reception room, where Hauke seemed to be explaining something to two elderly persons in a slow, earnest manner. 'There he is,' he said, 'the tall Frisian figure with the keen, grey eyes beside the thin nose and the sweeping forehead! He was the old man's servant and now has his own smallholding; he's rather young, I admit!'

'He seems to be about thirty,' said the Dike Superintendant, sizing up Hauke.

'He's hardly twenty-four,' remarked Manners, 'but the Pastor is quite right: all good proposals concerning dikes, sluices and so forth that were put forward in the name of the dike reeve were his; the old man wasn't up to much towards the end.'

'So, so,' said the Dike Superintendant; 'and you think he would be the right man to take over the duties of his old master?'

'He certainly would be the right man,' replied Jewe Manners; 'but he doesn't have what folk here call "clay under his feet". His father had about nine acres, and he may have about twelve acres himself; but until now, no one here has ever become dike reeve with only that much.'

The Pastor was just opening his mouth as if to object when Elke Volkerts, who had been present in the room for some time, suddenly stepped towards them: 'Would Your Honour allow me to say a word?' she said to the Superintendant; 'just so that a misunderstanding does not lead to an injustice!'

'Speak on, Miss Elke!' he replied; 'wisdom from the lips of a pretty girl is always worth hearing!'

—'It's not wisdom, Your Honour; I only want to speak the truth.'

'That, too, must be heard, Miss Elke!'

The girl glanced to the side once more with her dark eyes, as if to assure herself that no unwanted ears were listening: 'Your Honour,' she began, her breast heaving with emotion, 'my god-father, Jewe Manners, told you that Hauke Haien has only about twelve acres; that is true, at this moment, but as soon as need be, Hauke will have as many more acres to call his own as this farm has—my father's farm, now mine; that together will certainly be enough for a dike reeve!'

Old Manners turned his white head towards her, as if he had to see for himself who was speaking. 'What's that?' he asked, 'What are you saying, child?'

But Elke drew from her bodice a gleaming gold ring on a black ribbon: 'I am engaged to be married, Godfather Manners,' she said; 'here is the ring, and Hauke Haien is my fiancé.'

—'And when—I surely have the right to ask, having stood godfather to you, Elke Volkerts—when did that take place?'

—'That was a long time ago; but I was of age, Godfather Manners,' she replied; 'my father was already broken in health and, knowing him, I did not want to distress him any more with the matter; now that he is with God, he will know that his daughter is safe in this man's hands. I would have kept it secret for the whole year of mourning; but now, for the sake of Hauke and of the polder, I had to speak.' Then, turning to the Dike Superintendant, she added: 'I hope Your Honour will forgive me!'

The three men looked at one another; the Pastor laughed, old Manners contented himself with 'Hm, hm!', whilst the Dike Superintendant rubbed his forehead, as if about to make an important decision. 'Yes, my dear girl,' he said at last, 'but what about the rights of property here in the polder? I must confess, just now I'm not very well up in this complex business!'

'Nor need you be, Your Honour,' answered the dike reeve's daughter; 'I shall make over the property to my fiancé before the wedding. I have a little pride of my own,' she added, with a smile, 'I want to marry the richest man in the village!'

'Well, Manners,' remarked the Pastor, 'I think you'll have no objection, as godfather, too, when I join the young dike reeve and the old dike reeve's daughter in matrimony!'

The old man shook his head gently. 'And the Lord's blessing upon them!' he said devoutly.

But the Dike Superintendant offered the girl his hand. 'You have spoken wisely and truly, Elke Volkerts; I thank you for your well-founded declaration and hope to be a guest in your house in the future, too, and on happier occasions than today; but—that a man was made dike reeve by such a young girl— that's the amazing part of the matter!'

'Your Honour,' Elke replied, looking at the kindly Superintendant once more with her grave eyes, 'a woman must surely be able to help the right man!' Then she went into the adjoining reception room and, without a word, laid her hand in Hauke Haien's.

Some years had passed; a sturdy workman with his wife and child now lived in Tede Haien's little house; the young dike reeve, Hauke Haien, with his wife Elke Volkerts, was master of her father's farmstead. In summer, the mighty ash tree rustled in front of the house, as before; but on the bench which now stood beneath the tree, only the young wife was generally to be seen, alone, with some household work or other in her hands; their marriage was still lacking a child; but her husband had other things to do than sit before the door of an evening, for, despite the help he had given previously, there was still a deal of unfinished work dating back to the old man's period of office, with which he himself had not thought it wise to interfere at the time; now, however, all this had to be dealt with by degrees; he wielded a stout broom. Moreover, there was the running of the farm, which had been increased by the addition of his own property, on which he also dispensed with the services of a second man; and so, except on Sundays, when they attended church, man and wife generally saw each other only during the midday meal, hastily despatched by Hauke, and at sunrise and sunset; theirs was a life of continuous work, though a satisfying one.

Then a malicious jest began to make the rounds.—One Sunday, after the younger landholders from the fenland and upland villages had been to church, a group of the more unruly ones had remained drinking up at the inn; after the fourth or fifth glass the talk turned, not to King and Government—they were not yet so reckless then—but to local and senior officials, and above all, to communal taxes and levies; and the longer they talked, the less did these meet their approval, particularly the new dike taxes; all sluices and locks which had always been sound before were now allegedly in need of repair; on the dike, new places were always being discovered where hundreds of barrowfuls of earth were needed; to hell with the whole business! they grumbled.

'It's all thanks to that clever dike reeve of yours,' exclaimed one of the men from the upland, 'always walking around brooding and then sticking his nose into everything!'

'Yes, Marten,' said Ole Peters, who was sitting opposite the speaker; 'you're right; he's crafty—always buttering up the Dike Superintendant; but we're stuck with him!'

'Why did you let yourselves be saddled with him?' asked the other, 'Now you have to pay the price.'

Ole Peters laughed. 'Why, Marten Fedders, that's how things are with us, and there's nothing to be done about it; the old one got to be dike reeve thanks to his father, the young one thanks to his wife.' The roar of laughter which now ran round the table showed that the newly coined remark had met with approval.

But the remark had been made in a public house and it did not remain there; it soon spread in the upland village and down in the fenland village, as well; and it came to Hauke's ears, too. Once again, the procession of malicious faces passed before his mind's eye and he heard, even more mocking than it had been, the laughter at the inn table. 'Swine!' he cried, his eyes glaring balefully, as if he would have liked to have them whipped.

Elke laid her hand upon his arm. 'Let them be,' she said, 'every one of them would like to be in your shoes!'

—'That's just the point!' he replied, grumbling.

'And', she went on, 'didn't Ole Peters himself marry into property?'

'Yes, he did, Elke; but what he got by marrying Vollina wasn't good enough to make him dike reeve!'

—'Say, rather, *he* wasn't good enough!' Elke pulled her husband round, so that he was forced to see himself in the mirror, for they were standing between the windows of the room. '*There* stands the dike reeve!' she said; 'look at him; only the man who can wield office will hold it!'

'You're right,' he replied thoughtfully, 'and yet . . . Well, Elke, I must be off to the east sluice; the gates won't close again!'

She squeezed his hand. 'Come; look at me! What's the matter? Your eyes are so far away.'

'Nothing, Elke, you're quite right.'

Off he went; but he had not long left the house before the sluice repair was forgotten. Another idea, which he had only half-conceived and had carried about with him for years, but which had retreated entirely before the weight of daily business, now took possession of him anew, mightier than ever, as if it had suddenly grown wings.

Almost before he knew it, he found himself up on the main dike, a good distance to the south in the direction of the town; the village, which was at this end of the dike, had long since vanished from his sight on the left; on and on he strode, his eyes turned unerringly in the direction of the sea, to the wide foreshore; had anyone been walking beside him, he would surely have seen what fierce mental activity was going on behind those eyes. At last he came to a halt; here the foreshore diminished to a narrow strip beside the dike. 'It must be possible!' he said to himself; 'Seven years in office; they shan't say any more that I'm dike reeve only thanks to my wife!'

Still he remained motionless, his eyes roaming keenly and thoughtfully on all sides along the green foreshore; then he walked back until, here too, a narrow strip of green pasture-land replaced the wide stretch of land before him. Close by the dike, however, this was crossed by a strong current which separated almost the entire foreshore from the mainland, forming a *hallig*; a crude wooden bridge ran across the gap, so that cattle and hay wains and carts could be brought to the *hallig* and back again. Now the ebb-tide was running, and the golden September sun was gleaming above the strip of mud-flat—some hundred paces wide—and the deep channel in the middle, through which the sea was even now driving masses of water. 'That could be dammed up,' murmured Hauke to himself, after watching this spectacle for a while; then he looked up and, in his mind's eye he drew, from the dike on which he was standing and across the channel, a line along the edge of the severed area of land, around to the south and then back again to the east across the continuation of the channel and over to the dike. The invisible line which he had thus drawn represented a new dike, new in the design of its profile, too, which until now had existed only in his head.

'That would make a polder of about twelve hundred acres,' he said to himself, smiling; 'not exactly large, but . . .'

Then another calculation came to his mind: the foreshore here belonged to the community, individual members owning a number of shares according to the size of their property in the district or of other legal acquisitions; he began to calculate how many shares he had had from his father and how many from Elke's father, and what he himself had bought since his marriage, partly from a vague idea of future advantage, partly as his sheep-rearing increased. Already it was a respectable amount of land; for he had also bought all of Ole Peters's shares—Ole having been overcome by vexation when his best ram was drowned in a flood. But that had been a strange trick of fate: for, as long as Hauke could remember, even during high floods, only the outer areas had been inundated. What splendid cornfields and pastures that would make, what a fortune that would be worth, when it was all contained by his new dike! A feeling of intoxication rushed into his head; but he dug his fingernails into the palms of his hands and forced his eyes to see, clearly and calmly, what lay in front of him: a wide, dikeless expanse of land, exposed to Heaven alone knew what storms and floods in the next few years, on the farthest limits of which a flock of dirty sheep was now slowly wandering and grazing; and—for him— a mass of work, struggle, and trouble! Yet, in spite of all, as he walked down from the dike and towards the path which led across the fields to his house, he felt as if he were carrying a great treasure home with him.

In the entrance Elke came towards him. 'What was wrong with the sluice?' she asked.

He looked at her with a mysterious smile. 'We'll soon be needing another sluice,' he replied; 'and locks and a new dike!'

'I don't understand,' said Elke, as they went into the room; 'what do you mean, Hauke?'

'I want,' he said slowly, and stopped for a moment, 'I want the big area of foreshore that begins opposite our farm and continues out westward, closed in by a dike to form a regular polder; the floods have left us in peace for almost an age, now, but if a bad one comes and sweeps away the turf, the whole thing can be ruined at one fell swoop; only years of idleness could have let things go on like that till now!'

She looked at him, astounded. 'You're blaming yourself!'

—'Yes, I am, Elke; but until now, there were so many other things to be done!'

'Yes, Hauke; you've done enough, indeed!'

He had sat down in the old dike reeve's armchair, and his hands were gripping the sides of the chair firmly.

'Do you have the courage for it?' asked his wife.

—'That I do, Elke,' he said, quickly.

'Don't be too hasty, Hauke; that's a task that will make you or break you; almost everyone will be against you; they'll not thank you for all your pain and trouble.'

He nodded. 'I know,' he said.

'And what if it failed!' she cried; 'ever since I was a child, I have heard that the channel couldn't be closed off, and therefore no one ought to try!'

'That was an excuse for the work-shy!' said Hauke; 'Why shouldn't they be able to close off the channel?'

—'I didn't hear; perhaps because it runs in a straight line; the current is too strong.' A memory from the past came over her and an almost roguish smile shone out of her grave eyes. 'When I was a child,' she said, 'I once heard the farm-hands talking about it; they said that, if a dam was to hold firm, some living creature had to be thrown in and buried in the dam; when a dike was being built on the other side, a good hundred years ago, they said, a gipsy child was buried there, that they had bought from its mother for a large sum of money; but no woman would sell her child today!'

Hauke shook his head: 'Then it's just as well that we haven't a child; else they would absolutely demand it from us!'

'They shouldn't have it!' she cried, throwing her arms across her breast as if in terror.

Hauke smiled; but again she asked: 'And the awful cost of it! Have you thought of that?'

—'Yes, I have, Elke; what we get out of it will far outweigh the cost; and the costs for the upkeep of the old dike will largely be covered by the new dike, too; we shall do the work ourselves: we have more than eighty teams of horses in the district, and there's no lack of young hands here, either. At least, you shan't have made me dike reeve for nothing, Elke; I want to show them that I really am one!'

She had crouched down in front of him, looking at him anxiously; now she rose to her feet with a sigh: 'I must get on with the day's work,' she said, slowly stroking his cheek; 'and you must do yours, Hauke!'

'Amen, Elke!' he answered with a grave smile; 'There's enough work for both of us!'

— — And there was, indeed, enough work for both, but the heaviest load now fell upon the man's shoulders. On Sunday afternoons and often in the evenings, too, Hauke would sit, together with a skilled surveyor, deeply engrossed in calculating, drawing, and sketching; when he was alone he worked just as hard, often not finishing until well after midnight. Then he would tiptoe into their bedchamber—for the gloomy console beds in the living-room were no longer used during Hauke's day—and his wife, in order that he might rest at last, would lie there with eyes closed, feigning sleep, though she had only waited for him, her heart pounding; sometimes he would kiss her forehead and murmur loving words before lying down in hope of sleep which, often enough, came to him only with the first cock-crow. In the midst of a winter storm he would go out onto the dike, paper and pencil in his hand; would stand drawing and making notes, while a gust of wind tore the cap from his head and his long, pale hair flew about his flushed face; later on, as long as the ice did not thwart him, he would row out with a farm-hand to the mud-flats and, with measuring rod and sounding-line, measure the depths of the currents, of which he was not yet sure. Elke often trembled for his sake; but, once he was home again, he could not have discerned her anxiety save from the tight grasp of her hand or the gleam of her otherwise staid eyes. 'Patience, Elke,' he said, on one occasion, feeling that his wife could not leave him in peace; 'I must be sure of myself before I submit my proposal!' She nodded and let him alone. His visits to the Dike Superintendant in town did not become less frequent; all these and his work at the farmhouse and in the fields were always followed by his studies, which he pursued until far into the night. His dealings with other people, save those concerning work and business, ceased almost entirely; his dealings with his wife became fewer and fewer. 'These are bad times, and will remain so for a long time yet,' said Elke to herself and returned to her work.

Now, at last, the sun and the spring winds had broken the ice everywhere, the last preparations had been completed; the application to the Dike Superintendant for recommendation to a higher authority, containing the proposal for a dike enclosing the said foreshore, for the increment of the public good, especially for that of the polder and, no less, that of the government coffers—for these would benefit in a few years from the taxes payable on some twelve hundred acres—had been neatly written and, together with drawings and sketches of the entire terrain, now and in the future, and of the locks and sluices and all other relevant features, packed into a strong envelope and sealed with the official seal of the dike reeve's office.

'There it is, Elke,' said the young dike reeve, 'give it your blessing!'

Elke laid her hand in his. 'We shall hold together,' she said. —'That we shall!'

A mounted messenger then brought the application to the town.

'As you can see, my dear sir,' said the schoolmaster, breaking off his narrative and gazing at me in a friendly manner with his keen eyes, 'what I have related up to now, I have put together during the almost forty years of my working life here in this polder, from what has been passed on by informed people or the stories told by their grandchildren and great-grandchildren; what I am now about to tell you, so that you may link all this with the final events, was in those days, and is, even today, the talk of the entire fenland village as soon as the spinning-wheels begin to hum around All Hallows'.'

In those days, from the dike reeve's farmstead, some five or six hundred paces farther north, you could see, when standing on the dike, a few thousand paces out in the mud-flats and somewhat more distant from the shore opposite, a small *hallig*, known as 'Jeverssand' or 'Jevershallig'. It had been used by the grandparents of the people of that generation as a sheep pasture, for grass had grown upon it; but that was no longer so, for the low-lying *hallig* had been flooded by the sea several times, and that in midsummer, so that the grass had withered and become unfit for sheep pasture. And so, apart from the gulls and the other birds which frequent the shore, and now and then an osprey, no living creature ever visited the island; and on moonlit nights, from the dike, you could see only wreaths of mist passing over it, now thin, now dense. A few bleached bones of drowned sheep and the skeleton of a horse, it was said (though no one could tell how it came to be there), could be seen there when the moon was shining from the east upon the *hallig*.

Here, one evening, toward the end of March, the day-labourer from the Tede Haien house and Iven Johns, the young dike reeve's farm-hand, were standing motionless beside each other, staring across at the *hallig*, which was scarcely visible in the dim moonlight; something strange seemed to have riveted their attention. The labourer thrust his hands into his pockets and shivered. 'Come on, Iven,' he said, 'that bodes nothing good; let's go home!'

The other man laughed, though a shudder ran through him. 'Away with ye, it's a living creature, a big one! Who the devil can have driven it across the mud-flat! Look, now it's stretching its neck towards us! No, it's lowering its head; it's grazing! I didn't think there was anything there to graze on. I wonder what it can be?'

'What's it to us!' rejoined the other. 'Good-night to you, Iven, if you'll not come with me; I'm off home!'

—'Yes, yes; you've a wife waiting for you, and a warm bed! In my room there's nothing but the cold March air!'

'Good night, then!' called the labourer, as he trotted home along the dike. The farm-hand turned two or three times to watch him go; yet he himself remained where he was, held by a desire to see something uncanny. Then a dark, stocky figure came along the dike towards him from the village: it was the dike reeve's servant-lad. 'What d'you want, Carsten?' called the farm-hand.

'Me?—nothing,' replied the lad; 'but our maister wants to speak to you, Iven Johns!'

The farm-hand had turned his gaze towards the *hallig* once more. 'Right away!' he said; 'I'll come right away!'

'What is it you're looking at?' asked the lad.

Iven raised his arm and pointed silently to the *hallig*. 'O-oh!' whispered the lad; 'there's a horse—a white horse—walking; it must be ridden by the devil—how would a horse get to Jevershallig?'

—'Don't know, Carsten—if it's a *real* horse!'

'Yes, yes, Iven; look, it's grazing just like a horse! But who took it over there?—we don't have such big boats in the village! Maybe it's just a sheep; Peter Ohm says, in the moonlight, ten peat-stacks look like a whole village. No, look! Now it's jumping —it must be a horse, after all!'

The two remained silent for a while, their eyes directed only to what they could faintly see happening yonder. The moon was

high in the sky, shining on the wide sea, which was just beginning to drive the water of the rising flood-tide across the gleaming mud-flats. Only the quiet sound of the water reached their
ears, no animal cry was to be heard over the colossal expanse; in
the fenland behind the dike, too, all was empty: cows and oxen
were all in their stables. Nothing moved; only what they thought
was a horse, a white horse, still seemed to be moving yonder on
Jevershallig. 'It's getting lighter,' said the farm-hand, breaking
the silence; 'I can clearly see the white sheep-bones gleaming!'

'I see it, too,' said the lad, craning his neck; then, as if suddenly noticing something, he tugged the farm-hand by the sleeve.
'Iven,' he whispered, 'the horse's skeleton that was there, too—
where is it? I can't see it?'

'I can't see it either! Strange!' exclaimed the farm-hand.

—'Not so strange, Iven! They say that, on some nights—I
don't know when—the bones get up and carry on as if they was
alive!'

'So?' said Iven; 'That's just old wives' tales!'

'Maybe so, Iven,' replied the lad.

'But I thought you were sent to fetch me; come on, we must
away home! Nothing ever changes over there.'

The boy would not budge until the farm-hand had turned
him round by force and thrust him on his way. 'Listen, Carsten,'
said Iven, when the ghostly *hallig* was already a good way behind them, 'they say you'll try just about anything; I believe
you'd like to go and have a look at it yourself.'

'Yes,' replied Carsten, though immediately shuddering a little;
'yes, I would, Iven!'

'D'you really mean it?—Well, then,' said the farm-hand, after
the boy had emphatically given him his hand on it, 'we'll take
our boat out tomorrow evening; you row over to Jeverssand, and
I'll stay here on the dike in the meantime.'

'Yes,' answered the lad, 'I'll go. I'll take my whip with me.'

'You do that!'

They reached their master's house in silence and walked slowly
up the high mound towards it.

At the same time next evening, the farm-hand was sitting on the
great stone in front of the stable door, when the lad approached

him, cracking his whip. 'How strangely it whistles!' remarked Iven.

'Yes; just you watch out,' replied the lad; 'I've plaited nails into it!'

'Come on, then!' said his companion.

As on the previous evening, the moon was shining brightly high in the eastern sky. In a short time the two were out on the dike once more, looking out towards Jevershallig, which lay in the water like a patch of mist. 'There it is again,' said Iven; 'I was here after midday, and it wasn't there; but I could see the horse's white skeleton plain as ever!'

The lad craned his neck. 'It's not there now, Iven,' he whispered.

'Well, Carsten, what d'you think?' asked the farm-hand. 'Are you still itching to row across?'

Carsten reflected for a moment, then he cracked his whip in the air. 'Just cast off, Iven!'

Whatever it was walking about on the *hallig* yonder seemed to stretch its neck and turn its head towards the mainland. But they did not see it any more; they were already walking down the side of the dike to the spot where the boat was moored. 'Right, get in!' said Iven, untying the boat. 'I'll stay here until you come back. You'll have to moor the boat on the eastern side; folks have always been able to land there!' And the lad nodded without speaking and, taking his whip, rowed out into the moonlit night; meanwhile, the farm-hand strolled back beneath the dike and climbed up again at the spot where they had been standing before. Soon he saw the boat pull in at a dark, steep place with a wide channel leading up to it, and a stocky figure jumped ashore.—Was he right in thinking that the lad was cracking his whip? But it might have been the sound of the running flood-tide. Several hundred paces to the north he saw what they had taken to be a white horse, and now—yes! the lad's figure was walking straight towards it. Now it was raising its head, as if suspicious; and the lad—now he could hear it plainly—was cracking his whip. But—whatever was he thinking of?—He was turning round, going back the way he had come. The thing over there appeared to continue grazing, without a pause; no sound of whinnying was to be heard; now and then, something like white eddies of water seemed to flow over the apparition. The farm-hand stared across as if spellbound.

Then he heard the sound of the boat landing on the shore close by, and soon he saw the lad in the half-light, climbing up the dike towards him. 'Well, Carsten,' he asked, 'what was it?'

The lad shook his head. 'Nothing at all!' he said; 'I could still see it from the boat for a short time; but once I was on the *hallig*—damned if I know where the creature had hidden itself, the moon was shining bright enough; but when I reached the spot, there was nothing there but the bleached bones of half-a-dozen sheep, and a bit farther on lay the horse's skeleton with its long white skull, and the moon shining in its empty eye-sockets!'

'Hm!' said the farm-hand; 'did you take a good look?'

'Yes, Iven, I stood still; then a damned lapwing, that had cowered down to sleep behind the skeleton, flew up with a screech and gave me such a fright that I cracked my whip after it a few times.'

'And that was all?'

'Yes, Iven; that's all I know.'

'It's enough, too,' said the farm-hand, and he drew the lad by the arm towards him and pointed over to the *hallig*. 'There, d'you see something, Carsten?'

—'Well, I never—it's moving again!'

'Again?' said Iven; 'I've been looking over there the whole time, but it didn't go away; you made straight for the creature!'

The lad stared at him; suddenly there was an expression of horror on his usually impudent face, which the farm-hand did not fail to notice. 'Come on!' he said, 'let's get on home; from here it looks like a living thing, and over there, there's nothing but bones—that's more than you and me can fathom. But keep your mouth shut—you mustn't gossip about things like that!'

They turned away from the shore, the lad trotting at the other's side; neither spoke, and the fenland lay in unbroken silence beside them.

— —After the moon had waned, however, and the nights had become darker, something else happened:

Hauke Haien had ridden into town on the day the horse-market was held, though he had no business at the market; but when he returned home towards evening, he brought another horse with him; it was rough-haired and scrawny, so that every one of its ribs could be counted, and its eyes lay dull and deep in their sockets. Elke had come out of the front door to welcome her husband. 'Heaven help us!' she cried, 'what shall we do with the old nag?' For, as Hauke rode up to the house leading it, and halted beneath the ash-tree, she had seen that the poor creature was lame too.

But the young dike reeve leapt from his brown gelding with a laugh. 'Never mind, Elke; he won't cost much!'

Elke replied shrewdly: 'You know very well: the cheapest is oft the dearest.'

—'But not always, Elke; the animal is four years old, at most; just take a closer look at him! He's been starved and ill-treated; but our oats will do him good; I shall take care of him myself, so that they don't overfeed him.'

Meanwhile, the animal remained standing, its head drooping and its long mane hanging down beside its neck. While her husband was calling the farm-hand, Elke walked around the horse, examining it; then she shook her head: 'We've never had a horse like this in our stable!'

At that moment the servant-lad came round the corner of the house and stopped short, his eyes wide with fright. 'Why, Carsten,' cried the dike reeve, 'what's got into you? Don't you like my white horse?'

'Yes—oh yes, maister, why shouldn't I!'

—'Well, take the horses into the stable; don't feed them; I'll be there myself directly.'

The lad carefully took the white horse by the halter, then— as if seeking protection—hastily seized the bridle of the gelding, which had also been entrusted to his care. Hauke and his wife, however, went into the living room; Elke had placed a dish of beer gruel in readiness for him, and bread and butter.

He had soon eaten and drunk his fill, then he rose and began to walk with his wife back and forth in the room. 'Let me tell you, Elke,' he said, while the light of the evening sun played upon the tiles in the walls, 'how I came by the animal. I had spent a full hour with the Dike Superintendent; he had good news for me—one thing and another in my proposal will certainly be changed, but the main thing—my profile—is accepted, and the order to build the new dike should be here in the next few days or so!'

Elke sighed involuntarily. 'So, it's settled, then?' she asked, anxiously.

'Yes, wife,' replied Hauke; 'it will be a hard task, but I believe that's the reason why the Lord brought us together! Our farm is now doing so well; you can take a sizeable part of the burden on your shoulders; just think, ten years from now—the property will be quite different then.'

She had squeezed her husband's hand assuringly in her own hands as he began to speak; but she could not take any pleasure from his last words. 'Property—for whom?' she asked. 'You would have to take another wife; I can't give you any children.'

Tears started in her eyes; but he took her tightly in his arms. 'We shall leave that to the Lord,' he said; 'but now—and later, too —we're young enough to enjoy the fruits of our labour ourselves.'

She looked at him with her dark eyes for a long while, as he held her. 'Forgive me, Hauke,' she said; 'I'm a faint-hearted woman at times.'

He bowed his head to her face and kissed her. 'You're my wife and I'm your husband, Elke. And that's how it will always be.'

She clasped her arms firmly around his neck. 'You're right, Hauke, and whatever happens shall be for us both.' Then, blushing, she released him. 'You were going to tell me about the white horse,' she said in a quiet voice.

'Yes, I was, Elke. I told you already that I was overjoyed at the good news the Dike Superintendant had given me; and as I was riding out of the town, on the embankment behind the harbour, I met a rough-looking fellow—whether a vagabond or tinker or what, I couldn't say. He was pulling the horse behind him by the halter; but the creature raised its head and looked at me shyly; I had a feeling that it wanted to beg something of me—I was rich enough at that moment, after all. "Hey, neighbour!" I called, "where are you off to with the old nag?"

'The fellow stopped, and the horse with him. "To sell it," he said, giving me a crafty nod.

'"But not to me!" I said, laughing.

'"Why not?" he said; "it's a fine horse, worth no less than one hundred thalers."

'I laughed in his face.

'"Well," he said, "don't laugh so cruel; It's not the price I expect from you! But I've no use for the animal, it will go to rack and ruin with me; with you, it would soon look quite different!"

'Then I jumped down from the gelding and looked the white horse in the mouth and saw that it was still young. "How much do you want for it?" I cried, for the horse was looking at me again as if begging.

'"Master, you shall have it for thirty thalers!" he said, "and I'll throw in the halter into the bargain!"

'And then, wife, I shook the brown hand—it looked almost like a claw—that the fellow offered me. So now we have the white horse and, I think, cheap enough, too! The only strange thing was, as I rode away with the horses I heard the sound of someone laughing behind me and, when I turned my head, I saw the gipsy; he was standing there with his legs apart, his hands on his hips, and laughing after me like the devil.'

'Ugh!' cried Elke; 'I only hope the horse hasn't anything of his old master about him! I hope he may thrive for you, Hauke!'

'*He* shall thrive, at least, as far as I can afford it!' And the dike reeve went into the stable, as he had told the servant lad he would.

— —But he did not feed the white horse on that evening only—he did so from then on, never letting the animal out of his sight. He wanted to show that he had made a good bargain; the horse should be given correct treatment, at least.—And, after only a few weeks, the animal's condition improved; the rough hair gradually vanished and a smooth, dapple-grey coat began to appear, and when he led the horse around the yard one day, it strode, slender, on firm legs. Hauke thought of the outlandish horse-dealer. 'The fellow was either a fool or a rogue who had stolen it!' he murmured to himself.—Soon, whenever the horse so much as heard his footsteps approaching it would jerk round its head and greet him with a whinny; now he could see, too, that it had what the Arabs look for in a horse—a lean head, in

which a pair of fiery brown eyes gleamed. Then he led the
animal out of the stable and put a light saddle upon its back; but
scarcely was he seated when a neigh, like a cry of pleasure,
issued from its throat, and away it flew with him, down the
mound to the path and then towards the dike; but the rider sat
steady and, when they had reached the top, it fell into a light
step, almost dancing, its head turned towards the sea. He patted
and stroked the smooth neck, but there was no longer any need
for this caress; the horse seemed perfectly at one with its rider
and, after they had ridden some distance northwards along the
dike, he turned it gently and rode back to the yard.

The farm-hands were standing down below on the track,
awaiting their master's return. 'Now, Iven!' he called, jumping
down from the horse, 'you ride it out into the field to the others;
it will bear you like a cradle!'

The white horse shook its head and neighed loudly across the
sunny fenland whilst the farm-hand unfastened the saddle, which
the servant-lad carried away to the saddle-room; then it laid its
head upon its master's shoulder and contentedly allowed him to
stroke it. But when the farm-hand made to spring on to its back,
the horse suddenly leapt to the side and then stood still once
more, its beautiful eyes fixed upon its master. 'Oho, Iven,' exclaimed Hauke, 'has he hurt you?' and tried to help him to his
feet.

Iven rubbed his hip vigorously. 'No, maister,' he said, 'no
harm done—but it's the devil that rides him!'

'And I do, too!' rejoined Hauke, laughing. 'And now take him
by the bridle into the field.'

Somewhat shamefaced, the farm-hand obeyed, and the horse
meekly let itself be led away.

— —Some evenings later, farm-hand and servant-lad were
standing together in front of the stable door. The red glow of
the evening sun had faded behind the dike and, on the inner
side, the polder was already flooded by the dusk; only now and
then, in the distance, could be heard the bellowing of an angry
bull or the scream of a lark being attacked and killed by a weasel
or a water rat. The farm-hand was leaning against the door-post,
smoking his short pipe, though he could no longer see the smoke
from it. He and the servant-lad had not spoken a word to each

other. Something was weighing on the lad's mind, but he did not know how best to approach his taciturn companion. 'Iven!' he said at last, 'you know the horse's skeleton on Jeverssand?'

'What of it?' asked the farm-hand.

'Aye, Iven, what indeed? It's not there any more, neither by day nor by night; at least twenty times I've walked out to the dike to look!'

'The old bones have fallen apart, I suppose?' said Iven and quietly went on smoking his pipe.

'But I was out there by moonlight, too—there's nothing moving about on Jeverssand, either.'

'Yes,' said the farm-hand; 'the bones have fallen apart, so the horse won't be able to get up again!'

'Don't make jokes, Iven! I know, now; I can tell you where it is.'

The farm-hand turned to him abruptly. 'Well, where is it, then?'

'*Where indeed?*' echoed the lad meaningfully. 'It's standing in our stable; it's been standing there since it left the *hallig*. It's not without reason the maister himself feeds it; I *know*, Iven.'

The farm-hand puffed heartily into the darkness for a while. 'You're not very bright, Carsten,' he said at last; 'our white horse? If ever a horse was full of life, then it's that one! How can a young man of the world like you fall for such old wives' tales!'

— —But the lad was not to be convinced: if the devil had got into the horse, why shouldn't it be alive? On the contrary, that made it all the worse!—He shrank back in fear whenever he entered the stable of an evening, where the white horse was sometimes kept, even in the summer, and it turned its fiery head abruptly towards him. 'The devil take him!' he would grumble; 'We shan't be together much longer!'

And so he quietly looked for a new place of service, gave notice, and, at All Souls', began work as farm-hand to Ole Peters. Here he found willing listeners for his tale of the dike reeve's devil-horse; Ole's fat wife, Vollina, and her dull-witted father, the former dike agent, Jesse Harders, would listen to him, enjoying the thrill, and afterwards repeat the tale to anyone who harboured a grudge against the dike reeve or took pleasure in stories of that kind.

Meanwhile, the order for the building of the new dike had already arrived from the Dike Superintendant's office at the end of March. Hauke first called a meeting of the dike agents, and all had appeared one day up at the inn by the church and listened to him as he read to them the main items from the documents prepared until now: from his application, from the Dike Superintendant's report, and, last of all, from the final communication containing first and foremost the official approval of the dike-profile as proposed by him, whereby the new dike should not fall steeply, as before, but instead gradually slope down on the seaward side; but the faces of the listeners betrayed no sign of pleasure, nor even of satisfaction.

'Yes, yes,' exclaimed one old dike-agent; 'what did I tell you! And protesting won't be of any use—the dike reeve has got the Dike Superintendant behind him.'

'You're quite right, Detlev Wiens,' spoke up another; 'the spring repairs are due soon, and now a thousand-mile dike is to be built—everything else will have to be left till later.'

'You can finish the repairs this year,' said Hauke; 'work on the new dike won't start as soon as that!'

Very few of them were willing to admit this. 'But what about your profile?' said a third, introducing a new topic; 'the dike will be broader on the seaward side than Lawrenz's son* was tall! Where are we to get the materials from? When has the work to be finished?'

'If not this year, then next; that will mainly depend on ourselves!' said Hauke.

Grim laughter ran through the assembly. 'But why such needless work? The dike shouldn't be any higher than the old one,' cried another, 'and *that's* been standing for over thirty years now.'

'You're right,' replied Hauke; 'thirty years ago the old dike collapsed, and thirty-five years before that, and again forty-five years before that; since then, even the highest floods have left us in peace, though the old dike is still standing there, steep and badly designed. But the new dike will hold for hundreds and hundreds of years, despite such floods; it won't be breached, because the gentle slope on the seaward side won't give the waves any purchase; so that you shall gain safe land for yourselves and your children; that's the reason the commissioners and the Dike Superintendant are behind me; and that's why you should see it as being for your own benefit!'

As the members of the assembly showed no desire to reply immediately, an old, white-haired man rose from his chair: Elke's godfather, Jewe Manners, who at Hauke's request had continued to remain in office as dike agent. 'Dike Reeve Hauke Haien,' he said, 'you are causing us a great deal of worry and expense, and I only wish you had waited until after the Lord had let me go to my rest; but—you are right, and only an unreasonable man could deny it. We must thank God for every day that He has preserved for us that costly piece of foreshore against storm and high water, despite our idleness; but now the eleventh hour has struck, in which we ourselves must set to work and safeguard it ourselves to the best of our knowledge and skill, and no longer try God's patience. I am an old man, my friends; I have seen dikes built and broken; but the dike which Hauke Haien has devised by means of his God-given talents and succeeded in having approved for you by the commissioners—none of you will see it break during your lifetime; and if you yourselves have no wish to thank him, your grandchildren will not be able to deny him a wreath of honour later!'

Jewe Manners sat down again, took a blue handkerchief from his pocket, and wiped a few drops from his brow. The old man was still known to all as a man of competence and unimpeachable honesty and, since the members of the assembly were not inclined to agree with him, they continued to remain silent. Then Hauke Haien began to address the assembly; but everyone could see that he had turned pale. 'I thank you, Jewe Manners,' he began, 'for being here and for having spoken; you other gentlemen should at least see the building of the new dike— which is of course my responsibility—as an irrevocable fact; therefore let us determine what has to be done!'

'Speak!' called one of the assembly. And Hauke spread out the plan of the new dike on the table. 'Someone asked just now,' he began, 'where we shall find such large amounts of earth? As you can see, as far as the foreshore extends into the mud-flats, a strip of land has been left bare outside the line of the dike; we can take the earth from there, and from the foreshore that runs north and south from the new polder along the dike; as long as we have a firm layer of clay on the seaward sides, we can use sand on the inner side or in the middle! Now, first of all, we must choose a surveyor to plot out the line of the new dike on the foreshore. I'm sure that the man who helped me prepare the plan will be the most capable. Also, we shall have to employ cartwrights to make one-horse tip-carts for transporting the clay or other material; for damming up the channel and for the inner sides of the dike, where we shall have to make do with sand, we shall need several hundred cartloads of straw for topping the dike—I cannot say how many, as yet—perhaps more than we can spare in the fenland!—Let us consider how all this is to be procured and prepared first of all; also, a skilled carpenter must be charged with building the new sluice here on the west side.'

The members of the company had gathered around the table; they looked at the plan with indifference and began to speak, though they seemed to be doing so only for the sake of saying something. When the question of choosing the surveyor arose, one of the younger agents said: 'You have planned the work, dike reeve; you yourself must know best who is fitted for the task.'

To this, however, Hauke replied: 'Since you are all under oath, you must not be bound by my opinion, but only by your own, Jakob Meyen; and if your proposal is the better one, then I shall withdraw mine.'

'Well,' said Jakob Meyen, 'I am sure that yours will be in order.'

One of the elder agents, however, did not fully agree; he had a nephew, he said, the like of whom had never been seen here in the fenland for surveying: he was more capable than even the dike reeve's father, the late Tede Haien, had been!

The assembly then deliberated concerning both surveyors and at length decided that the task should be entrusted mutually to them. Then the question of the tip-carts, the delivery of the straw, and all other matters were dealt with in similar fashion; Hauke returned home almost exhausted, and at a late hour, on the gelding, which he still rode at that time. But as he sat in the old armchair, which had belonged to his predecessor—a weightier, though more light-hearted man—his wife was already at his side. 'You look so tired, Hauke' she said, brushing the hair from his forehead with her slender hand.

'A little, certainly!' he replied.

—'And is it going well?'

'After a fashion,' he said with a bitter smile; 'but I must push the cart myself—and be happy when it's not being held back!'

—'But not by all of them?'

'No, Elke; your godfather, Jewe Manners, is a good man; I only wish he were thirty years younger!'

Some weeks later, after the dike line had been staked out and the greater part of the tip-carts delivered, all the share-holders of the projected polder, as well as the owners of the lands behind the old dike, were summoned by the dike reeve to a meeting in the parish inn; the purpose of the meeting was to present to them a plan for the division of labour and costs and to hear any objections; for even the latter were required to bear their share of the work and costs, inasmuch as the new dike and new sluices would reduce the maintenance costs of the older dike-works. This plan had meant a great deal of work for Hauke and, had not a messenger and a secretary been assigned to him through the intercession of the Dike Superintendant, he would not have completed the task so quickly, although every day he again worked until far into the night. When, dead tired, he at last went to his bed, his wife was no longer waiting for him in feigned sleep as in the past; she, too, had enough daily work of her own, so that she lay at night in a sound sleep, deep as the deepest well.

After Hauke had read out his plan and once again spread out the documents—which, of course, had already been displayed for public inspection for three days here at the inn—on the table, two men, of grave appearance, examined with deference this work of painstaking diligence and, after careful consideration, agreed to their dike reeve's fair proposals; others, however, whose shares in the new land had been sold, either by themselves or their fathers or other, previous owners, protested at being involved in the costs of the new polder, which was no longer their concern, unmindful of the fact that, as a result of the new works, their old lands too would gradually be relieved of costs; some again, favoured with shares in the new polder, cried out that others were welcome to buy these shares from them, and have them for next to nothing; because of the unfair burden that would be imposed upon them, they said, they could not survive. But Ole Peters, who was leaning, grim-faced, against the door-post, broke in: 'Think it over first, then put your trust in our dike reeve! He knows how to reckon; he already has the most shares, he was clever enough to buy mine from me and, when he had them, he decided to make this new polder!'

Deathly silence fell over the assembly for a moment following these words. The dike reeve was standing at the table on which he had spread out his papers beforehand; he raised his head and looked across to Ole Peters. 'You know very well, Ole Peters,' he said, 'that what you are saying is slander against me; yet you say it because you know, too, that a large part of the mud you are throwing will stick to me! The truth is that you wanted to be rid of your shares and that I needed them at the time for my sheep-rearing; and something else: the blackguard remark that you made in the inn—that I was dike reeve only thanks to my wife—shook me to the core, and I wanted to show you all that I could be dike reeve by my own efforts; and so, Ole Peters, I have done what the dike reeve before me ought to have done. But if you bear a grudge against me because your shares now belong to me—you can hear for yourself, there are people enough who are offering their shares cheap, only because the work is now too much for them!'

A murmur of approval rose among a small section of the assembly and old Jewe Manners, who was standing among them, called aloud: 'Bravo, Hauke Haien! With God's help, you'll accomplish the work!'

But the business was not completed on that day, although Ole Peters said no more and the members of the assembly did not leave until supper-time; only at a second meeting was everything finally settled, and then only after Hauke had agreed to provide four teams in the following month instead of the three that should rightly have been his contribution.

The Whitsun bells were already ringing throughout the district when the work at last began; a line of tip-carts plied unceasingly from the foreshore to the dike-line to discharge their loads of clay, and an equal number was already on the way back to load anew on the foreshore; on the dike-line itself, men armed with shovels and spades were standing ready to carry the unloaded clay to its foreseen place and spread it evenly; huge waggon-loads of straw were brought up and dropped; the straw was needed not only to cover the lighter material, such as sand and loose earth, which was used on the inner side of the dike; single sections of the dike were gradually completed, and the sods of turf which had been placed on top were covered here and there with a firm layer of straw to protect them from the gnawing of the waves. Official overseers strode about everywhere and, whenever a storm was blowing, they would stand with their mouths wide open, shouting orders amidst wind and rain; the dike reeve rode among them on his white horse, which he now used at all times; and the animal and his rider flew back and forth as the dike reeve quickly and curtly issued his instructions, praised the workers, or, as sometimes happened, dismissed a man without mercy for being lazy or incompetent. 'That's no good at all!' he would shout; 'We'll not have the dike spoiled by your laziness!' They could hear the snorting of his horse in the distance whenever he rode up from the polder, and every man of them would increase his efforts. 'Move yourselves! The White Horse rider's coming!'

At breakfast time, when the workers were lying in groups on the ground and eating their morning crust, Hauke would ride alongside the unmanned works, and his keen eyes would see if someone had wielded his spade carelessly. Whenever he rode over to the men to explain how the work was to be done, they would raise their eyes to him and patiently continue chewing their bread; but a word of agreement, or even a remark, was never heard from them. Once, at that time of day—it was already late on in the morning—seeing that the work on one part of the dike was especially well done, he rode to the nearest group of workers, leapt from his horse, and asked cheerily who had performed such a neat piece of work; but they merely looked at him diffidently and grimly, and it was only slowly and almost unwillingly that they at length disclosed some names. The man to whom he had given the horse, which was standing quiet as a lamb, was holding him with both hands and gazing as if frightened at the animal's beautiful eyes which, as usual, were fixed upon his master.

'Well, Marten!' called Hauke, 'Why are you standing there as if you'd been struck by lightning?'

—'Your horse, maister—it's as quiet as if it was planning to work some mischief!'

Hauke laughed, taking the horse by the bridle himself, and the animal immediately rubbed its head fondly upon his shoulder. Some of the workers looked up shyly at the horse and rider; others, however, continued to eat their breakfast in silence, as if all this did not concern them, now and then throwing a piece to the gulls which had spotted the feeding-ground and, swooping down on their slender wings, almost touched the workers' heads. As if lost in thought, the dike reeve looked at the begging birds for a while, seeing how they snapped up with their beaks the crusts that were thrown to them; then he leapt into the saddle and, without looking back at the men, rode away; some words, which they now spoke aloud, sounded almost like mockery in his ears. 'What's that they're saying?' he asked himself aloud. 'Was Elke right, when she said that they are all against me? These farm labourers and smallholders, too—even though my new dike will bring prosperity for many of them?'

He put spurs to his horse, so that it rushed down into the polder as if possessed. He, of course, knew nothing of the uncanny aura which his former servant-lad had attributed to him; but the people ought to have seen him now, his eyes staring from his lean face, his cloak fluttering, and his horse flying like the wind!

——So the summer and the autumn went by; work had carried on until the end of November and then come to a halt because of the frost and snow; they had not been able to complete the work and therefore decided to leave the polder open. Eight feet high stood the dike; only to the west, where the sluice was to be built against the water, had a gap been left; further up, too, in front of the old dike, the channel had been left untouched. Thus the flood-tide was able to flow into the polder, as in the past thirty years, without causing much damage there or to the new dike. And so the work of human hands was left to God on high and placed under His protection, until the spring sun should enable the work to be completed.

——Meanwhile, a happy event had taken place in the house of the dike reeve: in the ninth year of their marriage a child had been born at last. It was red and wrinkled and weighed seven pounds, as is proper for new-born children when, as in this case, they are of the female sex; yet its cries had sounded strangely muffled, which was not to the liking of the midwife. The worst of it was that, two days after the birth, Elke lay in bed with a heavy puerperal fever; she was delirious and could not recognize either her husband or her old nurse. The tremendous joy which Hauke had felt on seeing his child had given way to gloom; the physician had been called from the town, he sat by Elke's bed, felt her pulse, prescribed medicines, and looked about him helplessly. Hauke shook his head: 'He can't help her; only God can help!' He had worked out his own conception of Christianity, but there was something that stopped him from praying. When the old doctor had driven away, he stood at the window staring out at the wintry day and, while the sick woman cried out in her delirium, he clasped his hands together; but whether out of devotion or simply in order not to sink in his dreadful fear, he himself did not know.

'Water! The water!' whimpered the sick woman. 'Hold me!' she cried; 'Hold me, Hauke!' Then her voice sank; it sounded as if she was weeping: 'Out to sea, out into the waters? Dear God, I shall never see him again!'

At this, he turned and pushed the nurse away from the bed; he fell upon his knees, put his arms around his wife, and drew her close to him: 'Elke! Elke! Don't you know me? I'm here with you!'

But she only opened wide her eyes glowing with fever and looked around her as if hopelessly lost.

He laid her back upon her pillows; then he wrung his hands together: 'Lord God,' he cried, 'don't take her away from me! You know I cannot live without her!' Then he appeared to reflect and added, in a lower voice: 'I know that You cannot always do as You would wish, not even You; You are wise beyond all measure; You must act according to your wisdom— O Lord, speak to me, if only through a breath!'

It was as if silence had suddenly fallen; he could hear only a gentle breathing. As he turned back to the bed, his wife lay sleeping peacefully; only the nurse was looking at him, her eyes filled with dismay. He heard the door close. 'Who was that?' he asked.

'It was Ann Grete the maid, master; she brought the warming basket.'

—'Why are you looking at me so fearfully, Frau Levke?'

'I? I was startled to hear your prayer, master; you will save no one from death with such a prayer!'

Hauke looked at her with his piercing eyes. 'Do you, too, attend the conventicle at the house of the Dutch tailor Jantje, like Ann Grete?'

'Yes, master; we both share the living faith!'

Hauke made no reply. The separatist conventicle movement, which at that time was developing vigorously, had flourished among the Frisians too; impoverished craftsmen or school-masters dismissed for drunkenness played the main role in it, and maidservants, young women, old women, idlers, and lonely people flocked eagerly to the clandestine meetings at which any one might play the priest. Among the members of the dike reeve's household, Ann Grete and the servant-lad, who was in love with her, used to spend their free evenings there. Elke, of course, had not refrained from making known to Hauke her doubts on this score; but he had said that one should not inter-fere in matters of religious belief: it did no one any harm, and it was better for people to be there than in the village ale-house!

And there the matter had remained, and so had he kept silent even now. But naturally, others did not keep silent concerning him; the words of his prayer had made the rounds from house to house; he had denied God's omnipotence; and what was a God without omnipotence? He was an atheist; that business of the devil's horse might well be true, after all!

Hauke heard nothing of this; he had eyes and ears only for his wife at this time; even the child no longer existed for him.

The old doctor came again, came every day, sometimes twice; then he remained a whole night, wrote a further prescription, and Iven Johns galloped off with it to the apothecary. Then his expression became more friendly, and he nodded confidently to the dike reeve: 'She's improving! She's improving! With God's help!' And one day—had his skill conquered the disease, or had the dear Lord been able to find a way to answer Hauke's prayer after all?—when the doctor was alone with the sick woman, he spoke to her and his old eyes smiled: 'Well, my dear, now I can say it to you without fear: today is a red-letter day for the doctor; your condition was very serious, but now you belong to us again, to the living!'

A flood of light seemed to break out from her dark eyes: 'Hauke! Hauke, where are you?' she cried and, as he rushed into the room in answer to her clear call and ran to her bed, she threw her arms around his neck: 'Hauke, husband, I am saved! I shall remain here with you!'

And the old doctor took his silk handkerchief from his pocket, wiped his forehead and cheeks, and, nodding, left the room.

— — On the third evening following this day a pious preacher —a slipper-maker who had been dismissed by the dike reeve— spoke at the conventicle in the house of the Dutch jobbing tailor, explaining to his listeners the nature of God: 'But he who shall deny God's omnipotence, he who shall say: "I know Thou canst not do as Thou willst"—we all know the unhappy wretch; he is a burden upon us all, like a stone—he has fallen away from God and seeks God's enemy, the friend of sin, to be his comforter; for the hand of man must have a staff of some kind to support it. But beware ye him who prays in that manner; for his prayer is accursed!'

— — This, too, ran like wildfire from house to house: how could it be otherwise in a small community? And it came to Hauke's ears too. He said not a word about it, not even to his wife; but at times he would clasp her firmly in his arms and draw her to him: 'Stay true to me, Elke! Stay true to me!' Then she would look up at him, her eyes filled with astonishment: 'True to you? Who else could there be?' After a short time, however, she understood what he meant: 'Yes, Hauke, we are true to each other; not only because we need each other.' And then they each went to their work.

This would have been well enough; but despite the activities afforded by his work, there was a loneliness about him, and a feeling of defiance and reserve towards his fellow men crept into his heart; only towards his wife did he remain always the same, and every morning and evening he would kneel in front of his daughter's cradle as if it were the source of his eternal salvation. Towards the servants and labourers, however, he became stricter; the clumsy and the slovenly, whom he had in the past quietly admonished, now trembled at the fierce lashing of his tongue, and sometimes Elke would go and quietly placate them.

With the approach of spring, the dike works began once more; in order to protect the new sluice which was now to be built, the gap in the western dike-line was closed by means of a temporary dike in the shape of a half-moon both inside and out; and with the sluice, the main dike gradually grew in height, with the work proceeding faster the higher it got. But for the dike reeve in charge, the work did not become any easier, for Ole Peters had been made dike agent in place of Jewe Manners, who had died that winter. Hauke had made no attempt to prevent his appointment; but instead of the encouraging words, accompanied by a friendly pat on his left shoulder, which he had so often received from his wife's old godfather, he now encountered furtive resistance and unnecessary objections from the old man's successor, which had to be countered by unnecessary justifications; for Ole, though admittedly an important man, had no talent where dike matters were concerned; moreover, the 'pen-pusher' was still a thorn in his side from earlier days.

The clear sky spread over sea and fenland once more, and the polder was again bright with sturdy cattle, breaking the wide silence from time to time with their lowing: above in the heavens the larks were singing without cease, though this was noticed only when their song had broken off for the length of a breath. There was no storm to interrupt the work, and the sluice was already standing, its beams still unpainted, not having needed the protection of the temporary dike for even one night; the Lord seemed to look favourably upon the new work. And Elke's eyes would smile at her husband when he returned home on his white horse after being out on the dike. 'You're a good creature, after all!' she would say, patting the horse on its smooth neck. But whenever she held the child to her bosom, Hauke would jump down from his horse and dandle the tiny creature in his arms; and whenever the horse held its brown eyes fixed upon the child, he would say: 'Come here; you shall have the honour, too!' and set little Wienke—she had been christened with that name—upon the saddle and led the horse in a circle around the mound. The old ash tree also had the honour at times; Hauke would set the child upon a swaying bough, rocking her gently, with Elke standing in the doorway, laughter in her eyes; but the child did not laugh—its eyes, with a tiny, delicate nose between them, would gaze dully into the distance, and the little hands made no attempt to grasp the stick which her father held out to her. Hauke paid no attention to this, for he knew nothing about children of such an early age; only Elke, when she saw the bright-eyed little girl in the arms of her servant-woman, who had given birth at the same time as she, would sometimes say sadly: 'My child isn't as far on as yours, Stina!' and Stina, shaking her tubby little son, whom she was holding by the hand, with rough affection, would cry: 'Yes, missus, children *are* different; that one, he used to steal the apples from the larder before he was two years old!' And Elke would brush the chubby little fellow's curly hair out of his eyes and then, secretly, press her silent daughter to her heart.

— —As October approached, the new sluice was already firmly in place on the west side in the main dike, which now met on both sides and, except at the gaps near the channel, ran down to the seaward sides with its gently sloping profile, topping the normal flood level by fifteen feet. From the north-west corner one had a clear view past Jevershallig and out into the mud-flats; but naturally the winds were stronger here, so that the observer's hair would stream out behind him; any one wishing to look out from this point had to keep a firm hold on his cap.

At the end of November, when rain and storm had set in, only the gully close by the old dike, through which on the north side the sea rushed through the channel into the new polder, still remained to be closed. On either side stood the walls of the dike; the abyss between them now had to be filled. A dry summer would have made the work easier; but, whatever the weather, the task had to be completed, for a gathering storm could endanger the whole enterprise. And Hauke did his utmost to complete the work now. The rain fell in torrents, the wind howled; but his lean figure on the spirited horse stood out, now here, now there, among the dark masses of men who were busily working up above and down below on the north side of the dike by the gully. Now he could be seen down below near the tip-carts which had to bring the clay from the foreshore; a dense cluster of carts had just reached the channel and the loads of clay were being thrown down. From time to time the harsh orders of the dike reeve, determined to be in sole command on this day, rang through the splashing rain and the roaring wind; he called up the carts by numbers, sending back those pushing to the front; whenever he shouted 'Stop!' work down below would come to a halt; 'Straw! A load of straw down there!' he would shout to the men working on top, and the straw would sweep down from one of the carts above on to the wet clay. Down below, men would rush to seize it and pull it apart, shouting to those above not to bury them. Then fresh carts would arrive, and once again Hauke was up on top, looking down from his horse into the pit at the men shovelling and spreading the clay; then he directed his gaze towards the sea. A keen wind was blowing and he could see the water's edge creeping steadily up the dike and the waves sweeping higher; he could see, too, that the men were dripping wet and scarcely able to breathe, toiling heavily in the face of the wind which cut off the very breath from their mouths, and in the cold rain which poured down on them. 'Keep at it, men! Keep at it!' he shouted down to them. 'Only another foot higher; that will be enough to hold back the flood!' The sounds of the men working could be heard despite the roaring of the storm: the splash of the masses of clay being tipped out, the clattering of the carts, and the swishing of the straw as it was thrown down went on without cease; from time to time one could hear the whimpering of a small brown dog, harried about, helpless and shivering with cold, amidst the men and the carts; suddenly, a heart-rending yelp from the little animal rang out from the bottom of the gully. Hauke looked down; he had seen the dog hurled down from the top of the dike, and a flush of rage swept suddenly over his face. 'Stop! Stop!' he shouted down to the men by the carts; they were tipping out the wet clay without cease.

'Why?' called a rough voice from below; 'Not for the miserable cur's sake?'

'Stop, I say!' shouted Hauke once more; 'Bring me the dog! I'll not have our work desecrated!'

But no one made a move; only a few spadefuls of heavy clay thudded beside the yelping animal. He put spurs to his horse, so that it gave a neigh, and plunged down the dike, the men falling back out of his path. 'The dog!' he bellowed; 'Give me the dog!'

A hand fell gently upon his shoulder, as if it were the hand of old Jewe Manners; but when he turned, he saw that it was only a friend of the old man. 'Take care, dike reeve!' murmured the man; 'You've no friends among these people; forget the dog!'

The wind was howling, the rain beating down; the men had rammed their spades into the ground, some had cast them aside. Hauke bent towards the old man. 'Will you hold my horse, Harke Jens?' he asked, and scarcely had the other taken hold of the bridle when Hauke leapt into the pit and took the whimpering little creature in his arm; at almost the same moment he was up in the saddle once again and galloping back to the dike. His eyes swept over the men, who were standing by the carts. 'Who was it?' he shouted; 'Who threw the creature in?'

For a moment all were silent, for the dike reeve's gaunt features were afire with rage, and they shrank back from him in superstitious fear. Then a bull-necked fellow stepped towards him from one of the carts. 'I didn't do it, dike reeve,' he said, biting off a quid from a roll of chewing tobacco and pushing it calmly into his mouth; 'but the one who did it did right; if your dike is to hold, a living creature must be buried in it!'

—'A living creature? What catechism taught you that?'

'None, master,' the fellow replied, an insolent laugh rising in his throat; 'our grandfathers knew it, who could surely equal you in Christian faith! A child is even better; but if there's none to be had, a dog will do well enough!'

'Enough of your heathen beliefs!' Hauke shouted at him, ''twould hold better if they were to throw *you* in!'

A shocked 'Aah!' rose from a dozen throats, and the dike reeve perceived grim faces and clenched fists all around him; he saw clearly that these were no friends, and the thought of his dike fell on him like a bolt of fear; what would happen if all of them now threw down their spades?—And as he glanced down once more he saw again old Jewe Manners's friend, walking among the workers, speaking to this one or that one, laughing with one, slapping another on the shoulder with a friendly smile and, one after the other, they picked up their spades again; a few moments later the work was under way once again.—What more did he want? The channel had to be closed off and the dog was hidden safe enough in the folds of his cloak. With a sudden resolve he turned his horse towards the nearest cart. 'Straw on the edge!' he cried imperiously and, almost mechanically, the carter obeyed; soon the straw swished down into the pit and, on all sides, each and every man set to work once again.

In this way they worked on for another hour; it was past six o'clock and darkness was already approaching; the rain had stopped and Hauke called the overseers over to his horse: 'At four o'clock tomorrow morning', he said, 'everyone is to be here; the moon will still be up and with God's help we shall finish the work! And another thing!' he shouted, as they made to depart; 'd'you know the dog?' and he brought out the trembling animal from under his cloak.

They shook their heads; only one spoke: 'It's been running around begging in the village for days; doesn't belong to anyone at all!'

'Then it's mine!' replied Hauke. 'Don't forget: tomorrow morning at four!' he said and rode away.

Just as he arrived home, Ann Grete came through the door; she was wearing clean clothes, and the thought flashed into his mind that she was going to the house of the conventicle tailor. 'Hold out your apron!' he cried and when, instinctively, she obeyed, he threw the little dog, besmirched with clay, into it. 'Take him to little Wienke; he shall be her playmate! But wash him and warm him first; that will be a work pleasing to God, the poor creature is frozen stiff!'

And Ann Grete had no choice but obey her master and did not attend the conventicle that day.

On the following day the last spadeful of earth on the dike was turned; the wind had dropped; gulls and avocets swept continually in graceful flight back and forth over land and sea; from Jevershallig could be heard the thousandfold cry of the ring-geese which were content to linger for the day on the North Sea coast, and, out of the white morning mist which covered the wide fenland, a golden autumn day slowly dawned and cast its light over the new work of human hands.

Some weeks later the commissioners came, together with the

Dike Superintendant, in order to see it; a great banquet, the first since the funeral banquet of old Tede Volkerts, was held in the dike reeve's house; all the dike agents and the most important landowners were invited. After the feast the carriages of all the guests and of the Dike Superintendant were made ready; the Dike Superintendant helped Elke into her gig, in front of which the brown gelding was stamping his hooves; then he himself jumped up behind and took the reins in his hands; for he wished to drive his dike reeve's clever wife himself. Off they all went merrily from the mound and out onto the track, up the path to the new dike, and then along the dike around the new polder. Meanwhile a light north-west wind had sprung up, and the flood was being driven against the north and west sides of the new dike; but it was plain to see that the force of the waves was diminished by the gentle slope; the commissioners echoed the words of praise spoken by the Dike Superintendant, so that the doubts hesitantly expressed by one or the other of the dike agents were very quickly quelled.

—That event, too, passed by; but the dike reeve experienced another satisfaction one day as he was riding along the new dike in quiet, contemplative mood. The question may, perhaps, have occurred to him, why the polder—which, had it not been for him, would not exist and in which his own sweat and sleepless nights were buried—had now at last been named 'New Caroline Polder' after one of the royal princesses; but it was a fact: the name was indicated in all relevant documents—in some, even, in red Gothic script. Looking up, he saw two labourers with their farming tools approaching, one about twenty paces behind the other. 'Wait for me!' he heard the straggler call; but the other man—who was now standing near a path leading down into the polder—called back: 'Another time, Jens! It's late now, and I have to dig clay here.'

—'Where?'

'Why, here, in the Hauke Haien Polder!'

He spoke in a loud voice as he trotted down the path, as if he wished everyone in the fenland to hear. For Hauke, however, it was as if he had heard his own fame proclaimed; he rose in the stirrups, set spurs to his horse, and gazed out steadily over the wide landscape to his left; 'Hauke Haien Polder!' he repeated quietly; it sounded as if the polder could never bear any other name! Let them all do as they wished; there was no getting round *his* name; as for the princess's name—would it not soon be simply mouldering away in old books? On went the white horse at a proud gallop; but in his ears the name still resounded: 'Hauke Haien Polder! Hauke Haien Polder!' In his imagination, the new dike grew almost to an eighth wonder of the world; the like of it was not to be seen in all Friesland! He slowed the horse to a prancing trot; he felt as if he were standing in the midst of all the Frisians; he towered above them by a head, and his gaze swept keenly and pityingly over them.

— —Three years had meanwhile gone by since the completion of the dike; the new work had proved itself and the repair costs had been extremely low; in the polder the white clover was now blossoming almost everywhere and anyone walking across the sheltered meadows would be met by a sweet-smelling cloud borne on the summer wind. Now the time had come to convert the previously 'ideal' shares into 'real' shares, and to allocate pieces of land, designated as theirs for ever, to all shareholders. Hauke had not been idle in acquiring some new parcels of land for himself; Ole Peters had doggedly refused to do so: he did not possess any land in the new polder. The allocation had not been possible without anger and dispute, but had nevertheless been completed; this day, too, now lay behind the dike reeve.

From now on he led a lonely life, fulfilling his duties as farmer and as dike reeve, and towards those who were closest to him; his old friends were no longer alive and he was not the man to find new friends. But peace reigned in his house, peace which his mute child did not spoil; she spoke very little, and the never-ending questions which are usual with lively children were infrequent, and mostly of a kind that the person questioned found difficult to answer; but her dear, foolish little face almost always bore an expression of contentment. She had two playmates, and these were enough for her; whenever she walked across the mound the little brown dog rescued by Hauke would leap around her—wherever the dog was, little Wienke was not far away. Her second playmate was a black-headed gull. Just as the dog had a name—Pearl—the gull's name was Claus.

Claus had been brought to the farm by an aged human agency: old Trin' Jans, now eighty, had no longer been able to take care of herself in her cottage on the outer dike; Elke was of the opinion that her grandmother's old maidservant could pass her few remaining days and die peacefully within their family and so, half by force, Hauke and Elke had brought her to the farm and installed her in the north-west room of the new barn which the dike reeve had had to build beside the main house some years before, when he had increased the size of his farm. Some of the maids had been given rooms next door and were thus able to help the old woman at night. Her old household implements were placed along the walls: a chest made from the wood of a sugar crate, above which hung two colourful pictures of her lost son, a spinning-wheel—long since disused—and a curtained bed, spotlessly clean, in front of which stood a stool covered with the white fur of the erstwhile Angora cat. But she had also possessed a living creature which she had brought with her: Claus, the gull, who had remained faithful to her for years and been fed by her; of course, when winter came he would fly south with the other gulls and return only when the sweet-scented wormwood blossomed on the shore.

The barn was built a little lower on the mound so that, from her window, the old woman could not look out across the dike to the sea. 'You keep me here as if I was in prison, dike reeve!' she grumbled when Hauke entered her room one day, and she pointed with her twisted fingers to the fields lying below. 'Where is Jeverssand? Over there behind the brown ox or the black ox?'

'What do you want with Jeverssand?' asked Hauke.

—'Jeverssand, nonsense!' growled the old woman. 'I want to see the spot where my son went to meet his Maker long ago!'

—'If that's what you want to see,' replied Hauke, 'you must go and sit under the ash tree, then you can see the whole ocean!'

'Yes,' said the old woman, 'yes, if I had your young legs, dike reeve!'

Such were her thanks—and remained so for a long time—for the help which the dike reeve and his wife gave her; but then, all at once, matters changed. One morning Wienke's little head peeped in to her through the half-open door. 'Well,' called the old woman, who was sitting upon her wooden chair, her hands clasped together; 'and what are you up to here?'

But the child came closer without saying a word and gazed at her unceasingly with her incurious eyes.

'Are you the dike reeve's daughter?' asked Trin' Jans and, when the child lowered her little head as if nodding, she added: 'Sit down here on my stool. That was once an Angora cat—as big as that! But your father killed him. If he was still alive, you could ride on him.'

Wienke turned her eyes to the white fur without a word; then she knelt down and began to stroke it with her little hands, as children do with a living cat or dog. 'Poor cat!' she said and continued stroking.

'So,' said the old woman after a while, 'that's enough for now; and today you can sit on him, too; perhaps that's just what your father killed him for!' Then she picked up the child by both arms and placed her roughly upon the stool. But when the child remained silent and still and only continued to look at her, she began to shake her head. 'You are punishing him, Lord God! Yes, yes, You are punishing him!' she murmured; then a feeling of pity for the child seemed to overcome her after all; with her bony hand she stroked the child's thin hair and the look in the child's eyes seemed to show pleasure at the caress.

From now on Wienke came every day to visit the old woman in her room; soon she began to sit upon the Angora stool of her own accord, and Trin' Jans would put small pieces of meat and bread, of which she always had a supply, into Wienke's little hands and have her throw them on to the floor; then the seagull would dart out screaming and with outspread wings from some corner or other and fall upon the morsels. At first the child was terrified and screamed at the sight of the huge, clamorous bird; but before long it was a familiar game and, as soon as she put her little head in at the door, the bird would dart to her and land upon her head or shoulder until the old woman came to her aid and the feeding could begin. Trin' Jans, who could not otherwise bear to see another so much as put out his hand towards her Claus, would now watch indulgently as the child gradually won the bird's affections away from her. He willingly allowed himself to be caught by the child; she would carry him around and wrap him in her apron, and when, at times, the little brown dog would prance around her and, jealous, leap up at the bird, she would cry: 'Not you, not you, Pearl,' and with her little arms she would raise the gull so high that he would free himself and fly away screaming across the mound, and then the dog, leaping and fawning, would attempt to usurp the gull's place in her arms.

If Hauke or Elke happened to see this odd quartet, the members of which had one defect in common, they would look at the child tenderly; but when they turned away their faces would reveal only an expression of pain which each, alone, bore away from the scene, for the words of release had not yet been spoken between them. One morning in summer, when Wienke was sitting with the old woman and her two pets on the great stones in front of the barn door, her parents walked by, the dike reeve leading his horse behind him, the reins over his arm; he intended to ride out on to the dike and had brought up the horse from the field himself; his wife had linked her arm into his. A warm sun was shining; it was almost humid and, from time to time, a gust of wind blew from the south-south-east. The child seemed to feel uneasy where she was sitting. 'Wienke wants to come!' she cried and, shaking the gull from her lap, she grasped her father's hand.

'Then come,' he said.

—'In this wind?' objected Elke. 'She'll be blown away!'

'I'll hold her tight; the air is warm today and the waves so pretty—she can watch them dancing.'

And Elke ran into the house and brought her daughter a scarf and a little hood. 'But there's a storm brewing,' she said; 'off with you both now, quickly, and come back soon.'

'The storm won't catch us,' laughed Hauke, and lifted the child up on to the saddle in front of him. Elke remained on the mound for a time and, shading her eyes with her hand, watched them trotting down the path and towards the dike; Trin' Jans was sitting upon the stone muttering inaudibly through her withered lips.

The child lay quietly in her father's arm; she seemed almost unable to breathe in the oppressive air of the approaching storm; he bowed down his head to her: 'Well, Wienke?' he asked.

She looked at him for a while. 'Father,' she said, 'you can do it! Can't you do everything?'

'Can do what, Wienke?'

But she did not speak; she seemed not to have understood her own question.

It was flood-tide; as they came up on to the dike the wide sea reflected the rays of the sun into her eyes, a whirlwind lashed the waves into a spiral and other waves followed and crashed dully on the shore; frightened, she put out her tiny hands and grasped her father's fist, with which he was holding the reins, so that the horse suddenly leapt to the side. Her pale blue eyes looked up at Hauke in bewildered terror: 'The water, father! The water!' she cried.

Gently he freed himself from her grasp and said: 'Hush, child, your father is with you; the water won't hurt you!'

She brushed her pale blonde hair from her forehead and ventured to look out at the sea once more. 'It won't hurt me,' she said, trembling; 'no, say it musn't hurt us; you can do that and then it won't hurt us!'

'*I* can't do that, child,' replied Hauke; 'but the dike we are riding on will protect us, and it was your father who planned it and had it built.'

She turned her eyes towards him as if she had not fully understood, then buried her strikingly small head in her father's wide cloak.

'Why are you hiding, Wienke?' he murmured; 'are you still afraid?' And a trembling little voice came from the folds of the cloak: 'Wienke doesn't want to see it; but you can do anything, can't you, father?'

A sound of distant thunder rolled up against the wind. 'Oho!' said Hauke; 'Here it comes!' and he turned his horse's head. 'Now let's go home to mother!'

The child took a deep breath; but not until they had reached the mound and the house again did she raise her little head from her father's breast. When Elke had taken off the scarf and hood inside, she remained standing in front of her mother like a tiny, mute pillar. 'Well, Wienke,' said Elke, shaking her gently, 'do you like the great ocean?'

But the child opened her eyes wide: 'It talks!' she said; 'Wienke's afraid!'

—'It doesn't talk; it only roars and rages!'

The child looked into the distance, then 'Does it have legs?' she asked again; 'Can it climb over the dike?'

—'No, Wienke; your father will see that it doesn't; he is the dike reeve.'

'Yes,' said the child and clapped her tiny hands, smiling foolishly. 'Father can do anything—anything!' Suddenly, turning from her mother, she cried: 'Let Wienke go to Trin' Jans, she's got red apples!'

Elke opened the door and let the child out. Then, closing the door again, she turned to her husband with a look of intense grief in her eyes, from which only courage and comfort had hitherto come to his aid.

He held out his hand to her and pressed her to him, as if no further words were needed between them; but, in a quiet voice, she said: 'No, Hauke, let me speak: the child that I bore you after so many years will always remain a child. Dear God! She is weak-minded; I had to say it to you sometime.'

'I've known it for a long time' said Hauke, holding his wife's hand tightly as she tried to remove it.

'And so we are alone, after all,' she went on.

But Hauke shook his head. 'I love her, and she puts her little arms around me and presses herself tight against me; I wouldn't forego that for all the treasure on earth!'

His wife stared darkly in front of her. 'But why?' she asked, 'What have I done wrong?'

—'Yes, Elke, I have asked the same question, too—of the only One who knows; but you know yourself, the Almighty does not give mankind an answer—perhaps because we would not understand it.'

Meanwhile he had taken hold of her other hand and he drew her gently to him: 'Don't be led away from loving your child as you do; you may be sure she understands!'

And Elke threw herself on to her husband's breast and wept her heart out, and was no longer alone with her grief. Then, suddenly, she smiled at him and, pressing his hand firmly, she ran out and brought her child from old Trin' Jans's room, took her upon her lap, and kissed and hugged her until Wienke stammered: 'Mother! Dear mother!'

In this way, the people on the dike reeve's farm lived quietly together; had it not been for the child, life would have been much the poorer.

Summer gradually drew to an end; the migrating birds had flown away, and the skies were empty of lark-song; only in front of the barns, where they were picking grains of corn after the threshing, could a few be heard as they flew away screeching; already everything was frozen hard. One afternoon, in the kitchen of the main house, old Trin' Jans was sitting near the stove, on the wooden step of a stairway which led up to the attic. In the last few weeks she seemed to have taken on a new lease of life; now she enjoyed coming into the kitchen from time to time to watch Elke going about her business; there was no longer any question of her legs not being able to carry her there, ever since little Wienke had one day taken hold of her apron and led her up to the house. Now the child was kneeling beside her, her impassive eyes staring into the flames which flickered from the opening of the stove; with one tiny hand she was holding the old woman's sleeve, with the other, her own pale-blonde hair. Trin' Jans was telling her a story: 'You know', she said, 'that I was housemaid to your great-grandfather, and I had to feed the pigs; he was cleverer than all of them—'tis a cruel long time ago, but one evening, the moon was shining, they closed the sluice and she couldn't go back into the sea. Oh, how she cried and pulled at her hard, rough hair with her fish-hands. Yes, child, I saw it and heard her crying! The ditches between the fields were all full of water, and the moon was shining on them so that they gleamed like silver, and she swam from one ditch to another and clapped her hands together, or what passed for hands, so that you could hear it from afar, as if she was praying; but those creatures cannot pray, child. I was sitting in front of my door on some beams that had been left there for building, looking far out into the fields; and the mermaid was still swimming in the ditches and, when she raised her arms, they glistened like silver and diamonds, too. At last I lost sight of her, and the wild geese and gulls, that I had not heard all that time, flew whooping and cackling through the sky once more.'

The old woman fell silent; the child had picked up one word: 'Could she pray?' she asked. 'What did you say? Who was she?'

'It was the mermaid, child,' said the old woman. 'They are fairy creatures, who can't go to heaven.'

'Can't go to heaven!' echoed the child, and her little breast heaved in a deep sigh, as if she had understood.

—'Trin' Jans!' said a deep voice from the kitchen door, and the old woman flinched slightly. It was the dike reeve, Hauke Haien, leaning against the dresser. 'What have you been telling the child? Haven't I told you to keep your fairy-tales to yourself or to save them for the geese and the hens?'

The old woman looked at him with a vexed expression and pushed the child away from her. 'They're not fairy-tales,' she muttered to herself; 'they're what my great-uncle used to tell me.'

—'Your great-uncle, Trin'? You said just now you had seen it yourself.'

'That's all one,' said the old woman; 'but you don't believe me, Hauke Haien; you're trying to make a liar out of my great-uncle.' With this she moved closer to the stove and stretched out her hands over the flames rising from the opening.

The dike reeve glanced towards the window; it was still scarcely dusk. 'Come, Wienke!' he said, drawing his weak-minded child to him; 'Come with me; I want to show you something from the dike outside. But we must go on foot; the white horse is at the smithy.' Then he went into the living-room with her, and Elke wound thick woollen shawls around the child's neck and shoulders; a moment later she and her father were walking north-west upon the old dike, past Jeverssand to a point where the mud-flats spread wide and almost out of view.

Sometimes he carried her in his arms, sometimes he led her by the hand; twilight slowly approached and, in the distance, everything vanished in mist and haze. But out there, as far as the eye could see, the streams in the mud-flats, swelling unseen, had burst the ice and, just as Hauke had once seen in his youth, wreaths of smoky mist were rising from the cracks, as before, and there again were the same uncanny, crazy figures, hopping towards one another, bowing, and then, abruptly, spreading out again in a frightening fashion.

The anxious child clung fast to her father and held his hand over her little face: 'The sea-devils!' she murmured through his fingers, trembling; 'The sea-devils!'

He shook his head. 'No, Wienke, neither mermaids nor sea-devils; there are no such things. Who told you about them?'

She looked up at him dully, but made no reply. He stroked her cheeks tenderly. 'Look again!' he said; 'only poor, hungry birds! See how the big one is spreading his wings just now; they are catching the fish that come to the cracks where the mist is rising.'

'Fish,' repeated Wienke.

'Yes, child, they are all living creatures, like ourselves; there is nothing else; but our dear God is everywhere!'

Little Wienke had fixed her eyes upon the ground and was holding her breath, as if looking, terrified, into an abyss. Perhaps she only appeared to be doing so; her father stared at her for a long while, then he bent towards her and looked into her little face, but the imprisoned soul within betrayed not a flicker of emotion. He lifted her up on his arm and pushed her frozen little hands into one of his thick woollen gloves. 'There, Wienke,' —the child clearly could not hear the tone of heartfelt intensity in his voice—'warm yourself in my arms! You're our child, our one and only . . . and you love us.' The man's voice broke; but the child pressed her little head tenderly against his rough beard.

And so they set off peacefully for home.

After New Year the house was visited by fresh anxiety; the dike reeve fell ill with marsh fever; he, too, lay at death's door and, after he had recovered thanks to Elke's care and attention, he scarcely seemed the same. His bodily exhaustion weighed upon his spirit, too, and Elke was disturbed to see how little interest he took in everything. But towards the end of March he felt an urge to mount his white horse and ride along his dike once again for the first time since his illness; it was afternoon and the sun, which had been shining before, was now long since hidden behind a dull haze.

During the winter there had been floods on several occasions, though these were not serious; only on a *hallig* near the other shore a herd of sheep had been drowned and a piece of the foreshore had been washed away; but on this side and in the new polder there had been no damage worth speaking of. The night before, however, a fierce storm had raged; and now the dike reeve had to ride out himself and inspect everything with his own eyes. He had already ridden round the new dike from the south-east corner, and everything was sound, but when he had reached the north-east corner, where the new dike joined the old, he saw that the new dike was undamaged, but where the channel had formerly reached the old dike and flowed alongside it, a wide stretch of the turf covering had been torn up and swept away, and in the body of the dike was a pit washed out by the flood; what was more: in the pit an entire labyrinth of mouse burrows could be plainly seen. Hauke dismounted from his horse and inspected the damage at close quarters; the damage caused by the mice was unmistakable and seemed to run on, invisible, through the dike.

He gave a violent start; he should have taken precautions against this happening even when the new dike was being built; since it had been overlooked at the time, it must be dealt with now! The cattle were not yet back in the fields and the grass was unusually sparse; wherever he looked, the landscape stared back empty and bare. He mounted his horse again and rode back and forth along the shore; it was ebb-tide and he could plainly see how, from outside, the current had scooped out a new bed for itself in the mud and had now launched an attack against the old dike from the north-west; the new dike, however, thanks to its more gentle profile, had been able to withstand the impact wherever the current struck it.

In his mind's eye the dike reeve saw a host of fresh toil and troubles rising before him; not only did the old dike have to be reinforced here, its profile had to be adapted to that of the new dike as well; but, above all, the channel, which had reappeared as a source of danger, had to be diverted by means of new dams or groynes. Once more he rode along the new dike up to the farthest north-west corner, then back again, his eyes fixed steadily upon the newly washed-out bed of the channel which could be seen plainly enough in the exposed mud-bank. The horse tried to gallop ahead, snorting and pounding his front hooves; but his rider held him back, for he wished to ride slowly; more, he wished to quell the ferment which was rising more and more fiercely inside him.

If another storm-flood came—like that of 1655, in which countless people and their possessions had been engulfed—if another came, as had more than once happened before!—a burning shiver ran through the rider's frame—the old dike would not withstand the thrust of the water hurtling up against it! What then—what would happen then? There would be only one single means—perhaps—of saving the old polder and the lives and property in it. Hauke felt his heart stand still, and his head, usually so steady, whirled; he did not utter the words aloud, but a voice within him spoke loud enough: Your polder, the Hauke Haien Polder, would have to be abandoned and the new dike cut!

In his imagination he could already see the surging flood-waters bursting through and covering the grass and clover with their salty foam. He dug the spurs into his horse's flanks and, with a cry, the animal galloped away along the dike and down the path towards the dike reeve's house.

Hauke arrived home, his head filled with fear and confused plans. He threw himself into his armchair and, when Elke entered the room with their daughter, he rose to his feet again, lifted the child up to him, and kissed her; then, with a few gentle slaps, he chased away the little brown dog. 'I must go up to the inn,' he said, taking his cap from the door-hook on which he had hung it a moment before.

His wife looked at him anxiously. 'What have you to do there? It will soon be evening, Hauke!'

'Dike matters!' he murmured to himself; 'I shall be meeting some of the dike agents there.'

With these words he went out through the door. Elke followed him and squeezed his hand. Hauke Haien, who at all other times had kept his thoughts to himself, was now eager to hear a word from those whom he had previously considered hardly worth including in a discussion. In the taproom he found Ole Peters sitting at the card table with two of the dike agents and a man from the polder.

'I suppose you've just been out there, dike reeve?' said Ole, picking up the half-dealt cards and throwing them down again.

'Yes, Ole,' replied Hauke. 'I was out there; it looks bad.'

'Bad?—Well, it will probably cost a few hundred squares of turf and a new layer of straw; I was out there too this afternoon.'

'It can't be done as cheaply as that, Ole,' said the dike reeve; 'the channel is there again and, even if it doesn't meet the old dike from the north side, it's striking it from the north-west!'

'You should have left it where you found it!' said Ole drily.

'What you mean is,' replied Hauke, 'the new polder is no concern of yours and therefore, it oughtn't to exist. Well, that's your own fault! But if we have to build groynes to protect the old dike, the green clover behind the new dike will more than make up for it!'

'What's that you say, dike reeve?' cried the dike agents. 'Groynes? How many? You're fond of tackling everything from the most expensive side!'

The cards lay untouched upon the table. 'I'll tell you something, dike reeve,' said Ole Peters, putting his elbows on the table; 'that new polder of yours is a bottomless pit that you've presented to us! All of us are still labouring under the heavy costs of your new wide dike; now it's devouring the old dike and you expect us to repair it! Luckily it's not as bad as all that; it has held this time and it will hold in the future! Just mount your white horse again tomorrow and have another look at it!'

Hauke had come to the inn from the peaceful atmosphere of his house; behind the still moderate words which he had just heard lay—he could not mistake it—unyielding opposition; he felt he still lacked his old strength so necessary to meet it. 'I shall do as you advise, Ole,' he said, 'but I fear I shall find it just as I have seen it today.'

—An uneasy night followed that day, and Hauke tossed and turned on his pillow, unable to find sleep. 'What is it?' asked Elke, herself unable to sleep for worrying about her husband; 'if something is oppressing you, then tell me about it; that is what we have always done.'

'Nothing of importance, Elke!' he replied; 'some repairs have to be made on the dike and on the sluices; you know I always have to brood over my problems during the night.' He said no more; for he wished to retain his freedom of action; unconscious as he was of it, his wife's clear vision and forceful spirit were a hindrance to him in his present weak condition, a hindrance which he involuntarily avoided.

— —The following morning, when he came out on to the dike again, the world was quite different from that which he had seen the previous day; it was fully ebb-tide, but it was still some time before noon and a clear spring sun was casting its rays almost vertically upon the wide expanse of mud-flats; the white gulls were sweeping calmly back and forth and, unseen, high above them in the azure-blue sky, the larks were singing their eternal melody. Hauke, who did not know how Nature can deceive us with her charms, stood upon the north-west corner of the dike searching for the new channel-bed which had so startled him the previous day; but at first, because of the rays shining down from the sun's zenith, he could not see it at all. Only when he shielded his eyes from the blinding rays with his hand was it unmistakable; yet the twilight shadows must have deceived him yesterday; the bed of the channel was now only faintly defined; it must have been the ravages of the mice, now exposed to view, more than the flood, which had damaged the dike. It would have to be attended to, of course, but by careful digging and, as Ole Peters had said, with fresh pieces of turf and a few loads of straw, the damage could be repaired.

'It wasn't so bad,' he said to himself, relieved; 'you fooled yourself yesterday!'—He summoned the dike agents, and without any objection—something which had never occurred before —it was resolved to carry out the work. The dike reeve seemed to feel an invigorating calm flow through his still weak body and, a few weeks later, the whole work had been neatly completed.

The year went on, but the more time passed and the more vigorously the newly laid grass grew through the layer of straw, the greater was Hauke's uneasiness whenever he walked or rode past this spot; at times he turned his eyes aside, or rode hard by the landward side of the dike; once or twice, when he ought to have gone there, he ordered his horse to be brought back into the stable, though it was already saddled; then, again, he would abruptly set out there on foot, though no work awaited him, simply in order to get away from the house quickly and unseen;

and sometimes he had turned back, unable to bear the thought of looking at the uncanny spot once more; in the end, he would have liked to dig up everything again with his bare hands, for this piece of the dike confronted him like a pang of conscience which had taken shape outside his mind. But he could no longer touch it with his hand; nor was he able to talk about it to anyone, not even to his wife. And so September arrived; a moderate storm had blown during the night and at last turned towards the north-west. On the following, dreary morning, at ebb-tide, Hauke rode out on to the dike and started in dismay as his eyes swept across the mud-flats; there, coming from the north-west, he suddenly saw once again, cut more deeply and sharply than before, the ghostly new channel-bed; no matter how hard he stared, it refused to disappear.

When he returned home again Elke took him by the hand: 'What is it, Hauke?' she asked, looking into his grim face; 'Not more trouble, I hope? We are so happy now; I have a feeling that you are at peace with everyone!'

But in reply to these words he could find no words of his own to express his vague fears.

'No, Elke,' he said, 'I have no enemies; but it is a heavy responsibility to protect our community from God's ocean.'

He freed himself from her arms in order to avoid his beloved wife's further questions. He went into the stable and the barns as if to check everything; but he was not aware of anything around him; he was merely anxious to soothe his pangs of conscience and persuade himself that they were an expression of morbid, excessive fear.

— —The year of which I am telling you [said my host, the schoolmaster, after a while] was the year 1756, that will never be forgotten in this district; that year saw a death in Hauke Haien's house. Towards the end of September, Trin' Jans, almost ninety years old, lay on her deathbed in her room in the great barn. At her request, they had seated her upright in her pillows, and her eyes gazed through the small, leaded panes out into the distance; there must have been a lighter layer of air in the sky above a denser layer, for it was as if the horizon were raised and, at that moment, the reflection lifted the sea above the top of the dike like a shimmering silver streak, so that it shone blindingly into the room; even the southern tip of Jeverssand could be seen.

At the foot of the bed little Wienke was crouching down, one hand tightly grasping that of her father, who was standing beside her. In the features of the dying woman the so-called Hippocratic expression* could already be seen, and the child stared breathlessly at the uncanny transformation, far beyond her understanding, of the unlovely but familiar face.

'What is she doing? What is it, father?' she whispered anxiously, digging her fingernails into her father's hand.

'She is dying,' said the dike reeve.

'Dying!' echoed the child and seemed to fall into a confused day-dream.

But the old woman moved her lips once more: 'Jins! Jins!' and then a scream, like a cry for help, burst from her throat and her bony arms reached out towards the shimmering reflection of the sea outside: 'Help mi! Help mi! Tha's floatin' oth'watter! . . . God hev mercy o' th'rest on'em!'

Her arms fell, and the bed creaked gently; she was no longer among the living.

The child gave a deep sigh and raised her pale eyes towards her father: 'Is she still dying?' she asked.

'No, she has finished' said the dike reeve and he took the child into his arms. 'She is far away now, with our dear God in Heaven!'

'With our dear God in Heaven!' she repeated and was silent for a while as if she had to think over the meaning of the words. 'Is it good, with our dear God in Heaven?'

'Yes, it's the best thing.' But the last words of the dying woman still resounded dully in Hauke's mind. 'God hev mercy o' th'rest on'em!'—the words echoed quietly inside him. 'What did the old witch mean? Can people foretell the future when they are dying— —?'

— —Soon after Trin' Jans had been laid to rest up by the church, talk arose more and more frequently about disasters of all kinds and strange vermin which were said to have brought fear to the people of North Friesland: certain it was that, on the third Sunday before Easter, a whirlwind had hurled down the golden weather-cock from the church spire yonder; and it was also true that, in midsummer, myriads of foul insects had fallen like snow from the sky, so that people had not dared to open their eyes, and afterwards the creatures had lain almost hand-high upon the fields, something which had never been seen before. Towards the end of September the first man and Ann Grete the maid had set off to market with corn and butter, and on their return they climbed down from the wagon, their faces white with fear. 'What's wrong? What's the matter with you?' cried the other maids, who had run out when they heard the wagon approaching.

Ann Grete, in her travelling dress, was out of breath as she came into the spacious kitchen. 'Well, tell us!' cried the maids once more. 'Whatever has happened?'

'Oh, may the Lord Jesus save us!' cried Ann Grete. 'You know old Mariken from the Ziegelhof Farm yonder, across the water—we always stand together with our butter baskets at the corner of the apothecary's shop, and she told me about it, and Iven Johns, too, he said: "There'll be a disaster!" he said, "a disaster over all North Friesland, Ann Gret', believe me." And'—she lowered her voice—'the dike reeve's white horse isn't as it should be, either!'

—'Sh, sh!' whispered the other maids.

'Yes, yes; what do I care! But over there, on the other side, things are much worse than with us! Not only flies and horrid creatures—but blood fell like rain from heaven; and then, on the Sunday morning after, when the Pastor picked up his wash-basin, there were five deaths-heads in it the size of peas, and everyone came to see it; in August there were horrible red-headed caterpillars swarming over the country, devouring corn and flour and bread and whatever else they could find, and no fire could destroy them!'

Suddenly Ann Grete broke off in her story; none of the other maids had noticed that the mistress of the house had come into the kitchen. 'What are you chattering about?' she asked; 'You'd better not let the master hear you!' And when they all tried to tell her what had happened: 'There's no need; I've heard enough of it; go back to your work, that will be more of a blessing for

you!' Then she took Ann Grete into the living-room and reckoned up the proceeds from the market with her.

Such superstitious gossip thus obtained no sustenance in the
house of the dike reeve; but in the other houses, the longer the
evenings became the more easily did it find willing ears. It lay
oppressively everywhere, and people whispered among themselves that a disaster, a dreadful disaster, would befall North
Friesland.

It was in October, before the feast of All Souls'. During the day
a heavy storm had blown from the south-west; in the evening, a
half-moon hung in the sky and dark brown clouds were scurry-
ing across it; shadows alternating with dim light flew over the
earth; the storm was growing in force. In the dike reeve's room,
the emptied plates were still upon the table; the farm-hands had
been sent into the stable in order to see to the cattle; the maids
had been instructed to look through the house and attics to
ensure that all doors and shutters were properly closed so that
the storm should not blow in and cause damage. In the house,
Hauke was standing beside his wife at the window; he had just
devoured his supper after having been out on the dike. He had
gone out on foot quite early in the afternoon; he had had sharp
wooden stakes and sacks filled with clay or earth piled in one
place or another where the dike appeared to be weak; he had
posted people everywhere to ram the stakes into the ground and
to pile up the sacks as soon as the flood-water began to gnaw at
the dike; most of the people he had positioned in the north-west
corner, where the old dike met the new, with orders that they
might leave their posts only in case of extreme peril. All this he
had left behind him; for, scarcely a quarter-of-an-hour before,
he had arrived home, wet and dishevelled, and now, listening to
the gusts of wind rattling the leaded panes, he was gazing, as if
absently, out into the stormy night; the wall clock behind its
glass window was just striking eight. The child, who was standing beside her mother, started and hid her face in her mother's
dress. 'Claus!' she cried, and began to weep; 'Where's my Claus?'

Her question was not unfounded for, just as in the previous
year, the seagull had not flown south this winter. Her father did

not hear the question, but Elke took the child into her arms. 'Your Claus is in the barn,' she said; 'he's warm there.'

'Why?' asked Wienke; 'is that good?'

—'Yes, that's good.'

The master of the house was still standing at the window. 'We can't wait any longer, Elke!' he said; 'call one of the maids; the storm will push the panes in—the shutters must be closed and barred!'

At a word from the mistress, the maid had run outside; from inside the room, they could see her skirts flying; but just as she had released the clamps, the storm tore the shutter from her grasp and hurled it against the window so that some of the panes splintered and flew into the room; one of the lamps was blown out and began to smoke. Hauke himself was obliged to go outside to help, and it was only with difficulty that the shutters, one after another, were fastened in front of the windows. As they pulled open the door on entering the house again, a gust of wind followed them so that the glass and silver in the wall cupboard jostled together; upstairs in the house the beams trembled and groaned above their heads, as if the storm were trying to tear the roof from the walls. But Hauke did not come back into the room at once; Elke heard him walking through the threshing-room towards the stable. 'The white horse! The white horse, Iven! Quick!' she heard him shout; then he came back into the room, his hair dishevelled, but his grey eyes gleaming. 'The wind has turned!' he cried, 'To north-west, and the water half as high as spring-tide! More than a wind!—We've never had such a gale as this!'

Elke had turned deathly pale: 'And you have to go out again?'

He seized both her hands and squeezed them, almost fitfully, in his own. 'I must, Elke.'

Slowly, she raised her dark eyes to his face and for a few seconds they looked at each other, though it seemed an eternity. 'Yes, Hauke,' she said, 'I know very well, you must go!'

There was a sound of hooves outside the door. She threw her arms around his neck and, for a moment, she seemed unable to release him; but only for a moment. 'This too is our battle!' said Hauke; 'You are all safe here; no flood has ever threatened this house. And pray to God that He may be with me!'

Hauke wrapped himself in his cloak, and Elke took a scarf and wound it carefully around his neck; she tried to speak a word but her quivering lips failed her.

Outside, the white horse gave a neigh, and it rang out into the howling storm like the blast of a trumpet. Elke had gone outside with her husband; the old ash tree was creaking as if it must burst asunder. 'Get on, master!' shouted the farm-hand; 'the horse is half-crazed; he could break the reins!' Hauke threw his arms around his wife. 'I'll be back again at sunrise!' he said.

He had already leapt upon his horse; the animal reared up on its hind legs and then, like a warhorse charging into battle, galloped with its rider down the slope of the mound and out into the night and the raging storm. 'Father, my father!' cried a child's piteous voice behind him; 'Dear father!'

Wienke had run after her father in the darkness as he galloped away, but after a hundred paces or so she stumbled over a heap of earth and fell to the ground.

Iven Johns, the farm-hand, brought the weeping child back to her mother; Elke was leaning against the trunk of the ash tree, whose branches were lashing the air above her, staring as if lost in thought out into the night into which her husband had vanished; whenever the roaring of the storm or the distant thunder of the sea ceased for a moment, she would start in terror; now it seemed to her that all the elements had determined to destroy him alone and would cease abruptly as soon as they had him in their grasp. Her knees trembled, the storm had loosed her hair and was playing with it wantonly. 'Here's the child, missus!' shouted Iven; 'Hold her tight!' and he placed the little girl firmly in her mother's arms.

'The child?—I'd forgotten you, Wienke!' she cried; 'God forgive me!' She pressed the child tightly to her breast, as tightly as only love knows how, and fell down upon her knees. 'Dear God and you my Lord Jesus—let us not be made widow and orphan! Protect him, dear God; only You and I know him for what he is!' And the storm gave no more respite; it raged and roared as if the whole world would perish amid a dreadful thundering clamour.

'Go back into the house, missus!' said Johns; 'Come!', and he helped her to her feet and led them both into the house and into the living-room.

— —The dike reeve Hauke Haien galloped on his white steed towards the dike. The narrow path was bottomless, for, in the last few days, the rain had fallen in torrents; yet the wet, sticky clay did not seem to cling to the horse's hooves, it was as if the ground beneath him was firm and summer-dry. The clouds lashed across the sky like a wild hunt; down below, the wide fenland lay like an unseen desert filled with restless shadows; from the water behind the dike, more and more terrifying, came a dull roar, as if it was determined to devour everything else. 'On!' shouted Hauke to his horse; 'Our most terrible ride ever!'

Then a cry, like a dying scream, rang out from beneath his horse's hooves. He jerked at the bridle and looked around him; a flock of white gulls, half-flying, half-driven by the wind, passed beside him close to the ground with mocking screams; they were seeking a haven inland. As the moon shone fleetingly through the clouds, he saw that one of the gulls lay trampled on the path; the rider thought he glimpsed a red ribbon fluttering from its neck. 'Claus!' he shouted; 'Poor Claus!'

Was it his daughter's bird? Had he recognized horse and rider and looked for safety with them?—The rider did not know. 'On!' he shouted once more and, immediately, the horse raised its hooves for a fresh gallop; then, suddenly, the storm dropped and was succeeded by a deathly silence, though only for an instant, then it returned with renewed rage; but the sound of human voices and the faint barking of a dog had reached the rider's ears and, as he turned his head back towards the village, he recognized in the moonlight, as it broke through the clouds, people working on high-piled wagons on the mounds and in front of the houses; in a flash he saw still other wagons driving in haste towards the high ground; he heard the bellowing of cattle as they were driven out of the warm stables and off to the heights. 'Thank God!' he said to himself, 'They're saving themselves and the cattle'—then, with a cry of fear: 'My wife! my child!—No! No! The water won't reach our mound!'

But all this was only a moment of time; the whole scene flew past him as if it were only a vision.

A fearful squall came roaring up from the sea, and horse and rider plunged towards it, down the narrow path to the dike. When they reached the top, Hauke halted his horse with a fierce pull at the reins. But where was the sea? Where was Jeverssand? Where was the other shore?— —He could see nothing but mountains of water ahead of him, rising menacingly against the night sky, seeking to pile themselves one upon another into towers and beating one upon another against the solid land. On they came, with crests of white, howling as if all beasts of prey in the wilderness were imprisoned within them. The white horse stamped with his hooves and snorted out into the tumult; but the rider was daunted, as if all human power was at an end here; as if darkness, death, and oblivion must now overwhelm them.

But then he reconsidered: it was a storm-tide; though he himself had never seen the like; his wife, his child were safe in their unassailable house upon its high mound; but his dike—his breast heaved with pride—the Hauke Haien Dike, as people called it—could now demonstrate how a dike ought to be built!

But—what was that?—He halted at the corner formed by the two dikes; where were the men he had posted here, the men who were to keep watch here?—He looked north along the old dike, for he had sent some few men there, too; but not a soul was to be seen, either here or there. He rode farther out, still he was alone; only the howling of the storm and the roaring of the sea, coming from an immeasurable distance, struck his ears with deafening force. He turned back his horse; once again he came to the abandoned corner and let his gaze run along the line of the new dike; he could see clearly: here the waves were rolling in more slowly, less violently; almost as if it were a different sea. 'That will hold!' he murmured, and something like laughter rose in his throat.

But his laughter died away as his eyes ranged farther along the line of his dike: at the north-west corner—what was that? A dark mass of teeming figures; he could see them busily jostling and heaving—no doubt of it, they were men! But what were they doing, what were they working at on his dike? And he dug the spurs into his horse's flanks, and away flew the animal with him; the storm was coming broadside on and, at times, the squalls of wind were so strong that they were almost hurled from the dike into the new polder; but horse and rider well knew where they were going. Already Hauke could see a few dozen men grouped together, working busily, and now he saw that a gully had been cut straight across the new dike. Roughly he jerked his horse to a halt. 'Stop!' he shouted; 'Stop! What devil's work are you at here?'

Startled at seeing the dike reeve suddenly in their midst, they had stopped digging. The storm had carried his words to them and it was plain that several of the men were eager to speak to him; but he could see only their violent gestures, for they were all standing on his left, and whatever they said was snatched away by the storm; now and then, the force of the gale would hurl the men tumbling against one another so that they crowded together in a dense flock. With a quick glance Hauke measured the gully and the height of the water which, despite the new profile, was splashing up almost to the top of the dike and spraying horse and rider. Only another ten minutes' work—that was clear—then the flood would pour through the gully and the Hauke Haien Polder would be buried beneath the waves!

The dike reeve beckoned one of the workers to the other side of his horse. 'Well, speak!' he shouted; 'What are you doing here, what's the meaning of it?'

The man shouted back: 'We're to cut through the new dike, maister, so that the old dike won't break!'

'What's that?'

—'Cut through the new dike!'

'And drown the polder?—Who the devil ordered you to do that?'

'No, maister, not the devil; Ole Peters, the dike agent, was here; he ordered it!'

The rider's eyes flashed with fury: 'Don't you know me?' he bellowed. 'Where *I* am, Ole Peters has no say in the matter! Away with the lot of you! Back to your posts, where I ordered you!'

When they hesitated, he plunged with his horse into their midst. 'Go back to where you belong—or go to the devil!'

'Take care, maister!' shouted one of the men and struck out with his spade at the horse, which was rearing like a wild beast; but a blow from a hoof knocked the spade out of his hand, and another man fell to the ground. Suddenly a scream was heard from among the rest of the throng, a scream such as only the fear of death can tear from a human throat; for an instant, all of them—the dike reeve and his horse, too—stood as if petrified; but one of the workmen had held out his arm like a signpost, pointing to the north-east corner of the two dikes, where the old dike met the new. Only the howling of the storm and the rushing of the water could be heard. Hauke turned in his saddle: what was that? His eyes widened: 'God in Heaven! A breach! A breach in the old dike!'

'Your guilt, dike reeve!' cried a voice from the throng. 'Your guilt! Carry it with you to God's throne!'

Hauke's face, crimson with fury, now turned deathly white; the moonlight shining upon it could not make it whiter; his arms hung limp by his sides and he was scarcely aware that he was holding the reins. But this, too, only for an instant; then he sat bolt upright and a deep groan escaped his lips; then he turned his horse without a word; the horse snorted and galloped with him east along the dike. The rider's eyes flashed keenly in every direction; his thoughts tumbled in confusion. What guilt should he carry with him to God's throne?—The cut through the new dike—perhaps they would have finished it if he had not shouted 'Stop!' but—there was something else and it thrust a burning arrow through his heart; he knew only too well—last summer, if only Ole Peters's malicious mouth had not then held him back—that was it! He alone had seen how weak the old dike was; he ought to have carried out the repairs despite everything. 'Lord God, I confess,' he shouted suddenly into the storm; 'I have failed in my duty!'

On his left, close by his horse's hooves, the sea was raging; in front of him, and now shrouded in complete blackness, was the old polder with its mounds and familiar houses; only from one direction was a light shining through the darkness. The sight brought comfort to his heart; to him the light seemed like a greeting from his wife and child. Thank heaven, they were in safety on the high mound. The others were surely in the upland village yonder; from there, more lights were shining than he had ever seen before; and even from high in the sky, no doubt from the church tower, light was shining out into the darkness. 'They must all have fled, all of them!' said Hauke to himself; 'The houses on many of the mounds will certainly be in ruins, and black years lie ahead for the flooded fields; sluices and drains will have to be repaired. We must bear the burden, and I shall help—even those who have injured me; only have mercy on us, Lord God!'

He cast a sideward glance at the new polder; outside, the foaming sea was raging but inside there seemed to be only the peace of the night. A cry of exultation burst unwittingly from the rider's breast: 'The Hauke Haien Dike will hold well enough; it will hold even in a hundred years!'

A thunderous roar at his feet woke him from these dreams; the horse jibed at going forward. What was that?—The horse leapt back, and he felt a piece of the dike crashing into the depths in front of him. He opened his eyes wide and banished all thoughts from his mind; at the old dike he halted; the horse had already stepped on to it with his front hooves. Without thinking, he jerked back the horse; the last cloud drifted away from the moon and the gentle star now cast its light upon the dreadful monster which, foaming and hissing ahead of him, was plunging into the depths and down into the polder.

Hauke stared as if bereft of his senses; a judgement flood it was, sent to swallow up man and beast. Again the ray of light flashed into his eyes; it was the same light that he had noticed before; it was still burning in his house and, as he looked down, heartened, into the polder, he saw that, behind the dizzying maelstrom that was plunging down in front of him, only a strip some hundred yards wide was flooded; behind it he could clearly see the path which led from the polder. But that was not all: a wagon—no, a two-wheeled cart—was racing madly towards the dike; a woman, and a child, too, were sitting in it. Then—was that not the yelping bark of a small dog, heard on the wind flying past? Almighty God! it was indeed his wife and daughter; already they were close to the dike, and the seething mass of water was rolling towards them. A cry, a cry of despair broke from the rider's breast. 'Elke!' he shouted; 'Elke! Go back! Go back!'

But neither sea nor storm showed mercy; his words were scattered by their frenzy; only his cloak had been seized by the storm, which had almost thrown him from his horse; and the gig raced without stopping towards the raging flood. Then he saw the woman stretching up her hands as if towards him: had she recognized him? Had her yearning and her fear for his life driven her from the safe haven of the house? And now—was she shouting a last word to him?—The questions raced through his mind, but they remained unanswered; her words to him, his words to her—all were lost; only a roaring tumult, as if the end of the world had come, filled their ears so that no other sound could be heard.

'My child! Oh, Elke! My faithful Elke!' he shouted into the storm. Again, a large piece of the dike in front of him plunged down into the depths and was followed by the thundering sea; he saw, one last time, the horse's head and the wheels of the cart emerge from the furious waves and, whirling round, sink again. The rider's staring eyes saw nothing more as he stood alone upon the dike. 'The end!' he said to himself in a low voice; then he rode to the abyss where, beneath him, the water, hissing uncannily, was beginning to drown his village; still he could see the light shining from his house, but to him it seemed soulless. He sat upright in his saddle and drove the spurs into his horse's flanks; the animal reared and almost fell backwards, but the strength of the rider pressed him down again. 'Onward!' cried the rider again, as he had so often done to urge the horse to a gallop: 'Lord God, take me; but spare the others!'

Another dig of the spurs; the horse neighed, outcrying the sound of the storm and the waves; then, from the crashing floods below was heard a dull thud, a brief struggle.

The bright moon looked down from on high; but below on the dike no further sign of life was to be seen save the wild waves, which had soon flooded the old polder almost completely. But still the mound of Hauke Haien's house rose above the flood, still the light shone from within and, from the upland, where one after another the houses grew dark, the lonely lantern still cast its flickering light from the church tower across the foaming waves.

The story-teller fell silent; I reached for the filled glass which had been standing before me for no little time; but I did not raise it to my lips: my hand remained upon the table.

'That is the story of Hauke Haien,' my host began again, 'to the best of my knowledge. Of course, the dike reeve's housekeeper would have told you a different tale, for this much is known, too: the horse's white skeleton was again to be seen on Jevershallig after flood-tide, as before; everyone in the village claimed to have seen it.—This much is certain: Hauke Haien, with wife and child, drowned in that flood; I have not been able to find even their burial place up in the churchyard; their bodies will have been washed out through the breach into the open sea and there, on the seabed, little by little returned to what they were made of—and so they found peace from the world. But the Hauke Haien Dike still stands even now, after a hundred years, and, if you intend to ride to the town tomorrow and have no fear of a half-hour detour, you will have the dike beneath your horse's hooves.

'The thanks of the grandchildren, once promised by Jewe Manners to the builder of the dike, were never paid, as you have seen; that, sir, is the way of the world: Socrates was given poison to drink and Our Lord Jesus was nailed to the Cross! We may not be able to go quite that far these days; but—to proclaim a man of violence or an ill-tempered, stubborn priest a saint, or make a respectable fellow into a spook, a ghost of the night, just because he stands head and shoulders above us all—*that* is possible any day.'

With these words, the grave little man rose to his feet and listened. 'Things have taken a turn,' he said and drew back the woollen curtain from the window; outside, bright moonlight was shining. 'See there,' he went on; 'the dike agents are coming back; but they are going their separate ways, returning home;—there must have been a breach on the other shore yonder; the water has fallen.'

Standing beside him, I looked outside: the upstairs windows were above the level of the dike; it was just as he had said. I picked up my glass and drank the rest. 'Many thanks for this evening,' I said; 'I think we can sleep in peace!'

'That we can,' the little man replied; 'I wish you a restful night with all my heart!'

——Going downstairs, I met the dike reeve in the entrance; he had come to take home a map which he had left behind in the taproom. 'All over!' he said. 'But our schoolmaster has told you a good yarn, no doubt; he's one of the enlighteners!'

—'He seems a very knowledgeable man!'

'Yes, yes, certainly; but seeing is believing; and over on the other side, the dike has broken—just as I said it would!'

I shrugged my shoulders. 'I shall have to sleep on it! Goodnight, dike reeve!'

He laughed. 'Good-night!'

———Next morning, by the light of a bright, golden sun which had risen above a scene of widespread destruction, I rode along the Hauke Haien Dike down into the town.

EXPLANATORY NOTES

Blond Eckbert

LUDWIG TIECK (1773–1853), one of the leading German Romantics, is perhaps best known for his re-creation of the fairy-tale as a genre with proper aesthetic status. He also wrote a number of longer narratives. *Blond Eckbert* is incorporated into Tieck's serial text *Phantasus*.

The Marchioness of O...

HEINRICH VON KLEIST (1777–1811) is often seen as marking the transition from the regulated world-view of Classicism to a modernity ruled by what he called a 'fragile arrangement'. *The Marchioness of O...* is one of his range of masterly contributions to the *Novelle* genre. He is also one of the greatest of German dramatists.

23 *Phantasus . . . Morpheus*: according to Ovid (*Metamorphoses*, xi. 641), sons of the Greek god of sleep, Hypnos.

Lenz

GEORG BÜCHNER (1813–37) is best known for his dramas *Woyzeck* and *Danton's Death* (*Dantons Tod*). These plays enact a struggle between a desire for revolutionary change and the irresistible force of socio-historical fatalism. Both plays also represent the sort of compulsion in the human psyche which is the keynote of *Lenz*.

58 *Lenz*: Büchner's narrative is based on an episode in the life of Jakob Michael Reinhold Lenz (1751–92), a leading dramatist of the *Sturm und Drang* ('Storm and Stress') movement.

60 *Oberlin*: Johann Friedrich Oberlin (1740–1826), pastor and philanthropist. Büchner bases *Lenz* on Oberlin's account of the writer's visit to Waldersbach in the inhospitable Steintal.

Kaufmann's: Christoph Kaufmann (1753–95), Swiss doctor and writer who coined the term *Sturm und Drang*.

66 *Stilling*: Johann Heinrich Jung-Stilling (1740–1817), Pietist doctor and writer who published studies of the Apocalypse.

The Idealistic period: in the second half of the eighteenth century Idealism held sway in the aesthetic and moral culture of Germany.

67 *'The Private Tutor' and 'The Soldiers'*: Lenz's two most celebrated dramas, *Der Hofmeister* (1774) and *Die Soldaten* (1776).

Old German school: artists of the fifteenth and sixteenth centuries, such as Altdorfer, Dürer, and Grünewald.

69 *Lavater*: Johann Caspar Lavater (1741–1801), Swiss pastor and philosopher, best known for his influential work on physiognomy.

74 *Arise and walk!*: echoing the words of Christ (Mark 2: 9 and 5: 41).

75 *Pfeffel*: Gottlieb Konrad Pfeffel (1736–1809), Alsatian writer.

the Wandering Jew: Ahasverus the Jew, said to have been made to wander eternally when he refused rest to Christ on the way to Golgotha.

76 *Friederike*: Friederike Brion (1752–1813), pastor's daughter from Sesenheim, famously courted by Goethe. The woman, alluded to elsewhere in the narrative, who subsequently became the object of Lenz's unrequited love.

The Jew's Beech

ANNETTE VON DROSTE-HÜLSHOFF (1797–1848) published poetry in various forms: lyric, ballad, and epic. A strong trait throughout is the demonic representation of the natural world, focusing in particular on her native Westphalia. *The Jew's Beech* is Droste-Hülshoff's only narrative text of stature.

96 *Niemand*: this translates as Nobody.

112 *the bridegroom in the Song of Songs*: this appears to be a conflation of imagery from the Song of Songs and from Psalms.

118 *le vrai n'est pas toujours vraisemblable*: 'the true does not always have the appearance of truth'; after the French aesthetician Boileau (1636–1711).

Tourmaline

ADALBERT STIFTER (1805–68) is perhaps best known for the *Novelle* collection *Coloured Stones* (*Bunte Steine*) of which *Tourmaline* is part. The collection as a whole aims to exemplify what Stifter calls a 'gentle law' behind the natural world and human affairs. Stifter also made a significant contribution to the *Bildungsroman* genre with his novel *The Indian Summer* (*Der Nachsommer*).

128 *the first two tales*: the stories *Granite* and *Limestone*.

Mozart on the way to Prague

EDUARD MÖRIKE (1804–75) wrote lyric poetry, fairy-tales, and a *Bildungsroman*, *Nolten the Painter* (*Der Maler Nolten*). He is representative, in many senses, of the 'Restoration' period in mid-nineteenth-century German culture. His poetry and prose alike tends to achieve a balance in form and content between Romantic and Classical tendencies.

166 *una finzione di poeti*: a poets' fiction.

Prater: the park in Vienna famous for its amusements.

170 *per marca*: for each lesson.

171 *'Belmonte and Konstanze'*: an alternative title for Mozart's *Singspiel*, *Die Entführung aus dem Serail*.

'Cosa Rara': a light opera by Martin y Soler.

173 *Kapellmeister*: the conductor or leader of a *Kapelle*, or court orchestra.

175 *Unter den Linden*: the main boulevard in the centre of Berlin.

Sanssouci: the palace of the Prussian kings in Potsdam.

'Tarar': opera by Mozart's rival Salieri (1750–1825).

182 *Hagedorn, Götz*: the writers Friedrich von Hagedorn (1708–54) and Johann Nikolaus Götz (1721–81).

187 *figli di Nettuno*: sons of Neptune.

188 *saltarelli, canzoni a ballo*: respectively, lively dances and polyphonic dance songs in the Italian style.

191 *Masetto* and *Zerlina*: betrothed peasants, characters in *Don Giovanni*.

the song:

> Dearest sisters, born to love,
> Pluck the halcyon days of youth!
> If you bow your heads in yearning,
> Helpful Cupid is nearby.
> > Tra la la!
> O, what joys await you all!

194 *Ninon de Lenclos . . . Madame de Sévigné . . . Chapelle*: the fashionable hostess Ninon de Lenclos (1615–1705), the celebrated letter-writer Madame de Sévigné (1626–96), and the poet Chapelle (1626–86) were all leading lights in seventeenth-century Parisian society.

197 —*here . . . sea*: Karl Wilhelm Ramler (1725–98), translator and imitator of Horace and other classical poets. The relevant passage from Ramler's translation of *Ode* iii. 4. reads:

> —hier, der auf der Schulter
> Keinen unthätigen Bogen führet!

Der seines Delos grünenden Mutterhain
Und Pataras beschatteten Strand bewohnt,
Der seines Hauptes goldne Locken
In die kastalischen Fluten tauchet.

198 *À la bonne heure!*: 'In good time!' 'Excellent!'

da Ponte . . . Schikaneder: Lorenzo da Ponte (1749–1838) was the librettist for a number of Mozart operas, including *Don Giovanni*; Emanuel Schikaneder (1751–1812) wrote the libretto for *The Magic Flute*.

199 *Monsieur Bonbonnière*: Mozart's nickname for Salieri, who would gorge himself on sweets.

201 *phlogiston*: in early chemistry, the principle of inflammability.

Stephansplatz: the square around St Stephen's Cathedral in the centre of Vienna.

209 *Prince Esterhazy*: Prince Miklós József Esterházy (1714–90), patron of the arts. Haydn was for thirty years conductor of his private orchestra.

your quartets: the six Mozart string quartets dedicated to Haydn.

211 *Florentine master*: a reference to the famous salt-cellar by Benvenuto Cellini, held at that time in Schloss Ambras near Innsbruck.

213 *Leporello*: Don Giovanni's manservant.

Sillery: A kind of champagne.

214 *the priest*: da Ponte, who converted from Judaism to Catholicism and became a priest.

218 *Chevalier Gluck*: the composer Christoph Willibald von Gluck (1714–87).

Clothes Make the Man

GOTTFRIED KELLER (1819–90) created a number of cyclical texts, most famously *The People of Seldwyla*, which is based in and around a hypothetical small-town community in Switzerland. Like *Clothes Make the Man*, the other tales in the cycle satirize the bankruptcy at the foundations of bourgeois culture. Keller also published a monumental *Bildungsroman*, *Green Heinrich* (*Der grüne Heinrich*).

221 *[title]*: the German title (literally, 'Clothes Make People') derives from *vestis virum reddit* in Quintilian's *Institutio oratoria*.

228 *Bocksbeutel*: (literally, 'billy-goat's bag') a flask of Franconian wine, so called because it resembles a goat's scrotum.

228 *Pütschli-Nievergelt*: Keller frequently uses playful names. This combines a diminutive form of *putsch* with 'Never-repay'.

231 *Praga or Ostrolenka*: sites of battles between Poland and Russia in 1831.

232 *Nettchen*: diminutive form of Annette.

238 *the youth at the parting of the ways*: a reference to Hercules, who is said to have stood at the crossroads of the paths of virtue and luxury.

243 *Pool of Bethseda . . . thirty years*: the Biblical pool which had healing powers. The old man in fact waited thirty-eight years in vain for his turn at the pool, an ironic allusion to Böhni's perseverence.

245 *Carbonari coat*: the type of cloak worn by a member of the Carbonari, an association akin to the freemasons, whose members disguised themselves as charcoal-burners (*carbonari*).

The White Horse Rider

THEODOR STORM (1817–88) set the majority of his many *Novellen* in his native Schleswig-Holstein. They are typically tales of lost love or of alienation in family and communal life, invariably overlaid with a sense of existential transience. The stories often have lyrical elements, and Storm was also an accomplished lyric poet.

263 *halligen*: a *hallig* is a small island without dike protection off the North Sea coast of Schleswig-Holstein.

265 *polder*: an area of coastal farmland won through dike construction.

Plattdeutsch: the Low German dialect spoken in various forms in large areas of Northern Germany.

267 *Hans Mommsen*: the autodidact Hans Momsen (1735–1811) was one of the sources for the figure of Hauke Haien.

270 *boy wonder from Lübeck*: Christian Heinrich Heineken (1721–5), a famous North German *wunderkind*.

305 *white cloths*: this refers to the superstitious ritual of covering mirrors and other reflective surfaces in a house where a death had just occurred.

325 *Lawrenz's son*: Laurentius Damm, a man living in Hamburg around 1600, is said to have had a son over nine feet tall.

355 *Hippocratic expression*: the face of one at death's door (after Hippocrates who first described it for medical purposes).

THE WORLD'S CLASSICS

A Select List

JANE AUSTEN: Emma
Edited by James Kinsley and David Lodge

J. M. BARRIE: Peter Pan in Kensington Gardens & Peter and Wendy
Edited by Peter Hollindale

WILLIAM BECKFORD: Vathek
Edited by Roger Lonsdale

JOHN BUNYAN: The Pilgrim's Progress
Edited by N. H. Keeble

THOMAS CARLYLE: The French Revolution
Edited by K. J. Fielding and David Sorensen

GEOFFREY CHAUCER: The Canterbury Tales
Translated by David Wright

CHARLES DICKENS: Christmas Books
Edited by Ruth Glancy

MARIA EDGEWORTH: Castle Rackrent
Edited by George Watson

ELIZABETH GASKELL: Cousin Phillis and Other Tales
Edited by Angus Easson

THOMAS HARDY: A Pair of Blue Eyes
Edited by Alan Manford

HOMER: The Iliad
Translated by Robert Fitzgerald
Introduction by G. S. Kirk

HENRIK IBSEN: An Enemy of the People, The Wild Duck,
Rosmersholm
Edited and Translated by James McFarlane

HENRY JAMES: The Ambassadors
Edited by Christopher Butler

JOCELIN OF BRAKELOND:
Chronicle of the Abbey of Bury St. Edmunds
Translated by Diana Greenway and Jane Sayers

BEN JONSON: Five Plays
Edited by G. A. Wilkes

LEONARDO DA VINCI: Notebooks
Edited by Irma A. Richter

HERMAN MELVILLE: The Confidence-Man
Edited by Tony Tanner

PROSPER MÉRIMÉE: Carmen and Other Stories
Translated by Nicholas Jotcham

EDGAR ALLAN POE: Selected Tales
Edited by Julian Symons

MARY SHELLEY: Frankenstein
Edited by M. K. Joseph

BRAM STOKER: Dracula
Edited by A. N. Wilson

ANTHONY TROLLOPE: The American Senator
Edited by John Halperin

OSCAR WILDE: Complete Shorter Fiction
Edited by Isobel Murray

VIRGINIA WOOLF: Mrs Dalloway
Edited by Claire Tomalin